THE NIGHT OF THE DANCE

THE NIGHT OF THE DANCE

JAMES HIME

ST. MARTIN'S MINOTAUR ✹ NEW YORK

www.minotaurbooks.com

Library of Congress Cataloging-in-Publication Data

Hime, James L.
    The night of the dance / James Hime.—1st ed.
      p. cm.
    ISBN 0-312-31322-5
    1. Washington County (Tex.)—Fiction. 2. African American men—Fiction.
3. Ex-police officers—Fiction. 4. Missing persons—Fiction. 5. Sheriffs—Fiction.
6. Retirees—Fiction.   I. Title.

PS3608.I47N54   2003
813'.6—dc21

2002037195

10 9 8 7 6 5 4 3

For Paulette,
my wife, my best friend, my inspiration in all things, for going on thirty years now

ACKNOWLEDGMENTS

THERE REALLY IS A BRENHAM, TEXAS, AND I HAVE VISITED IT A FEW TIMES. I even know a handful of people there, and they are all wonderful, peace-loving, tolerant folks who keep civil tongues in their heads, which is just another way of saying that the people and events depicted in this work of fiction are wholly the products of my imagination and not in any way based on reality. I hope the good men and women of Brenham will take no offense in my choice of setting. I certainly meant none.

I have lots of folks to thank.

First, thanks to my wife, Paulette, to whom this book is dedicated, for enduring in a good-humored way everything that comes with being Mrs. James Hime and for being supportive during all those months in which I was consumed by the low-probability challenge of writing and publishing a first novel. I have never written words to a better purpose than the poetry I wrote to win your heart, dear, nor shall I ever.

Also, thanks to my writing teacher, Chris Rogers, from whom I learned the fundamentals of mystery writing; to my cousin Anita Groves for help with all the health-care stuff; to my Tanglewood Boulevard running buddy, Carla Tenison, for her insights into the cattle market; to my old friend Michael Skelton for being an early and very blunt critic and for introducing me to John Clutterbuck; to Clutterbuck for introducing me to a number of people who were important in getting this book published and for reading and providing helpful comments on early drafts.

Thanks to Michael Connelly for the introduction to his agent, Philip Spitzer, and an enormous *muchos gracias* to Philip, who took a chance on me, told me he would sell this book, and then went out and did it.

Thanks to my St. Martin's editor, Kelley Ragland, and her colleague Benjamin Sevier for believing in the book enough to want to take it on, for working hard to make it a better read, and for putting up with all my dumb first-time-author questions. Y'all have been great, and I appreciate it more than you can ever know.

Thanks as well to all my friends—my former partner, Tom Bacon, and his parents, Dana Hock (who encouraged me to go back to writing when the Internet thing turned to dust) and her friend Phyllis, Debbie Emory,

George Lancaster, Hasty Johnson, Mr. and Mrs. Clayton Stone, and Matt Silverman—for slogging through earlier versions of the book and telling me what you thought. Your encouragement meant worlds to me.

Finally, thanks to the entire Hines family, in both the broader and narrower senses, for taking back the prodigal son and not begrudging him his creative-writing ambitions.

Houston, Texas
October 2002

THE NIGHT OF THE DANCE

PROLOGUE

THE CALL FROM DISPATCH IS SUCH A PROVOCATION IT CAUSES HIM TO JERK THE cruiser off the street into a parking lot, slam the transmission into PARK, and just sit there, working up a major case of the red ass.

He can tell already what this is about, been down this road many a time, thinking now that when a man abides in a world that's bathed in racism, invisible yet still there all the time, like the radiation from the stars, so that he's always awash in it, he develops his own sensing mechanism attuned to it. He can calibrate it and triangulate it, can measure its strength.

It's like he's got some kind of racism meter, built right into his brain, and it tracks down the racism in the world as it pertains to him, giving him readings. When it's stronger, when it's weaker.

When there's a concentrated burst of it coming from somewhere close, taking dead aim at him, penetrating the cells in his body.

Sheriff's Deputy C. Livermore Thomas breathes deep, thumbs the mike.

"C'mon, Darlene, gimme a break."

"Sorry, Clyde."

"Sorry, huh. Saying it don't make it so, Darlene, don't believe I hear no 'sorry' in your voice. You know what I *do* believe though? I believe ol' Clyde's being jacked around, you know what I'm sayin'?"

He waits for her to come back at him, thinking if she disses him, gives him any kind of a reason *at all* to think she might be dissing him, he's just going to rip this mike, cord and all, out of the radio, chuck it out the window.

She says, "You know what the sneaker ads say, Clyde. Just do it, okay?"

His racism meter gives him another reading, needle all the way over in the "they really fuckin' with you now" zone. He's thinking, *Okay, got to stay cool, come on back at old dispatch now, stand up for your human rights, use a little sweet reason.*

Whine some even.

"*Come on.* I'm meetin' Sonya for lunch in, what"—he checks the dashboard clock—"less than an hour. I can't go chasin' all the way out to the county line on account of some fool say he turned up a suspicious-looking *boot.*"

"The man says it looks peculiar. He's 'fraid it might be a body."

"It's a boot, out in a pasture, nothin' suspicious about it. Some country folks threw their trash out, old boot was part of it, that's all. You from the country, Darlene, you know what I'm talkin' 'bout here."

"Clyde, all I know is he's worried enough about it to call it in."

"Darlene, this here's Washington County, okay? We don't have no real crime 'round here. For sure ain't no dead bodies, except those in the grave-yard. This fool you say called in, he ain't tryin' to drill a oil well in a grave-yard is he?"

"No."

"Well, there you go then."

"Clyde, just get your ass out there, check it out, okay?"

Now *that* moves the needle on the racism meter. All she said was "ass," but Clyde knows she was thinking "black ass." She like to said it, too.

Clyde sets his jaw, thumbs the mike. "Get somebody else. How 'bout Jake?"

"Workin' a speed trap, out on Thirty-six. Citin' 'em so fast, he's gettin' writer's cramp."

"So what, if it's a real dead body and all out yonder?"

"Pays the bills, Clyde."

"What about the sheriff then?"

"He's in some meeting over at the bypass, told me not to disturb him for nothin' short of Bonnie and Clyde."

"Darlene, this here is bullshit and you know it. You keep treatin' me this way, disrespectin' me and all, I'm gonna know you a racist like everybody else in this cracker town, you know what I'm sayin'?"

"Clyde, I'm fixing to read the directions to you. You ready to write 'em down?"

"Yeah, but this is bullshit."

He scribbles down the route while she reads it to him. "Okay, I got 'em. But this here is bullshit plain and simple."

"Over and out, Clyde."

"Over and out your own self."

Clyde spikes the microphone off the front seat, pulls a U out of the parking lot, headed west now, punches the accelerator. He's thinking, *Sonya's a pro, she'll understand, plus she's seen this sort of thing before where we're concerned, many a time, many a time indeed.*

But the thought of being late sets his teeth to grinding. He hates being late worse than anything. His mama had drilled it into him, ever since he was little, running around barefoot in the dirt yard out front of their shot-gun house up in Oak Cliff. She said cleanliness was important all right, but it was punctuality that was next to godliness.

Once he gets to the city limits Clyde kicks the cruiser, and directly he's howling down the road doing ninety. He hits the siren, the lights. *That's right, let's give the taxpayers their money's worth.*

Now he's out in the country, no neat little rows of houses with landscaped yards out here, instead there's farms, ranches, cows, yard dogs, double-wides set way back from the highway with great big satellite dishes next to them, guys in straw hats and overalls driving farm equipment down the side of the road.

The scenery whips by and all around smoke hangs so thick in the air it blocks out the sun, renders the sky metallic, the color of corrugated tin or old asphalt, like the sky of another time, some primordial time when the world was young, primitive, volcanic.

Clyde hangs a left on Farm Road 390, part of the "Bluebonnet Trail," according to the sign. "Damn if these people don't love their bluebonnets," he says.

A half-mile farther on there's another left, this one onto a dirt road, barbed-wire fence running down both sides. It goes for a ways, then there's a break in the fencing on the right, got a cattle guard there Clyde has to rumble over, then on to another dirt road, this one winding through a dusty pasture, leading up a short hill.

"Yo, check out this road, man."

Bouncing over this rutted-out mess, little more than a cow path, Clyde can't go faster than twenty, else he's apt to bust something loose from the undercarriage. As it is he's being tossed around in his seat as if his cruiser were a carnival ride even though he's barely going funeral procession speed.

Crabbing along like this, he realizes, the siren and the lights, they're idiotic. *Better kill the lights and the sound before somebody sees me. There's no taxpayers out here anyhow, just these cows standin' around with their tails switchin' back and forth. And, man, talk about dry.*

Clyde checks the rearview, nothing to be seen but a cloud of dust.

He's thinking, *Goddamn this for the jive bullshit it is.*

He lurches over the hill, then another quarter-mile downhill into a pasture where there's half a dozen guys in coveralls and hard hats standing around, leaning up against their pickups, parked this way and that. There's a bulldozer and a sizable area, maybe a couple acres, where the weeds and grass have been scraped away leaving dry brown dirt.

Clyde parks the cruiser, gets out. A big guy walks up, got a face the color of a raw beef brisket. What with his red face and blue coveralls, the matching hard hat, the white lettering that says "Mexia Drilling Company," reminds Clyde of the American flag.

The flag-colored guy sticks his hand out for a shake. "Peter Wells," he says.

"Deputy Clyde Thomas. Pleased to meet you."

"Thanks for coming. It's over here."

Brisket Face leads Clyde across the cleared patch.

"We've been working this spot for two days, clearing it and leveling it. Got a new well planned. Drilling's supposed to begin next Wednesday. I was walking the perimeter when I looked down, saw the toe of a cowboy boot stickin' up out of the ground."

"Cowboy boot, huh?"

"Yeah. I thought it looked suspicious."

" 'As what I hear. This being like out in the country and all, maybe somebody just dumped a load of trash with a boot in it, here in this pasture. You think of that?"

"Well, yeah. But no one's living around here. There's no houses or nothin'."

"Uh-huh."

"And we haven't turned up any other trash since we been out here pushing dirt around. Struck me as strange so I'm thinking better safe than sorry."

"Better safe than sorry, huh. That's a good one. You make that up?"

"Well, no—"

"Why don't you just show me where the boot is at?"

The oil driller stops at the edge of the cleared area, points downward. "That's it."

Just like the man had said, there's the toe of a cowboy boot sticking up a couple inches out of the ground.

Clyde leans down, getting himself a closer look. "Can I get a shovel from y'all?"

"Sure. Hey, Dennis," Peter Wells hollers, "fetch a shovel over here, will ya?"

Another flag-looking guy—same beef-brisket face, blue duds, belly on him big enough to have its own gravitational field—ambles over with a shovel.

Clyde takes it, starts scraping at the dirt around the boot, a couple feet on either side, looking for the rest of the trash pile, sure it's there.

He's thinking, *Finish this bullshit up and still get lunch with Sonya.*

The shovel catches a few times, but on rocks and roots, not trash. Clyde tosses the shovel aside. He pulls out a handkerchief, wipes his brow, trying to think it through.

You could just jerk the boot out of the ground, see if anything is attached, like somebody's leg maybe. But if it's a body then you'd be messing with a crime scene right here in front of these oil guys with their side-of-beef faces and their blue jumpsuits, make great witnesses for some defense lawyer.

Or else you could back up, get a warrant, do a full crime-scene search, take a day, involve half the department.

Yeah, and if it turns out to be nothing but a stray boot you'll be catching shit about it for weeks.

The thing is to check it out, but not disturb nothin' too much.

Clyde fishes in his pocket for a knife, kneels down, starts cutting the boot where the upper is sewed to the sole. He cuts around the toe and down each side about an inch. Pockets the knife, bends the upper back from the sole, peers in. Has to get down on one knee real close, squint. "Motherfucker."

"Excuse me?"

Clyde straightens back up, looks at the Brisket Twins. "I think we might have ourselves a potential crime scene here, which means I need to get me a search warrant, alright? Now why don't the two of y'all just back up a ways while I go call this in? Don't touch nothin' and don't be walkin' around here none, you know what I'm sayin'?"

Back at the cruiser, he leans in, grabs the mike. "Yo, Darlene."

"Come in, Clyde."

"I got me a honest-to-God dead person out here. Or at least part of one."

"Do what?"

"I said it looks like the tip is gonna check out. Now maybe it ain't exactly Bonnie and Clyde, but why don't you find the sheriff and tell him to get out here, you know what I'm sayin'? And call the DPS, see if they can locate us a forensic anthropologist."

"A what?"

"A forensic anthropologist."

"How you spell that?"

"Shit, I don't know. Look it up."

Clyde signs off, says to himself, *A man don't need a warrant to make notes, take a few snaps, right?* Clyde goes to the trunk, pulls out a camera and a notebook. He checks the camera for film and batteries, starts back to where the boot is.

He's thinking, *Now wouldn't that be something? A no-shit homicide, right here in Pig Fart, Texas, real-live police work to be done, instead of days of doing nothing but handing out traffic tickets to Billy Bobs in pickups.*

He's thinking, *This might actually turn out to be kind of cool.*

At that moment, less than a mile away, a tall, lean, gray-haired man with blue eyes and a jaw on him that looks like it belongs on Mount Rushmore, a retired Texas Ranger dressed in rancher's khakis, is hauling hay to his cattle, trying to get his chores done so he can go down to Houston, see his daughter, sick these many months in a hospital down yonder. He labors away in the heat and smoke, oblivious to Clyde's discovery, to the implications of it for him.

He won't stay that way for long.

1

ON THE MORNING HE LEARNS ABOUT THE SHERIFF'S BOYS FINDING SISSY Fletcher's body, the smoke is worse than ever, has worked its way through the window unit into his bedroom, its smell factoring into his dreams like sounds sometimes do, waking him up. His subconscious mind registers it, tells him get up, something's on fire.

But once he's awake he knows nothing's on fire, leastwise not in these parts. He lies there, thinking it's too early to get up.

He listens to Martha's breathing, deep and steady, not quite a snore but almost, in the twin bed on the other side of the room. It's a sound he's listened to in the predawn for a lot of years, and he tries to follow the memory of it backward in time, tries to get it to carry him to thoughts of a day when Martha and he were younger and life hadn't used them up so much, thoughts so pleasant they might settle him down some, help him sleep.

In the end it's no use, his mind has gotten going on matters from this time right here. He decides that if he's going down that road he might as well do it over a cigarette.

That thought gets him up.

Soft as a big man can, trusting in the darkness to feel and memory, Jeremiah Spur fetches his work clothes hanging organized and handy in the closet where he had left them the night before. Knowing when he hung them there that even if he were to sleep all night he'd probably need to get dressed before Martha turned over for the first time.

He picks his way to the kitchen, starts the coffee machine. He strips out of his pajamas, folds them, lays them in the bottom of a kitchen chair, pulls on his khakis, buttons his work shirt. He taps his package of Camels in the palm of his hand until the coffee is done, then tucks the cigarettes into his shirt pocket, pours himself some black, takes his boots in one hand, mug in the other.

He pads his way across the family room in his stocking feet, has to clamp the boots between his elbow and his rib cage to free a hand, open the back door and keep it from banging, waking Martha up.

He drops into his straw-bottomed rocker that sits out on his back porch, pulls on his boots, drinks his coffee, rubs his eyes.

Duke gets up from the other side of the porch, stretches his body, its color that of a Zulu potentate, walks over head low, tail going from side to side. Duke plants himself next to the rocker, his back to Jeremiah, offering his head up to get scratched.

Jeremiah drains the coffee, hawks and spits, lights a cigarette. Sits there smoking, scratching Duke behind the ears, below the jaw, down his old black neck. Directly he can tell from the way the world is stirring out beyond the rail fence, birds calling some, chickens starting to make a racket, it's fixing to be light.

There'd been many a time, working some case or other as a Ranger, when he had been up and about this time of day, or even earlier. He had been partial to the predawn in those days, liked being up before the rest of the world got going. Bad guys still snoring away, dreaming their bad guy dreams, him wide-awake, tending relentlessly to the business of reeling them in.

But those days have been over for some months now. Giving up that life had been like having an arm sawed off. Not that he had any choice in it if he was to have any hope of managing all the forces that have him in their grip. You get to a certain point where you can't go on pretending that those other problems would somehow magically get better.

Life has taught Jeremiah Spur a thing or two, like miracles can happen, you just can't plan around them.

So he had had to quit. But, Lord, how he missed it.

He's being weak-minded, and he shakes his head over it. He stubs out the cigarette, flicks the butt out into the yard.

Not much for an old rancher to do this hour of the day but wait for the sunrise, except there won't be a sunrise worthy of the name. Instead, the sky lightens by degrees from complete black to a gray, the color of a cinder block, and there it stays. Somewhere out there you know the sun is up, but you can't see it. All you can see is smoke.

He wonders, *How many days are left to Elizabeth to see a sunrise or a sunset?* It's a bitter thought.

They say the fires are down in southern Mexico somewhere. Peasant farmers clearing woods and jungle, burning trash. Making new fields for various crops. The weatherman on Channel 13 allowed as how there's some kind of high-pressure system positioned over the central Gulf, redirecting the jet stream. Pumping smoke from the Mexican peasant fires and heat from the Mexican desert all the way to Texas, way up past his ranch even. They say smoke fouls the sky all the way to Dallas and beyond.

The very air of the Earth has become pestilential through acts of God and man. It smells like a trash fire, you can't stand to be outside for any length of time. Causes even a smoker's eyes to itch, throat to burn. He's lived in Washington County some forty years and he's never seen the likes of it.

Once it's light enough to see he gets up, takes his Stetson off a wall peg, puts it on.

He and Duke walk to the pickup he keeps parked just beyond the rail fence, Duke taking the tailgate in one jump. They'll drive the place. Check on the cattle.

The drought has scorched the pastures, turned them brown, cracked them open, cracks big enough to drop a pullet in. The weatherman says that the Gulf high-pressure system is pushing all their rain way north, up toward Kansas. Until that system breaks up or moves off, they would be getting plenty of smoke, plenty of heat, but the one thing they won't be getting is the benefaction of rain.

He parks near a copse of scrub oak, lets the engine idle. Lights a cigarette, eyes the cattle that huddle around looking lean, sickly. Hardly moving.

He gets out of the pickup, walks around to the back. Opens the tailgate, muscles a hay bale to the ground. Flicks his pocketknife, cuts the cord so that the hay falls loose. Now the cattle can feed.

In a better year he'd work his herd at the end of the month, cull the fall-borne steers for market. He could do that this year too, he supposes, but they aren't going to fetch much. Maybe thirty head, weighing four hundred pounds, four twenty-five each on average. With cattle prices at less than fifty cents a pound, he won't gross more than six, seven thousand bucks, a piddling anthill compared to his bank debt piled up like the Rockies. In a better year, he'd do twice that.

Jeremiah says to himself it's all kind of academic anyway. His hay will last him maybe another month, then he'll have to start selling his herd for what he can get. Lots of cattlemen had already been forced into it, that's why beef prices are what they are.

Won't be long before he'll have to go into town, see the bankers about cutting him some slack. It's a melancholy thought, hard for a man to abide, especially a Texas Ranger. A man who never used to have to give an order more than once.

He slips the pickup into gear and drives down to the tank. Parks, gets out. Duke hits the ground, starts running the perimeter, nose close to the surface, snorting.

Ordinarily it's a ten-acre tank, largest on his place. Now it's shrunk to maybe four.

He picks his way down to the water's edge. The cattle's hooves have chopped up the mud near the water. He spits in the water, looks up at the cinder-block sky.

For six months he's been pouring everything he has into this place, into his family. In every respect it has done nothing but get worse. The way things have been going, he figures he might as well have stayed a Ranger. Kept the paycheck.

It's a new thing to him, this sense of being a failure. Never had to struggle with anything like it before.

Don't be so damn weak-minded, Jeremiah.

He whistles Duke up, they drive back to the house. Walking through the backyard, Jeremiah's boots kick up little dust clouds with every step. Duke follows him as far as the back porch. Jeremiah pulls the screen door open, goes into the kitchen.

The house is quiet, Martha still in bed, sleeping off yesterday's fifth of vodka.

He goes to wash up, sees the message light blinking on the machine. Glances at the wall clock. Only reason someone would call this early must be bad news from the hospital. He hits the PLAY button.

"Morning, Jeremiah. This here's Dewey Sharpe. Sorry to call so early, but I was just wonderin' if you'd have time to come into town this morning. We got ourselves something of a situation here I'd like to visit with you 'bout. Give me a call and let me know if you're gonna be around today."

The man leaves a phone number and the machine clicks off. Jeremiah Spur pours some corn flakes and milk, swings a leg over the back of a kitchen chair, sits down to eat.

He can't imagine what the sheriff would want from him.

2

"NOW *THIS* IS MR. CHOCOLATE AND *THIS* IS MR. VANILLA AND *THIS* IS MR. Strawberry and *this* . . ."

A singsong voice is coming from behind the counter at the Big Scoop Ice Cream Parlor. Every now and then Jeremiah can see the chanter herself, working her way down a row of short freezers that runs along the back wall, a little gray-haired lady dressed in blue gingham, calling out the flavors, pointing at the freezers with a bony forefinger, her arm pumping up and down, like she was hammering a nail into a two-by-four.

". . . and *this* is Mr. Chocolate Fudge and *this* is Mr. Neapolitan and *this* . . ."

Jeremiah reckons maybe she forgot he's sitting out here drinking this cup of coffee she sold him ten minutes ago, or maybe she hasn't forgotten and it just doesn't inhibit her, the thought of a total stranger listening in on her peculiar ritual.

He has set up shop in the booth farthest from the front door, established for himself a good view of the whole place, except a few parts in back where the chanting is coming from. Choosing such a seat is so old a habit he hardly even thinks about it.

He sits with both elbows on the table, sips his coffee, wanting a smoke, but there are no ashtrays on the tables. It's not like he has *seen* an actual NO SMOKING sign but these days you can't be too careful.

". . . and *this* is Mr. Rocky Road and *this* is Mr. Coffee and *this* is Mr. Butter Pecan and *this* . . ."

It feels odd to be sitting here, drinking coffee in an ice cream parlor at a little past nine o'clock on a weekday morning. Better than being at the county courthouse though. Jeremiah hasn't been down yonder since he retired, got no particular desire to be seen walking around there in civilian clothes, no gun belt, no badge. No official business to attend to. He would have drawn lots of stares down at the courthouse.

He is used to being stared at, had been stared at plenty in his life, but in the past it had always been for the right reasons.

Through the front windows Jeremiah watches Sheriff Dewey Sharpe pull up in his brown and yellow county cruiser, open the door, heave himself out of it. Open the back door of the cruiser, fetch out a black attaché case, stroll into the restaurant.

Inside the door he hollers, "Howdy, Miss B."

"And *this* is Mr. Spumoni—good morning, Dewey—and *this* is Mr. Lime Sherbet . . ."

The sheriff spies Jeremiah, gives a little wave, ambles over, drops into the opposite side of the booth. Sets the attaché case down, sticks out his hand to be shook. He is a man of manifold physical imperfections the most pronounced of which include his beer gut, multiple chins, fireplug build, cheap haircut, mouth full of yellow teeth that look like a "Before" picture in an orthodontics textbook.

"Thanks for coming," he says. "You ever been here before?"

"No."

Dewey jerks a fat thumb over his shoulder. "That there's Miss Baker. She owns the joint. She inventories the stock first thing in the morning." He drops his voice, leans in. "She's a couple enchiladas shy of a combo plate."

"I think I seen her at church. Don't she have a grown son who's kinda slow?"

"Yeah. I fixed him up with a job on the lube rack out at the county garage. Changing oil on highway maintenance equipment is about all he's fit for."

"You reckon she'd mind if I smoked?"

"Oh, hell no." He turns around, hollers, "Hey, Miss B? Could we trouble you for an ashtray?"

Directly the ice cream lady appears with an ashtray and a cup of coffee for the sheriff. "Will we be seeing your sister today?"

"I 'spect she'll be along after a while."

"Good. She's so sweet. She tells me when they have the sales on down at the pharmacy."

Then Miss B disappears, goes back to her freezers and her chanting. "Now *this* is Mr. Peppermint and *this* is Mr. Rum Raisin and *this* . . ."

Jeremiah lights up a Camel, eyes the sheriff.

Dewey slurps his coffee, gestures outside. "Man," Dewey says. "This smoke is just gettin' worse and worse. I guess it ain't gonna get no better 'til we get some rain."

Jeremiah is wondering why he agreed to get together with this fat fool, this walking disgrace to law enforcement, a peckerwood who doesn't even have the courtesy to be on time. He takes a drag. "I've got fifteen minutes. You want to talk about the weather, that's up to you. Makes me no never mind. But I'm leaving in fifteen minutes."

"Okay. Sorry."

The sheriff pulls a case file out of the attaché. Sets it on the table, squares it up in front of Jeremiah.

"Here's the deal," he says. "Three days ago a work crew preparing an oil-well drilling site over near Gay Hill called us in to check out a suspicious situation, cowboy boot sticking up out the ground. Upon investigating, we turned up a human skeleton. Preliminary forensics establish it's Sissy Fletcher."

"Jim Fletcher's daughter?"

"Yep. You remember when she just up and disappeared about ten years ago?"

"I recollect it some. When was it exactly?"

The sheriff flips open his file.

"And *this* is Mr. Pistachio, and my goodness, Mr. Pistachio needs to be *replaced* . . ."

"She was last seen February 11, 1989."

Jeremiah flicks the ash off his cigarette, thinks a minute. "I was down in Laredo, workin' the Jalisco Diablos Gang drug case. I wasn't gettin' home much, just a day or two ever' now and then."

"Well, here's the upshot of it. She was last seen that night, at the rodeo dance. She didn't come home that night nor the next night neither. The guy she was living with reported her missing on that Monday, the thirteenth. The next day her pickup was stopped down at the border, near McAllen. A Meskin kid from here in town was at the wheel. Claimed he found it with the keys in the ignition over on the near north side of town, was headed south with it, was gonna sell it. He got sent up for grand theft auto."

"Do they have anything to tie him to the Fletcher girl?"

"Just the truck, but he was a suspect all the same. Our office—that was back when Pat Patterson was sheriff—worked the case locally for a couple weeks, but couldn't turn nothing useful up. She just seemed to have vanished. Since the eleventh was the last day of the rodeo, there was some theorizin' that maybe she had run off with one of the rodeo cowboys that was at the dance that night. It took a month to track all them rascals down but none of them would own up to so much as having met her. By then, with no better suspect than the Meskin kid, and nothin' to go on as to him but the truck, and no ransom note, no body, the whole investigation just kinda fizzled out, ever-body waitin' for the next thing to happen. Ever-body figured she'd surface somewhere sooner or later, maybe in Canada or something. Now she turns up in some pasture halfway to Somerville ten years later on my durn watch."

Jeremiah smokes, squints at the sheriff, grateful now that he has had a close look at what passes for law enforcement in Brenham that the crime rate is low around here.

In the back, roll call is over for the day. The ice cream lady has taken to singing to herself. Sounds like "You Are My Sunshine."

Dewey's eyes shift and his hands fidget. "So, anyway, I bet you're wondering what this has to do with you. What I want to know is whether I could get you to give us a hand with this sucker. This ain't typical of the murder cases we usually get, you know, where the perp's locked up before the body's cold. On top of that, we got us a victim whose daddy is a pretty big deal in these parts. So I'm thinkin', I could sure use the help of your own self seeing as how you had all them years as a legendary Texas Ranger."

Dewey slides the file Jeremiah's way. Jeremiah can see the fat on the sheriff's ring finger has all but swallowed up his wedding band.

Jeremiah stops the file, pushes it back. "It don't seem all that big a mystery to me. Find the Mexican kid. He's your killer."

"But it's like I said, we didn't have nothin' on him but the truck. Plus this was his first offense and there ain't nothin' to suggest he was the type to off somebody, then bury 'em way out in the country, just to steal their ride. And on top of that his alibi for the night of the dance, it's tight as a tent rope in the rain."

Jeremiah shrugs. "I reckon. Anyway you can forget about me. I'm retired. Nothin' but a rancher now."

"But you ain't been retired long, right? What, six months?"

"Sheriff, you got a homicide. Handle it by the book. If you folks ain't up to it, call the Rangers. They'll put a man on it."

"Yeah, take control of it, push me and my people aside."

Jeremiah stubs out his cigarette. "A thing can only be what it is, Dewey."

"I didn't want to get into this, but I reckon I got to be blunt. It's like this—I know what folks around here are sayin' these days. I'm probably looking at an opponent in the primary next year. I can't do nothin' right, and Joe Bob Cole—well, people talk about him like he's Eliot Ness or somethin'. Now, maybe I ain't the world's greatest living cop, can't hold a candle to the likes of you, but I've been the best sheriff this county's had in twenty years, better than Pat Patterson ever was by a damn sight. I just need a little something good to happen so as to change the way folks see me."

Jeremiah's impatience sets his jaw to working. "Like I said. I'm retired."

"Please, just take the file, look it over." Dewey gives it another little push. "Think on it some."

Against his better judgment, Jeremiah takes the file, starts thumbing it. Crime scene pictures: yellow tape, rags, bones in a dusty grave. All that's left of a preacher's daughter, buried in the earth ten years ago, now come back to complicate Jeremiah's life.

He knows for a fact he doesn't need any more complications.

But he's thinking how much he misses it. God help him, he does miss it so.

He tells himself it's shameful for a grown man to be so weak-minded.

He looks up. Dewey is staring out the front window, watching a young woman, a good-looking blonde, park a silver Ford Explorer and get out. Jeremiah knows her. She works the cash register down at the Medical Arts Pharmacy, where Jeremiah goes to get Martha's high blood pressure medicine. Name of Cindy Miller. She looks about as much like Dewey Sharpe as she does Muhammad Ali. She walks into the Big Scoop, eases into a booth down at the far end.

Jeremiah looks down at the case file, runs a big weathered hand down its length. Thinks about the debts he can't pay, about his wife, her troubles, how they're getting worse to the point where sometimes he doesn't feel like he knows her anymore. Thinks about his daughter, how little time she's got left on this earth.

Tough on a man to lose a daughter. Something Jim Fletcher knows a thing or two about.

A phrase comes to him from way back in his past, all the way back to high school.

"Centrifugal force" is the phrase. That's his problem. Too much centrifugal force in his life.

You ain't on the payroll no more, Jeremiah. You don't have a dog in this fight.

He thinks about Sissy Fletcher, ending up like this, about Sissy Fletcher's daddy, losing a daughter in such a fashion. What a thing to have to live with.

He thinks about the killer, maybe walking around town this very minute, feeling good about getting away with it. Passing folks on the street, saying howdy, just as smug as he can be with his secret. Maybe even attending services in Dr. Fletcher's own church on Sunday, sitting in a pew, listening to the sermon, smiling to his criminal self about what he had done, how he never got caught.

Jeremiah tells himself that life always has centrifugal forces. Maybe you just notice them more when you're cut loose from your center of gravity.

A thing can only be what it is.

He picks his hat up from off the seat, takes the file in his other hand. "When do you need this back?"

"Whenever you're done. Take all the time you need."

Jeremiah stands up, puts on his hat. "I got to go."

Jeremiah walks out the ice cream parlor, gets into his pickup. Duke has been sleeping on the front seat. He sits up to get a head scratching.

As Jeremiah pulls out of the parking lot, he notices Dewey is lumbering toward that blond-headed girl that works over at the pharmacy.

3

DEWEY DOESN'T COMMENCE TO BREATHE NORMAL UNTIL HE HEARS THE DOOR close behind Captain Spur. He had been sitting there puckered up the whole time, shoulders all in a bind, holding his breath, watching the man smoke his cigs, wondering if the tough old bird really meant what he said about being retired, not willing to help, practically making Dewey beg him.

Dewey doesn't like to beg. He finds it stressful.

Dewey is thinking how he must have sounded, his desperation leaking out in his voice there toward the end. He figures Jeremiah Spur isn't likely to respect a man much who comes across as that weak, but Dewey can live with that so long as the captain will lend a hand.

But will he?

No way to read a guy like that, face as expressive as a frying pan, eyes of a world-champion five-card-stud player, saying nothing about what's going on in his mind.

Still Dewey nurtures the feeling there had been something there, some reason to hope old Jeremiah was wrestling with it. Maybe it was the way he had run his hand down that case file.

And he *had* taken the file with him when he left.

Dewey snaps the attaché case shut, heaves himself out of the booth, puts Jeremiah Spur out of his mind.

Time to see about practicing a seduction on Miss Cindy Miller. He's feeling like today's the day he'll finally set sail on the S.S. *Dewey-Screws-the-Blond-Chick*.

Cindy is down yonder, in the booth at the far end, smiling his way. He grins back, starts walking over, affecting his best peace officer swagger, admiring her visage every strutting step of the way. Blond hair, long graceful neck, skin that is perfect as only the skin of a young woman can be, a woman too young to have collected the assorted wrinkles and spots and blemishes that get displayed on the surface of an older woman barring the vigorous and repeated application of cosmetic substances.

But the main thing is her eyes. They make Dewey feel like he's looking down from space at two little cloudless Earths, clear blue water wrapped around one dark continent, places of mysterious beauty to be explored and conquered.

Now that he's gotten within sniffing distance he can tell she's wearing perfume, makes her smell like a flower, gardenias he's guessing from what little he knows of flowers. He is thinking what it would be like to take her across the highway to the Adobe Inn, peel all the clothes off her, get her between the sheets with that gardenia smell.

Dewey is working at his number one goal in life, which is to become a practiced seducer of women, conqueror of hearts. Brazos River Valley Don Juan. He's just this close. The uniform, the hat, the badge, the boots, the gun—basically the whole Sheriff Dewey Sharpe package—gets him a ways there.

But not all the way to the barn.

Dewey knows that what's going to get him all the way to that room over at the Adobe Inn with Miss Cindy Miller is Power.

A man can tell this is so by a sideways glance at recent events, what's been in the newspapers, on TV and everywhere else you turn. They prove it up pretty as you please.

Power. Like the man said, the greatest aphrodisiac.

Dewey is in possession of Power here in Brenham, Texas, population 11,952. He knows he's within a gnat's eyelash of being a bedroom black belt, just needs a touch of conversational pixie dust, ounce or two of charisma. Personality is what ties it all together.

In the past it was always his savoir faire that let him down, crapping out on him at the moment of truth like it had some kind of fuse in it that blew at just the wrong time.

"So how you doin' this mornin'?" he says as he slides next to her in the booth.

"Fine," she says, melting him halfway to his boots with her smile.

They talk small awhile about the weather and what have you, until Dewey decides to make his move. "You give any thought to that little subject I raised the other day?"

"Dewey, I kind of hoped I had heard the last of that."

"Come on. You being in the medical profession, you know better than to load it up with a lot of emotional overburden. It's just a natural act, 'tween two consenting adults. No harm in it. Least not in comparison to its pleasurable aspects."

She ducks her head some, looks at him out from under her yellow bangs, gives him a little smile that adds twenty beats a minute to his pulse rate. "Dewey, I work the counter at the pharmacy. That doesn't make me a member of the medical profession. I do think you're just as sweet as can be.

You know I do. But I am seeing someone, don'cha know. And, besides, you're married."

"Yeah, well, so what? That don't mean there can't be no me and you."

"Dewey, we've been friends a long time, and so we should stay. I can't treat Hollis . . ."

Dewey snorts, shifts around so as to ease the load off his piles which have of late taken to tormenting him. "I'll tell you what, you lose that jerk and see how much happier you are. If he cared half as much about you as he did about himself it'd be different."

"Oh, that's just his way. Being such a natural-born talent at surgery and all, having the power to heal folks, working under all that pressure."

Dewey forges ahead like he hasn't heard her leaping to Hollis's defense, her brows all knitted together above her Planet Earths. "Top of that, the man is without a doubt the worst wing shot ever was. You shoulda seen him out on the County Hospital Board charity dove hunt last fall. I was next to him in the tree line. The guy went through about three boxes of shells, never busted one bird all day. Not one. He couldn't hit a bull in the ass with a tennis racket."

"Well he grew up in the north, don'cha know. Didn't learn to hunt until . . ."

"It was like he was puttin' in for the People for the Ethical Treatment of Animals Marksmanship Award."

"Dewey, it really doesn't matter to me whether . . ."

"And don't go thinkin' he's some kinda sure thing, just 'cause he's a doctor. There's law enforcement crawling all over the health care bidness, on account of Medicare fraud and whatnot. I see it in the papers all the time. It's even money he ends up in the penitentiary, married to the man with the most cigarettes."

"But Hollis is just the most honest man. Look, none of this matters two cents anyway, since you're married."

"Oh, hell, Claudia and I ain't hardly even on speaking terms."

"How come?"

"She's been on a tear ever since I accidentally pissed on her cockatiel."

"Do what?"

Dewey shifts around some more in his seat. Swallows some coffee. "See, she's got this damn cockatiel at the house. Used to belong to my bitch sister-in-law, Janice, lives up in Austin. Janice bought the bird, then come to find out she had to give it away, her kids was allergic to it or something. So what's she do? She palms it off on Claudia. God Almighty, I hate that bird, have ever since I first laid eyes on it."

"Did you say you had an accident on it?"

"Yeah, but it wasn't my fault. See, the deal is, I'm somewhat given to sleepwalkin'. Have been all my life. Sometimes when I sleepwalk I dream I'm goin' to the bathroom. When that happens, well, I just let 'er rip wherever I happen to be standin' at the moment. I don't know no better 'cause I'm asleep, you see."

Cindy nods, watching him tell his tale. Now that he's into it, Dewey's not sure this story is setting the right tone, forming the proper prelude to a belly-bumping session over at the Adobe. But he's gone this far, so he reckons he's got to finish.

"The other night I was walkin' 'round the house in my sleep and wouldn't you know I had my bathroom dream when I was standin' over the bird cage."

"Oh, my word."

"I swear, you never heard such squawkin'. Woke up both me and Claudia. She accused me of doin' it on purpose. Didn't even want to hear my side of the story. Anyway, can't hold a man to account for what he does in his sleep, can you?"

"I guess not."

"No, you can't. It ain't fair. But she don't care. She's got her panties all twisted up and that's it."

"Did she make you move out or anything?"

"Naw, she's just been a bitch with handles for about twenty-four hours a day."

"She'll get over it."

"Don't care if she does or not. I ain't gonna be home that much during the next few weeks anyhow." Dewey drops his voice, looks around. He can hear Mrs. Baker in the back singing "Jesus Loves Me." "I'm workin' a big murder case."

"Really?" Cindy whispers back. "What can you tell me about it?"

Dewey knows word's bound to be all over town by now, but he figures to act real secretive anyway, on account of it will make him seem more important. "Well, I'm not supposed to say nothin' yet, but since I trust you and all . . . You remember Sissy Fletcher?"

"Sure. She was a couple years ahead of me in high school."

"We found her remains buried out near Gay Hill. Somebody caved her skull in."

Cindy's eyes widen. She leans in. The smell of her perfume, the closeness of her body—it's just about all Dewey can do to keep his hands off her.

"So that explains it," Cindy says.

"Explains what?"

"Why you and Captain Spur were visiting when I arrived."

Dewey is wondering how in the world she can have known Dewey was talking to Jeremiah Spur about . . .

She says, "Can you tell me what he knows about it?"

"About what?"

"You know. About his daughter. And Sissy."

"Whose daughter?"

"Come on, Dewey. Captain Spur's daughter."

"What about her?"

Cindy draws back some. "You mean you don't know?"

"Cindy, I swear to God, I got no idea what you are talking about."

"Okay, you know Captain Spur's got a daughter, Elizabeth."

"I don't know her, but I've heard tell of her. I've heard she's real sick in a hospital down in Houston."

Cindy nods, yellow hair swinging around. "Yeah, that's her. There've been rumors around town for years. People say she was the last person to see Sissy Fletcher before she disappeared."

"Do what?"

"Word is somebody saw just the two of them. Late the night Sissy disappeared, after the rodeo dance. In Sissy's pickup truck, don'cha know."

Dewey is thinking hard about the file he handed over to Jeremiah Spur. "There wasn't nothin' about that in the case file."

"Maybe the police didn't talk to the right people last time. And you know what else? Not long after Sissy turned up missing, Elizabeth moved out to California."

"News to me."

"And listen to this—did you know she's a lesbian?"

"The hell you say."

"Swear to God."

Dewey is quiet now, turning all this over in his mind. Cindy takes a swallow from her mug, wipes her mouth. "Listen, Dewey, it's been fun chatting, but I need to scoot. I have to get back, finish up some stuff. I'm getting off early today."

"Oh, yeah?" Dewey stands up to let her out, not thinking about Sissy Fletcher and Elizabeth Spur now, thinking instead if Cindy's taking the afternoon off maybe they could spend a couple hours together, over at the Adobe. He's supposed to play golf this afternoon, but to hell with that. Besides, he could still get over to the club this evening for cocktails and a few hands of gin rummy.

"Hollis is taking me to Houston for dinner and a baseball game. See ya." Her lips brush his cheek on her way past.

"Great. That's just great."

Dewey slumps back down in the booth, watches her get into her SUV, tight skirt straining against her thighs, her hips. She drives away, leaving him behind alone, still breathing her perfume, molars grinding.

"Damn Hollis. Goddamn piece of shit Yankee bastard."

The S.S. *Dewey-Screws-the-Blond-Chick* has just taken another torpedo below the waterline, leaving Dewey feeling like a loser, sexual frustration eating him alive.

Not only that, now he's got this new angle to figure in the Sissy Fletcher business.

He scratches his head, wondering just what was all that about Jeremiah's sick daughter, anyway? Her, a lesbian? Dewey isn't even sure he's ever met one of them.

And if everybody knows she was the last person seen with Sissy Fletcher, how come no one questioned her, got her statement, during the first go around?

Dewey's no professional cop and he knows it. Owes his job to political pull, got appointed sheriff a few years back when the former sheriff was bounced out over the death in custody of a black prisoner. But even someone with lawman credentials as suspect as Dewey's could tell from reading the Fletcher case file that the first investigation had been downright spotty. Lacking in leadership. Misdirected as all get out. Word back then was, if you needed something from old Sheriff Patterson, you had best look for him down at Skeeter's Ice House, and it had better be before noon. He preferred to spend his time down there, getting drunker than a waltzing piss ant, instead of doing police work, having to mess around with victims and criminals and such.

But still and all . . .

Dewey stares at the floor, wondering how much of this old Jeremiah knows. Maybe he knows it all, doesn't want to get involved because of something about his daughter and Sissy Fletcher. Jeremiah sure was quick to finger that Mexican kid, trying to make him out as the killer. Dewey shakes his head at this thought, because it doesn't seem like the Jeremiah Spur he has heard tell of for so long.

Dewey looks around, listens to Mrs. Baker singing, sounds like "The Teensy Weensy Spider," thinks maybe the reason he's not getting anywhere with Cindy Miller is because of the atmosphere. Maybe that's what's spoiling it.

He had picked this place because it's out here at the bypass, near Cindy's pharmacy, not much chance they'd run into Claudia way out here. Claudia works in town, at the antiques store across from the courthouse. She never comes out this way.

Dewey decides he needs to find another spot for his little get-togethers with Cindy, someplace with a little romance to it, more conducive to triggering some kind of howling hormonal surge in a woman. This joint ain't getting it done.

As he gets up to leave, Dewey is thinking it's been a rough morning.

4

JEREMIAH SPUR AND HIS DOG DUKE ARE DOING SEVENTY DOWN HIGHWAY 290, smoke getting thicker the farther south they go, blocking out the sun, making the whole world feel strange, artificial, like some Hollywood set where they're getting ready to film something, a battlefield scene maybe.

Jeremiah smokes a Camel, thinking some about the dead girl buried in the pasture, then telling himself to get his mind off that case file and back on his own daughter.

They call it acute myelocytic leukemia, and it's damned nasty. Maybe fifteen thousand folks a year get it in America. Two-thirds of them are dead inside of twelve months.

It's pretty much a death sentence, is what it is.

Elizabeth found out she had it late last year. Went to see her doctor with a spot on her arm that wouldn't heal, they ran a few tests and then bang. There she was with it.

Jeremiah takes the Loop around to Fannin, turns north toward the Medical Center, a bunch of hospitals and parking structures all coveyed up together. He pulls into the M. D. Andersen garage, takes the ramp up to the floor one down from the top where there are no other cars parked and Duke will have some shade.

He pulls into a space, rolls the windows down halfway, lights a cigarette, sits and smokes, Duke lying on the seat watching him.

His mind slides back to the Fletcher girl, trying to remember her. Seems like he must have met her. He recollects now that Elizabeth and Sissy had known each other, but just how well he couldn't say. Sissy had been, what, five, six years older than Elizabeth? No bigger than Brenham is, he wonders if maybe they had even been friends.

It seems like something he should know about his own daughter. If he hadn't been on the road so much when she was growing up, he would have been able to keep up with that kind of thing.

He asks himself whether it would matter if they had been friends and decides maybe it would. Maybe he'd somehow owe it to Elizabeth to help the sheriff out. He figures to raise the matter with Elizabeth, if she feels up to talking about it.

"Okay," he says to Duke, flicking the cigarette butt out the window. "I'm goin' in. You just sit here now, you hear?"

The place is a rat's maze of halls going every which way, here and there a set of elevators, stripes of different colors on the walls, supposed to help guide you. He knows the layout now, not apt to take a wrong turn, get lost for a half hour like he did the first time he came down here.

Directly he finds Elizabeth's room, pushes through the door. Sees she's sleeping.

Amanda sits on the other side of the room by the window reading a magazine. She's a sight to behold what with her crew cut, rings and studs stuck in her ears and lips and eyebrows and such. Jeremiah is never sure what the right protocol with her is, whether to shake her hand or give her a hug or just exactly what. This morning she looks tired, eyes red from too little sleep.

She puts the magazine down, starts to stand when he walks in. Jeremiah takes off his hat, motions her to sit, eases around the foot of the bed, where Elizabeth is hooked up to various tentacles of medical science, machines and IV drips.

"Howdy," he whispers. "How's she doin'?"

"Better. At least she's been able to rest some. The morphine helps."

"How're you doin'?"

He gets a weak smile back. "Okay. I'm just tired."

"Why don't you go get yourself a cup of coffee or somethin'? I'll sit here a spell."

Jeremiah eases into the armchair, looks at his sick daughter's face. The cancer, those terrible hard drugs they use on her, they've made her so frail, seems like she has to work hard just to breathe. Seeing her so makes him feel helpless.

It's a feeling he purely hates.

He turns to look out the window, searching for some kind of distraction, not wanting to think of his daughter dying on him. Her room is on the top floor, higher than all the other buildings around. When it's clear outside you can see all the way downtown, where the tall office towers are clustered, but today the smoke from the Mexican fires blocks the view, and he can't see a thing north of the Rice University campus.

It's noontime, the street down below thick with traffic. It's a mystery to Jeremiah how folks can live in this town. All the people, forever getting in one another's way. The fuss they make all hours of the day. He would be crazy inside of a week.

"Is it still smoky out there?"

He turns around and there's Elizabeth, awake, watching him.

"Oh, hi, honey. I didn't know you was awake."

"I just woke up. Thanks for coming. How's the smoke?"

"Oh, hell, worse than ever. We ain't seen the sun since last Saturday. Gonna be that way 'til we get some rain, I reckon. I swear them Mexicans is trying to kill us."

Then Jeremiah thinks about what it is he just said. He swallows, stares down at his boots, boots he now sees somehow still have the dust from the yard on them. He's gone and tracked that dust in here. Just like a dumb ass old rancher to pull a stunt like that. He turns his hat around and around in his hands, unsupplied with words.

Jeremiah is thinking he needs to forget his disreputable-looking boots, summon up something to say, force it out, talk to his daughter. He looks up. "So, how you doin'?"

"Oh, you know, 'bout the same. I get the treatments twice a week. It's only chemo now. They stopped the radiation for good, or so they say. The doctor is supposed to be in later, talk about where we go from here." She pauses, seems to be catching her breath. "It's been almost six months. They say after that length of time there's not much point in continuing with the chemo."

They're silent until she speaks again. "Papa, how's Mama?"

"She's hurtin', honey. She still don't know how to handle you bein' sick and all."

"Have you had any luck, you know, trying to keep her sober?"

"None to speak of. She said she'll go with me, see the preacher about it. About that, and ever-thing else what's troublin' her."

"That's good. That's a start."

"Speakin' of the preacher, here's somethin' you might be interested in. The sheriff's boys found a body buried out in a pasture a couple days ago. Remember Sissy Fletcher?"

Jeremiah sees Elizabeth's eyes flicker. "Yes."

"It was her remains. The sheriff asked me this morning to give 'em a hand with the case."

Elizabeth closes her eyes, sinks back in her pillow for a bit, opens them again. Jeremiah can see the pain living in her, like some evil spirit that has moved in and won't leave.

"Papa, I thought you were retired."

"Well, I am. But they sure seem to need the help."

Elizabeth closes her eyes again. "So, are you planning to give them a hand?"

"It's against my better judgment to. Kindly got my hands full at the moment."

"Yes, you do." Elizabeth opens her eyes, shifts so she can fix Jeremiah full on with a look. "One of the things dying does for you is—no, now, just listen to me, okay?—it frees you up to be candid."

"If you say so, honey."

"Well, I do. So let me be candid with you, as hard as that may be for the both of us. Papa, I'm sure they could use your help. But right now you need to keep your priorities straight. Your priorities are Mama and the ranch."

"Them's my thoughts exactly."

"Besides, nothing good can come from digging around in the past. Especially where Sissy Fletcher is concerned. Take my word for it."

Jeremiah turns his hat around and around in his hands, not used to advice on how to live his life from his daughter, not sure how to respond to it. "I reckon."

The door opens, a nurse walks in, pulling a cart loaded with pills and syringes and the like.

Elizabeth smiles her weak little smile. "At last. I was beginning to wonder if you all had forgotten about me."

The nurse smiles back. "We never forget you, child." She looks at Jeremiah. "Could you excuse us for a few minutes?"

Jeremiah gets up, walks out the door, into the hallway. All around there are doctors and nurses, attending to the business of the cancer ward. They're so busy they hardly look his way, but he's conscious of the dust on his boots, the Camels in his shirt pocket. He's thinking how much he hates hospitals. Hates them and fears them. He turns his hat around in his hands, stays close to the wall, out of everybody's way.

Judging by Elizabeth's reaction, he reckons he had better reconcile himself to steering clear of the Fletcher case. He supposes it's better that way, but he can't help but feel a twinge of regret.

It is a fact, he says to himself, that a thing can only be what it is.

5

THE BIGGEST OFFICE IN THE COURTHOUSE, BIGGER EVEN THAN THE COUNTY
judge's, is a corner job on the second floor belonging to George Barnett,
Washington County district attorney, going on thirty-five years now.

It's an office that has always struck Dewey Sharpe as more trophy room
than lawyer's office and to give himself something to do while George jaws
away on the phone Dewey sits across from George's cherry-wood partner's
desk, with its hand-carved trim and the ball and claw feet, counting
George's trophies.

Starting with seven presidents of the United States of America and going
from there down through the ranks, United States senators, governors, lieu-
tenant governors, attorneys general, judges, state legislators, famous smiles
on famous men, plus a woman or two, that had had their pictures taken
with George. All personally signed, the big-deal politician in the picture
going to the trouble to convey something heartfelt or jocular to George,
proof of George's access to the power of the signer.

There were plenty of courthouse legends about how the DA had used
each of those fine public servants somehow or other along the way, and
how they in turn had used him back, and then given him their pictures to
display on his wall so as to underscore his long tenure and the influence
that comes with it. To make the point for the benefit of all who enter his
presence that George Barnett is a Great Man.

All these famous men and women—well, two women—are obliged to
share George's walls with an animal head collection, trophy mounts of
mule and whitetail deer, an elk, some kind of African antelope, and one of
those wild pigs from South Texas, as well as the entire bodies of ducks,
quail, a bass, and two rainbow trout. These were animals that had once
walked the Earth's land or flown the Earth's air or swam the Earth's waters
and that owing to some wicked twist of their own fate had happened to
cross paths with the DA only to be killed by him for the sport of it.

Dewey's a hunter and a fisherman too so he's not being judgmental.
Might be a tad envious though.

The wild pig is the most recent addition to the George Barnett Collection, and it's so ugly it seems to Dewey that it must have been created by

God on one of His more pissed-off days. The name it goes by is "javelina," one of those Mexican words, where you don't say the "J" like a "J," instead it comes out like an "H." George had had the thing mounted with its fangs bared, and a cigar wedged between its teeth.

The pig and the DA look so much alike they could practically be kin— coarse black hair slicked back, malevolent eyes, big snout, bared fangs, cigar. The DA is too smart not to know this, and the pig has a place of honor on the wall just above the DA's head.

The fact that Dewey can see as far as the wall is itself something of a miracle what with a thick cloud of cigar smoke churning in the room. The DA looks to be on about his fourth stogie of the day even though it's barely eleven o'clock. The room stinks something fierce and Dewey's nose is about to itch plumb off.

Dewey drums his fingers on the arm of his chair, wondering how much longer he is going to have to wait for the DA to get off the phone. It's already been nearly half an hour since he was shown in and still George is cocked back in his big leather chair, hand-tooled snakeskin boots up on the desk, puffing away, sweet-talking Lamar Jackson, the editor of the *Brenham Gazette*.

Goddamnit, Dewey says to himself, *he's stealin' my thunder. Lamar ought to be interviewing me. It's my department what found the body.*

If George didn't practically run the damn county, Dewey would up and leave.

Finally the DA closes the conversation, leans forward, hangs up. He takes his cigar out of his mouth, turns his snout to one side, coughs, spits little flecks of tobacco out. He looks at Dewey, makes no move to get up, offer his hand.

"Hello, Dewey," he says. "How the hell are you?"

"I been worse."

"My guess is you been better too, my boy. I got your message that you had told Jim y'all had dug up his daughter."

"That's right. Soon as we got the ME's report, saw the match on the dental. Went over to the church office. Seen him there."

"What about the brother? I forget his name."

"His name is Martin. Jim said he'd talk to him himself."

"How'd Jim take it?"

"Better than I would have if it had of been me. Said it was tough on him, havin' to reopen that part of his life after all these years. Said some kind of quotation, something some German said about staring at some abyss too much. I said to him what's a abyss? He said it's a big hole."

"Uh-huh."

"I think he must have done the better part of his grievin' long ago."

"Hell, Sissy gave him plenty of cause to grieve while she was still alive."

"I reckon."

"Hard to understand how a man as fine as Jim Fletcher could produce a daughter like her. Him a genuine man of God, her such a public sinner. Putting real energy and enthusiasm into it. Strange, don't you think?"

"Yep."

"Well, I'll give him a call later."

"I'm sure he'd appreciate that."

"Listen, my boy." George swings his boots to the floor, sits upright, elbows on the desk, stubby finger pointing at Dewey. "I assume you know this case will be attracting considerable attention."

"What do you mean?"

"Lamar was just saying he expects the Houston press to pick it up. As though he won't have a hand in that. Hell, I wouldn't be surprised if we had TV camera crews up here in a couple days. Now what I'm wondering is . . ." The intercom cuts him off.

"Mr. Barnett?" a tinny voice asks.

"What is it, Brenda?"

"I got the governor's office on line one. Returning your call."

" 'Scuse me a second," he says to Dewey, takes the cigar out of his mouth, picks up the handset, punches a flashing button on the phone.

"This is George Barnett. Yes, I'll hold . . . Good morning, Governor. How are things in Austin? . . . Yes, sir, we got it here too. Probably will until we get some rain, at least that's what they say. . . . Yes, sir. Our cattlemen are sure feeling it. Listen, I know you're busy, and I appreciate your calling me back. I thought you'd like to know, our Sheriff's Department found Jim Fletcher's daughter's remains a couple days ago . . . Yes, sir, buried in a pasture over on the west side of the county. You know where Gay Hill is, where we had that barbecue fund-raiser for you? . . . Yeah, that's what it looks like. . . . The sheriff and I were just fixing to talk about that, as a matter of fact. . . . You read my mind, Governor, that's just what I was thinking. I appreciate the offer. How about Frank Cade? You think you could get the Rangers to free him up? . . . I couldn't agree more, Governor. We appreciate the help. I'll pass it along to Sheriff Sharpe. Yes, sir. Okay, thanks again for calling and tell the missus I said 'howdy.' "

George hangs up, sticks his cigar back in his mouth, looks over at Dewey.

"That was the governor," he says, as if Dewey hadn't just sat through his end of the entire conversation.

"How does the governor know Jim Fletcher?"

"Jim was an assistant minister in the church the governor attended growing up."

"Is that a fact?"

"He offered up the Rangers."

"I don't think I need the Rangers."

"Look, Dewey, like I was saying, this case'll be on many a radar screen on account of Jim Fletcher being such a big deal in town and the church and all."

"That don't mean we automatically got to call in the Rangers."

"It might not be such a bad idea, though, when you take into account it's not the kind of case we typically get around here. It'll be built on forensic and circumstantial evidence, no eyewitnesses. On top of that, you're not gonna be able to count on much help from the folks who knew Sissy, once you go pawin' around in her past. There's plenty there that folks in this town would just as lief be let alone."

"You can get folks to talk if you go about it right."

"How would you know?"

Dewey hesitates, fidgets. Tries to think of what to say. "Well, you can."

"Look, I just wonder if y'all wouldn't be better served to get yourselves some help from some high-powered investigative types, like the Rangers. The governor says he can shake Frank Cade loose from over in San Antonio."

"I hear what you're sayin', but I say we ought to keep this local. In fact, just this mornin' I took it up with Jeremiah Spur."

The DA visibly starts. "You did what?"

"Discussed it with old Jeremiah. Talked to him 'bout comin' out of retirement, givin' us a hand, consultin' some."

"Shit, Dewey." The DA puffs out some cigar smoke, snout pointed at Dewey, wild pig eyes boring in, looking at Dewey like he's some kind of lower life form.

"What's the matter? You got a problem with Captain Spur?"

"Why would I have a problem with him? Was a time, I'll grant you, when Jeremiah would have eaten this case up. And if he was to get involved it would please the governor, too, for sure. Jeremiah always has been one of his favorites."

"Glad you like the idea."

"Not so fast." The DA's puffing up a storm now. "Captain Spur happens to have a few problems of his own, like a daughter that's took bad sick with the cancer. From what I hear, the doctors don't know how much longer she's got. And his wife's not exactly handling it too well. Besides, he's in the same money bind as every other rancher in the county, what with the drought and the sorry state of the cattle market and so on."

"So you think it's apt to be a tough sell."

"Shit, Dewey, what am I sayin' here, huh? Jeremiah Spur isn't cashing the state's checks anymore and he's got his hands more than full already. I'd be astounded if he'd lift a finger on this thing."

"But, George . . ."

"Shut up, Dewey. There's something you need to understand. Maybe you can coax Jeremiah into this. I for one am not holding *my* breath, but I guess you can try to do anything you think you're big enough to do. But one way or another, my boy, you better get yourself some help. And do you want to know why?"

Dewey stares at the floor. "No, but I got a feelin' I'm fixin' to learn."

"Because everybody in this town knows you can't find your ass with both hands, that's why. So you take this case on by your fundamentally incompetent lonesome and it gets fucked up, I will personally see to it that Joe Bob Cole is the next sheriff of this county. And you know good and goddamn well I can do it. So for your own good, to provide you the cover you need, you ought to let me give Frank Cade a call."

The abuse has set the tips of Dewey's ears on fire. He swallows, tells himself to take it easy, says, "I get the message, George."

The DA coughs, spits more tobacco flecks on the floor, works his tongue around the inside of his big lips. "Alright, then. But there's another thing we need to discuss. Word is Clyde Thomas found the body, so he's all over you, wanting on the case."

"True enough."

"But unless I miss my bet you don't want the voters to be all confused about who's in charge, especially if the Rangers get involved, huh? So I'm betting if you had your druthers, you'd druther he kept his distance."

Dewey can't for the life of him figure out where this is heading.

"Well, my boy?"

"There's somethin' to what you say."

The DA stubs out his cigar. "Thought so. I've said you all should call in some help and I meant it. But whether y'all handle this yourselves, or get the Rangers in, or ever-how you do it, y'all are gonna need us to help clear out ever-what procedural underbrush there is. Make sure if you do arrest somebody you'll have a tryable case."

"I reckon."

"I'm not asking for your agreement, Dewey. I'm telling you how it's going to be. The best lawyer we got is Sonya Nichols, and I'll let you have her. But only on condition that Clyde Thomas ain't got a thing to do with this investigation, on account of their personal relationship raises what might be called the appearance of impropriety. Having them two lovebirds working together would raise eyebrows. You with me?"

Dewey's not quite sure what the DA is getting at, decides a little candor won't hurt, George having been so candid with him. "Sounds like a bullshit reason to me."

"Of course it's bullshit. You know it's bullshit and I know it's bullshit. If your nigger deputy thinks about it for five seconds he'll know it's bullshit too. So how do you think he'll react?"

"Like he always does. He'll go flappin' around, callin' me and you and ever-body else he can think of a rascist."

The DA nods his head, grabs a new cigar out of a box on his desk, leans back in his chair, commences to unwrap it. "Seems likely, doesn't it? With any luck he'll go off like a Roman candle, quit or give you a reason to fire his miserable black ass. Then we'll finally be shed of that goddamn pain in the ass nigger that you had the questionable judgment to hire in the first place."

"I see what you're sayin'."

"Good. Now we're done. Oh, and Dewey," the DA says, putting his feet back up on his desk as Dewey stands to leave. "I'm only going to say this one more time. Do not fuck this up. Take my advice. Call in the Rangers, my boy. Call in Frank Cade."

"'Ppreciate the advice, George."

Well, Dewey thinks as he closes the DA's office door behind him, *I ain't inviting the Rangers in, I don't care if it harelips George Barnett and the governor and the pope hisself. Them boys would shove me out the way so fast it'd make me swimmy-headed.*

Dewey knows George Barnett thinks he runs this county, and he takes a dim view of folks who ignore his advice. He's not above having his political machine teach Dewey a lesson, instruct him on the consequences of turning a deaf ear to the DA. The only way Dewey can be sure George won't have a grudge to nurse is to come to heel.

Just like the DA to suggest Frank Cade, too. Cade may be a Texas Ranger and all but everybody knows George has Cade in his pocket, uses him for opposition research on potential opponents, all kinds of stuff. Dewey has never been able to understand how come a guy like George could lead the likes of Frank Cade around by the nose.

Dewey clumps downstairs, out of the courthouse, into the hazy Texas morning, smoke and haze so thick you can't see the sun, yet it's still so cotton-picking *hot.* Gonna be near a hundred today.

The other strange thing was the way the DA had acted at the mention of Jeremiah Spur, like Dewey had just uttered a cuss word in polite company. Dewey had heard some stories over the years, about there being some kind of history between the DA and the Spurs, but he'd never put much stock in them.

Then again, maybe George had heard this rumor of Cindy's, that Elizabeth Spur had been the last person seen with Sissy, and that was what caused the DA to flinch at the sound of Jeremiah's name. But that doesn't strike Dewey as too likely, since there had been no mention of any such thing in the original investigation report and the DA had not brought it up himself.

No, Dewey figures, that one little lead may not be much, but it's his very own and he intends to keep it to himself for the time being, give him a leg up on everybody that thinks he isn't up to tackling this here case.

He decides that before he has any kind of confrontation with Clyde Thomas he needs to get himself something to eat. He heads across the street to the Farm-to-Market Café, thinking, *It's only May and already it's hotter than a buzzard's crotch.*

6

CLYDE THOMAS STEERS HIS CRUISER INTO THE PARKING LOT OF UNCLE FRED-die's Wine and Spirits, parks, gets out. Pushes his way through the door.

The clerk behind the counter looks up from his comic book, hollers out, "Here come da judge!" Guy's grinning like a hound dog eating a canned ham.

It's the same deal with the few black guys around town Clyde counts as friends, him having to live with this "here-come-da-judge" stuff on account of that black guy on the Supreme Court up in D.C. Clyde's "C" stands for "Clarence," making him "Clarence Thomas," like the Mr. Justice. Folks years ago took to calling Clyde "the Judge."

"Yo, Jasper. What's up?"

Jasper hauls himself off his stool, sticks his hand out to give Clyde a shake. "Nuthin', man. Just here fightin' this cash register is all. What's up with you?"

Clyde styles back to the soft drink case, helps himself to a Coca-Cola, looks around at the racks of whiskey, beer cases stacked one on top of the other, ready for the brothers to come in, buy them, take them home, drain them, seek relief from their dead-end lives, their boredom with their own minds. He comes back to the front of the store.

"What's up with me," he says, "is basically the same ol' shit, you know what I'm sayin'? 'Cept for the murder case I'se workin'."

He pops the top on his Coke, pushes his hat back on this head, takes a swallow.

"No shit?"

"No shit, man. Got a call on Monday, some oil workers were scrapin' 'round in a pasture out Gay Hill way, turned up a suspicious-lookin' boot. Dispatch knew right off, thing to do was put the department's best man on the case."

"That's you, huh."

"Who else would it be? Turns out that boot was on the bony-ass skeleton of a local preacher's daughter, got herself disappeared a few years back, been missin' ever since. She'd been offed."

"Who done it?"

"Don't nobody know. That's why I'se workin' the case, see. It's a big 'un, too, lots of pressure, her daddy big stuff here in Shitberg. You heard of Jim Fletcher?"

"Yeah, man. That the girl's daddy?"

"That's right. That's high profile, you know what I'm sayin'? That fool sheriff I work for been hintin' 'round maybe he ought to be runnin' the show, 'stead of me. Only he ain't a real cop. He's more like a politician, got hisself elected a cop."

"Uh-huh."

"He try to take my case away, he's gonna have a big-ass problem."

"That's right."

"Now, you know what I'm here for, and it ain't this can of soda pop."

"Yes, sir. You be wantin' to know if I'se clean."

Last year Clyde's fellow deputy Bobby Crowner had pulled Jasper over for running a stop sign, caught a whiff of what was in the car, busted him for possession, two joints and two rocks of crack. The only reason this kid's not up in Huntsville right this minute, getting himself an advanced degree in the criminal arts and sciences on full scholarship from the state of Texas, was on account of Clyde vouching for him with his lady friend, Sonya, over in the DA's office.

Clyde knows Jasper and his mama from church, knows Jasper's no hoodlum, just never had any kind of fair shake, no male role model to ride his ass, keep it on the straight and narrow. Clyde swore to Sonya he'd make sure the brother stayed clean.

They pled him out, got him ninety in county and the rest probated. Clyde saw to it he got into treatment, then fixed him up with a job. Had to lean on old Freddie pretty hard before he came through, had to promise Freddie he'd keep an eye on the kid, make sure he didn't backslide, start financing his appetite for drugs out of Freddie's till.

Clyde has pledged to himself, This one they gonna save. This brother's gonna make it. Next fall, Jasper would start classes over at Blinn County Junior College, start working toward his degree in something legitimate, something that will get him out of this dump, help him start a life somewhere like Houston maybe.

"Well, is you?"

"Yes, sir. Just clean as can be."

"Let me look in your eyes. You ain't clean, I can see the crack in there, swimmin' around like dog shit."

He looks into Jasper's eyes, sees they're clear.

"Okay. You better stay clean. I find out you ain't, you know what'll happen?"

"Yes, sir. You gonna find me, whip my punk ass like a natural man."

"You got that right. And that is at a minimum."

Clyde's cell phone chirps. He reaches down, unhooks it, says, "Deputy Thomas."

"Clyde? Where are you?" It's Billie the brain-dead receptionist from down at the office, the one with the tonal inflection, makes all her sentences sound like questions.

"I'm over at Uncle Freddie's. What you want?"

"The sheriff was lookin' for you a while ago, says for you to come in for a visit?"

"Alright. I'll be there directly." He hangs up, reaches into his pocket for his money clip, peels off a buck, flips it to the kid, heads for the door, says, "See you around, Jasper. Don't do nothin' that'll make me have to come jump up and down on yo' ass."

"Don't dash yet, man. You got a quarter comin' back."

"Keep it."

"Thanks, man. Hey, Judge."

"Yeah?"

"Everybody say since you shaved yo' head, y'all look like Michael."

Clyde stops, turns back. He whips off his Stetson, shows off the top of his head, all shiny, smooth as a river rock. Sets Jasper to whooping such that Clyde can still hear him, even after Clyde's out the door, back in the parking lot.

Clyde slides behind the wheel of his cruiser, heads off toward the courthouse. He takes no notice of the two white men sitting in the pickup truck parked across the street such that they can watch the liquor store, even though it's not a part of town where a couple white ranchers ordinarily go to sit in their vehicle.

Not all the black folks treat Clyde like a star, even though when he landed here he was the first black deputy in Washington County since Reconstruction, if then. There wouldn't be one yet if a black man hadn't died in custody six years ago. Body so busted up when the cops finally got him over to the emergency room, it looked like the brother had been set upon by a pack of gorillas swinging tire tools.

Next thing the Sheriff's Department knew, FBI, Department of Justice, braless reporter women from the Eastern press, civil-rights types from over in Houston, they were all over their asses, had the heat turned way up. Cost the sheriff his job.

One of the consequences was the feds put the squeeze on the new sheriff, Dewey Sharpe, saw to it he hired a black man on as a deputy.

Clyde had been working traffic up in Dallas, heard about the job. He was tired of taking shit from the DPD racists, thought it'd be preferable to hang out with the cross-burners in Hootersville for a while. Clyde likes the way the gig's been going. Especially since he got to know Sonya, started seeing her.

But some of the brothers around town didn't much care for him taking up with Sonya. Between that and his position in law enforcement, it put some distance between them and him, caused them to regard him with a measure of suspicion, like he'd turned against his own people somehow.

He also knows his thing with Sonya puts a bull's-eye on him too, so far as some of the local hardcase rednecks go, but his thinking is, he's the one has the uniform, the squad car that can go 150 miles an hour, the Glock nine-millimeter. Ain't much they can do about it.

As he drives back to the office he commences to whistle a tune. Clyde thinks life is working out just fine.

Like most folks who entertain such notions, he would feel differently if he had access to more complete information.

7

MARTIN FLETCHER WATCHES THE BIG BLACK DEPUTY WALK OUT OF THE LIQUOR store, get in the squad car, take off leaving rubber on the street, going fast toward town.

He turns to look at Dud Hughes sitting over on the passenger side with his John Deere baseball cap shoved back on his head, sleeves of his khaki shirt rolled up to his elbows. Martin says, "Did you see how that nigger carried himself?"

Dud's got his eyes fixed on his wristwatch. He looks up at Martin, says, "What do you mean?"

"I'm talkin' about how he walked. Even though he's a cop, he walked like he was a pimp or a drug pusher or something. You know, it's just natural for them folks to walk like criminals, even when they supposed to be the law. Niggers."

"Look, Martin, I was busy timin' him like you asked me to do, so I can't say I made much of a study of his walk. You want me to watch the nigger walk, you got to do your own timin'."

"What was it then, eight minutes maybe?"

Dud Hughes checks his watch again, lips moving in silent calculation. "Pretty good guess, partner. Closer to seven and a half."

"Musta known the guy behind the counter, stopped to visit some."

"Uh-huh. Martin?"

"What?"

"I'm real sorry 'bout Sissy."

"You done said that."

"I just wanted you to know."

"Fine. Don't bring it up again."

"Okay. Martin?"

"Now what?"

"I don't git it."

"What don't you git?"

"I don't git how you figger to make enough knockin' off a liquor store to do anybody any good."

Martin sighs, scratches at his long black beard, which looks to most folks like it could stand to be trimmed. His beard gives him a wildness of appearance, a look reinforced by his eyes, which burn in his head as though what they see stirs an anger deep within him.

He cranks the driver's-side window down, leans out, spits a stream of tobacco juice, uses the sleeve of his denim work shirt to wipe the excess off his mouth, contemplates his Dud Hughes problem, the upshot of which is that the man is fence-post dumb, lacks the brain for finance. Martin can only hope Dud's propensity for violence will offset his intellectual shortcomings.

Martin knows Dud loves him like a brother. If Martin asked Dud to kill a man for him, Dud would have it done by sundown. But if Martin asked Dud to solve a problem in long division he might well be in his dotage before Dud ever got back to him.

But old Dud's about the only guy around here Martin can rely on to be of use in Martin's life's work, his God-given mission to throw off the chains that the evil, atheistic government has wrapped around the white man, and Martin's grateful to have the help, especially now that God has this very week gone out of his way to get Martin's attention, focus him on the need for action. Soon.

Martin leans out of the cab, spits again, turns to Dud. "Let's see if I can 'splain it to you. Thing about armed robbery is—no wait, think of it this a way. If I was to take you down to my father's church, set you behind the organ, open the hymnal up to the 'Doxology,' could you play it?"

"Do what?"

"Could you play the organ? Could you play the 'Doxology' on the organ if I was to set you in front of it?"

"No, I reckon not."

"That's right. Not unless you have some lessons first. And practiced at it some."

"What's that got to do with doin' this liquor store over here in nigger town?"

"What it has to do with it is, armed robbery's like playin' a musical instrument, except there ain't no place to go to get armed robbery lessons. You got to be self-taught. And you got to practice."

"Practice?"

"Yeah, like with this here liquor store." Martin jerks his head in the direction of the store, which sits across the street with its pink and green trim, its burglar bars in the windows, its hand-drawn signs advertising malt liquor specials hanging catty-wompass on the walls. "You figger the job out, pull it off, walk away with the contents of the cash drawer, don't get caught. That's like learnin' to play 'Chopsticks.' Come on."

Martin opens the door, starts to get out.

"Where we goin'?"

"To check it out. Let's go."

The liquor store sits by itself, vacant lot on one side, abandoned auto repair shop on the other, rows of shotgun shacks back behind it and then farther down the street on the left-hand side, houses with paint blistered up and peeling off, tarpaper roofs.

Down yonder Martin can see laundry hanging limply from clotheslines, the smoky air so still nothing moves, not so much as a strap on a pair of overalls, the clotheslines themselves tied between trees and the posts of crooked porches weighed down with old furniture, major appliances, like faceless angular beasts that have been cornered just across the border of a closed and broken land, now silently guarding the secrets they left behind, on the other side of the screen door.

There are no signs of life on the street here at midday beyond a few black kids riding around on beat-up old bicycles, chasing one another, fighting in the dirt.

Inside the store it's cool and dark. Rows of liquor bottles line the walls, beer cases are stacked on the floor, the aisles are filled with racks holding cheap wines, cases of soda pop, a couple shelves of snack foods. There behind the counter is a black guy reading a comic book, watching them some.

Dud stops at the counter. "How you doin', boy?"

"Help you?"

Martin says, "Where you keep the soft drinks?"

"'Frigerator case. Back o' the sto'."

Martin walks to the back, gets a Dr Pepper out of the cooler. Hollers back at Dud, "You want anything?"

"Yeah. Git me a Lone Star."

"Comin' up."

Martin grabs the beer, turns, looks around, sees a storeroom in the back, might be a safe in there. No security camera, no security at all that Martin can see. Could be the clerk has a piece tucked away somewhere behind the counter.

He heads back to the front.

"That be a dolla seventy-nine."

"Pay the man," Martin says to Dud.

Dud reaches for his wallet, says, "That cop what was just in here."

"Who, Clyde?"

"I reckon. Deputy sheriff."

"Yeah. That be Clyde."

"He a friend of yours?"

"Yeah, man. He like a big brother to me."

"Uh-huh."

"Peoples around here, they call him da Judge."

Dud collects his change and his Lone Star, starts for the door. "Is that a fact? He don't look like no judge I ever seen. Looks more like a convict to me."

"He ain't no convict."

"Yeah, well, we'll see you."

Back in the truck, Martin puts the can in the drink holder, cranks the engine, pulls his truck out onto the street.

"Nothin' to it," he says. "Wait 'til just before closin' time, middle or end of the month. On payday, day the welfare checks are cut. Walk in. Put the muzzle of my three fifty-seven Magnum between the eyes of that blue gum behind the counter. Get his attention focused on that. It's nothin' but a short little black tunnel, but he'll be thinkin' it's big enough, long enough to take him straight to Jesus, if I was to put enough pressure on the trigger. He'll hand us the cash drawer. We take the money. Leave. Slick as a whistle."

"Like learnin' to play 'Chopsticks,' huh?"

Martin's not listening to Dud. He's wondering whether he ought to just do the guy behind the counter, better not to have any witnesses. He can feel the big gun recoiling in his hand, smell of cordite in his nostrils now, just driving down the street, thinking about it.

He doesn't have to decide this very minute. He'll make his mind up then, standing over that boy.

"Martin?"

"Yeah?"

"I said just like learnin' to play 'Chopsticks.' "

"Huh? Yeah. That's the idea."

"Bet there ain't that much in the till."

"Excuse me?"

"You know, it'd be nice to have a little extra left over, help out with the bills."

"So?"

"I'm just sayin', you'd git more money from a bank."

"What?"

"I always wanted to do a bank job."

"You don't know nothin' about nothin', do you?"

"I'm just sayin'—"

"Come on. I'll show you what I'm talkin' about."

He takes a left at the next intersection and heads back into town.

Inside of a half hour they're standing in the marble lobby of the First State Bank of Brenham, Martin and Dud leaning over the table where the deposit slips are kept, pretending to be filling one out.

"Okay," Martin whispers. "Over by the door, a guard with a gun."

"It's just one guy."

"Yeah, but you got to figger out some way to deal with him."

"Be easy to take him out with an automatic weapon."

"That would make a lot of racket, too, now wouldn't it?"

"Well, yeah."

"Might have the cops swarmin' all over the place. Now, looky here, how many security cameras you see?"

Dud looks up, glances around the room, pretends he's stuck trying to figure a sum. He looks back down. "Four."

"Wrong. There's six. One in each corner, two behind the counter."

"So they got security cameras."

"Yeah, and little buttons under the counter they punch, send a signal to the cops. See anybody you recognize?"

"Yeah. Behind the counter. Lisa Winkelford, or she used to be Lisa Winkelford, before she married that guy, what's-his-name, the plumber. You know who I mean."

"Let's go."

They wad up their paperwork, head for the door, nod to the guard on their way out into the parking lot.

"So," Martin says, "you got your basic armed guard. And your basic video security system, silent alarm and whatnot. And your basic employees, know what we look like, how we walk, talk, dress, that sort of thing. So you got all that. Now here's a question for you—what time of day do banks open?"

"In the morning, 'bout nine."

" 'Til when?"

"I dunno. Middle of the day."

"Middle of the day. Broad daylight. People around then, customers, passersby who can watch you come and go. And they got exploding dye packs, other stuff, makes it easy to get caught if you don't know what you're doin'.."

"So it's tougher."

"You bet it's tougher. Like playin' the 'Doxology.' You don't just up and do it 'cause you decide to do it. Takes planning, practice."

"Well, let's get the practice then. I'm itchin' to do a bank."

They keep quiet until Martin has pulled his pickup out of the bank parking lot.

Then Dud says, "Plannin' and practice, huh. Like you been sayin' about any kind of a target we might decide to go after."

Martin shrugs. "Well, that's a little different, I reckon. My point there is more, you got to seek the guidance of God Almighty if you want to be assured of success, light a fire that will lead to the liberation of the people."

"You still think that's where them boys up in Oklahoma went wrong?"

"Absolutely. I don't think they had taken God's wishes into account, 'specially in light of the day-care center bein' there and all. We can't be goin' around pickin' targets without guidance from the Lord or it'll end up counterproductive. All Oklahoma did was drive all the patriots underground. So in my daily prayer sessions, I been seekin' the Lord's will in this thing, try to make sure we're a hunnerd percent certain."

"I don't see how you can ever be a hunnerd percent sure about such a thing."

Martin pulls up at a stoplight, looks over at Dud. "Well, you can. This business with my sister for example."

"I didn't think you wanted to talk about her."

"I don't. But here's the deal. The fact she's been gone all these years and now they dug her up—it's like God's tryin' to say somethin' to me, you know? Send me some kind of message."

"What kind of message?"

"I don't know exactly. He's got somethin' He wants me to do, some kind of mission He wants me to go on. I'm still prayin' on it."

The light turns green and Martin pulls through the intersection. They drive into the service station where Dud had left his pickup to have the tires balanced. They can see it parked off to the side.

"Looks like they done finished," Dud says. He opens the door to get out of the truck.

"Dud?"

Dud gets out, looks back in at Martin. "Yeah?"

"Where is the sheriff's office at?"

"Do what?"

"The sheriff's office. Where's it at?"

"I don't know. The county courthouse, I expect. How come?"

"I had a dream last night. About Oklahoma City. I dreamed I was there. Only . . ."

"Only what?"

"Only it wasn't the federal building that got blowed up. It was the Washington County courthouse."

"I don't reckon I get it."

"I dreamed that God spoke to me."

"How do you know it was God?"

Martin shrugs. "You just know."

"What did He say?"

"He called me His Messenger. He said, 'Martin Luther Fletcher, thou art My Messenger. You must take My message to My people.' "

"How come Him to pick you?"

"Beats me."

"Well, then, what's His message?"

"I ain't completely for sure."

"I hope you don't mind my sayin' so, but that's pretty weird, Martin."

"Was the sheriff's boys dug my sister up."

"I know."

"And they operate out the courthouse."

"I reckon they do."

Martin shifts his gaze off into the far distance. "I think God is tryin' to tell me somethin', Dud."

"Whatever you say, Martin." Dud turns to walk off.

"Hey, Dud!"

Dud turns around, walks back to the truck. "Yeah?"

"What are you doin' tonight?"

"Nothin', I reckon."

"Good. I'll be by to pick you up at nine o'clock."

"Why?"

Martin smiles. "Today's pretty much the middle of the month."

Then he shifts the truck into drive and pulls away.

8

GEORGE BARNETT WHEELS THE BIG BLACK LINCOLN INTO THE BLUEBONNET ICE Cream Company parking lot, navigates into a space that lets him watch the front door by looking in the rearview out the back glass, figuring there's less chance he'll get spotted that way. He leaves the engine running, needs the air-conditioning to stay on, else he'd be prostrate from heat stroke inside of five minutes.

He reaches inside his coat pocket and plucks out a Cohiba, a genuine bootleg *Habano*, still in its little box, part of a supply his oil man cousin smuggled in from London last month. He lights it, sits back to puff and wait.

Directly there is motion reflected in his rearview mirror and the sizable frame of Joe Bob Cole emerges from the ice cream plant, makes his way across the parking lot toward George through the incessant smoke and haze that smother creation like a curse straight from God's lips.

Joe Bob opens the passenger's side door, sets himself inside, his weight rocking the big car when he hits the seat. He reaches over with his right hand to shake George's, using his left hand to scratch a long black sideburn that's flecked with dandruff.

"Howdy, George. Nice of you to call, offer to buy my lunch."

"Don't mention it," George says around his cigar, slipping the car into reverse, then pointing it out the parking lot, headed east. "I thought we might get a ways out of town so we can have some privacy. Maybe head over to Bertha's in Hempstead."

"Works for me. Chicken-fried steak there has always been pretty reliable."

"So how's the ice cream business?"

"It's been better. We strugglin' to maintain our market share, what with the Germans hammerin' away with their big national advertising campaign and them hippies up in Vermont confusing the American public with their environmentalist crap. And then you got the media gettin' everybody all stirred up about low-fat diets, so nobody—"

"Joe Bob." George takes the cigar between two thick fingers, points his snout at the big man, staring at him to get his attention.

"What?"

"It was a rhetorical question. I don't give the remotest shit about the ice cream business, okay?" George bites down on his cigar, rolls the driver's-side window down a couple inches to let some of the smoke inside his sedan escape, join the smoke in the outside world.

"Okay. Sorry."

"Something I do care about, however, is whether you got the *huevos* to bump off that ridiculous amateur Dewey Sharpe in the primary next year."

"I don't reckon I can miss, what with your help and all."

"My boy, you are so right. You don't know how right you are."

"Meaning what, exactly?"

"Meaning I'll lay odds that before the day's out there is going to be a major change in personnel in the Sheriff's Department."

"George, I have no idea what you're talkin' about."

"I believe, my boy, that I have engineered it such that your old friend Clyde Thomas is probably going to take the sizable bait I've dangled in front of his pork chop-eatin' lips and quit. Today, more'n likely."

Joe Bob stares out the window in silence. George can see he is trying to calculate how this might be a good thing for his candidacy, trying to puzzle it out in that pea brain of his. George puffs on his cigar, lets the silence drag out.

Finally Joe Bob clears his throat. "George, you sure that's a good thing? I mean, lots of white folks around here was going to vote against Dewey on account of they can't stand that black bastard."

George takes a final pull on his Cohiba, flicks the butt out the window, shoots Joe Bob a sideways look. "We'll be at the restaurant in a few minutes. Then I'll explain it to you, my boy."

George doesn't get back into the subject until the waitress sets the chicken-fried steaks down and fetches the ketchup bottle. He says, "Now, like I was saying about that boy Clyde. I'll grant you with that attitude of his, plus his shacking up with my best assistant DA, he sticks in the craw of a good many of the white people. But that is not the main point at the moment."

"What would the main point be then?"

"The main point is"—George lowers his voice, leans in some—"the main point is . . . and if you ever repeat this I'll say you're a lying sack of shit . . . the main point is he's a pretty good cop. Easily the best there is in the department. The rest of them don't know any more about police work than they do about the culinary practices in the Hebrides. Which is to say, were they to find themselves with a high-profile criminal case, say a murder case, they are likely to make a major display of their incompetence. Pave the way for a reform campaign based upon your well-earned reputation as a crime-fighter."

Joe Bob shrugs. "I still don't get how this is all that helpful. There ain't no crime around here anyhow to speak of."

"Well, now, you're wrong about that too, my boy."

George lays down his utensils, takes a drink of iced tea, sets the tea glass down, clears his throat. "Two days ago a body turned up in a pasture over near Gay Hill."

Now Joe Bob lays down his fork and looks back at the district attorney.

George locks eyes with Joe Bob. "Now it was our man Clyde that turned the body up, and I expect him to quit his job because Dewey is gonna take him off the case. At my suggestion, of course."

"Okay. Whose body was it? Or you want me to try and guess that too?"

George is watching Joe Bob closely now. "You want to take a guess? Got any idea who might have been shallow buried out yonder?"

George waits, but Joe Bob keeps still.

"It was Sissy Fletcher," says George. "She was a close friend of yours, as I recollect."

"We knew each other."

"That's one way to say it. Another way would be to say you were fucking her. And still another way would be to say you had an 'adulterous affair,' which, if memory serves, was the turn of phrase your wife's lawyers selected for the divorce papers."

"You got a hell of a memory, George."

"Divorce papers that were served pretty much the exact same day your wife got a manila envelope full of mighty interesting pictures delivered to her front doorstep by a person or persons unknown. Not long after that Miss Alicia Fletcher dropped your ass. And just a little while later that *same* Miss Fletcher disappeared altogether."

"What's your point, George?" Joe Bob is tensing up now, face all clouded over.

"And unless I am mistaken it was you that worked the case for Pat Patterson when she went missing. Even though some folks might have thought that was a mighty peculiar way to go about staffing such a thing under the circumstances."

Joe Bob's eyebrows arch. "That's kind of a funny thing for you to say."

"How come?"

"'Cause Pat told me it was you who suggested he put me on the case."

George chuckles. "That old drunk never could be trusted to keep his mouth shut, even when he was told to."

"And it was you told him nobody ought to bust a gut on it, seein' as how she had more than likely up and quit this town like she'd been threatenin' to do for years, just run off with some bull rider."

"I'll grant you, that's what I thought at the time. But now, of course, you got to ask yourself, who would of wanted to see her dead?"

Joe Bob snorts. "The line of people would of stretched around this here restaurant."

"And you'd of been standin' in it."

"What the fuck is that supposed to mean?" The clouds have descended on Joe Bob's face again and he looks like he's fixing to erupt, brows all furrowed, fists clenched on either side of his plate of half-eaten chicken-fried steak.

"You got any idea who might of done her in, Joe Bob?"

"No, sir, I don't."

George looks at Joe Bob hard, pinning him down with his wild pig eyes. He lets the silence grow between them. Then he leans back.

"That's what I'd sure like to believe. Because I can't be throwing my weight behind a man who's got secrets that might be embarrassing to the both of us were they ever somehow to come out."

"Ever-body's got a secret or two, George. As I recollect you might have some your own self. Like what it might have been would have caused *your* wife, just a couple years before my wife dumped me, to drive her Lincoln into an overpass pillar going about a hunnerd miles an hour—"

"Watch it, boy. Don't fuck with me."

"—not wearing her seat belt. But you can quit worrying about whether I'm the one that planted Sissy Fletcher out in that pasture. It ain't me that done it. You need suspects, you'll find there are plenty around here who took as bad from her as I did."

"Okay. Fine. I can't exactly say I figured you for it, although if I had of been in your shoes, I don't know that I wouldn't have been tempted. I just wanted to hear you say you were clean."

Some of the tension leaks out of Joe Bob's posture. "So you really think Dewey and the boys gonna screw the pooch on this Sissy Fletcher deal, huh?"

"They got no more chance of finding the killer than the man in the moon."

"That's too bad," Joe Bob says, a little uncertainly. "That means her killer gets away with what he done."

George shrugs. "I'm not sure anyone ought to care about a murder that's ten years in the past."

"Kind of a strange position for a district attorney to take."

George shrugs again. "The fact that no one should care doesn't mean folks won't. They will care, something fierce. Which is just fine, speaking in strictly political terms, since all Dewey and his group of dimwits are going to do is stumble around, in all likelihood make asses of themselves. At the same time old Dewey's in a pickle because if he brings somebody in from the outside it just points up how he ain't up to his job."

"Somebody from the outside?"

"Yeah."

"Like who?"

"Like Frank Cade."

"How is old Frank?"

"He's good. We went spring turkey hunting together last month, up in Hamilton County. He killed himself a nice gobbler."

"He's always been your boy, ain't he?"

"Me and Frank got ourselves an understanding. Anyway, I offered to get him involved but Dewey wasn't havin' none of it. I didn't figure he would. Plus I went out of my way to insult him, made like I thought he was too much of a fool to take this on himself. Took a sledgehammer to his pride."

"So he's gonna go it alone."

"He'd like to. But see, that's the problem. Even Dewey's not such a fool that he doesn't know he ain't up to it. Get this." George leans back in, lowers his voice. "He wants to try to get Jeremiah Spur to help out."

"You're shittin' me."

"Not for a minute. The way he sees it, he can get Spur to consult, leverage off the man's experience, up the odds he'll crack the case, but keep all the credit to himself. Not a bad plan when you think about it."

This news appears to arrest the relaxation process that had begun to take hold in Joe Bob. "Well, shit, if that happens, Dewey'll come out looking like a hero."

George leans back again, waves dismissively. "Oh, don't go getting your bowels in an uproar. Spur ain't about to have a thing to do with this."

"How do you know?"

"Two reasons. He's distracted. And he's compromised."

"Do what?"

"Never mind. There's just no way Jeremiah Spur is gonna have anything to do with any investigation into the death of Sissy Fletcher."

"You sound like you know more than you're sayin'."

"All you need to know is that Jeremiah Spur ain't a factor."

"Which means he stays out."

"Yep."

Joe Bob scratches a sideburn, causing dandruff to shower onto his cheap suit. "And since Dewey ain't callin' in the Rangers that means Dewey is on his own, assumin' Clyde Thomas does like you say and goes back to the watermelon patch."

"Yep."

"Which means the case is apt to go unsolved."

"I'd lay heavy odds on it."

"Which means I'm gonna whip Dewey's ass in the primary next year."

"Don't forget to mention me in your victory speech."

Joe Bob grins wide. "It'll be a pleasure, George."

Dewey Sharpe is sitting in his office when there's a knock on the door and Clyde Thomas sticks his head in. "Yo, Sheriff, you lookin' for me?"

"Yep. Have a seat," Dewey says.

Clyde pulls up a chair.

Dewey clears his throat, fiddles with a pencil, doodles some. "I paid a call on George Barnett this morning, wanted to get his take on staffin' the Fletcher case. He feels right strong about it, stronger than nine feet up a bull's ass."

"So what, man?"

Dewey hurries on. "Well, he's all over me to call in the Rangers, for one thing. And he says we got to work with someone from his office, make sure there's no foulups legal-wise. He's offered up Sonya, keep us straight in that department."

"You got a point you tryin' to get to, huh?" Clyde says, his jaw muscles clenching.

"It's like this, Clyde—George don't want you and Sonya workin' the same case."

"What the fuck?"

"I'm sorry, Clyde, but I don't got much choice but to respect George's judgment on this. His office is gonna have to try any case we develop and he's right concerned that y'all's relationship might screw things up."

It gets quiet, Clyde just sitting there, Dewey concentrating on playing with his pencil. Then Clyde jumps to his feet, sends his chair hurtling backward against the far wall. He leans over into Dewey's face, his eyes wild, jaw muscles working.

Dewey shrinks back, thinking, *This guy's about to come across this desk, beat the everliving shit out of me.*

"Don't jack me off, Dewey," Clyde says. "Fact that I'm goin' out with Sonya ain't got shit to do with it."

"Now, goddamnit, Clyde . . ."

"Shut up, man. I ain't through by a damn sight. You think I'm stupid, huh? Nigger too dumb to know when the white man is fuckin' with him, right? You figure I'll just lie down for all this garbage you running at me about screwin' up the case, all that bullshit, just bitch out, right? Just go back to steppin' and fetchin' for yo' fat country-fried ass. Well, I ain't, motherfucker."

"Look, Clyde, you really need to settle down."

"Yeah, well, that's what you think, man. You know what, man? I don't need this shit. I fuckin' quit, man. You can have my badge, you know what I'm sayin'?"

Clyde spins around, kicks the chair out of the way, charges out the door.

"Well," Dewey says under his breath, "there goes the black vote."

The sound of the door slamming rings in Dewey's ears for a long time.

9

JEREMIAH SPUR PULLS OFF THE COUNTY ROAD INTO HIS DRIVEWAY, STEERS THE truck behind the house, parks, gets out, Duke hitting the ground behind him.

The garage door is up but Martha's car is gone. Jeremiah figures she probably left to go run errands or something. Things have gotten so bad lately that Jeremiah is just as happy she's not around, a realization that comes with a little jolt of guilt.

In the kitchen there's a pot of something simmering on the stove, potato soup judging from the smell of it. He notices the message light blinking on the answering machine and punches the button, drawing himself a glass of water while the thing plays.

"Hello, Martha, Jeremiah. This is Jim Fletcher. I just wanted to confirm our appointment tomorrow morning at ten o'clock. No need to call me back—if I don't hear from you, I'll assume you're coming. I'm looking forward to seeing you. Thanks and have a nice evening."

Jeremiah has been wondering should he call Dr. Fletcher, offer to postpone, what with the preacher's daughter having just turned up dead. He takes a long drink of tap water, looks out the kitchen window at his dusty fields stretching up the little hill behind his house.

That's the thing about a pro, he thinks. He gets the job done. Lawmen, preachers, whatever. Pros are tough-minded that way.

Soon he and Duke are back in the pickup, bouncing through the dust headed to the back pasture. The rest of the world will spin as it may, but Jeremiah Spur's got a busted fence post needs fixing. The cattle watch them as they go by. In the rearview, Jeremiah can see Duke back there nose up, taking in whatever smells are riding the sooty air.

He pulls to a stop next to the fence, parks, unloads the gear he needs. Duke drops to the ground, trots off.

Jeremiah clips the barbed wire from the busted fence post, gets the posthole digger, commences to dig. The hardpan fights back. Sweat boils out of him, darkens his khaki shirt. The hazy air unstirred by breeze, the sticky afternoon heat have him wheezing.

It takes him twenty minutes digging to get the old fence post loose. He wrestles it out, tosses it aside with a grunt, mixes the concrete, pours it in, positions the new post, at first just eyeballing it up straight, then clamping a level against it, using his free hand to straighten it further.

He reaches for his handkerchief, wipes his face, leans against the pickup, looking to rest, smoke a cigarette while the concrete dries. He puzzles over Elizabeth, at her reaction to the mention of Sissy Fletcher. He's not quite sure what to make of it.

Jeremiah can read a man pretty fair. But women—damn, why are they always so powerfully hard to figure? His own flesh and blood even.

It wasn't always so where Elizabeth was concerned. The two of them used to communicate right well back when she was young. Living out in the country, on a ranch, it gave him a chance to teach her stuff, about horses, for instance, how to ride them, care for them. The two of them had ridden together from the time she was five. It gave them a common language, a language Martha did not comprehend and that was accordingly somehow more special to them, a tongue foreign to all but lovers of horses.

It was natural that her love of horses had led her to barrel racing. Looking at the images of the past that populate his mind he can still see her plain as day, fifteen years old, at the Washington County rodeo, up on her quarter horse Polly, leaning hard into the big horse's neck until their forms merged, whipping around those red and white barrels while he sat up in the grandstands listening to Martha's whispered prayers for her safety. Elizabeth had looked every bit the part too. Had a face full of freckles, wore her hair pulled back in a ponytail under her Stetson, a Western shirt with fake pearl buttons, jeans held up by a hand-tooled belt fastened with a big silver belt buckle, black Tony Lama lizard-skin boots he and Martha had given her one Christmas.

She rode better than the boys did and by God if she hadn't roped better than all but one or two of them. She never got tired of proving it to them, neither.

But then she got older, changed somehow. Sure, they all do, but this had been pretty stark. She spoke the language of horse lovers less and less until she ceased to speak it altogether. Over the course of some months it was as though she had become some other person, a stranger to her parents, almost like the old Elizabeth had broke apart into a billion pieces, broke such that no amount of horseback rides together through spring pastures quilted with bluebonnets could fix her back the way she'd been.

Or maybe the old Elizabeth was still in there somewhere, but some kind of wall Jeremiah couldn't see had come whanging down between them. For a while he took to the notion that it was just teenage rebellion. She and her mother got to where they couldn't talk to one another, just as likely as not their conversations would end with their backs turned one against the other, each hollering to be heard over the other.

He had tried his darnedest to understand it but he never could.

It strikes him as odd that the God that had given him discernment of livestock and criminals saw fit to deny him discernment of his own child.

A thing can only be what it is.

He flicks the cigarette butt on the ground. He likes it out here where it's quiet, just the *thump thump, thump thump* of the rocker arm over at Frank Gibson's pulling oil out of the Austin Chalk, and Duke barking away at something on the other side of a little hill in his pasture. He checks the fence post, tests to see if he can string the wire, but the concrete hasn't fixed yet. He lights another Camel, leans against the truck.

One day, when Elizabeth was a senior in high school, she up and announced she was leaving, going off to San Francisco as soon as she graduated, surprising Jeremiah that she would want to go live in a place she had never seen. He hadn't wanted her to go but he didn't have the words to get her to stay. By then she and her mother weren't on speaking terms, hadn't been for months.

He remembers driving her to town the day she left, waiting with her in the pickup for the Greyhound to arrive, carry her up to Dallas. He had thought that there were some things he probably ought to say to her as she took her leave but his mind was altogether blank. They sat there in silence, waiting for the bus, him smoking one cigarette after another, staring out the windshield, his brain as empty as a widow's bed.

Directly the bus pulled up. He fetched her bag from the back of the pickup, carried it to where the bus driver was loading luggage for folks.

She was fixing to board when she turned to him, asked if she could hug him. It had surprised him, her feeling the need to ask first. He dropped his cigarette on the pavement, ground it out with the toe of his boot, hugged her hard. He could smell her hair spray, her perfume.

He can smell it to this day.

While she was hugging him back she said, "I wish you'd quit smokin', Papa. It's gonna kill you."

He didn't have the words for what was in his heart, so he just said, "Take care, honey. Call us ever-when you get there."

They heard from her now and again, but hardly ever saw her. When they did, at Christmas or whatnot, she seemed completely different.

For one thing, if you hadn't known of your own knowledge she had grown up on a ranch in Texas, you never could have guessed it. She didn't talk Texan anymore, it was some other language she spoke, more correct in her English and pronunciation. She didn't care to go riding, didn't even want to spend time with Polly, except to see her for a minute or two, stroke her big nose, give her a carrot.

And then there was the other thing.

It occurs to Jeremiah that old Duke is still over yonder somewhere barking up a storm, straining at it out here in this heat. *Damn dog's gonna bark himself silly.*

Elizabeth hadn't been gone but a couple years when they got her letter. It had come on a Saturday when he happened to be home. Martha read it once, then handed it to him and went to lie down. He remembers sitting in his rocker reading it no telling how many times, not quite knowing what to think.

It took him many a day of studying on it before he got used to thinking of his daughter as a homosexual. But poor Martha, she had taken it terrible hard, such that she's not over it to this day, bless her heart.

Relations between Elizabeth and her mother, poor as they were, worsened still, what with Elizabeth wanting to bring Amanda home whenever she came. Martha wasn't having any of it and the two of them dug in from there.

Martha never seemed to want to discuss the matter and he, well, he had never been much of a talker, certainly not about that sort of thing. His devoted observance of the virtue of silence, his mastery of the by now mostly forgotten practice of keeping still when you don't have anything much to say, had always stood him in good stead as a Ranger, but had come to seem like something of a liability in family matters.

And then last year Elizabeth had called, said she had cancer, said she was "coming home to Texas to die." Had said it just so, matter-of-fact like.

He has never been able to get out of his head how she had hugged him, had asked him to stop smoking. Then got on the bus. And now she has come back after all these years but only because she is dying.

Now Duke's barking sounds downright frantic. Jeremiah is thinking what in the world could it be out here this time of year that . . .

Snake season.

Jeremiah grabs the shovel out of the pickup, starts running after his dog. On the other side of the rise he can see Duke down near a brush pile Jeremiah cut a while back, a mound of dead mesquite, scrub oak. Ordinarily he would have burned it by now, but what with the drought, the fire risk was such that he had decided to put it off.

Duke is down there barking for all he's worth, hair up on the back of his neck, mouth dripping foam.

"Duke!"

The big black dog gives no sign of hearing him. He barks furiously, focused on something over by the brush pile.

Jeremiah's nerves set to tingling. He starts running hard.

Then he hears the rattle going. He doesn't see the snake until he's twenty yards or so away, then there it is, low against the ground, the same color as the dried-up pasture, folded back on itself strike-ready, maybe fifteen feet from his dog, rattle going fast. It is a big damn snake, maybe six feet long.

Automatically Jeremiah's right hand drops to his hip where his Colt Commander .45 used to ride. All he comes up with is belt loop.

Jeremiah forces himself into a walk, figuring if he were to run up on Duke, Duke would close on the snake, charge into strike range, put himself between Jeremiah and the rattler. Jeremiah has seen it happen before. Dogs are like that.

He works his way to within ten feet of Duke. The rancher edges forward, a little at a time, eyes always on the snake.

"Easy, boy, easy. Easy now, Duke." Duke is lunging in and back, in and back. The snake's head twitches, darts, measuring the distance to the big Lab.

Jeremiah closes on his dog, grabs his collar, hauls him backward. Even with Jeremiah's fist around his collar Duke continues to lunge, wanting back at that snake, his collar twisting and turning in Jeremiah's hand, Jeremiah straining to overcome Duke's ninety pounds of thrust, the two of them kicking up dust clouds as they go. Jeremiah backs him up, away from the snake, out of strike range, drops to a knee, one hand on Duke's hindquarters, pushing down hard.

"DUKE! YOU SIT! SIT NOW, YOU HEAR?"

Now the dog eases off, sits, sides heaving.

"Good boy. That's a boy. Good boy. Now stay."

Duke is panting now, saliva running down his neck. Then he closes his jaws, leans forward, a growl growing deep in his throat.

"STAY!"

Jeremiah waits until he knows he'll be obeyed. Then he gets up, shovel in hand, walks back to where the snake is, moving slowly, carefully so as not to provoke a strike, getting just close enough in and then quickly raising the shovel up over his head with the blade pointed toward the snake, bringing it down fast, catching the rattler right behind its head. The long brown and black body whips back and forth until at last it becomes still.

Jeremiah pokes around, looking for a nest, thinking he's got to get back out here in the next couple days, torch this brush.

He walks back to where Duke sits, sets the shovel down, looks his dog over.

"What'd you want to go and scare me like that for?" Jeremiah whispers as he checks the dog out. "Don't do that no more, y'hear? Don't know what I'd do if—"

It's a weak-minded thought he cuts short, feeling like an idiot, out here in a pasture whispering to a dog.

Still he can't get it out of his mind, how it was the last thing she did, just before she got on the bus. She had hugged him and asked him to stop smoking.

10

IT'S NEAR SUPPERTIME WHEN JEREMIAH PULLS HIS PICKUP BACK BEHIND THE house. He gets out, walks to a cabinet on the porch, pulls out a forty-pound bag of dog food, sets out a bowl of chow and some fresh water for Duke.

The pot of soup still sits on the stove, a bowl and a spoon next to it along with a plate of corn bread. Jeremiah washes up, helps himself to some supper, carries it on a TV tray into the living room.

He finds Martha right where he expects to, on the couch over to the left of the door, dressed in a flowered housedress. As poorly lit as this room is, still you can tell her hair has commenced to thin and it could use some looking after. She hasn't been much of a mind lately to apply makeup, the flush in her cheeks coming from liquor.

She stares across her tray at the television, itself the only source of light in the room, some kind of game show playing there, sound off.

This is how she takes her meals, has for many a year. She once told Jeremiah she got into the habit of it when his job took him out of town for long stretches of time, leaving her with no company for supper. Jeremiah places a certain value on his time to himself so it was a while before it occurred to him that in sharing this with him she may have been lodging some manner of grievance.

Jeremiah sets his tray down, eases into his armchair, starting to feel some soreness now in his shoulders from the afternoon's effort. He starts to say something to her about having killed a big snake in the back pasture this evening but thinks better of it.

He pinches off a bite of corn bread, says, "How was your day?"

"Fine," she says, not looking his way. "Did you make it down to the hospital?"

"Yep."

They eat awhile. Then Martha asks, "How is she?"

"Weak, but I don't think she's in no pain to speak of. They give her lots of painkiller. Not much else can be done I reckon. They've quit the chemo. No point in it."

Martha gets up, leaves with her tray, comes back, carrying a full tea glass, the smell of the vodka working its way over to Jeremiah.

"She ain't got much longer, Martha. I know she'd like to see you."

Martha is quiet so long Jeremiah begins to wonder if she heard him. Then she says, "Not while that other one is there."

"You mean Amanda?"

"Who else would I mean?"

"From what I can tell she's a pretty nice gal."

Martha sips her drink, stares at the television playing across the room. "I heard in town today Sissy Fletcher turned up buried over near here somewhere."

"Yep. Almost to Gay Hill. I thought maybe Jim'd druther postpone our session, but he left word on the machine we should come ahead on."

"I'd be surprised if he could keep his mind on his business."

"He must think he can."

Martha sips at her drink. "Well, I guess we're going then."

Jeremiah clears his throat. "The sheriff visited with me this morning about this Sissy Fletcher thing. The forensics make it plain it was homicide."

"What a surprise."

"The sheriff's concerned he can't get the job done hisself."

Martha shifts some. "How predictable. Don't tell me, let me guess. He would be ever so grateful if you would put your life on hold for a while, give them a hand."

"Well, I ain't gonna. I told him, call the Rangers."

"Oh, really."

The sound of her voice, the edge that's in it, makes Jeremiah wonder how much vodka she has poured down her whistle already this evening. "I don't believe I ought to be getting in the middle of that."

She turns, looks at him, the light from the television illuminating half her face, the other half dark, in the shadows, as though she were wearing some kind of mask over it.

"Oh, come off it, Jeremiah. You'll do it. First I imagine you'll wrestle with it some. Not for the reason most folks would—the fact that if anybody had it coming to them, Sissy Fletcher did."

"While I can't say I remember all that much about her, I am given to understand someone crushed her head like it was a melon. Nobody has that coming to 'em."

"Just as I was saying. A victim's a victim in your book. Fact that she was evil through and through—well, that's essentially irrelevant, isn't it? Not a factor. No, the reason you'll wrestle with it is, you've been telling yourself you have certain duties to your family, and they take priority."

"And that's a fact."

"Yes, it is a fact. But let's don't lie to ourselves about the rest of the facts. Someone's been murdered. The local police, who are never anything but a bunch of amateurs to your way of thinking, need help. A killer's out there, and somebody has to be the one to bring him to justice. It's the call of another duty, isn't it? Turning away from one duty to respond to the other—isn't that what makes you Jeremiah Spur?"

"I hear what you're sayin'."

"At the end of the day, you'll do it. It's like my daddy used to say, the older a person gets, the more like himself he becomes. More than likely it's your fate to go do this thing."

"I'm sorry. I reckon I'm not following you on that last thing there."

"I'm talking about fate. You'll help the sheriff out because it's your fate to do it."

"I've never much cottoned to it, the idea of fate."

"Doesn't matter whether you have or not, it's a force in the universe every bit as real as magnetism or gravity. Your life, my life, all our lives, they're fate's unfinished business. Now fate has landed Sissy Fletcher's corpse in your path. It ought to be interesting to see where things go from there."

She turns away, stares at the television across the room. On the TV screen a group of young people are silently gallomping around in what looks to be some kind of sitcom.

Jeremiah polishes off his meal, takes his plate and bowl to the kitchen sink, heads out to the back porch to rock, smoke, scratch Duke behind the ears.

He can't help but think that married life with Martha has certainly seen its better day and yet he's got feelings for her, once the prettiest thing in three counties. She could have had anybody for a husband. She chose Jeremiah of her own free will, and then she had given him a great gift—she had given him her youth, making a life for them out here, raising their daughter, practically all by herself.

It had just flat used her up.

Jeremiah has long believed that a person is the sum of their antecedents. He's the sum of his, she's the sum of hers, they are powerful and inescapable. Her antecedents made her what she is.

Maybe tomorrow will help them get to the bottom of her melancholy. He's heard tell Jim Fletcher is good at it.

Now his mind is back to the Sissy Fletcher business, Martha's reaction to it, stranger in a way even than Elizabeth's, all this nonsense about fate. He doesn't see any connection between him and the Fletcher girl whatsoever.

Martha has always had a peculiar sort of mystical side, her seeing a batch of preternatural forces at work in the world—angels, miracles, omens and the like. Phenomena that don't exist for Jeremiah.

But his fate all tangled up with Sissy Fletcher? That notion strikes him as far-fetched, and he figures he most likely has the vodka to thank for it.

That file is still sitting out yonder on the floorboard of the pickup.

"Good night," Martha calls out to him, her words a mumbled slur.

"Good night."

A man with the sense God gave a doorknob would just leave it be, let that file sit out there all night until he can deliver it back to that fool sheriff.

Then again, the way Elizabeth and Martha reacted . . .

Hell. A quick look-see can't hurt.

Jeremiah stubs out his cigarette, heads to the pickup, wondering despite himself if it's just one more step in fate's direction.

11

DEWEY SHARPE PUSHES THROUGH THE LOCKER-ROOM DOORS GLAD TO BE SHED of the golf course. He knows if a man sets out to play a game of golf, he had better prepare for it by concentrating his mind solely on his golf game, not let a ceaseless swarm of distractions from down at the office pester him, send his mind off in forty eleven different directions.

That Sissy Fletcher mess was hard enough to set aside. But then Clyde had gone and pulled that Mount St. Helen's routine in his office and the entire department was in an uproar about it. Word that Clyde had quit was already buzzing around town.

So Dewey had paid the price for his inability to focus his scrambled mind. Four and a half hours of atrocious golf.

Now he is ready for some heavy-duty nineteenth hole action here in the locker room of the Brenham Country Club where there must be twenty-five guys this evening, doing the locker-room thing, drinking, smoking, belching, playing cards, telling jokes, the air heavy with the smell of beer and cigar smoke.

Dewey sees a group playing dominoes off to one side, pretends he doesn't notice Joe Bob Cole over there drinking a beer with one hand and scratching himself under the armpit with the other.

On the television behind the bar a baseball game is going, Atlanta against somebody. No one is paying it any mind except Rufus Marsh, who may or may not already be fifteen sheets to the wind.

Rufus is the dean of the BCC alcoholics, a scotch-and-water guzzler with a nose that looks like a ripe eggplant, a scrawny body that has a great distended gut cantilevered off its front, and a cough that reminds Dewey of a flooded lawnmower somebody is trying to pull start. Day in, day out, the man sits there on his barstool, proceeds to get and stay drunker than any-body else, a fine service which the other boys appreciate since it allows them to say to themselves so what if they get drunk now and then at least they aren't as bad as old Rufus.

The other thing about Rufus is that sometimes it seems like he has crossed over to some other plane of consciousness not accessible by the sober or by those who merely overindulge on occasion, and in so doing has achieved a sort of transcendent perspective. Every once in a while he will dismount from his barstool and deliver himself of a statement that strikes everybody within earshot as damned near oracular. Then he'll climb back up on his barstool and not say another word for weeks on end.

Dewey can see Stan Rainwater, Leslie Payne, Barry Tillman, his old running buddies from high school, grouped around a card table way at the back. Dewey swings by the bar, collects the gin and tonic the bartender has waiting for him, strolls through the room, shaking hands, slapping backs, finally making it to the table and taking a seat.

"Howdy, boys."

They howdy him back.

Dewey looks at Leslie, says, "What are you waitin' for, Payne? Run 'em."

Leslie and Stan finish shuffling their decks of cards, commence to deal.

"How'd you play?" Barry says to Dewey.

"Like a real A-rab. Shot a forty-three on the front, goddamned forty-five on the back. Hit two Oh Be on thirteen."

Dewey collects his cards, looks them over, discards one.

"Hey, Sheriff," Stan says, "I hear you finally got your nerve up, fired that black deputy."

"Maybe you ain't heard, you damn insensitive Indian, they don't like to be called black no more." Stan's about one-sixteenth Cherokee which makes him an Indian in Dewey's book. "They prefer 'Aferkin American.' Anyhow, I didn't have to fire him. He got pissed off and quit."

"Quit, huh."

"Yeah. Didn't care for how I was staffin' a case."

"Wouldn't have been the Sissy Fletcher case, would it?" Barry says.

"My, but word do get around, don't it?" Dewey says.

Leslie discards the jack of clubs.

Dewey picks it up, says, "Say, Leslie?"

"What?"

"Where's the farmer take his cotton?"

"You're shittin' me. You holdin' jacks?"

" 'Fraid so." Dewey lays them down. "Gin rummy."

"Shit."

Dewey produces a cigar from his shirt pocket, lights it up. Few hands of cards, a couple of stiff toddies (*Hey*, he thinks, *I ain't nowhere near as bad as ol' Rufus*), a cigar, makes for the perfect evening. Tomorrow he'll most likely be sorry, since the problem with a cigar is your mouth tastes like you're still smoking it two days after you've stubbed it out. But what the hell.

He says, "You know, since you brung it up, I got a question for you boys that bears on the Fletcher thing."

"Go ahead on."

Dewey shuffles. "Okay. I heard this here rumor from one of my confidential police sources? Said Jeremiah Spur's daughter was the last person seen with Sissy the night she turned up missing. Y'all ever heard any such a thing before?"

"Not me."

"Nope."

"Negatory."

"Well, me neither. All afternoon, while I was supposed to of been thinking about my golf swing, keeping my head still and so forth, I've been cogitating on this, trying to figure out how you go about running such a story to ground. Suddenly it come to me."

He deals, sets the deck down, turns the top card up.

"What's that?" Leslie says.

Cigar between his teeth now, Dewey gathers his hand, starts arranging it. "When y'all go home this evening, ask your wives if they've ever heard of this here story. If they ain't, say to them to ask their friends. Then y'all let me know what y'all learn."

"What's that gonna get you?" Stan says.

"Here's how I got it scoped. I figure among us our wives got something like a hunnerd years of gossip stored up in their heads, rattling around in there with recipes, relative's birthdays, list of three thousand chores they need us to do. Somewhere laid up in their heads may be some piece of information, some kind of a lead that would help me run this rumor to ground, and I aim to coax it out if I can."

"What makes you think our wives would know any such thing?" says Stan.

"On account of the victim was a woman. You know as well as I do all these women do all day long is sit around and talk about one another. Must of been just as true ten years ago when Sissy Fletcher disappeared as it is today. And if I'm right about that then they would have sat around and talked about who saw who and who said what to who and so forth and so on."

"I follow you."

Dewey says, "Glad you see my point. Now if I'm wrong about our wives, and *they* ain't heard nothin' useful before, but they were to start talkin' to the women *they* know—well, we're lookin' at tappin' the mother lode of gossip is all."

"Well, now, ain't you the master detective?" says Barry.

"I'm plenty better than I been gettin' credit for, that's for damn sure," says Dewey, fishing for a card. "I just needed me a chance to show it."

He takes a swallow of his gin and tonic, eyes his cards, puffs on his cigar, feeling right satisfied with himself. He believes he'll just have himself a large time tonight.

After a couple hours Dewey has worked his way into his fourth drink and is beginning to struggle some keeping track of the cards, when behind him he hears Joe Bob Cole say, "Well, looky here, if it ain't the top lawman in Washington County. If you in here playin' cards with your blow buddies you must have 'bout cracked the Sissy Fletcher case."

All of a sudden it gets real quiet, no sound to be heard except the TV going above the bar and Rufus Marsh coughing his flooded Briggs & Stratton cough.

Dewey looks up, sees Stan, Leslie, and Barry making a close study of their hands.

Dewey sets his cards down, swivels.

Joe Bob is propped up against a row of lockers, half-empty Lone Star bottle clutched in a hairy paw, staring down at Dewey like he's contemplating a stray yard dog. He's big enough to play tackle for the Cowboys and so ugly it makes your molars hurt just to look at the man. Got greasy black hair combed back fifties style, ridiculous black sideburns running way down past his earlobes, looks like a cross between a grown Beaver Cleaver and a Hell's Angel. His right jawline is etched with a red scar, a lifetime souvenir from a barroom fight he got himself into just before landing his former position as Sheriff Pat Patterson's chief deputy and thumb-breaker.

"You talkin' to me?" Dewey says.

"I was just sayin' you must be closin' in on Sissy Fletcher's killer, on account of why else would you have time to spend your en-tire afternoon out here?"

The room stirs some, guys talking low.

"Don't you worry none, Joe Bob, we're workin' the case."

"Workin' the case, huh? Well, you coulda fooled me. I thought you was just fuckin' off, like the brain-dead peckerwood ever-body in this town knows you is."

Some guys laugh at that.

"We'll find the sumbitch that done it. Don't you fret." Dewey is trying real hard to show some confidence, some professionalism, though he's not quite sure it's working.

Joe Bob sneers, looks around. "Yeah, well, don't let your mouth overload your ass. What you need to understand is we all sure lookin' forward to you arrestin' a suspect. Ever-body'll sleep better."

Sounds of agreement from around the room.

Joe Bob turns to go, then turns back. "Oh, one other thing. Word is you finally got rid of that nigger deputy. Me and some of the other boys was real glad to hear that. Only thing we can't quite figure out is what took you so long seeing as how law enforcement is white people's work."

"Law says I got to be an equal-opportunity employer. I am. Always will be."

"Well ain't you just so politically correct? You know what? Folks around here don't have much use for it, the political correctness. In fact, you ever hear the story old Brewster Cramer used to tell 'bout when he was in the State Legislature? Wasn't that long ago."

Now Joe Bob has the floor, has everybody's attention, has turned away from Dewey. "Ol' Brewster said one time this colored woman representative from Houston comes walkin' up to him on the House floor, says, 'Mr. Cramer,'" Joe Bob says, talkin' in dialect now, "'I wanna ask you somethin'. I be understandin' you gets elected by tellin' peoples in yo' districk you hate niggers.' You know what he said to her?" He turns back to Dewey.

"No."

"He said, 'No, ma'am, that ain't right. That is not how I get elected. I get elected by tellin' folks in my district I hate niggers more than my opponent does.'"

Lot of guys laugh, whistle, bang their hands on tables, lockers.

Joe Bob grins. "That's how you get elected 'round here, partner. See ya around."

"Goddamnit," Dewey says to himself, "that's enough."

He pushes back from the card table, gets to his feet. "Wait a second, Joe Bob. I want to ask you somethin'."

"Take it easy, Dewey," Leslie whispers.

"Shut up," Dewey whispers back.

Joe Bob stops, turns around, looks Dewey over. "Go ahead on. Ask."

"You a proud, patriotic, love-it-or-leave-it American, am I right?"

"That I am." Joe Bob looks around the room. "I believe ever-body here could attest to that."

"It ever occur to you what it would be like in this here country if there wasn't anybody but white folks?"

"Sure. It'd be like paradise."

"So you'd like it better."

"Absolutely."

"It'd be better without Michael Jordan. Emmet Smith. Bill Cosby. Colin Powell. You'd be just as proud of America if all the Olympic gold medals that was ever won by colored Americans was won for Russia because they was all Russian instead."

Joe Bob stands there looking at Dewey like he has lost his mind, hauling out this line of reasoning here in the most segregated place in the county.

But Dewey's not finished. "Have I got it about right, Joe Bob? America would be a better place if Tiger Woods was a Frenchman, is the way you see it."

Joe Bob sneers. "That boy makes my ass hurt. Him and his orang-a-tang pump ever-when he sinks a long putt."

There's some snickering around the room at that.

Dewey is unfazed. "He's a hell of a ball striker, Joe Bob."

"Hey, Joe Bob."

Everybody turns to see Rufus Marsh up off his barstool, inserting himself into the proceedings.

Joe Bob pivots his way. "What?"

"If I was a bettin' man," Rufus says, "I'd bet that if God was to offer to make you a nigger in exchange for which He'd give you Tiger's golf swing, you'd be crossin' the color line goin' the wrong direction so fast it'd make us all swimmy-headed."

This observation from the Barstool Oracle is greeted with more howling laughter and table banging. As Rufus climbs back up on his barstool, Joe Bob stalks out of the room.

Dewey sits back down, turns back to his cards. Directly it gets quiet again.

Leslie Payne looks at him like he'd just announced he planned to give up golf, start taking ballet lessons. "Goddamn it, man, what has gotten into you?"

"Shut up and deal."

"You can't go around talkin' like that."

Dewey looks over at Leslie, says, "The thing of it is, what you don't know, what nobody in here but me knows, is that Clyde Thomas ain't a bad guy. I've worked with him for five years and, yeah, he's got an attitude problem, but he's also all kinds of smart and a pretty good cop. I sort of feel bad about what happened between him and me and I guess that's what made me do it."

"That and about four drinks."

"Yeah, that too, and the fact that I didn't want that big tub of lard over there to get away with shootin' off his mouth like that about the coloreds. It just ain't right."

"This is Washington County, Dewey. It ain't Massachusetts. He can shoot his mouth off like that all he wants. It's a damn good thing Rufus Marsh rode to your rescue. Rufus got it about right, too. If God would give me Tiger Woods's golf swing I'd gladly let him turn me into any kind of nigger Meskin chink frog wop raghead mongrel mixture that made Him happy."

"Are we gonna play cards or what?"

Leslie shuffles, looks around the room, leans over, says, "One thing's for sure, Dewey. Maybe folks around here can forget you're some kind of closet liberal. But an unsolved murder, that they ain't forgettin.' Looks like the road to reelection runs through Sissy Fletcher's grave."

"Thanks for the directions, Leslie," Dewey says.

He bites down on his cold cigar, tries not to let on as to how he feels, decides maybe he'll do some serious drinking this evening.

12

"PISS POOR IS WHAT IT IS. JUST PISS POOR."

Jeremiah Spur leans forward, sets the case file down on the coffee table alongside his yellow legal pad and his Wilson Feed and Supply ballpoint pen, absentmindedly squares everything up flush with the table edge. Leans forward, gets into his thinking position, elbows on his knees, twirling his reading glasses between his thumb and his forefinger, staring at the floor for a spell. Then he sits back.

"I seen some mighty marginal police work in my day, but by God if this 'un here don't beat all," he says out loud.

Calls for a cigarette.

He lights himself a Camel, tries to find a bright side to look on, thinks about the forensics work that had been done just this week, judges it to have been carried off tolerably well. At least the sheriff's boys had had enough sense to call in a specialist, a forensic anthropologist Jeremiah's worked with before, a good hand, does nice work.

Seems that move was the particular inspiration of this deputy that found the body, this Clyde Thomas fellow. Jeremiah doesn't recollect ever having met the man, but he's heard tell of him, seen him around town on occasion. Big strapping black kid, favors that basketball player a bit, what's his name from Chicago. Jeremiah's been given to understand that Clyde's a pretty fair cop too, learned something about law enforcement when he was with the Dallas PD.

Jeremiah taps the ash off his smoke into an ashtray, reaches for the file.

The local ME, Dr. Alan Hutcheson, had ruled it death by blunt force trauma to the head. The back of the victim's skull had been caved in, one blow that was as fatal as fatal could be, delivered by someone standing behind her, off to the left some.

Jeremiah's high school physics may be old and yet they still apply.

F=MA. Force equals mass times acceleration.

Pretty simple equation, as equations go. The natural science of murder is the same as that of the rest of the universe. Accelerate a big enough object into the back of a person's head, the skull collapses in on the brain, the brain sustains mortal injury, ceases to function. Just like that a person is plucked from the ranks of the living, becomes nothing but a memory to everybody who ever knew her.

Consigned to a narrow grave, little more than a ditch, carved into a pasture, left there for the livestock to walk over her night and day.

It says here that Doc Hutcheson thought the killer had something of a height advantage, based on what he could learn by studying the point of impact, the fractures radiating out from it and so forth. Since the dead girl had been about five-five, the ME made the killer in all likelihood to be north of six feet.

Which means she could have been killed by just about any male in Washington County, or by any of five or six dozen females.

The dental work is what established that these were the remains of Alicia Fletcher, once known to all and sundry as "Sissy."

It is not a "body" in any proper sense of the word, this pile of bones, these clumps of hair, the soft tissues having long since decomposed away. A skeleton is the proper name for it, done up in western gear like some kind of twisted goat roper Halloween joke—western shirt, leather jacket, boots, jeans, had fifty-three dollars and thirty-seven cents in them, some wadded-up beer tickets from the rodeo dance, a driver's license, credit cards, a pocketknife. Wasn't any purse or wallet, but if she'd been killed in a robbery they wouldn't have found the cash on her.

Jeremiah flips a page on the legal pad, studies his blue scrawl written there. The top button of her jeans was snapped, the belt buckle fastened. Her jacket had been zipped all the way up, closed leather providing some protection for the upper garments from decay. Based on some torn threads, missing buttons, the ME had delivered himself of the view that her shirt had been ripped open, although he allowed as how he could not be one hundred percent sure, given the condition of things. Her bra snap was undone too.

A ripped shirt and an unsnapped bra suggest a sexual element, now, doesn't it? Jeremiah leans forward in his thinking position again, getting his brain closer to his heart so the blood will flow better.

Could she have been raped, then murdered after getting herself dressed back up? Or was she raped, then bludgeoned, then dressed back up by her killer?

That doesn't seem to make a lot of sense to Jeremiah, doesn't match up with his experience. Women that are raped and then murdered are almost always found undressed, certainly not with britches on them.

Maybe there was no sexual assault. Maybe it had been consensual sex. Or maybe she had consensual sex with one person, and was murdered by someone else altogether.

Jeremiah is thinking it's all guesswork pure and simple since these bones were buried back when the governor's daddy was president, no tissue or body fluids left for analysis after such a span of time. All there is to go on is the condition of the victim's clothing. It's apt to be mighty thin, any conclusion that's based upon the likes of that.

Aside from this little bit of detail, the crime-scene search didn't turn up anything to speak of except for a peculiar-looking blue button. The boys found it by the skeleton's right side, near a pocket on the victim's leather jacket. There's an enlarged photo of it in the file. Jeremiah flips over to it.

It's a big old blue button that doesn't match any of Sissy Fletcher's clothing. It doesn't look to Jeremiah like a shirt button, or like the kind of button that would be found on any garment common to these parts. Jeremiah is a lot of things but a button expert is not one of them. He decides this evidence is beyond his ken, figures that the sheriff will no doubt send the button down to the DPS crime lab in Houston, see if they can trace it.

He stubs out his cigarette, flips back to the crime-scene photographs, parsing them for the secrets they might reveal to an eye trained to look for them. They chronicle the corpse's emergence from the parched ground. Little by little the dusty ground yielded up these lonely bones, a grisly striptease. He studies the sketches that had been made out there, turns them around in his hands, holds them this way and that.

Jeremiah is thinking as crime scenes go, this one here is pretty tame. It's as though she'd been laid to rest, face up, hands folded in front of her. None of the usual blood and gore on account of the body had been buried there so long ago.

Jeremiah focuses back on his notes. Yep, he concludes, the forensics work, that crime scene search, that there is in pretty good shape, considering it was done by a department run by that idiot Dewey Sharpe.

But the work, if you can call it that, that had been done ten years ago, wo-howdy.

Joe Bob Cole had run the case, and based on what little Jeremiah had heard about the man, Jeremiah had never figured him for smart. Looking at this file, Jeremiah concludes that Joe Bob's brain must roll around in his head like a BB in a boxcar.

Jeremiah picks himself up off the couch, goes out to the porch to sit in his rocker, smoke a cigarette.

They had naturally suspected the family first. Sissy hadn't been married, but she had been living with a guy, name of Greg Johnson. Jeremiah wonders if it's the Greg Johnson he knows, the veterinarian who treats Jeremiah's cattle from time to time. He's a taxidermist too, old Greg is. He works over on the west side of town, has a veterinary clinic and a taxidermy shop, side by each, with a sign that runs over the top of both their doors, says "Either Way You Get Your Dog Back." The walls are hung with pictures he's taken of scenes out West, wildlife, landscapes, and so forth. He's a pretty good photographer, put himself through veterinarian school doing weddings and such.

He'd be about the right age to be the same Greg Johnson.

Greg claimed in his statement that Sissy had left for the rodeo dance before he did, said they arrived separately, left separately, barely saw each other while they were there, that such comings and goings independent of one another wasn't uncommon for them since they both liked to maintain their freedom. He allowed as how after the dance he went home with a drinking buddy and the both of them stated that they had stayed up late drinking bonded whiskey, that Greg had spent the night on the couch there, then drug his hungover ass home the next day.

When Sissy didn't come home Sunday night, he made a stab at looking for her but didn't have any luck at it. Reported her missing the next day.

Jim Fletcher and his son Martin had been questioned, but they weren't what you'd call likely suspects, given who Jim was and seeing as how Martin was just sixteen years old at the time. And on top of that they were alibi'd by one another. So the questioning was none too rigorous, fell way short of exacting. Dr. Fletcher had said he had worked late that Saturday evening in the church office on the next day's sermon, as he does customarily. Martin had been too young to go to the dance, had stayed home, read his Bible, went to bed about eleven o'clock.

A search of the place where Sissy and Greg lived didn't turn up anything useful, although since all her duds and boots and whatnot were still there somebody should have figured that maybe she hadn't vamoosed after all.

When Sissy's pickup was found down near the border with the Mexican kid at the wheel it was brought back to town, dusted for prints. That turned up nothing pretty much, just Sissy's and the Mexican kid's and a mess of other latents they had run through the FBI's computers, but that didn't yield a match.

Not another lick of forensic work was done on the pickup.

That more than anything tells Jeremiah that Joe Bob and his boys had defaulted to the notion that she must have took off, else why wouldn't they have checked the truck for bloodstains, hairs, fibers, and whatnot?

Joe Bob and them did talk to some folks that had seen Sissy at the rodeo dance, that thought that maybe she had been drinking but wasn't drunk. A couple people said they might have seen her leave the American Legion hall early, while the dance was still in full swing, maybe with another gal in tow, but no one could be sure about it.

The Sheriff's Department tracked down most of the rodeo riders too, itinerant guys with pockmarked faces and missing teeth who had moved on down the circuit, following the rodeo through the dirt arenas of rural

Texas, a traveling troupe beset by creaking joints and drinking problems. None of them would own up to having seen Sissy.

Jeremiah smokes, listens to the cicadas sawing away out there past the porch light, Duke lying over yonder on his side, paws jerking back and forth, chasing jackrabbits in his sleep.

Jeremiah is thinking this case is going to require someone to start pretty much from scratch. It will be no easy chore, trying to figure out who killed a woman way back in 1989 with no more than this to go on.

Ten years is a long time. People move on, die off. Memories weaken, fail altogether. The whole trail turns to ice.

And as to ever-what relationship there may have been between Sissy Fletcher and his own wife and daughter, Jeremiah cannot find so much as a whisper of it in this sorry excuse for a case file.

Jeremiah glances at his watch. Almost ten o'clock. Time to be getting on to bed. He rises and stretches.

As he switches off the lamps in the family room, he decides that fate is going to have to try harder than this if it aims to rope him into this here case.

13

THE LAW SAYS LIQUOR STORES GOT TO CLOSE BY TEN O'CLOCK, AND MARTIN
has timed it such that he wheels the pickup into the empty lot across the
street from Uncle Freddie's Wine and Spirits at a quarter till. He parks
where they can watch the store through the windshield, kills the headlamps,
hits a couple switches with a gloved hand, sliding the windows down partway so he can listen better, hear the traffic sounds coming from the street,
get an informed sense of the neighborhood's comings and goings.

He cuts off the engine.

There are two cars parked out front of Uncle Freddie's and some move-
ment inside the store although what with the burglar bars and the neon
beer signs hanging in the windows it's pretty near impossible to make out
what's going on inside.

"Can you see anything?" he says to Dud.

Dud peers through the windshield. "I'm guessing there's at least a couple guys in there plus ever–who is behind the counter."

"Damn. I 'uz hopin' it'd be empty long about this time of night, nobody
in there but that monkey-faced kid we saw today. Guess some soul brothers
needed a nightcap."

Martin reaches over, opens the glove box, pulls out a pouch of Red Man,
helps himself to a chaw, offers some to Dud.

Dud shakes his head. "No, thanks. Maybe we ought to call it off. Come
back again tomorrow."

"No. That we ain't gonna do. We'll just wait 'til they clear out, make our
move right before closin' time, like I planned it."

Martin can feel the hesitation in Dud's silence, knows the man is working his way up to saying something.

"Okay, Dud. Let's hear it."

"Hear what?"

"Come on. I know you're over there worrying somethin'. Out with it."

Dud clears his throat. "Well, Martin, you the brains of this operation and
all but I still don't much cotton to the notion of running over yonder
wearing gloves and ski masks and jackets and whatnot. I mean, what if

somebody sees us out here runnin' around in the damn heat with ski equipment on, calls the cops while we're in there?"

Martin spits a juice stream out the window. "You see any witnesses hanging around outside the ones that are in that there liquor store?"

"No, Martin, but it's dark and this is nigger town and seein' as how they all black they might blend in. Darkness to a colored man is like a mesquite thicket to a whitetail, it gives 'em cover. There might be fifty of 'em just hanging around in the shadows and we'd never know it. They bound to pay attention to a couple guys wearin' this kind of rig runnin' around their neighborhood. Niggers may not be all that smart but even they can figger out that that ain't normal behavior for Brenham, Texas, in the middle of May."

"This whole operation ain't gonna take more than five minutes. Even if they is a coon or two lurking back up in the bushes somewheres, how they gonna get to a phone in time to call the cops?"

"That ain't a problem. They'll use their cell phones."

Martin spits out the window again. "Their what?"

"Their cell phones. Ever-body's got a cell phone these days."

"I ain't got a cell phone."

"You ought to get yourself one, Martin. My cousin Arlene's got one. She was tellin' me just the other day how much she loves it, how she can use it to call her mama while she's driving down the street. And she got herself a deal too, got eight hunnerd minutes a month for just thirty-nine ninety-five and they all but give her the actual phone."

"Okay, fine, you've made your point. So what would you suggest we do then?"

"Well." Dud thinks for a few seconds. "What if we was to pull around yonder"—gesturing now, to the back of the store—"and look for a back way in?"

Martin is starting to get exercised, Dud taking it upon himself to armchair quarterback Martin's plan. Dud suddenly forgetting his place in the chain of command, becoming all critical, volunteering his thoughts without any kind of invitation.

It's impertinent, and it's made worse by the fact that Martin sees the sense in it.

Of course it's a good idea to try to find a back way in, do what they can to avoid getting spotted. Martin wishes he had thought of it first.

But that isn't the point really, not in Martin's eyes at least. The point is that Martin is God's Messenger, leastwise according to the dream he had last night. Not Dud. And what's the use of being God's Messenger if you can't get your orders carried out by somebody as simpleminded as Dud? Dud flunked out of third grade, never made an A in school in anything other than shop class.

Dud says, "Hey, look."

Two men walk out of the liquor store one right after the other, brown paper bags clutched in their hands. They visit with one another for a minute outside the door, then knock their fists together, get in their cars, drive off.

Uncle Freddie's parking lot is empty now and Martin can see lights being switched off in the store, way in the back.

He spits his wad of tobacco out on the ground. "Get your ski mask on," he says.

In five seconds they're out of the pickup, running across the street, their guns still tucked in their belts. By the time they get to the front door, the store is dark except for a few lights up front and the neon beer signs. Martin presses up close to the glass, sees the kid who minds the register coming around the counter, fiddling with a ring of keys.

Martin puts his shoulder into the door, busts through, whips his gun out, and throws down on the cash register kid who freezes at the sound.

"Up with your hands, boy," Martin says, nervous and excited now that they're actually doing it, his nerves causing him to dance toward the kid, his .357 Magnum held in both hands, pointed between the kid's eyes, backing him away from the door, Dud coming barreling through it behind him.

The black kid's mouth makes a big O, his eyes locked on Martin's gun, eyes like two hen's eggs lying in a black nest. His hands fly into the air, key ring dropping to the floor, as he backs away from Martin.

"Oh, oh, oh, mister, please don't shoot me. Lord, Lord, please don't shoot me."

"Shut up." Martin looks back over his shoulder at Dud. "Close the door. Find the light switch and cut it off."

"Lord, Lord, I'se 'fraid uh this. I tol' Mama not to make me take this job, sooner or later somebody come along—"

"Shut up," Martin says again, cocking the hammer, looking hard at the kid. "Kill the lights!" he says over his shoulder.

Dud says, "I can't find the switch."

Martin looks at the black kid over the gun barrel. "Where's the light switch at?"

"It's over yonder. By the do'. Lord, Lord. Help me, Jesus."

"Okay. I got it." Now the only illumination in the place is furnished courtesy of Budweiser, Coors, Miller Genuine Draft.

"Okay, good. Now get over here, get these keys up off the floor, go back and lock that door. Then keep an eye on the street."

"Lord, Lord, help me, Jesus. Help me."

While Dud secures the front door, Martin sizes up the kid, his eyes adjusting to the darkness now, able to see pretty good from the beer sign light. The kid is the same one they saw in here earlier today, all right. The boy is scared half to death, knees literally shaking, lips trembling, praying to the Lord.

Martin is relaxing some now, his nerves commencing to settle, thinking, *This boy is all mine, he's gonna do just like I tell him to.* Martin congratulates himself on catching him clean, out here in the open. No chance for him to get to a gun or a baseball bat or some such hidden behind the counter. He will not be a problem.

Martin lets the hammer down on his revolver. "What's your name, boy?"

"Jasper Jefferson, suh."

"Well, Jasper, in case you ain't figgered it out yet this here is an armed robbery. You ever been robbed before, Jasper?"

"No, suh. Oh, Lord. Oh, Lord, Lord."

"Alright, let me 'splain it to you. This is how it goes. I hold this gun on you and tell you what to do, and as long as you do like I say and don't give me no trouble you get to keep your brains inside your head. Is that clear?"

"Yes, suh."

"Is the cash drawer locked?"

"No, suh."

"Alright then. Keep your hands up high while I go behind the counter."

Martin eases around the counter, keeping the gun trained at Jasper. He pushes a couple of buttons on the cash register. "Jasper, how do you—Wait a minute, here we go." The cash drawer pops open.

"You keep your hands up nice and high for me, okay, Jasper?"

"Yes, suh. Oh, Lord, help me, Jesus."

Martin reaches in, grabs the folding money, wads it up, stuffs it into the pocket of his windbreaker, leaves the coins where they are.

Martin is starting to look around for a safe behind the counter when he hears a car coming down the street, then headlights wash the store.

From over at the door Dud says, "Martin!"

Martin brings a fist down on the countertop. "What did I say about names?"

"Sorry. But a car just pulled up. Somebody's gettin' out. It's a nigger woman."

Jasper says, "That my mama. She come to pick me up after work. Help us, Lord. Oh, sweet Jesus."

Martin tries to think, but nothing comes to mind other than that Dud had said his name and that changes everything. No way this ends clean now.

He can hear the woman banging on the front door. "Jasper! You in there? You let me in this minute."

Martin looks at Jasper. "You stay quiet. Maybe she'll go away."

"You don't know my mama. The good Lord didn't put no give up in her. She stay up all night if she have to just to get a good look at my eyes when I comes in from bein' out somewheres. Oh, Lord, Lord."

The banging and hollering stops. "What's she doin' now?"

Dud peers through the front glass from his position, half-crouched behind a stand of snack foods. "She's foolin' around in her purse. She's taking somethin' out and . . . it's a cell phone. See, I told you them things is everywhere. Even the niggers got 'em."

The phone behind the counter rings.

Martin steps toward Jasper, sticks the muzzle of his pistol in his ear, grabs his shaking bicep in a powerful grip. "Answer it. Tell her you got a bit more to do before you close up. Tell her to come back in a half hour. No, wait. Tell her you're gonna let her in so she can wait inside."

"No! I ain't lettin' you hurt my mama."

"Jasper, you best better do what I say or I'll be hurting both you and your mama. Answer it!" Martin pushes Jasper behind the counter, gun barrel digging into Jasper's ear.

Jasper picks the handset up. "Uncle Freddie's. Hi, Mama. No, ma'am, I ain't done yet. Gonna be a little while."

Martin whispers. "Tell her you're gonna let her in."

Jasper hesitates, so Martin digs the pistol into Jasper's ear some more.

The light from the beer signs plays off Jasper's face, making him look like a desperate clown in a wretched carnival. He looks like he's fixing to bust into tears. "No, don't wait in the car. I'll open the do', you can come inside. Yes'm."

Jasper hangs the phone up. "Help us, Jesus," he whispers.

Martin gestures at Dud, telling him to open the door, let the woman in.

Dud slides over, throws the lock, opens the door up, staying low, out of sight.

A black woman in her early fifties, a purse hanging from her arm, steps through the door. "Jasper, why all the lights off, baby? How can you see?"

Her eyes adjust and she sees Martin holding a gun to her Jasper's head. She screams, "Oh, my God!"

Dud slams the door shut behind her, sticks his gun in the small of her back.

Martin says, "Lady, you better shut up and do exactly like I say."

"Oh, my God. Oh, my God. Please don't hurt him. Please don't hurt my boy."

"I need you to shut up right now, ma'am, you understand me?"

Martin reaches in his windbreaker, fishes out a roll of duct tape, tosses it to Dud.

"Take her in the back, wrap up her hands and feet, and tape her mouth shut. Then get her car keys and move her vehicle back behind the store. And bring me the duct tape when you're done."

Dud prods Jasper's mother with his pistol. "You heard the man. Go on. Git."

Martin turns his attention back to Jasper.

"You ain't gonna hurt her, is you?"

"This place got a safe?"

"A what?"

"A safe. With money in it."

"No, suh. The cash drawer is all. You ain't gonna hurt my mama, is you? Oh, Lord. Oh, Lord."

"Lie down on the floor here."

"Do what?"

"Lie down on the floor. No, facedown. That's it. Put your hands behind your head. Now, don't move."

Jasper's down on the floor now, mumbling his prayers and beseeching the Almighty. Martin looks around behind and under the counter, opens drawers. Nothing.

Dud walks past on his way to the parking lot, drops the duct tape on the counter.

Martin looks up. "You see a door that leads out back?"

"Yeah."

"Alright then. Bring her vehicle around back and then bring mine." Martin hands Dud the keys to his pickup. "You see anything that looks like a safe?"

"Naw. I didn't see nothing that looked like that. One thing I do know, though."

"What's that?"

"Banks got safes."

"You want to give it a rest?"

"Hey, I'd love to rob a place with a safe. They ain't got one here, near as I can figger."

"Just go move the vehicles, okay? Then knock on the back door. I'll let you in."

Martin takes the duct tape, straddles Jasper, brings the clerk's arms down his back to his waist, wraps his wrists tight with the tape. He jerks Jasper to his feet. "Let's go back here and check on your mama."

They stumble through the store, tripping some in the inadequate light.

Dud had left a bare ceiling bulb burning in the back room. Jasper's mama is all trussed up, leaned up against a stack of beer cases, eyes wide, breathing hard behind the duct tape stretched across her mouth.

"Lie down," Martin says to Jasper. "On your face."

Martin wraps duct tape around Jasper's ankles. Then he looks around the storeroom. Nothing here but stacks of cans and bottles, beer, wine, whiskey, all of it meaningless to Martin, since he's a teetotaler. He checks the corners, examines the rafters, scrutinizes the walls.

No luck on the safe. The kid had told the truth of it.

Dud knocks at the back door. Martin walks over, throws the deadbolt, lets his partner in.

"Both vehicles out back now?"

"Yeah. You find a safe?"

"Don't seem to be one."

"Okay, then, let's get out of here."

"What kind of car does the nigger woman drive?"

"It's a big ol' El Dorado. I'm guessing an '87."

"Good. Hang on a second."

Martin walks over to where Jasper lies all taped up, leans over, brings the pistol butt down on the back of the kid's skull with a crack. Jasper goes limp. Then Martin pivots, swings the pistol around hard, catching Jasper's mama on the temple. She slumps over. They're both motionless now, lying there, a trickle of blood coming out of them where Martin's pistol had made contact.

"Help me load them two in the trunk of her Caddy."

Dud's eyes light up. "You gonna do 'em?"

"Just help me load them like I asked."

"You gonna do 'em, ain't you?"

"I don't got much choice, since you called my name." Martin nods in the direction of the black kid. "He heard you call me 'Martin.'"

"Man, alive."

Once they have the Jeffersons loaded up and the trunk lid shut, Martin takes the keys from Dud. "You know where the Lutheran Church out in Gay Hill is?"

"Sure."

"Okay. Meet me in the parking lot there in two hours."

14

SONYA NICHOLS IS JERKED AWAKE NOT LONG AFTER MIDNIGHT BY THE TELE-phone's relentless ringing, the sound unnaturally loud in the quiet of the hour, the stridency of it stirring anxieties buried so deeply within her that they have no name.

She reaches over, snaps on a light, checks the time, grabs the receiver.

"Hello."

"Sonya?"

"Yes. Who is this?"

"This here's Deputy Bobby Crowner. Sorry to call you at this hour, but I thought maybe you would know where I can find Clyde."

"Hang on a second."

She puts the telephone on hold, turns around, gives Clyde a shake, not surprised he's still asleep. The man could sleep through a cannonade.

"Clyde. Clyde! Wake *up!* Telephone!"

Clyde shifts around, mumbles, "No more, baby, I needs to get my rest."

"Don't flatter yourself, okay? Clyde. *Clyde!*"

She whacks him in the rib cage a couple times with the receiver. "Wake up, damn it. Bobby Crowner's on the phone. He's looking for you."

Whacking him seems to be working, since he's rolling over now to reach for the phone. "Okay, okay, you don't have to go gettin' abusive. Who'd you say it was?"

"Bobby Crowner. From down at the office."

Clyde sits up, rubs his eyes, yawns, takes the receiver up against his ear. She reaches over, punches the blinking red light, pulls the sheet up around her shoulders, turns her back to the light.

"Yo, Bobby, what's up, man? Why you want to go callin' me so late?"

Clyde listens for a few moments, then sits up straight, wide awake now, eyebrows furrowed, paying close attention.

" 'Xactly when was it she called?"

He leans over, looks at the alarm clock. "Okay, I'm on the case. I be checkin' out Uncle Freddie's first, then I be callin' in."

Clyde stretches across Sonya to hang up the phone, swings his legs over the side of the bed, reaches down to the floor, picks up his jeans, commences to wrestle them on.

"Clyde, what's going on?"

"Jasper Jefferson's sister done called the office a little while ago, said Jasper ain't come home from work tonight. His mama went down to the liquor sto' to pick him up, and they both been missin' for a couple hours now."

"Oh, God. I hope Jasper hasn't relapsed on us."

"Me too, baby."

"If he has we won't have any choice but to send him up."

Clyde leans over, gives her a kiss. "Let's don't jump to no conclusions just yet. I'll call you later."

"Okay."

He leans over her, kills the light, heads for the front door.

Inside of twenty minutes Clyde is pulling his Z-28 to a stop in front of Uncle Freddie's. He opens the car door, starts to get out. Hesitates, says to himself, "Maybe Mr. Glock would like to go along fo' the ride."

He reaches behind the passenger seat, fishes out his holster. Pulls out the Glock, black steel gleaming under the dome light, checks to make sure the ammunition magazine is topped up, stands up out of the car, straps on his piece, looking around the vicinity.

The street is empty this time of night, no cars coming or going, nobody around at two o'clock in the morning, the only relief from darkness coming from the few streetlights that haven't fallen victim to vandals chucking rocks.

He goes to the front window, tries to see inside the liquor store but can't make out anything through the plate glass since it's blacker than a cat's asshole in there beyond the neon beer signs which themselves do more harm than good so far as seeing past the front window is concerned. He tries the front door but the place is locked up tighter than a miser's wallet. Clyde ponders whether to bust the door down, tells himself one big kick right there where the deadbolt goes into the door frame ought to just about do it. He backs away, gets set to find out what a size twelve Air Jordan can do to the front door of a liquor store, then changes his mind, decides to take a look out back first.

He eases around back, eyes adjusting to the darkness behind the store where the light from the street can't reach. He sees a door, goes up, tries the knob.

It's unlocked.

He pulls his Glock, backs up against the wall, pausing to listen hard for any sound that somebody inside might be making. He grips the gun in both hands against his chest at a forty-five-degree angle, finger on the trigger, holding himself still so he can hear, his heart beating fast.

It hits him hard and sudden, how long gone his edge is, lost on account of the years he's spent in this chicken-shit country town. He is thinking damn if he ain't the fool, pulling up in front of the store like that, sitting there checking his weapon with the dome light on, in full view of anybody who could have been lurking around, looking for a chance to gut-shoot a cop. He's lucky somebody hasn't already surprised him from out of the shadows that are all around, shot him deader than a rump roast. He looks around the area behind the store quickly, half-expecting to have to drop, roll, fire his pistol at somebody stalking him from somewhere beyond the corner of his eye.

He hasn't done anything like this since he was a rookie learning the basics of cop work, back at the DPD training facility, and he's thinking, damned if it don't show, his lack of recent experience at this sort of thing.

A sour taste marks fear's arrival, bile working its way into his mouth, making him want to spit. He steadies his breathing, crouches down, steps quickly inside the door, keeping low, holding the revolver out now, turning this way and that, ready to plug a breaking-and-entering son of a bitch, telling himself to get a good look before he pulls the trigger, make sure he doesn't fire a round into Jasper or his mama by mistake.

Dark as it is back here he can still see by the little bit of light that bleeds in from the front, see well enough to tell there's nobody in the back room. He eases forward to the door that leads to the front of the store. Real quick he's through it the same way, down low, pivoting and keeping the Glock out front, cupped in the palm of this left hand, right index finger primed on the trigger.

He moves fast across the rows of liquor bottles and beer cases, works the room until he's satisfied no one's there. In the front of the store he feels along the wall for the light switch, finds it, flicks it on. Sees the cash drawer standing open, paper money gone.

He walks around behind the counter, finds the phone, calls the office, Bobby picking up on the first ring.

"Yo, Bobby."

"Hey, Clyde. Whatcha got?"

"Not sure yet. I'm at Uncle Freddie's. Ain't no sign of Jasper or his mama. Looks like somebody done boosted the contents of the cash drawer."

"What are you gonna do now?"

"Have a look around. Call Freddie, would you? Ask him to come down here, bring his keys. And call Wanda Jefferson. Tell her I'll be by to see her in an hour or so."

"What do you reckon became of Jasper?"

"I ain't got no idea just yet. If he done fell off the wagon he might have hepped himself to some of the money out this cash register and dashed, would be in Houston by now, restocking his crack supply. But I can't imagine his mama bein' an accessory to it, churchgoin' lady like she is, and she ain't around here either."

"Right. Okay, I'll call Freddie and Wanda."

Dud Hughes comes to with a jerk, looks around, first rattle out of the box wondering how he's come to be out here in some church parking lot in the middle of nowhere, in the dead of night, asleep at the wheel of Martin Fletcher's pickup truck.

Then he gets his bearings, recollects that he had driven out here like Martin had asked him to, just before Martin himself had driven off in that Cadillac with the two colored folks stuffed in the trunk.

Dud flicks on the dome light, looks at his Timex. Half past two. He is wondering what has become of Martin. Dud would like to get on home, get some sleep in his own bed instead of propped up in this truck with his neck all twisted up. He's wishing Martin would show up.

And while he's at it, Dud would also like to have some idea how much liquor store cash money Martin is toting around in his jacket.

He cuts off the light, gets out of the truck. That's when he sees Martin, sitting on the tailgate, shoulders slumped, one hand gripping the truck next to him, the other working the back of his neck.

Dud walks back to where Martin is sitting. Martin doesn't look up or respond or even act like he knows Dud is there. He just sits there like he's in some kind of trance.

"Hey, Martin. How come you didn't wake me up? And what'd you do with that nigger kid and his mama?"

Martin looks up, but Dud can't tell much by looking at his face. It's too dark out here, the smoke and haze blocking out the moon. The darkness renders Martin featureless, hollows out his eyes above his black beard.

Martin says, "I seen me a vision, Dud."

"A vision?"

"Yeah. The Angel of the Lord spoke to me out of the flames."

"What flames? You start a campfire or somethin'? I ain't seen no flames."

"The Angel of the Lord said to me to quit procrastinatin', stop messin' around with armed robbery."

"What about the bank job?"

"He said God saw to it we botched this one tonight, and that's a sign we ain't s'posed to pull off no bank jobs. God wants me to get on with my mission."

"I thought the liquor store was Chopsticks for the bank job. I kind of had my heart set on it."

Martin shouts, "God don't want us to do no bank jobs! He wants me to get on with my mission! That's what the Angel done tol' me!"

The sound of his voice echoes off the side of the little Lutheran Church and travels out across the graveyard that's next to it, and beyond that to the pastures that lie all around, dark and empty except for shapes that might be cattle and might be brush.

"Okay, okay, you don't have to get all exercised. I was just askin'."

Martin goes back to staring at the ground, rubbing the back of his neck.

Dud decides to risk another question. "What mission you talkin' about, Martin?"

Martin gets down off the tailgate, walks a little ways off, says softly, "They shouldn't of dug her up, Dud. They should of just let her be."

"Who? You mean Sissy?"

"She was just fine where she was. No one missed her. Not even Daddy. He made out like he did, but he didn't really."

"She was kind of a handful, as I recollect."

Martin turns toward him. "The sheriff found her and dug her up and it's a sign from God, pointin' me in the direction of His will. I been like Jonah, tryin' to shirk my duty."

"Jonah? Oh, you mean the guy the whale ate? You seen him tonight too?"

"Now we got two dead folks and they was mostly innocent and the Angel of the Lord says that's a sign, a sign that it's high time I got on with it. Bring the message of God to the world, act like a patriot, like McVeigh was."

"Maybe they was mostly innocent, but I mean, sumbitch, they wasn't nothin' but a couple niggers. Ain't likely they'll be missed much. Don't be so hard on yourself."

Dud is thinking, *If we got to give up on the bank job, can't there be a reason better than that? Why give up on all that money just because of a couple of dead coons?*

Martin says, "I'm releasin' you from your duties to me, Dud."

"Do what?"

"I said you're free to go. You don't have to help me out no more."

"I don't get it. On account of how come?"

"What I got to do is for the most part a one-man job. You don't need to get involved in it. Once I done it, I'm headed out of here and I ain't comin' back. You can stay behind, look after my family. I'll give you the ranch."

"Martin, you gonna really leave your family?"

"Luke fourteen: twenty-six, Dud. 'If any man come to me, and hate not his father, and mother, and wife, and children, and brethren, and sisters, yea, and his own life also, he cannot be my disciple.'"

Dud knows the verse Martin is quoting. Dud doesn't claim to be any kind of Bible scholar, but it never made any sense to him that Jesus would say such a thing. Jesus had better family values than that, or at least it seems to Dud that he must of.

"Martin, I hope you don't mind me sayin' so, but you ain't makin' a lot of sense right now. You best better go home, get some sleep. You'll feel better in the mornin'."

"I'm makin' plenty of sense to me."

"Well that makes one of us. And anyhow, the deal where you and me is concerned is this. You 'bout the only friend I got around here, and I'll be danged if I'm a-hangin' around this here county if you're headed off somewheres else. You don't want to tell me what your mission is, that's fine with me. I'm still your partner in it."

Martin starts walking back toward Dud. "Even though you don't know what you're gettin' into, you still want to partner up with me on it?"

"Yep." Dud is thinking, *Maybe if I give old crazy Martin a hand here with this mission of his, he'll repay the favor, work with me on knocking over a bank.*

He draws close to Dud, almost close enough for Dud to see his face, but his eyes stay in shadows above the black beard that makes him look so wild.

"Okay," Martin says. "I can tell you mean it."

Martin puts his hand on Dud's shoulders, says softly, "You know, none of this woulda happened if they had just let her be. Now I got to stop 'em from gettin' any further than they got already. I know now what God wants me to do. The Angel quoted me a verse from Isaiah. Isaiah five: twenty-five."

"I bet to qualify to be an angel you got to know the entire Bible."

"This here verse is significant, because I had done memorized it myself. It goes: 'Therefore the anger of the Lord was kindled against His people, and He stretched out His hand against them and struck them; the mountains quaked, and their corpses were like refuse in the streets.'"

"Wo-howdy."

"Yeah. Wo-howdy. God tol' me to memorize that verse, the day the feds got theirs in Oklahoma City for what they done in Waco. And I didn't know why until just this week. Now I know what it means."

"What's it mean?"

"It means that it's the will of God, you and me got to blow up the Washington County courthouse."

Martin takes his hand off Dud, turns, walks off a ways, his head bowed.

It seems to Dud that Martin is getting weirder by the minute. The notion that God wants him to take out the county courthouse strikes Dud as completely crazy. He shrugs. "Like I said, your mission is your mission, and we partners in it. But I'll be danged if I see the sense in blowin' up that place in particular."

Martin turns back. "You fancy you're smart enough to know the mind of God?"

"Well, no."

"No, you ain't. None of us is. All I know is, He has sent me the message in such a fashion that He knows I'll get it loud and clear."

"Can you make any sense of it?"

"I might could if I had all the facts God has. Maybe there's an ATF office there, some kind of infiltration by the Justice Department, the FBI. That would be enough since they all disciples of the Antichrist. Or maybe it's just because it's a symbol of man's turnin' away from God, turnin' toward the gummint, to worship it. God told the people of Israel when they asked for a king the first time they didn't need one on account of they had Him. But they insisted on a king, so He give 'em Saul, and I don't think He's been happy about man havin' to have a gummint to lean on ever since that happened. And of course you recollect what happened to Saul."

Dud doesn't even know who Saul is. "You bet," he says.

"So it could be that, I reckon. I just don't know. There is one thing I do know though."

"What's that?"

"It's their command and control center for this business about my sister. And God wants to put a stop to that."

"But I don't understand why."

Martin stands in silence for a bit. The he says, "He has His reasons. Come on. Let's go home."

15

THE LAST THING DEWEY SHARPE REMEMBERS SEEING BEFORE HE PASSED OUT last night was Claudia, wearing a bathrobe, her hair in curlers, staring down at him from behind a mask of face cream, arms folded across her chest, her posture setting on Maximum Reproach.

This morning, Dewey is in a world of hurt.

He had spent the night on the couch in his golf clothes, and now his eyelids are fluttering, and even before he is full awake he knows he's afflicted with a museum-quality hangover. The back of his head feels like it's caught in a vise and his mouth tastes like the inside of a Mexican's tennis shoe.

He stays on the couch, too miserable to get up, ankle over to the medicine cabinet, until well after Claudia leaves for her weekly Bible study. Finally he tells himself to get going, face the music, so he unfolds his body off the couch a joint at a time like a man would unfold a rusty lawn chair. Picks his way to the bathroom like he is walking through a minefield.

What a sight he is, staring back at himself from the medicine cabinet mirror. His eyes look like two piss holes in the snow. He gulps down three ibuprofen, proceeds to take a long hot shower, hoping it'll ease the headache. It seems to help some.

But then it comes roaring back before he can finish dressing.

"Why don't the damn Advil work?" he says out loud.

It puts him in mind of a sermon he heard Dr. Fletcher preach last year, about how God is like this great big cosmic mechanical engineer, sin being one of His best designed creations. Each sin has its own punishment built into it, so that there's no real need for a hell. If you commit a sin you get to pay the price for it right here on Earth. Dewey sends up a little prayer complimenting the Almighty on how well designed the sin of drunkenness is, appending a humble plea for relief from his current suffering.

Dewey decides the thing he needs most is some food, maybe something spicy, something that would wake his liver up so it'll get off its ass and get the job done.

He drives over to the Waffle House on the bypass, settles into a booth so bright yellow he leaves his dark glasses on rather than risk being blinded by it, orders up a plate of *huevos rancheros* from a chewing gum–smacking waitress with a mustache. Directly she delivers them up, and it takes a pot and a half of black coffee to wash them down.

As soon as he walks into the office the receptionist, Billie Clifton, hands him a stack of message slips, the top one saying that Captain Spur had called, that he wants to come by this afternoon, visit some about the Fletcher case.

Great, Dewey says to himself. *Just what I need.*

When he walks into his office Clyde Thomas is sitting there waiting for him.

Dewey says to himself, *This day just keeps getting better and better.*

"Mornin', Sheriff," Clyde says.

"Mornin'." Dewey eases around behind his desk, lowers himself into his chair.

"Yo, Sheriff. You ain't lookin' so hot. Y'all come down with a case of the Bombay flu last night?"

"Clyde, why don't you state your business?"

"Fair enough. I been up all night, workin' an apparent robbery and missin' persons situation. Overnight somebody done boosted the cash over at Uncle Freddie's package sto' and on top o' that, the kid that minds the place and his mama done up and disappeared, along with the mama's car."

"Maybe they decided between them to pay the kid a bonus out of Freddie's working capital and then relocate out of Brenham."

"It's a thought. Jasper's a crack addict in recovery and I wouldn't put it past him. But not Missus Jefferson, no sir. She's one of God's saints. Maybe Jasper backslid and she's out there tryin' to find him, but I would have thought if that was the case she would have phoned in, kept her daughter up on her doings."

"So I take it you know the two of 'em."

"Yep. They personal friends of mine."

"You were up all night workin' this?"

"That's right."

"Turned up anything so far?"

"Naw, I ain't got shit. Talked to Freddie, and he says Jasper checked in at about eight o'clock last night. That's the last he heard from him. Jasper's sister Wanda said her mama left the house about nine forty-five, goin' to pick up Jasper jus' like she does every night he works. She never showed back up. Wanda ain't got any idea where they might have gone off to. She said her mama didn't have no bags packed or nothin'."

"What about the scene?"

"Back door unlocked, cash drawer standin' open, no whip out in it, jus' some coins. Spot of somethin' on the floor in the back room, might a been blood. I got the ME checkin' it out. I didn't have no proper crime-scene gear last night, jus' a couple of Q-Tips and a baggie, so I'm goin' back for another look this mornin'."

Dewey takes a long look at Clyde before he speaks again. "You strike me as mighty industrious for somebody who up and quit on me yesterday."

Clyde clears his throat, runs a hand over his smooth head, leans forward, looking up at Dewey now from under his eyebrows. "Sheriff, I'm, uh, I'm real, real sorry about that. I done lost it at you, and all you was tryin' to do was do yo' job. I was way out of line, and I just feel real bad about that, you know what I'm sayin'?"

Dewey is not believing this. An actual apology spilling out of the mouth of C. Livermore "Clyde" Thomas. Call CNN.

"You sorry you quit?"

"Yeah, Sheriff. I'd like to unquit if it's all the same to you. Besides, we got some kind of crime spree goin' on around here all of a sudden. Seems to me y'all could use some mo' help, take a little of the load off the other boys. How 'bout it, Sheriff?"

Dewey's thinking he needs to sort through the politics of this, and now is not the time to do it, not with a Force Five hangover messing with his mind.

"Tell you what, Clyde. You go on, see what you can find out about the Jeffersons. I'll take your application for reinstatement under advisement."

"Okay, Sheriff. You the man." Clyde gets up and heads for the door.

"Hey, Clyde?"

"Yo."

"Cut the lights on your way out the door, would you?"

"No problem."

After Clyde lets himself out, Dewey sits in his office, eyes closed, lights off, feet on the desk, waiting to start feeling like maybe he won't die today, his stomach making a sound like somebody's test-firing a jet engine way off in the distance, giving him doubts about his decision to start the day off with a big ass plate of huevos rancheros.

Another Friday. Another go around of the Dew-Man versus the Hangover.

On top of that, looks like there's another major crime here in town, the second to turn up inside of a week. Plus Jeremiah Spur's planning to come by this afternoon. Dewey knows the guy doesn't much care for him anyhow, and now how is he going to react, seeing Dewey in the state he's in?

Dewey in the meantime has to try to sit on the knowledge that old Spur's daughter might be a witness in this Fletcher business.

The thing about a hangover is, it just flat takes all a man's energy away, leaves him no energy for doing anything but sitting here in the dark, trying not to move. His stomach gurgles and growls, feels to him like a cloud of interstellar gas is beginning to form itself up under his belt buckle.

Well, maybe I do get myself overserved once in a while. But I ain't as bad as old Rufus Marsh. Now there's a guy with a drinking problem.

His phone rings but he ignores it. Directly there's a knock at the door and it opens a crack. Dewey's wondering why it has to be so damned bright out there.

"Sheriff?" Billie Clifton's voice and a teased-to-within-an-inch-of-its-life hairdo enter the room at about the same time.

"What is it?"

"Sheriff, I got Leslie Payne on line two? He says you're gonna want to hear what he has to say?"

"Billie?"

"Yes, sir?"

"Would you please tell me something?"

"Yes, sir?"

"Why do all your sentences sound like questions?"

"Do what, Sheriff?"

"Never mind. Forget it. I'll talk to Leslie."

Dewey swings his feet to the floor, pauses to wait for the room to stop rotating.

"You okay, Sheriff?"

"I'm fine. Just got a headache, is all."

"Okay."

Dewey lifts the receiver. "Hello."

"Hey, Dewey, it's Les."

"How you doin'?"

"Better'n you, I'll bet. I don't recall the last time I saw you drink so much."

"I been worse. You got something you need to tell me?"

"Yeah. Your hunch paid off. I was talkin' to Lynn this morning at breakfast about, you know, the Sissy Fletcher thing? The rumor 'bout her and Elizabeth Spur?"

"Yeah?"

"Lynn had heard it."

"No shit."

"And get this—she had heard who it was that seen 'em together that night."

"So—who was it?"

Leslie is snickering. "Man, this is too good."

"What? Come on, spit it out."

"The one that seen 'em was Lucy Brackett."

"Fuck you, Payne. I am in no mood for this bullshit today."

"It's not bullshit. That's what Lynn says. Story is that Lucy saw 'em together while she was driving home after she closed up shop that evening."

"You're telling me this is straight? Not some kind of get, you just havin' yourself some fun at my—"

"No way. That's what Lynn said. Seems like you better check it out, Sherlock."

"If I find out you're jerking me around, I swear to God—"

"Go get 'em, you master detective you."

Leslie is still snickering when Dewey hangs up the phone.

Dewey looks at his watch. Nine-thirty. He figures it's another half hour before the video store opens.

He leans back in his chair, closes his eyes, the gas cloud under his belt buckle growing steadily. It feels like it's pushing his vital organs around, rearranging them inside his stomach, moving the lower intestines on top of the upper ones.

Just his luck his eyewitness would be Lucy Brackett, the meanest woman in creation, the woman everyone calls the Beta Bitch, owner of I Love Lucy's Videos, Brenham's only video rental store.

Numerous women in Washington County have low opinions of Dewey, but hers is by far the lowest, right down there in the same zip code as whale dung. While she's as mean as a snake and pretty much an equal-opportunity shrew, she has her stinger out especially for Dewey on account of he dated her daughter Susan in high school. Lucy happened to come home early one evening, walk in on them while they were getting it on. Not an insignificant lapse in a Southern Baptist home.

She is the reason Dewey doesn't rent videos.

The vise has Dewey's head in its grip again, his stomach feels like it's going to expand until it fills the room—he loosens his belt and unsnaps his pants, but not even that seems to help—and in twenty-seven minutes he has to go pay a call on Lucy the Beta Bitch Brackett for the first time in over fifteen years.

But he doesn't have any choice whatsoever—Jeremiah Spur will be coming by this afternoon. If there's anything to this rumor that's going around, Dewey needs to know it before he talks to the old Ranger.

At a few minutes before ten o'clock, he walks blinking into the squad room, the brightness of it causing him to reach for his dark glasses and pop them on his head. He looks around, sees the room is empty, everybody out on patrol.

Billie asks him if he's feeling better as he passes through the reception area.

"Yeah, some. Listen, I'll be out for a while. Got to follow up a clue on the Fletcher case."

"Okay, Sheriff? I hope your headache gets better?"

Dewey slides into his cruiser, starts the engine, turns the air-conditioning up full power. He tries to focus his mind, come up with a line of questioning for the Beta Bitch, instead finds himself fretting that she's going to ride his ass about the Susan thing.

I Love Lucy's Videos is located in a strip shopping center on Market Street, south of town. It's a narrow little shop jammed between a store where everything is priced at a dollar and some kind of other store that sells comic books, has posters of various superheroes and demons in the window. Pimply faced teenagers smoke cigarettes on the sidewalk out front. As Dewey pulls up in the cruiser they put out their smokes, hop onto bicycles, and pedal off. He can't understand why they aren't in school.

A bell hanging from the top of the door announces Dewey's arrival. Way in the back, Lucy Brackett appears from out of a storeroom behind the counter. She stops, leans against a wall, smokes her Camel, and regards Dewey with undisguised hostility.

She is ugly enough to make a freight train take a dirt road, rail thin, gray hair, yellow skin, small, brittle, bilious features. Her mouth is permanently set on "sneer" and is surrounded by a mess of tight wrinkles that wouldn't be there if she had smiled on average as much as once a year since the Eisenhower Administration.

"Howdy, Mrs. Brackett." Dewey doesn't dare call her Lucy.

Watching him the whole time, she takes a last pull on her cigarette, puts it out in an ashtray overflowing with butts. The smoke hangs thick in the place, making Dewey's headache worse. His bowels are bucking and kicking, causing him to wonder whether he should have stopped by the men's room on his way out of the courthouse.

"Dewey Sharpe," she says in a tone of voice that you might use to address a cockroach just before you stomped it with your boot. "What the hell do *you* want?"

Dewey elects to forgo the pleasantries. "I don't know if you've heard or not, but we discovered the remains of Sissy Fletcher buried in a pasture over to the west side of the county earlier in the week. I'm headin' up the investigation, and I just wanted to ask you a question or two. Have you got a minute?"

"You hide from me for fifteen years, *after* I catch you molesting my Susan, and then you come around looking for my help on some case you're supposedly working?"

"How is Susan, by the way?"

"Git out."

"Mrs. Brackett, I—"

"I said git out."

"Look, Mrs. Brackett, I know you don't care for me much, and I'm sorry 'bout what happened between me and Susan but—"

"But nothing. If you don't leave, I'll call the law."

"I am the law."

"In your dreams, Dewey. You ain't the law. You're just a reprobate in a brown uniform. You were as sorry as the day is long when you were growing up and you're just as sorry this very minute. Everybody in this town knows it. You're the biggest joke in a town full of jokes."

Dewey starts walking to the back of the store, but slowly, like you'd approach a rabid animal or a 450-pound grizzly bear. The Beta Bitch watches him with her witch eyes. The pressure in his gut just keeps getting worse and worse and walking seems to add to it somehow.

"I've heard it said around town that you saw Sissy Fletcher and Elizabeth Spur together the night that Sissy disappeared."

The Beta Bitch fires up another Camel, starts smoking it, holding it with her thumb on the bottom and three fingers across the top. "I thought I told you to git."

"Mrs. Brackett, if this information that our, uh, sources have volunteered is correct, that makes you a material witness to a murder investigation."

"So what?"

"So if you don't give me your statement voluntarily, I can get a court to order you to. That'd be a mess of trouble for the both of us."

Now Dewey's stomach is beginning to out-and-out hurt from the gas. He's thinking that maybe he ought to try to let just a little out, since there's no way anyone could smell anything in here, what with all this smoke. He decides not to risk it, that it would be better to try to tough it out a while further.

"I might of seen something like that," she says at last.

Talk about reluctant.

"Can you tell me about it?"

"It was a long time ago. I don't know what I can remember."

"Just tell me what you can recollect." Damn, his stomach hurts. He has never had this problem with huevos rancheros before.

"Well, it was late. I had closed up the shop—we close at eleven o'clock on Saturday nights. I was driving through town, headed home. I pulled up to a stoplight, next to a pickup. It was Sissy Fletcher's truck—I recognized it because she was a regular customer of mine. She was partial to some of your racier fare."

Dewey leans against the counter, shifting his weight, trying to relieve the pain in his lower intestines. He knows he ought to be taking down what the Beta Bitch is telling him, but he's in too much discomfort.

"Go on."

"I was in my Oldsmobile so I couldn't see anything except the passenger's side. I looked up and I could see Elizabeth Spur sitting there."

"You sure it was her?"

"Of course I'm sure. She and Susan were in 4-H together for years."

"Okay. So she was in Sissy's pickup. Do you remember anything else?"

"Only that it looked like she was crying."

"Do what?"

"She was crying, I think. I remember she looked over and saw me looking at her. And she looked away real quick-like, and put her hands to her face, like this." The Beta Bitch covers her face with her hands.

"Then what?"

"Then the light changed and Sissy pulled away, real fast. Last thing I saw they turned west, headed out toward Gay Hill."

"Why didn't you tell this to the police when Sissy disappeared?"

"They never asked."

Oh, wow, Dewey thinks, it's coming back. *That really hurts.*

"You didn't go to them with what you knew?"

"Look, Dewey, do you have any idea how many times I've been ticketed for renting R-rated stuff to sixteen-year-olds? Like the cops don't have nothin' better to do than harass the small-business owner. Why should I do anything to help them out?"

It is all Dewey can do to keep from bending over double, clutching at his belly. He backs up and leans against a wall, feeling weak, sweat breaking out on his temples. He knows he has to let just a little of the pressure leak away, else he's liable to explode.

The Beta Bitch looks at him, the question on her face even before she says, "You don't look so good."

Maybe it hits the wall or comes out of his backside funny because he's all twisted up on the inside. Whatever the reason, it makes a sound like a beach ball being run over by a tractor-trailer rig.

Lucy Brackett's left arm shoots out, yellow finger making for a bony exit sign.

"Excuse me," he says meekly.

"Git out!" she screams. "Git out right now!"

"Yes, ma'am," Dewey says, and turns and heads for the door, clutching at his gut.

16

CLYDE HEADS STRAIGHT FROM DEWEY'S OFFICE TO HIS DESK, WHERE HE scratches around looking for a phone book, finally finds one over on Jake's desk covered up by a sports magazine. He thumbs through it until he finds the phone number of the Bethel Baptist Church. He dials it up. A secretary answers the phone, says the church name.

"This here's Clyde Thomas. Dr. Flatley in this mornin'?"

"Yes, suh, Judge, jus' a minute."

Directly the Reverend Dr. Ebeneezer Flatley's great baritone booms down the line. "Good mornin', Judge. I assume you are calling about the Jeffersons."

"That's right, Dr. Flatley. You done heard, huh?"

"Wanda called me right after you left her house this morning. I went over and sat with her until daybreak. We prayed together for the safe return of her mother and brother. Read the Bible. Nothing beats the Twenty-third Psalm at a time like this, no sir. I told her to fear not, for the Lord is with her. She was grateful for that, but she would have preferred that her mama be with her. Bless her heart. She is mighty worried, that child is, yes sir, mighty worried."

"That's what I know. I told her to chill, I'm on the mother—I'm on the case."

"That's good, Judge, that's real good. So how can I help you, Judge?"

"Well, sir, I needs to know if there is anybody out there amongst the children that might of been in the vicinity of Uncle Freddie's last night, seen anything of what went down. But we a little covered up with work around here, you know, just at the moment, and doin' a do' to do' is gonna take a lot of time, you know what I'm sayin'?"

"I believe I do."

"I was wonderin' if maybe you could get the word out, let folks know I'm workin' the case and would 'preciate a call if anybody seen anything."

"Happy to oblige, Judge, happy to oblige. I'll get the telephone tree on it."

"Telephone tree, huh. What's that?"

"Oh, it's a little system we got worked out over here to communicate with the flock. We call three of the ladies, and they call three more of the ladies, and then the nine of them call three more, and before you know it everybody has been contacted. We use it for potluck suppers, election day, that sort of thing. Works pretty good most of the time."

"That'd be just the thing, Dr. Flatley. If y'all turn anything up, y'all can reach me through dispatch here at the office."

"Alright, Judge. Good luck and God bless you, my boy."

Clyde hangs up, dials the ME's office. Dr. Hutcheson's secretary says he's in the lab, working on what Clyde had brought in early in the morning.

"When you 'spect he'll be done?"

"I'd give him another half hour."

"I'm gonna come on over then." He grabs his hat, heads out the door.

Dr. Hutcheson is a big, fit-looking guy in his middle forties, dark-headed with just a touch of gray at the temples. He gets up from his desk, offers up a hand, gestures for Clyde to help himself to a chair, hands him a sheet of paper to read.

"It's blood, alright," the ME says. "Type O positive. And it's fresh. Probably not more than twelve hours old. And there's one more fact here."

"What would that be?"

"Whoever was bleeding in the back room of Uncle Freddie's has sickle-cell trait."

"Say what?"

"Sickle-cell trait. You've heard of sickle-cell anemia, right?"

"Sho'. My uncle on my mama's side, he had it. It's damn nasty."

"Well, folks get that if they have inherited a sickle-cell gene from both their parents. Now if a person inherits a sickle-cell gene from only one parent, that gives them sickle-cell trait. Their red blood cells have half normal hemoglobin and half hemoglobin S. Other than that, they're perfectly healthy."

"Do that mean what I think it mean? That blood come out a black person?"

"That'd be my guess, although there's a three percent chance it came from an Asian."

"Bullshit, Doc. Ain't no Chinaman ever been in that part of town, much less inside Uncle Freddie's storeroom."

Clyde leaves the hospital parking lot, headed back over to Uncle Freddie's, all set to do a daylight crime-scene search, make sure he didn't miss anything in the first go 'round. On his way he radios in an APB on Mildred

Jefferson's 1987 El Dorado, now that he's got sufficient evidence to back him up.

Clyde has to admit the only reason he didn't APB it already, he had half-expected Mildred and Jasper to show up by now. He had been inclined to believe Jasper had cleaned out the cash drawer, pulled a Daryl Strawberry, gone back to doing blow. Clyde's been around enough addicts to know what they are truly like. They walk right along the edge of disaster every minute of every day, always just one moment of weakness away from going back. And if Jasper's mama had showed up and found him and the money gone, she wouldn't necessarily have seen the wisdom of siccing the cops on him just yet. She would have gone looking for him herself, tried to straighten it all out before Jasper ended up in Huntsville on a parole violation send-up.

That's not the way it looks now, though, unless the two of them got into a fistfight there in the back of the store, a mental image Clyde cannot quite conjure up.

He parks in the vacant lot across the street from the store, fetches his crime-scene gear from the trunk, walks across the street, studies the parking lot. Nothing useful here, cracked asphalt not giving up any clues. He takes a close look at the front door, CLOSED sign hanging on it, Freddie keeping the place locked up this morning at Clyde's request. The front door shows no signs of having been forced or jimmied.

Clyde concludes that either the perp came in the front door before Jasper could get it locked, or he made his way in through the back.

Clyde goes around back to have another look. He checks the grounds around the place, eyeballs the back door too, sees no signs of forced entry. He unlocks the back door with the key Freddie had given him, uses a handkerchief to twist the doorknob, walks in, flicks on the light, prowls around the storeroom looking in corners and such.

"What the hell is this?" he says out loud.

He bends down, gets a closer look at something lodged between a couple stacks of malt liquor cases, reaches in his pocket, pulls out a pencil, pokes at it.

"Roll of some kind of tape that don't look like it belongs here," he says to himself. He uses the pencil to pick it up, drop it into a plastic evidence bag.

He moves up to the front of the store, makes a mental note to get somebody down here to dust everything for prints.

Clyde can feel it, the pressure of trying to locate these missing folks, not sure anyone would care enough to do anything for them if it wasn't for him. It's not like the powers that be in this white man's town would be getting all up in arms over a couple black folks disappearing along with the cash from a black man's liquor store. So it's his baby to rock, and that makes him wish he had more experience at this sort of thing.

Moving around the store scoping everything out, it occurs to him there's an oddity to the timing, two people going missing the very week the most prominent missing person in Washington County history turns up dead in a pasture. Just the juxtaposition of events sets Clyde to wondering if there might be some kind of connection between the two cases, although not a single other thing points that way.

Clyde's walkie-talkie crackles. "Deputy Thomas. Come in Clyde Thomas."

He yanks the radio off his belt, pushes a button, says, "Yo, Darlene. What's up?"

"What's your twenty, Clyde?"

"I'm over at Uncle Freddie's processin' the scene. I'm gonna need you to patch me through to DPS forensics before long, order me up a fingerprint tech."

"Happy to do it. You wanna do that now, or call Dr. Flatley back first?"

"He call already?"

"Yeah, just now. Says he has somethin' for you."

"Roger. I'll call you back. You got his number?"

Clyde scribbles the number down, signs off, makes the call on his cell phone. Dr. Flatley is on the phone right away.

"Yo, Dr. Flatley, this here's Clyde returnin' yo' call."

"Good, thank you, Judge. I do believe we may have something for you."

"That's mighty quick work, Dr. Flatley."

"That's the telephone tree for you, son. I have to say that as good as the system is, it works even better when the subject is something like this, as opposed to who is going to bring the potato salad to the Juneteenth picnic. There is a catch though."

"What do that be?"

"Well, this is more of an anonymous tip as opposed to something somebody themselves eyewitnessed, and the person who has provided us with the information would rather they stayed out of the equation, if you follow my meaning."

"We can live with that."

"Excellent. In that case, then, word is that you might want to have a visit with a local character by the name of Lamont Stubbs. It comes to pass that he has a habit of hanging around that particular block on King Street late of an evening."

"Is that a fact?"

"It's something to look into. I'd check it out if I were you."

"Thank you, Dr. Flatley. You've been mighty helpful. Let me know if you hear of anything else." Clyde ends the call, thinks to himself, *I declare, Lamont Stubbs, the blackest man in Washington County, maybe in the whole state of Texas, nigger's so black he's almost purple.*

Clyde has had his eye on Lamont for a while now. The guy has a day job working a shammy cloth down at Mr. Sparkle's car wash. But it's what he does at night that interests Deputy Thomas. Lamont's said to be a seller of weed and other controlled substances to the adolescent population of Brenham, including, according to Clyde's snitches, Jasper Jefferson himself, back before Jasper got his ass busted and twelve-stepped. Clyde has long wanted to haul Lamont down to the county lockup but never has been able to catch him dirty. Getting a probable cause handle on Lamont has been like trying to frisk a wet seal.

Clyde locks up the liquor store, gets back in his cruiser, radios in a fingerprint request, asks them to dust the cash register, the doors, the countertops, light switches, a roll of duct tape he took from the scene. Then he sets out in search of Lamont Stubbs.

He starts at the car wash, where they say he isn't there, it's his day off.

Then he checks Lamont's crib, a shack on the near north side, weeds in the yard, chained up dog out in the back that sets to barking when Clyde pulls up in the squad car.

Clyde mounts the porch, gives the door a thorough beating, hollers out, "Lamont! Open up! I needs to talk to you." He beats the door until finally it opens a crack, part of a woman's face peeking out. Bloodshot eyes, hair a mess, looks like a junkie.

"What you want?" she says.

"I'se lookin' for Lamont."

"He ain't here."

"You mind if I come in, check things out?"

"Suit yo'sef." She pulls the door open, Clyde steps through into the gloom. He looks around at the peeling wallpaper, broken-down furniture, empty malt liquor cans scattered everywhere, ashtrays full of cigarette butts, fried chicken buckets left on the floor. The place is a real dump. Clyde doesn't understand how people can bear to live their lives this way. He walks through the house, tries not to step on any of the trash and debris all over the floor, no telling what would come off onto his boots.

The woman stays by the front door, hands up on her shoulders, like she's trying to keep warm even though it's got to be ninety degrees in here, just a couple ceiling fans turning, trying to fight off the heat. She's wearing long sleeves, no doubt to hide her needle tracks, would probably have long sleeves on even if she was out in the middle of the Gobi Desert at high noon.

Once he is satisfied Lamont is not on the premises, Clyde goes back to the front door. "So where's he at?" Clyde says.

"I dunno. Lef' a while ago. He say somethin' about goin' car shoppin'.'"

"Car shoppin', huh."

"He say his ride is gettin' old."

"He don't need a new ride. He need a new crib."

The woman gives him a shrug, like she doesn't see the need for either one.

Clyde heads out the door. "You see him, you tell him Deputy Clyde Thomas would like to have a word with his sorry ass."

Clyde starts making the rounds of the car lots, finally finds Lamont sitting behind the wheel of a used Lexus in a lot over on the bypass, a big four-door luxury sedan as black as Lamont. Clyde walks up to the driver's side, watches Lamont admiring the feel of the leather, the dashboard gleam. Clyde can see the sticker is asking for $25,999.

Clyde leans down, takes a look at Lamont. "Yo, Lamont."

Lamont doesn't even look up. "Yo, Judge."

"You thinkin' about buyin' the car?"

Lamont sighs, like his patience is being tried by a dimwit. "No, man. I'se gonna buy the car. I'se thinkin' about pussy."

"Well how about you takin' a break from yo' fantasy life and givin' me a moment of yo' precious time?"

"How come? I ain't done shit."

"No one says you did, Lamont. What you wanna go gettin' all defensive on me for? I just got a couple questions I'd like to ask is all."

"Like what?"

"Like whether you might of been hangin' around the vicinity of Uncle Freddie's last night, say around ten, ten-thirty."

"I don't know."

"How can you not know?"

Lamont looks up at the big cop for the first time. "My watch is broke."

Clyde leans in, face close to Lamont's, so close now he can hear the other man's breathing. Clyde looks over Lamont's shoulder, turns his head to the back and the front, admiring the automobile. "This sho' is a mighty fine car. Lexus makes a good automobile. More'n could be afforded by most men, make their livings rubbin' the water off white folks' rides. You know the best thing about the Lexus, Lamont?"

"What would that be?" Lamont looking at him, suspicion in his eyes.

Clyde grabs the back of Lamont's neck, slams him into the steering wheel. "The feel of the steering wheel, motherfucker."

Lamont howls, sits back, blood busting loose from his face. "Oh, man! You went and broke my nose!"

"And I ain't done breakin' shit. You just keep jivin' me, you'll see what I'm talkin' 'bout." Clyde reaches around the back of Lamont's head again.

"Okay, goddamnit, fuck," says Lamont, leaning away from Clyde, one hand cradling his face, the other fishing out a handkerchief, wiping at the blood that is running down. "I'll talk to you if you want. Jesus! You don't have to resort to no po-lice brutality, man."

Clyde straightens up a bit. "That's better. Now was you or wasn't you hanging 'round Uncle Freddie's last night, 'bout ten o'clock?"

"I might a been 'round there 'bout then. From a little after ten on prob'ly." Lamont dabs at his nose with his handkerchief.

"You notice anything goin' down at Uncle Freddie's?"

"I seen a couple cars leave."

"When?"

"I don't know. Maybe ten-thirty."

"Two cars."

"That's right. No, wait. A pickup and a car. That's it. I think the car was a El Dorado. I can't be sure. It was dark, man."

"You sure the other vehicle was a pickup?"

"Yeah, I'se sure."

"What kind was it?"

"Fuck if I know, man. I ain't got no interest in redneck transportation. It was white. That's all I know."

"Could you tell anything about who was in it?"

"Just a guy. One guy. And another person in the El Dorado."

"You didn't see no one else?"

"No, man. A dude in each vehicle. That was it."

"You notice anything else?"

"Look, it was dark, alright? Only reason I noticed what I did, they was skinnin' it back pretty good when they pulled out of Uncle Freddie's, and I caught me a look when they went under a streetlight."

"Which way'd they go?"

"The other direction from me. Off toward Burleson."

Clyde straightens up, figures that's about all he's apt to get out of this lowlife with the busted-up face. "The Washington County Sheriff's Department appreciates yo' cooperation, Lamont. You think of anything else, you give me a call, you know what I'm sayin'? And you might want to have somebody take a look at yo' nose. Looks like you might of broke it."

When he gets back to the office Clyde phones the Department of Motor Vehicles, asks for a list of all the pickups in Washington County, their owners and addresses. The woman up in Austin tells him it'll be late that evening before they can run it all through the computer, fax it down to him.

Next he phones Sonya, makes a date for lunch, figuring to go home after that, get a nap, come back in the evening to see what the DMV and the fin-gerprint techs have turned up.

He's headed out the door just as a big craggy-faced rancher toting a briefcase is heading in. The rancher stops, holds out his hand, says, "I'm Jeremiah Spur. You must be Deputy Clyde Thomas."

"That's right." Clyde takes the big leathery hand and gives it a firm shake.

"Pleased to meet you," the big man says. "Just wanted you to know, you did a good job on the Fletcher thing."

Clyde thanks him and walks off, a little puzzled as to how the man could know what he had done on the Fletcher case but other than that feeling pretty fine to have the kind words of a legendary lawman like Jeremiah Spur directed at him.

17

THE RECEPTIONIST WITH THE HAIR PILED UP TO HIGH HEAVEN, MAKEUP TROW-eled on thick as spackling, says, "Yes, sir, Sheriff," into the phone, hangs up, looks at Jeremiah, working her chewing gum like one of Jeremiah's Santa Gertrudis cattle works her cud.

"He asked if you would take a seat, Captain Spur, says he'll be right with you?"

The way she says it makes it sound doubtful, but Jeremiah surmises that's just her manner of making a declarative statement. He sets himself down on one of the old chairs with the torn fabric they got out here, puts the briefcase on the coffee table which is nicked and dinged and has water rings on it.

In no time his mind takes him back to this morning's session with Dr. Fletcher.

It just about hadn't happened. Martha declared when she got up this morning that she thought it was nothing but a waste of time and they ought to call up Jim and tell him to forget it. But Jeremiah stood his ground, argued that it couldn't hurt to go see what the man had to say. It took a while but at last she agreed to it.

He and Martha arrived at straight up ten o'clock. On their way through the narthex they passed a sign that said "Memorial Service for Alicia Fletcher, Sanctuary, 10:00 A.M. Saturday morning, May 15, 1999."

Dr. Fletcher's secretary had showed them into the preacher's study, where he was sitting behind his desk doing paperwork. Jeremiah had never had occasion to be in there before. Dr. Fletcher's office was like a little library, thick carpeting on the floor, cool and dark, blinds drawn against the Texas heat that was already building up outside and beginning to wear everything down like the curse of some long-forgotten deity, books all around, table lamps lighting the place, framed prints on the walls of Bible scenes, the Sermon on the Mount, the Last Supper, the Crucifixion, the Empty Tomb. It looked to Jeremiah like a good place to take a nap after a big lunch.

Dr. Fletcher got up from his chair, a big, broad-shouldered man with a head full of white hair, great big man-of-God smile, his years of ministering to other folks' needs showing themselves in the lines in his face. He was dressed in a dark blue business suit made of some kind of very fine fabric, tie to match. He came over to greet them, shake hands with Jeremiah, give Martha a hug.

The secretary made room for them on a couch where some clothes had been laid out, some suits, shirts, a big blue wool overcoat, and whatnot. As she picked up the stack of clothes she said to Dr. Fletcher, "Is this what you wanted me to send off to charity?"

"Yes, please, Ann." Turning then to the Spurs, he asked, "Can we get you all a cup of coffee?"

The secretary left with the clothes and their coffee orders, and they made themselves at home on the couch, Dr. Fletcher seated in an armchair on the other side of a coffee table with a Bible and a box of tissues on it.

Once his secretary finished serving them coffee and left again, closing the door softly behind her, the preacher commenced the proceedings. "Thank you all for coming in. Martha, I know this is painful for you, and to you I am particularly grateful. Why don't we get started with a prayer?"

They held hands and prayed, and then they got down to business, Dr. Fletcher starting off by asking after Elizabeth and then speaking of the pain of seeing a child in the grip of a terminal disease, the parents' daily struggle to live with the knowledge of impending loss, the need for the healing of old wounds before death's curtain descends and forecloses that option, the natural desire for avoidance, all this leading to reliance upon a crutch. A crutch such as alcohol.

Jeremiah thinks about how Martha looked, listening to all this. She had seemed out of patience with it almost from the start, had sat through it in silence, giving him the impression she would have walked right out but for her respect for the preacher. Then Dr. Fletcher had said, "I am familiar with that ultimate pain, the pain of a lost child. It's as much pain as a person can endure and while over time it may recede, it will never completely go away. There is nothing that ever fills the void that loss creates, and there is no escape from that pain to be found in a whiskey bottle. For if there were, you wouldn't be in pain now, and I long ago would have taken to drink myself."

It was as if Martha had not thought about what Sissy's loss had meant to Jim Fletcher before this, so wrapped up in her own troubles she was, and this seemed to soften her some, driving her to the tissue box, fetching one out, dabbing at her eyes with it. Jeremiah decided to step in, give his wife a moment to collect herself.

He said, "Jim, we just want you to know how sorry we are about Sissy."

The preacher nodded, gave a little wave of the hand, a gesture that said he knew they were sorry, they didn't need to say it out loud.

Jeremiah kept going. "I've talked to the sheriff about the case some. I told him I thought his department needs some help, ought to ask the Rangers to lend a hand."

"Dewey does have his shortcomings as a peace officer."

"Dr. Fletcher, as a peace officer, he couldn't pour piss out of a boot with the instructions written on the heel, if you'll pardon my being frank about it. To his credit, I think he knows that. He's gone so far as to ask for my help on it."

The preacher sat back, made a temple with his fingers, frowned at Jeremiah some from behind it. "Is that right?"

"Yes, sir. But I told him my plate's mighty full at the moment, and he ought to bring the Rangers in. That's what they're there for."

The preacher leaned forward, elbows on his knees. "Jeremiah, I have to tell you, I completely agree. You've got more than enough to worry about. You don't need such distractions right now, and you certainly shouldn't do it out of some felt need arising from our friendship. Sure I'd like to see her killer brought to justice, any father would. But—although it's a trite thing to say, I'll say it anyway—that's not going to bring Sissy back. And what's important in your life at this particular time is that you focus on your own family. They need you. Really and truly they do."

"Yes, sir."

Then the preacher turned to Martha, spoke to her in his great, tender, man-of-God way, encouraged her to pray over her situation, seek out a twelve-step program, learn what life is like without alcohol, not let her pain swamp her existence.

All things considered it ended pretty positively, Martha willing to give a twelve-step program some thought. Dr. Fletcher assigned them some Bible study to do, advised them to pray on a regular basis.

It was all over in about an hour and it ended like it began, with a prayer. They said their good-byes and left for home.

After Jeremiah dropped Martha off at the house, he came back to town to talk to the sheriff.

Directly Dewey emerges from somewhere in back. They howdy, shake. Dewey leads Jeremiah back to his office and closes the door, Jeremiah takes a seat, produces the Fletcher file out of his briefcase, hands it across the desk to Dewey.

"Did you read it?" the sheriff asks, taking the file, setting it on top of his desk.

"Yep."

"What d'you make of it?"

Jeremiah shrugs, reaches for a cigarette. "You got your work cut out for you."

"How's that?"

"Outside of the forensics, which don't tell you much more than the cause of death, you ain't got much to go on. A ten-year-old murder, witnesses scattered to the four corners of the Earth if they're still alive, memories of them what are still around weakened by the passage of time. It's a real mare's nest."

Dewey's hands go to his temples, and he starts working the skin there. "Then what would you do if you was me?"

"I stand by my original suggestion."

"The Rangers?"

"Yep."

"Did you hear we're workin' another case, by the way?"

"Nope."

"Somebody robbed a liquor store over in the colored part of town. The boy who minds the place and his mama are both missin'. I've put Clyde Thomas on it full-time."

"Is that a fact? I just met him out front, by the way. Seems like a good hand."

"He's smart enough for a, uh, you know."

Jeremiah looks around for a place to tip his ash, gets up, grabs a metal trash basket, sits back down with the trash can at his feet. "So you got your multiple investigations goin' on. Probably the first time that ever happened to you, huh?"

Dewey nods.

Jeremiah takes a pull, blows smoke out his nostrils. "Even more reason to bring the Rangers in. You're gettin' short-handed."

"What about you?"

Jeremiah stubs the cigarette out on the inside wall of the trash can. "I got my own rats to kill, Dewey."

Dewey drops his hands to his desk, picks up a letter opener, commences to fumble with it, uses it to scratch a spot on his back, pulls it back, studies it like somebody had just handed it to him and told him it had been retrieved from the lost continent of Atlantis. He glances up, a funny look on his face, then goes back to studying the letter opener. "I been doin' some legwork myself, and there's somethin' I need to tell you."

"Okay."

"I got an eyewitness that says the last person to see Sissy alive might of been your own daughter, Elizabeth."

Jeremiah reaches for his pack of Camels, shakes one out, lights it up, adjusting himself to the revelation that Dewey has just so reluctantly delivered himself of. "I have to tell you, Dewey, I got my substantial doubts about that. Who's the witness?"

"Lucy Brackett, the woman what owns the video store. She claims she seen Elizabeth in Sissy's pickup sometime after eleven o'clock, the night Sissy disappeared. Pulled up next to 'em at a stoplight, saw Elizabeth on the passenger's side. Claims she could see her clear as a bell, could tell Elizabeth was upset about somethin'."

Jeremiah is thinking that this cannot be because if it were true Elizabeth would have said something when he was visiting with her yesterday. "So your witness is sure about this? She seen it all crystal clear, even though it was the middle of the night?"

"Mrs. Brackett's prepared to swear to it, I do believe. Jeremiah, I reckon what this means is . . ."

Jeremiah smokes his cigarette, watches Dewey.

Dewey clears his throat. "What this means is we need to talk to Elizabeth. Based on what I've heard about how sick she is, uh, we sort of need to talk to her right quick."

Jeremiah sits and smokes, thinking maybe it's those drugs they got her on, put some kind of chemical stranglehold on her memory. Could have been all the years gone by plus the drugs plus the pain adding up to a sum that equals the loss of recollection. Maybe that would explain it, why Elizabeth hadn't seen fit to share this with him.

Or maybe there's something she doesn't want him to know.

Thirty-five years as a lawman should have made him tough-minded enough to look at it, the fact his daughter might be a witness to an old, old crime right here in their hometown, with a modicum of objectivity. But it seems he can't. All he can think of is how badly he wants to shield her from this, spare her some bumbling, painful interrogation, her all hooked up to her hospital tubes, fretting about her appearance, fighting off the pain of the cancer that is killing her, while this damn fool sheriff or one of his idiot deputies tries to take her statement.

He's a lawman. But damned if he isn't a father too.

A thing can only be what it is.

"I'm not sure I can allow that, Dewey. She's in a lot of pain, they got her on some serious drugs, and she shouldn't ought to be bothered with this. There ain't a way in the world she's got a thing to do with it."

"You know better than that, Jeremiah. We don't have no choice but to get her statement, and you can't really stop us."

Jeremiah says to himself, try to be tough-minded, face up to the fact this changes everything he had thought about this situation up to this instant. "I don't want her troubled by this any more than is absolutely necessary, you hear?"

"I understand."

"You gonna be the one to talk to her?"

"I thought maybe I'd ask Sonya Nichols from over at George Barnett's office to handle it for me. Thought maybe a woman might have better luck at it."

"Okay, but include me in. I intend to be there too."

Dewey goes back to scratching himself between the shoulder blades with the letter opener. After a minute, he says, "I ain't sure that's such a good idea, Jeremiah. I mean, with all due respect, I wonder how easy it's gonna be for her to level with us, if her own father is there in the room too."

Jeremiah is thinking to himself, *Shit, if this don't beat all.* He knows he hasn't got but one thing to use as leverage, and he hasn't got much choice but to use it.

"Tell you what. You let me sit in on that interview, and I'll give you a hand with this here case."

Jeremiah can see this perks Dewey up. Although he pretends to be turning it over in his steel trap of a mind, Jeremiah can tell he's a buyer at this price.

"Fair enough," Dewey says. "But we need to get movin' on this."

"Alright then. Get ahold of Sonya, tell her we can go tomorrow after the service for Sissy is over. Tell her to meet me in the parking lot at the church around eleven o'clock, and to bring the case file with her."

"I'll let her know."

"I don't like this, but I'm gonna go along with it. And there's something you need to understand. I want you to get her statement, then I want you to leave her alone."

"So long as she tells us the truth, we ain't got no problem with that."

Jeremiah stubs out his cigarette, stands up to go. "She's dying, Sheriff. What reason does she have to lie?"

As he leaves the sheriff's office, Jeremiah is asking himself that same question.

18

CLYDE DOESN'T WORK THE LATE SHIFT MUCH, PREFERRING TO TRADE IT TO
Bobby Crowner for the weekend shift, free up his evenings for pursuits
more natural to a man than cop work. Bobby is always ready to make the
swap, since he has another job down at Wilson Feed and Supply, lets him
work Saturdays to enhance his cash flow. Even when Clyde does pull a
night shift it's usually out on patrol, not here in the office.

So it feels little funny to Clyde, walking in here at a time of night when
he would ordinarily be shooting pool somewhere or having dinner over at
Sonya's, all the desks empty, nobody around except Sammy the night dispatcher who's working in a booth in the back. Clyde has come in this evening not because he and Bobby traded out, since they didn't and Clyde is
supposed to have the night off, but because he wants to see what came in
this afternoon by way of reports from the DPS and the DMV.

His IN box has them, a report from the fingerprint guys and a fax from
over at the DMV. He takes the fingerprint report, scans it, scratching his
shaved head while he reads the jargon about loops, whorls, all the technical-
ities of it.

The cash register was covered in prints, most of them Jasper's. They had
lifted a couple of completes and a couple of partials off the duct tape, but
they didn't match any of the other prints from Freddie's. Nothing useful to
speak of turned up anywhere else.

Clyde sets the fingerprint report aside, goes to the DMV fax. He flips
through it, thinking, man, there's a lot of pickups around here. The list runs
on for seven, eight pages, twenty-five names per page, a couple hundred
white pickup trucks in Washington County alone, north of five hundred if
you throw Waller and Burleson Counties in too.

Clyde scans the first few pages, then stops at a familiar-sounding name.
Martin Luther Fletcher, gives an address over on Farm-to-Market Road
511. That rings a bell with Clyde. He thinks Sissy Fletcher had a brother,
seems like his name might have been Martin. Sets Clyde to wondering
once again, could there be some kind of connection between this liquor
store job and the Sissy Fletcher murder? Seems like a long shot but there's

something about it Clyde can feel in his gut, although his brain's telling him the two don't have a thing in common other than this weird timing.

Clyde is jotting himself a note to get the fingerprint techs to compare these prints with those in the Fletcher file when his phone rings.

He answers it, says, "Clyde Thomas."

"Hey, Clyde. It's Bobby."

"Yo, man. What's up?"

"I got a tip on an abandoned vehicle up toward Gay Hill. Some kid phoned it in. Thought I'd run up there for a look-see. You want to ride along?"

"Sho', man. I'se just sittin' here messin' with some papers."

"Pick you up in ten minutes."

When Bobby Crowner pulls up to the curb at the courthouse, Clyde is already outside waiting. He opens up the passenger door, gets in.

Clyde says, "So you got yo'self a phoned-in tip."

Bobby steers the cruiser around the block, headed northwest. "Like I said, some kid phoned it in."

"Where we goin'?"

"I don't know the exact location. What he give me was more like general directions, down some back road over toward Gay Hill."

"Kid say what he was doin' out there this time of night?"

"It's Friday night in the country, Clyde. What do you think he was doin'?"

"Fuck if I know, man. I grew up in Oak Cliff."

"See, that's where I got some kind of an edge at least. I ain't as smart as you but I know the local ways of things. I grew up in these parts."

"So what's goin' down for a kid on Friday night 'round here in Pigville that takes him out to the boondocks, man? Ain't no video arcades, movie theaters out there. Hell, there ain't even any lights."

"Well, this kid in particular I'm guessin' . . ."

Clyde interrupts. "You don't know who it was?"

"Naw. Was a 'nonymous call, patched through to me by the dispatcher. The kid called nine one one, said he wanted to report something suspicious but didn't want his name associated with it. Anyway, I figger this kid is seventeen, eighteen, somethin' like that. A kid like that would get in his car with his girl, maybe with a buddy and his girl too, ice down some beers in the back, beers they would have scored through an older brother or somethin', drive around some, then head out somewhere lonesome to park."

"Park?"

"Yeah, you know, pull over down some dead-end road or out in a cotton field, or maybe over at the golf course. Drink some beer, neck some, try to feel off his girlfriend."

"That's the big Friday night deal around here, huh?"

"Yep. What did you all do in Oak Cliff when you was growin' up?"

"Pretty much the same thing. Only we wasn't goin' for just a feel. And it wasn't in no cotton field neither. Wallowin' 'round in some cotton field like some kind of farm animal, that ain't no way to treat a lady."

"Where did you go then?"

"They got motel rooms up there, you can rent 'em by the hour, you know what I'm sayin'?"

"That sounds about your speed."

They drive along in silence for a while, Clyde trying to decipher that last remark.

They're leaving the city limits now, headed for the countryside, dark as all get out except where the headlights go, smoke and haze blocking out all the light from the moon and the stars. All the time he's been down here in Washington County, Clyde still isn't accustomed to how dark country nights get. Not like Oak Cliff, streetlights up that way keep some illumination on the street after sundown. Out here it's end-of-the-world dark outside of little specks of light up near ranch houses set way back from the road.

Maybe it's the hour, or maybe it's on account of it being so dark, or maybe it's just that he's feeling it, the week's effort, but it all has Clyde wondering suddenly what he's got to show for his years in this wide-spot-in-the-road town. He has spent a lot of his life around here, keeping the peace for folks. He's not sure he can say exactly what's been in it for himself other than the pay envelope the sheriff hands him twice a month, an envelope with so little money in it he fibs to his mama about how much he makes rather than suffer the embarrassment of having her know.

He can feel the alienation beginning to set in again, the knowledge that nothing is as certain in his life as his separation from others. Separated from his black brothers by the uniform, nothing but a sign to them that he has turned his back on his own race, and that makes him worse than the white man in the eyes of some of them.

Set apart from the white man by the color of his skin.

"Let me ask you somethin'," he says to Bobby.

"Go ahead on."

"What do folks think about me?"

"You mean folks around here?"

"Hell, yes, I mean folks around here. Where else would I be talkin' about? Anchorage, Alaska?"

Bobby cogitates some, then says, "Well, you know Clyde, most folks ain't gonna give you much of a fair shake on account of what you are."

Bobby slows the cruiser, pulls off the highway, onto a country road.

Clyde says, "You grew up around here, huh?"

"Yep. That's how come I know all these back roads, see."

"So what do *you* think about me?"

"Come on, Clyde. We're friends. Coworkers."

" 'Friends,' huh." Clyde pauses. " 'Friends' is how it is, huh. Tell me somethin'."

"What?"

"You ever said the word 'nigger'?"

Bobby glances over at Clyde, then goes back to looking out the windshield. "You see a gate over there on the right anywhere?"

"You ain't answered my question."

"What question?"

"You ever say the n-word? Nigger."

"Clyde, I hate to be the one to break it to you, but this here is rural Texas. People say that word as often as they say 'Bible' or 'football' or 'beer' or any other kind of word. I grew up here, lived here a long time before I ever met you. What do you think?"

"Have you said it in the last year?"

"Maybe."

"What about the last month?"

"Come on, Clyde."

"The last week?"

"Yonder it is."

"That's what I figgered. I bet you say it all the time."

"Clyde, why do you want to go startin' this when we got work to do? You want to get the gate or what?"

Clyde looks out the window at the darkness all around. "How'd you know where to find this place?"

"Like I said, I grew up around here. I used to come out here and park too."

Bobby pulls up in front of the gate. Clyde gets out to mess around with the chain that holds it closed, trying to see what he's doing by the headlights, finally gets it unhooked, swings it wide. Bobby pulls through the gate, shifts the cruiser into reverse so Clyde can see by the taillights to relatch the gate. In front of the car the land slopes down away from the headlights into blackness.

"Whose place is this?" Clyde asks when he gets back in the cruiser.

Bobby slips the cruiser into gear, starts driving along a dirt road. "I ain't completely for sure. Could be the Swiss guy. It's close to his place anyhow."

"The who?"

"It's a man from Switzerland. I heard he has himself some hotels over yonder, and he's richer than God. I met him once. Nice feller, got him a thick German accent, talks like a Nazi in a war movie. Bought about three hundred acres out here, oh, maybe twenty years ago. Runs some kind of European cattle on it, but he don't get over here much himself so he has some hands that do it for him. I forget what you call 'em, his breed of cattle that is. They all white. Like an albino cow. I remember now. They're called Simmental. That's it."

"Y'all probably think they prettier that way, huh?"

"What do you mean?"

"A cow that's all white. Prettier than a regular ol' black Angus cow, got more sex appeal. Lookin' at a cow that be all white, probably give y'all a hard-on, huh? Y'all be tempted to go parkin' with a cow like that, it bein' all white and beautiful and shit."

"Come on, Clyde. Give me a break."

"I'm just sayin'."

"Nobody wants to go parkin' with no cows."

"Right now I don't see no cows of any color. Fact of the matter is I can't see shit. How much farther you think?"

"There's a little ol' dried up creek bed down at the bottom of this hill, got trees all around it. That's where the kid said they found the car."

"How far we from where the Fletcher girl was buried?"

"It's about a mile as the crow flies over yonder way I reckon."

Bobby drives along the dirt road and directly they're at the bottom, down in the creek bed. That's when they see it for the first time.

Bobby says, "It looks like someone set it on fire."

He works the cruiser around so that the headlights shine on what looks like a Cadillac with scorch marks all over it. In the dark it's hard to tell. Clyde and Bobby get out, walk up to it.

Bobby bends down, looks at the back. "Cadillac El Dorado, alright."

Clyde walks around the car, shining his flashlight in, tries the door. It opens up. "The inside's all burned out. Just springs, all the upholstery be gone. Looks like it caught fire there and spread 'round the outside. You smell gasoline?"

"Uh-huh."

"Somebody done torched it for sure."

"Can you see anything else?"

Clyde shines his light around. "Not much of nothin'. Everything pretty much been charbroiled." He leans over, shines the light on the steering column. "Looky here. Still got the keys in it."

He retrieves them, backs out of the car, holds them up to get a good look at them in his flashlight beam.

"Can you tell anything from 'em?"

"Naw, man, just a ring o' keys, got the ignition and the trunk key here, looks like a couple house keys maybe."

"Do you think this is Mrs. Jefferson's automobile?"

"It's a El Dorado, I'm guessin' late eighties. It's probably it."

"It's kind of weird, don't you think?"

"What's that?"

"Us finding it out here so close to where Sissy Fletcher was buried."

Clyde runs the flashlight beam up and down the car's length. "Yeah."

"Where do you reckon the people went?"

"Beats the shit outta me."

Then Clyde has a thought. He walks around back to the trunk, hands the flashlight to Bobby. "Here you go. Hold this on the trunk for a minute."

Clyde inserts the trunk key in, tries to open it, but the key won't turn. "It ain't gonna budge. Fire musta froze it up. You got a tire tool?"

"Yeah. Hang on."

Bobby walks back to the cruiser, leaves Clyde standing in the wash from the car headlights, feeling weird about being out here in the middle of nowhere, standing next to a burned-out vehicle in the pitch-black night on land owned by a Swiss guy that runs white cows. Clyde's skin is beginning to crawl, wondering what's in the trunk.

Directly Bobby comes back, tire tool in hand, hands it to Clyde.

"Okay," Clyde says. "Gimme some light. Lemme see if I can pop this sucker."

Clyde works the tire tool under the back of the trunk lid, then jerks up hard on it. The lid springs open. Bobby brings the light over and they both look in.

Clyde says softly, "Motherfucker."

Bobby takes a look, hands Clyde the flashlight without saying a word, goes off in the dark somewhere to puke.

Clyde stares inside the trunk, then stands back, drops the flashlight down by his side, and shouts, "Motherfucker!" It's the only thing that breaks the silence, except for the muted sounds of Bobby spitting up in the bushes.

Clyde goes back to the cruiser, leans in, grabs the radio. "Sammy, this is Clyde."

"Come in, Clyde."

"I got me another dead body situation over here at Gay Hill, only there's two of 'em this time. Hard to tell from the condition the bodies is in, but

I'm guessin' it would be Jasper and Mildred Jefferson. You want to patch me through to the DPS crime lab?"

Once he gets through, Clyde requests a forensics team, tells them where he'll meet them, signs off, gets out of the cruiser, leans against it with his head hanging, feeling empty inside, wondering who would have done something like this to these folks, these fine folks.

He thinks about the last time he saw Jasper, just yesterday. He had thought for sure they were going to save the kid, had him all straightened out, had him working a good steady job, and now this. Somebody had set Jasper and his mama on fire and left them out here for Clyde to find, black bodies locked up in a black trunk on a black night.

Clyde would like nothing better than to haul off and hit someone.

"Clyde?"

Clyde looks up, sees the outline of Bobby in the dark there, thinks maybe he's done being sick for now. "Yeah. What?"

"I'm sorry I used that word."

"Do what?"

"I'm real, real sorry. I ain't never gonna use that word again. I swear to God."

Clyde doesn't respond, is quiet for a while, just looks at the outline of Bobby standing there in the dark, faint smell of vomit on the man. All Clyde says is, "We might as well get the search started."

"Okay."

"You hold the flashlight while I look around."

19

JEREMIAH SPUR WHEELS HIS PICKUP INTO THE CHURCH PARKING LOT, SLIDES into a space next to Frank Gibson's Town Car, mentally notes the convenience of it since the Gibsons are carrying Martha home after the reception that follows the memorial service.

As for Jeremiah, he's got to go down to Houston with Sonya Nichols.

Jeremiah takes his Stetson off as they walk into the narthex, Martha at his side holding his elbow. They sign the guest book, then enter the sanctuary nodding this way and that to folks they know, giving them a little wave, half a smile, the solemn howdy you dispense at funerals, different from any other howdy in the measured way it's done, the restraint in it that says it's nice to see you again but don't you just hate the reason we're here. They take their usual spot on the far end of the last pew, where Jeremiah can see the whole place and be the first one out the door when the service is over.

This church with its stained glass, oak pews lined with red cushions, matching red carpeting on the floors, great big gold cross up behind the pulpit where Dr. Fletcher stands to preach, it had been Martha's church when she was growing up, so naturally it had become the place in which Elizabeth was baptized and confirmed. Jeremiah can still remember the day she was confirmed, her standing up in front of the congregation on a little step stool behind the pulpit reading the confirmation class's custom-made affirmation, the little barrel rider looking so out of place, so uncomfortable in her starched white dress, hair pulled back, her voice tripping over the words.

Jeremiah sits in his pew watching the folks file in, thinking back to yesterday evening, his conversation with Martha after he got home from his visit with the sheriff.

He found Martha sitting at the kitchen table still dressed in the nice clothes she had put on that morning for the meeting with the preacher, a cup of coffee in front of her. Jeremiah thought maybe that showed some progress already since most days she would have been busy wrapping herself around a vodka tonic by then.

There was some redness around her eyes and a box of tissues on the table.

"I'm home," he said, and then felt dumb for having said it on account of she could see that for herself.

She looked up, actually sort of smiled at him, a melancholy smile for sure, but he'd take that. Her smiles of whatever stripe were rare these days. He missed the Martha that used to smile and laugh. This Martha seemed to have forgotten how.

He went over to pour himself a cup of coffee, then came back to sit with her.

"What you been doin'?" he asked.

She looked at him with her red-rimmed eyes, said, "I've been sitting here pretty much ever since you left. Been sitting here thinking."

" 'Bout what?"

"About our visit with Jim. About what he said. You know what?"

"What?"

"Jim Fletcher is as smart as a tree full of owls."

"I agree. I'm curious why you would say it though."

She looked out the window, toward the back pastures where the smoke lay heavy and moved near a copse of trees over by the tank, their shapes blurred by the haze, made indistinct, less like cattle than the ghosts of cattle.

"He gets at his point by indirection. It didn't even dawn on me until after we got home that much of what he said about Elizabeth's cancer could have been applied word for word to her life, to the way she lived it. Not to mention how we, or at least I, have reacted to it. How I have chosen to deal with it."

To give himself some time to digest this Jeremiah reached for his cigarettes, shook one out, lit it up, got up to fetch an ashtray from the other side of the room.

She said, "Of course, it's his job to counsel people in times like these, and he's good at it. But in this case his counsel has all the more impact since he has been through something like our own experience himself. So it has set me to thinking. And that's what I've been sitting here doing."

"Which leaves you where?"

She took a sip of coffee, looked over at Jeremiah for a spell, then said, "It seems to me there's a lot to what he says. And I hate to admit it but I've about concluded that I've spent too many years trying to avoid dealing with the facts of life where Elizabeth is concerned. And now that she's not going to be with us much longer, I need to . . ." Her voice began to falter. "I need to . . . do what I can about . . . about that."

She pulled a tissue out of a box, dabbed at her eyes. "I want to see Elizabeth, as soon as I can. Would you take me down there tomorrow, after the memorial service?"

"I'd be tickled to carry you down yonder. But I can't tomorrow. Even though I got to go myself."

"What do you mean?"

"I got to pay her a visit tomorrow but it ain't a social call."

Jeremiah took a drag on his Camel, set it down in the ashtray, rubbed his hand over his forehead. He told her what the sheriff said. She kept still, watching his face during the telling of it.

He finished up, telling her he insisted on being in the room during the interview. He stopped with that, decided he'd best leave out that piece where he had to swap his help with the case in order to make the deal.

"So," he said, "I told Dewey I'd carry this lady assistant DA down yonder to talk to Elizabeth tomorrow. It's apt to be hard enough on her, goin' through that with me in the room. The honest truth is I don't think the both of us should be there."

She just sat in her chair for a while after he spoke, dabbing at her eyes, not looking at him much, instead looking out the window toward the back, toward where the cattle stood like ghosts.

Then she said, "Jeremiah, I . . ."

"Yeah?"

But she fell silent again, staring out the window, distracted by exactly what Jeremiah couldn't say.

At length she got up, took her coffee cup to the sink, said with her back to him, "I knew you couldn't keep your distance from this business."

"I intended to. The problem is, it ain't keepin' its distance from me."

"Which is no surprise. Like I told you, it's your fate or destiny or whatever you want to call it that's driving you and this mess together." He could hear shortness of temper in her voice.

Jeremiah figured he had to keep going despite the warning signs. "You'd know more about that than I would. But since we've been drug into it, I'm just wonderin' if you can recollect anything from that night, the night Sissy Fletcher disappeared."

"So now you're going to take my statement, I guess."

"That's not exactly what I'd call it. I could just use some help here with the facts is all. As I recollect I was out of town at the time, workin' a case."

"Yes, you were, not that there was anything unusual about that. Even though it was a weekend night, you couldn't see your way clear to get home."

"Drug cartels work weekends. That meant I had to, too."

They'd had this fight too many times already, the one about how being a Ranger wasn't a nine-to-five type of deal. No sense in belaboring the point.

Martha had gone to the coffeepot, turned it off. She poured out the rest

of the coffee, washed the pot, began to dry it with a dish towel. She sighed
a few times, said, "I don't know. I think I can remember a little. It was a
long time ago."

"What can you recollect from it?"

"It was Elizabeth's senior year in high school. The main thing I remember about it is that she went to the dance with some friends from school."

"Do you remember who?"

She went to the cupboard, pulled down an iced tea glass that had little
yellow daisies on the side, filled it with ice from a tray out of the freezer, the
ice hitting the sides and bottom of the glass, making a sound like a musical
instrument that needs tuning. "No. I really don't. Too many years have
gone by, I guess."

She fished her vodka bottle and the tonic out of a cabinet, poured first
the one until the level was about halfway up the daisies, then topped it off
with the other.

Jeremiah watched her fixing her drink and thought a thing can only be
what it is. "Do you remember anything about when she came home?"

"I think I had gone to bed already. I don't remember being up. She had
a midnight curfew that she was good about minding, so she would have
been in by then."

"Are you sure about that?"

"Yes. Pretty sure. Even if I was in bed already, I wouldn't have gone to
sleep before she got home. I could never get to sleep until after she was
home safe. The time or two she did stay out past midnight, I generally sat in
the family room, waiting for her."

"I kind of recollect that."

"So I seem to recall her coming in, going to her room, shutting the door.
Then again, maybe that's just my mind, telling me that's what would have
happened, making it seem like a memory."

"Anything else?"

"I think I remember hearing her crying, in her room. But then again
maybe that's me imagining things. She was a lonely teenage girl, a misfit
among her own people, even more so than we knew then, I suppose. It
wasn't any wonder that she cried, that she cried a lot. There's nothing suspicious about that, no matter what that sorry excuse for a human being
Lucy Brackett may say."

Martha finished mixing her drink and came over to sit at the kitchen
table.

Jeremiah glanced at the clock, checking to see what time of day she
elected to have her first drink. Four-thirty. Well, maybe it was some
progress, he decided.

"Did she ever say anything to you about what might have happened that night?"

"Not that I recall. I don't think Sissy Fletcher came up. Not that she would have."

"Why's that?"

Martha took a swallow, put the glass down on the table, ice clinking inside, and gave him a hard look. "Because I had made it clear to Elizabeth she was not to have anything to do with Sissy. Ever. She was to steer as wide of her as she could."

"On account of how come?"

Martha took another drink. "Jeremiah, it's a commonplace that everybody hates to speak ill of the dead, but since you're about to be wallowing in this sorry mess, there's something you need to understand. Sissy Fletcher was a dirty leg."

Jeremiah didn't know which was more surprising, his wife knowing that phrase, or her application of it to Jim Fletcher's daughter. "That don't seem . . ."

"Trust me on this, Jeremiah. She was. If you had been home more often you'd probably have known that already. Everybody in town knew it, with the possible exception of her father. I say 'possible' because even he must have had his suspicions."

"You seem pretty sure."

"Oh, yes. And on top of that she had some kind of agenda. She used her body to destroy men. She hated men."

"What makes you say that?"

Martha sipped her drink, stared out the window. "It's just a fact. If you don't believe me, ask around. Ask Joe Bob Cole."

Jeremiah was sitting there in silence, parsing through this pronouncement, when she spoke again.

"If you want to know the truth of it, I think that whoever killed Sissy Fletcher ought to get a medal for it. She was the worst thing ever to happen to this town."

"The law don't see it that way."

"I thought that's what you'd say."

They sat in silence, her sipping her drink, Jeremiah having another cigarette.

"Jeremiah?" she said.

"Yeah."

"You go do this, this interview, if you have to. But I want to see my daughter."

"Okay."

"I want to see her this weekend."

"Alright then. We'll go back on Sunday."

"Fine."

Now Jeremiah sits in the back pew of the First Church of the Lamb listening to the organ music, watching the congregation file in, thinking that had been about the end of it. He hadn't been able to coax anything else out of his wife, and she'd refilled that glass with the daisies on it and drained it and then refilled it over and over until there wasn't much left for her to do but stagger off to bed.

So his wife's hearsay was that the preacher's daughter had been a woman who was given to sleeping around, but who had hated men for some reason. That combination of facts doesn't make sense to Jeremiah. It seems to him like the two things would have precluded one another.

Revelations along such lines do things to a man's perspective, sitting here at the deceased's memorial service. They sure do.

Getting close now to time for the service to start, lots of people are coming down the aisles in a last-minute kind of hurry, looking for a spot where they can sit. Some of these folks are ranchers Jeremiah knows, local politicians, bankers, storekeepers, people Jeremiah's been around all his life, ever since he first arrived here in some cases.

But few of them would Jeremiah out-and-out call his friends.

Yonder comes the sheriff and a tall, good-looking redhead, must be his wife, and it certainly is not that blonde Dewey was snuggled up with over at the ice cream parlor. After that of all things comes the ice cream parlor lady herself, leading a grown man by the hand. Something about that young fellow strikes Jeremiah as funny. He shuffles along, halfway slumped over.

Jeremiah leans over to Martha and whispers, "Is that Mrs. Baker's son with her, the one that's supposed to be dim-witted?"

"Yes," she whispers back to him. "I think his name is Charlie."

"He ain't a bad-lookin' kid."

"Why should he be?"

"Well, I heard he was retarded. Most folks like that, they look kinda funny."

"From what I hear, he's not retarded. He's just kind of a slow learner."

Jeremiah can see that Charlie Baker is upset about something, wiping his nose with his sleeve, making little sobbing sounds as his mama leads him down the aisle. "He looks like he's been cryin'," he whispers to Martha.

Martha takes a look. "He sure does," she whispers back. "That's a little strange. Every time I've ever seen him, he's always seemed pretty happy."

"Seems kind of odd he'd be so upset about someone who'd gone missin' ten years ago, especially since neither of 'em is kin."

Martha shrugs. "I seem to recollect they were close to one another though."

Directly everybody's in their places, settling in noises coming from all around the sanctuary, people shifting in their pews, whispering. The organ music stops for a few moments, then begins again, louder, more energetic this time. The music director comes walking down the center aisle, followed by the choir, then the ministers. The choir cranks up "When I Survey The Wondrous Cross," and the congregation stands and joins in.

Once the hymn is done and the choir and everybody have found their places at the front, they all sit down in unison. Then there's the pastoral prayer, the Lord's Prayer, another hymn, the order of service foreordained by the brown and yellow program Jeremiah keeps stashed in the pew back in front of him where it'll be handy in case he needs to refer to it to anticipate what's coming and have the hymnal ready and whatnot.

By and by Dr. Fletcher takes the short walk up the steps to the pulpit, lays his Bible down, squares his reading glasses. "May the Lord be with you."

The congregation says back, "And also with you."

"Good morning. Thank you for coming. Please turn in your Bibles to page nine-thirty-seven and join me in reading from the Book of Matthew, chapter seven, verse one."

The preacher pauses while folks rustle around, finding the right page. Then he starts to read, everybody else joining up in a ragged group mumble.

"Judge not, that you not be judged. For with what judgment you judge, you will be judged; and with the measure you use, it will be measured back to you."

The preacher closes his Bible and says, "May the Lord add His blessing to the reading of His Word. Amen.

"This is a morning for remembering, not for judging. The playwright Tennessee Williams once said something to the effect that time consists only of the present, which is so fleeting that we can barely grasp it before it leaves us and becomes the past, and the past itself, which exists only in our memories. All there is of my daughter, Alicia Fletcher, at least all there is on this earth, exists now in the past, in the world of our memories of her, and of what she meant to us.

"And lest judgment try to force its way in where it is unwelcome, let us remember the words of Christ as set forth in the Gospel according to Saint Matthew.

"And so I would like to say a few words in loving remembrance of my daughter."

Jeremiah is thinking that the reading of Matthew chapter seven, verse one, strikes him as a mighty odd opening salvo for a memorial service. He allows as how it might make a modicum of sense given what Martha told him yesterday evening about the morals Sissy displayed while she was alive.

Jeremiah looks around the church, wondering if it was true, that everybody else had known all the things Martha had said about the dead girl. Then his mind tells itself to be still, listen to the preacher.

Jim Fletcher is saying, ". . . was born in Midland, Texas, on February fifth, 1964, but grew up here in Brenham. She was named for her mother's grandmother, who was one of the pioneers who first settled the Texas high plains. Sissy lost her own mother, my wife Theresa, when she was only fourteen years old. After that she became the lady of our house, watching over me and her brother Martin, who was just five years old at the time, and who was the first to call her 'Sissy.'

"Sissy attended Brenham High School where she was a cheerleader, a member of 4-H, a features editor of the yearbook, and the homecoming queen in 1981. She was also an active member of the youth choir and a number of the youth groups here at the church.

"She graduated from high school in 1982 and went to Austin to attend the University of Texas before returning home in 1984."

Dr. Fletcher pauses a moment or two, looks to be collecting himself.

"Those of you who had the pleasure of knowing her when she was growing up will remember her as the best friend of the small and weak and the implacable opponent of the big and strong.

"One spring, when Sissy was about sixteen, a mourning dove built a nest in a potted plant out on our back porch. The dove laid her eggs as they are wont to do at that time of year and pretty soon she had a bunch of baby birds in that nest. Sissy would come home every day from school and spend hours watching that mama with her babies.

"One day she came home from school and the mama bird was there, but the babies were gone. Sissy asked our maid Lilly what had become of the baby birds, and Lilly told her a cat had sneaked up and eaten the babies while the mama was away.

"Well, those of you who knew Sissy will not be surprised to hear that she was heartbroken, not just for the baby birds, but for the mama bird as well. That mama bird would sit in that nest, grieving in her simple, birdlike way for the loss of her young ones, and Sissy would sit in the family room, watching that mama bird for hours, feeling sympathy for it. She desperately wanted to find some way to comfort that bird. Finally she decided she would take some birdseed out to it, a little bit every day.

"One day I was walking through the house, and I looked out the back window and there was Sissy, sitting on the porch, that mourning dove resting in her hand, while Sissy stroked it and whispered to it.

"Whatever else she may have been, Sissy was the personification of kindness, especially when it came to the weak, the small, the helpless. While the rest of her was complicated—and like a lot of very intelligent people, she was very complicated—this part of her, perhaps the most precious part, was simple.

"Sissy was taken from us just a few days after her twenty-fifth birthday. She was missed then and she is missed today. But now, at last, we know she is in a place where the helpless, where children, are never, ever . . ."

The preacher suddenly stops. He clears his throat. He stands there in the pulpit, the lights overhead catching them now, the tears running down his face.

It is graveyard quiet in the sanctuary.

Dr. Fletcher closes his Bible, walks back down the pulpit steps, takes his seat.

The music director gets back up, leads them all in "Amazing Grace." Then Dr. Fletcher's assistant minister gives the benediction, thanks them all for coming, and invites them next door to the parsonage for the reception.

Jeremiah walks Martha out into the parking lot to wait for the Gibsons, putting his Stetson on once he has cleared the church. He positions himself and Martha at the rear of his pickup, so the Gibsons can't miss them on their way through the parking lot.

He glances at her, sees her expression. He says softly, "The look on your face would send Duke under the porch if he saw it."

She whispers, "That was the worst service I ever sat through. I didn't know Jim Fletcher was capable of anything that awful."

"It was his own daughter, Martha. He's allowed."

"I wonder if there's any way to get out of going to this reception."

"You ought to go, pay your respects."

"You're not going."

"That's different."

"I knew you'd say that. I just want to go home."

Jeremiah looks back toward the street, sees a gold sports car pull up to the curb. A tall young woman carrying a briefcase, wearing a businesslike suit, gets out the passenger's side, walks his way, followed by the deputy Jeremiah had run into yesterday, him getting out the driver's side and sashaying over with her, decked out in his brown uniform with the yellow trim, got his Stetson on.

Jeremiah watches them walk, thinking the deputy's got some strut to him.

The woman with the briefcase walks up, offers her hand, says, "Captain Spur, I'm Sonya Nichols. It's a great pleasure to meet you, sir. I believe you've met my gentleman friend, Clyde Thomas."

20

"PLEASED TO MEET YOU," JEREMIAH SAYS TO SONYA. "I'D LIKE YOU TO MEET MY wife, Martha. Martha, this is Sonya Nichols and Clyde Thomas."

While Martha shakes Sonya's hand warily, Jeremiah turns to Clyde, sticks his hand out. "Nice to see you again."

Clyde returns the shake, says, "How y'all are, man?"

Behind him Jeremiah hears the sound of paws scraping in the bed of his pickup, it registering on him that Duke is back there, probably just waking up from a nap, reacting to the sound of Jeremiah's voice. Jeremiah turns around, sees Duke get up, stretch, shake all over. Duke looks over his way, sees Clyde, and that's all it takes.

Duke sets to barking his loudest and most agitated bark, standing at the back of the pickup bed, teeth bared, eyes fixed on Clyde.

Jeremiah says, "Maybe we ought to move away from the pickup."

He starts to walk away, bringing Clyde and Sonya with him.

Clyde stops, looks back at the pickup, says, "What's wrong with yo' dog, man?"

"He's kind of territorial. Plus he don't much care for black folks."

Jeremiah takes Clyde by the elbow, starts walking him away from the truck.

Clyde glances back over his shoulder at the pickup where Duke looks like he's about to take to the air. "That dog be a racist motherfucker, man."

Sonya says, "Clyde!"

Jeremiah squints at Clyde. "No he ain't. He just don't like black folks. And if you ain't more careful with your language around my wife, Duke's gonna be about the last thing you have to worry about."

Clyde squares off. "What's with the tone of voice, man? Ain't you a little on the old side for that kind of hostility? I mean, what you gonna be backin' it up with, huh?"

"Maybe you and me ought to go across the street and find out."

They stand there eyeing one another, the muscles in Jeremiah's jaw working. Behind him Duke is barking like he's lost his mind, specks of foam flying from the corners of his mouth. People are pouring out of the church, slowing down when they get to the parking lot so as to get an eye-ful of this scene.

Sonya steps forward, puts her hand on Jeremiah's arm. "Please forgive him, Captain Spur."

Clyde says, "Forgive *me*?"

Sonya ignores him. "He hasn't had any sleep for two nights running. He's working a double homicide, armed robbery case."

Jeremiah isn't quite through sizing Clyde up yet, keeps eyeing him. "This that liquor store business the sheriff mentioned to me?"

"Yes, sir. Clyde just found the bodies last night. I want to go over it with you in the car on the way to Houston. Clyde wants that, too."

Jeremiah loosens up some, looks at Sonya. "Alright then. We probably ought to go on and git, before Duke jumps that tailgate and we have to pry him off your friend here. Did you bring the Fletcher case file?"

"Yes, sir."

"Good. Let me see to my wife a second."

Jeremiah goes back to where Martha's standing, joined now by the Gib-sons. Duke has finally barked himself out, but he's still on his feet, growling at Clyde.

Jeremiah speaks to the Gibsons, then turns to Martha. "We're fixin' to mount up. I'll tell Elizabeth we're both comin' back tomorrow."

Martha looks up at him, her eyes a little welled up. "Please take it easy on her."

"That's why I'm gonna be there. To make sure it goes easy."

Jeremiah looks back at Sonya, who is kissing Clyde good-bye. "You ready?"

"Yes, sir."

They head for Jeremiah's pickup.

Sheriff Dewey Sharpe spoons himself some mashed potatoes and gravy, straightens up from the dining-room table, checks the immediate vicinity to make sure no one's in earshot, leans over to his wife, Claudia, who is helping herself to a piece of cherry pie, and mumbles, "It's like the line from that Kenny Rogers song."

"What line?" she whispers back.

"It's a ill wind that blows no good. Ain't that right?"

"What do you mean?"

"I mean that if we hadn't of dug Sissy Fletcher out of the ground last Monday we wouldn't be eatin' so high on the hog today."

"Dewey!" she hisses back. "Show some respect."

"I'm 'bout to show this grub a whole lot of respect. When I'm done with this I'm gonna come back and get me some more and I ain't leavin' here 'til I'm as full as a tick. Come on, let's find us someplace to sit so we can have at this food with both hands."

Dewey's got one paw clamped around a sweating glass of sweet tea, the other holding a dinner plate heaped with food. Fried chicken, mashed potatoes, black-eyed peas, jalapeno corn bread, cream gravy on everything. Dewey isn't much of a green vegetables man. He prefers his food fried and in reassuring shades of yellow and brown. If it doesn't taste good with cream gravy on it, or hot sauce, or both, Dewey doesn't want to have anything to do with it.

He leaves the dining room, navigates through the crowd that packs this little parsonage with its overstuffed furniture, its Bible verse samplers on the walls, its doilies, its theology and philosophy books everywhere, pictures arranged just so, conveying a sense of simple dignity, just what you'd expect to find in Dr. Fletcher's house.

Folks from all walks of Washington County life are in here cheek by jowl, brought together to eat potluck and visit on account of a girl long since dead.

Over yonder is George Barnett talking to Dr. Fletcher himself. The Gibsons and Martha Spur are off in a corner on the other side of the room. Dewey had seen Jeremiah leave with Sonya so he knows the old Ranger is on his way to Houston to take his daughter's statement, wanting to get it behind him so bad he blew his chance to graze on these free victuals, an error in judgment if ever there was one in Dewey's view.

There's the state representative, the state senator, the congressman from down in Bellville, some guy that had been introduced to Dewey as the governor's chief of staff, the superintendent of schools, Bert Wilson of Wilson Feed and Supply, and every minister from every church in town, both the white folks' churches and the ones the colored folks attend, along with a bunch of other ministers from out-of-town churches, some as far away as Louisiana and Arkansas judging by the tags on the cars outside.

Dewey spots a couple of empty armchairs on either side of a table over by a set of French doors in the family room, gives Claudia a little nudge with his elbow, a little jerk of the head, using his body English to steer her in that direction.

The sheriff falls heavily into one of the armchairs with his elbows held high and out to the side to keep his meal from tipping off his plate and his tea from spilling. He sets his tea glass down on the table, squarely on top of a religious magazine, Billy Graham's smiling face making for a nice coaster. Claudia takes the other armchair.

Directly Dewey is showing so much devotion to his food that he doesn't notice he and Claudia are fixing to be joined by another couple of mourners until it's too late.

He hears someone say "Hi, Dewey" in a familiar little singsong voice, looks up to see Cindy Miller, staring down at him with her Planet Earth eyes, holding two matching plates of rabbit food, all carrot sticks and celery and lettuce and the like. Her boyfriend, Dr. Hollis Watson, the Yankee surgeon, pulls a couple of chairs up and arranges them so they can sit and visit with the Sharpes.

Dewey has the feeling that maybe this isn't such a good thing that's getting ready to happen right here.

Cindy takes her seat, hands Hollis his plate of vegetables, no doubt fresh, no doubt grown in somebody's home garden right here in Washington County, utterly inedible so far as Dewey is concerned.

Cindy reaches over, offers a hand to Claudia. "Hi. I'm Cindy Miller. This is my friend, Dr. Hollis Watson. Dewey, I think y'all may know one another."

Dewey shakes the man's hand. "Yeah, we met on a dove hunt last fall. How you doin', Doc?"

"Great, thanks."

"How's the doctorin' business?"

"It's fine. But we're not having the record year you law enforcement guys are."

"Yeah. We seem to be blessed with an overabundance of crime these days."

They're quiet while they eat for a few moments.

"Wasn't that a lovely service?" Cindy asks.

"Very moving," Claudia replies. "Almost enough to make you forget what kind of person Sissy really was."

Dewey shoots her a look that says, *Now* who isn't showing the proper respect? "Remember," he says through a mouthful of mashed potatoes, " 'judge not.' "

"Sounds like she had quite a way with animals, or birds at least," says Dr. Watson, forking some salad into his mouth.

"That was a sweet story about her and that mourning dove," Cindy says, nibbling at a carrot stick as if to haul off and eat the whole thing in the bite and a half that would be required would cause her instantly to swell up four dress sizes.

"I never heard of a wild dove lettin' a person hold it before," Dewey says.

"That's not your style, is it, Dewey, to go around holding doves in your hand?" says Dr. Watson. He turns to Cindy and says, "Dewey would rather rain lead death on doves. He's a heck of a wing shot, I believe is the term, right, Dewey? You must have shot two dozen birds at the charity hunt last year. Even though the bag limit is about half that as I understand."

"Dewey's got a history of pretty rough treatment of the members of the bird kingdom, don'cha know," Cindy says. "He was telling me just the other day how he relieved himself on Mrs. Sharpe's cockatiel."

"Excuse me?" Claudia says.

Dewey shrinks into his armchair, wondering how to extricate himself from this nightmare of a conversation, but not coming up with a plan, what with him being boxed into this corner, a plate of half-eaten chow on his lap.

Cindy just keeps going. "I've been wondering, Mrs. Sharpe, does it make a bird smell bad for it to be peed on?"

"I beg your pardon?" Claudia says, looking first at Cindy, then at Dewey.

"Well," Cindy says, "I mean, I'm just curious because my little brother accidentally peed on a hair dryer once and every time we used it after that it smelled awful. I was just wondering whether you would have the same problem with a cockatiel. Not that you'd use a cockatiel to dry your hair, of course."

Dewey looks at Claudia, gives a little shrug that says *I don't know what she's talking about,* even though Cindy had already said she got the story from him.

Then Dewey hears another familiar voice say, "Hi, Dewey. Hi, Cindy."

He looks up to see Mrs. Baker from the Big Scoop Ice Cream Parlor, her son in tow. "Hi, Mrs. B," Cindy says. "Is your son feeling better now? I noticed he seemed kind of upset, you know, in the memorial service."

"Oh, yes. It's just that he so loved Sissy, and he misses her very much," she says.

She turns to her son, who is standing behind her, hunched over, a dull look on his face. "Charlie, say 'hi' to Sheriff Sharpe."

"How you?" Charlie says, his eyes locked on something down near his feet.

Dewey wishes they would just disappear, but it would be impolite not to speak. He says, "Fine, Charlie. How are things down at the garage?"

"Pretty good I reckon."

"I dropped my cruiser over there this mornin' for an oil change. When can you get to it, do you think?"

He shrugs, says, "This afternoon, prob'ly."

"That'd be great. Good seein' you."

Dewey goes back to his food, hoping they'll take the hint and move on off.

Mrs. Baker says, "My goodness, where are my manners? Charlie, I don't believe you've met the sheriff's sister, Cindy."

"Sister?" Claudia and Hollis Watson say the word in unison.

Mrs. Baker doesn't seem to notice them. "Cindy, this is my son Charlie. Dewey, I hope we'll be seeing you and Cindy for coffee again this week. Bye-bye now." Then she moves off, dragging Charlie behind her.

Cindy says, "Dewey, did you tell that nice lady I'm your sister?"

Dewey turns to Claudia and says, "Honey, I know this must all seem kind of confusing, but I promise I can explain everything."

Claudia stares back at him, her eyes growing hard. Then she stands up, towering over Dewey, looking him in the eye as she drops her pie plate into his lap. It lands in his mashed potatoes, sends a spray of creamed gravy across the front of his suit, his shirt, the tie he had bought just last week at Krepke's Men's Clothing for $29.95.

"You can walk home, mister," she says. "I'm taking the car."

"Wait a minute," he says, struggling to set his plate down, trying to get his feet under him, wiping at the cream gravy on the front of his suit with a napkin, following her as she crosses the room through the crowd.

Even though she has a head start and is longer-legged than he is, he has just about caught up to her when a short black man in a clerical collar steps in front of him, blocks his path.

"Hello, Sheriff."

Dewey hits the brakes before he slams into Dr. Ebeneezer Flatley, smears the reverend with cream gravy. "Howdy, Dr. Flatley."

"I wonder if I might have a word with you, please, sir?"

Dewey looks past Dr. Flatley, trying to keep Claudia in sight. "As a matter of fact, I was just fixing to leave . . ."

"It won't take but a minute. My, oh my, what happened to your nice suit? And I bet that was a very beautiful tie."

Dewey would like to try to catch up to Claudia, clear up this Cindy Miller mess, but Dr. Flatley seems pretty insistent, and what with him being a real influence on the voting predilections in the darker precincts, Dewey figures he best better give him a minute or two, rather than risk offending the man.

"Oh, that," Dewey says, looking down at his suit front. "I kind of had a accident."

"Yes, sir, I do believe you did. By the way, do you know Martin Fletcher, the son of my good friend Jim Fletcher?"

Dr. Flatley takes Dewey's arm, turns him forty-five degrees, forcing him to look up into the face of a tall, wild-looking young rancher with a long scraggly black beard.

"I think we met a few years back. How you doin', Martin? Sorry about your sister." Dewey sticks out his hand, gives Martin a shake.

"Thanks."

Dewey can't help but notice there's something funny about Martin's eyes, the way they sink back behind his eyelids and kind of dart around.

"Martin and I were just visitin' about the brutal murders of those sweet people from my flock, Mildred and Jasper Jefferson, whose deaths have compounded the tragedy of an already very, very tragic week. I trust Clyde Thomas has been keeping you apprised of his investigation, Sheriff?"

"Yes, sir. He's been working that case nonstop. I get the feelin' he's makin' good progress too. By the way, Martin, Clyde's the one what found your sister's remains, and he's pitchin' in on that case when he's got the time."

Dr. Flatley says, "So what's your take on the Jefferson case?"

Dewey looks around, lowers his voice, motions the preacher and Martin to come in closer. "I probably ought not be tellin' y'all this, but I guess there ain't no harm in it. It looks to us like the Jeffersons might have been bound with some kind of tape, then shot execution style, like a mob hit or somethin'. That's the preliminary forensics anyhow. On top of that Clyde found a roll of duct tape in the back of Uncle Freddie's—that was the liquor store where Jasper worked, Martin, where the cash drawer was robbed. We was able to lift some fingerprints from it that don't match Jasper's or anybody else's who worked at the store. You heard 'bout the condition of the bodies when Clyde found 'em?"

Dr. Flatley nods. Martin just stares at him through slitted eyes.

"Well, Clyde told me this morning the medical examiner says they was shot in the trunk of Mrs. Jefferson's Cadillac before they was set on fire. The floor of the trunk's got a couple bullet holes in it. We're guessin' it was a pretty big handgun, fired at point-blank range, a forty-five or maybe a three fifty-seven Magnum, we ain't for sure yet. We retrieved a couple slugs from the scene and we're checkin' the ballistics."

"Why would someone shoot those poor people, then set them on fire?"

"We figger ever-who done it must of been covering their tracks from the liquor-store holdup."

Dr. Flatley looks thoughtful. "Lord have mercy. What a thing to do to a person, isn't that right, Martin?"

Martin says, "It's pretty awful, alright."

"How about that Clyde Thomas, though, finding them folks so fast? He's a good man, don't you think, Sheriff?"

"Well, sir, he has his moments. He's apt to be a handful sometimes, when he can't keep that street attitude of his under control. He quit on me this week, behaved pretty offensively in the process. Called me some names I didn't much care for."

"But he's a good police officer, isn't he, now? Wouldn't you agree with that?"

"Hard to argue with that, Dr. Flatley."

"And according to him he said he's sorry, asked for his old job back. Now, I would have to say, with all the crime that has afflicted us here in Brenham of late, you can use all the good hands you can get, can't you?"

Dewey looks at the preacher, then back at Martin who is staring down at him, his eyes boring into Dewey, studying him close, like he were looking at something exotic and unexpected, an Australian bushman with a bone stuck through his nose or something.

There's definitely something weird about the man, Dewey thinks. If it weren't for the fact that Martin Fletcher is the preacher's boy, Dewey would swear that he had been dabbling in recreational pharmaceuticals.

Dewey looks back at Dr. Flatley. "We been busy lately, that's for sure."

"That's what I know. I also know you could do yourself a world of good with my congregation and their friends if you were to reinstate Clyde Thomas, let him work the Jefferson case full-time and, of course, continue to help you all try to find Martin's sister's killer as his availability allows." Dr. Flatley gives Martin a kind smile and a nod.

"Yes, sir."

"They'd be sure to remember your sound judgment come next spring, in the primary election."

"Yes, sir."

"Good, good," Dr. Flatley says, patting Dewey on the shoulder. "I'm glad we agree. Now you might want to go ask Lilly if she's got some club soda you can put on that gravy spot before it stains your suit. I fear that tie is probably beyond redemption."

"Yes, sir," Dewey says for a third time. He nods at Martin, then he fights his way through the crowd to the front door, out to the porch, where he can plainly see the empty spot in the church parking lot where Claudia's Oldsmobile had been parked.

Dewey starts walking toward home. He's thinking he's going to be so deep into Claudia's doghouse he's going to need a Rand McNally map to find his way out.

Martin Fletcher felt his pulse rate jack up and the room begin to lurch around while the sheriff was talking. He began to feel light-headed, like he might sick up.

He watches the fat sheriff waddle off, people maneuvering to stay out of the way of his suit front covered with cream gravy. Once Dewey disappears out the front door, Martin turns back, realizing Dr. Flatley has just said something to him, but he hasn't heard what it was.

"Beg your pardon?" Martin says.

"I was just saying, if we had to rely solely on the good sheriff there to keep the crime rate down in Washington County, I do believe all would be lost."

"How do you mean?"

The preacher gives a little shrug. "I just mean his crime-fighting skills are mighty lacking, mighty lacking indeed. It's a good thing he's got a man like Clyde Thomas to fall back on in these particular times. If anybody can bring some justice to the Jefferson family, it would be Clyde."

"You feel like he can get the job done then?"

"Yes indeed, sir, yes indeed. He's got the brains and the experience. And I'll tell you something else."

"What's that?"

"If that sheriff would get out of Clyde's way, he'd have your sister's murder solved too. I guarantee it."

"He's that good, is he?"

"Folks around here don't realize how smart he is. The way he expresses himself tends to obscure it. He sounds like a kid from the ghetto sometimes, which is what he is, but still, he's most capable."

"Is that a fact? Good to have a man like that around, I reckon. Well, thanks for comin', Dr. Flatley."

"Don't mention it, son. Say, you look a little pale. Are you okay?"

"I'm fine, sir. Just workin' me up a little headache is all."

"Okay. You take care now. And God bless you."

Martin moves off, looking for Dud, finally finding him in the kitchen chowing down on a plate of barbecued brisket, potato salad, pinto beans.

"Hey, Martin," Dud says. "What's wrong, partner? You ain't lookin' too good."

"Come here a second, would ya, Dud?" Martin takes him by the arm, guides him around the corner and into the pantry, pushes him back in there, closes the door behind him, gets up close to Dud's face.

"What's up, Martin?"

"You didn't by any chance leave that roll of duct tape in that liquor store the other night, did you?"

Dud puts his fork down in his plate, reaches up under his Stetson to scratch.

"Martin, the way I got it remembered you had the tape last. You was usin' it to tie up that kid while I went and moved the vehicles."

Now it's Martin's turn to reach up, scratch his beard, think back.

"Come to think of it, I believe you're right."

"How come you to ask?"

"I think we might have ourselves a problem."

"Like what?"

"Like I think the cops found that duct tape, done lifted some finger-prints off it."

"What are we gonna do now?"

"We gonna have to accelerate the plan. What are you up to this after-noon?"

"Not much of nothin' I reckon."

"Good. We need to make that feed store run. We got to kick this thing into high gear."

"Okay. I'll come by your place at two."

"See you then." Martin walks out of the pantry thinking, *Corpses like refuse in the streets.*

21

MERGING HIS PICKUP ONTO HIGHWAY 290 HEADED TOWARD HOUSTON, JERE-
miah Spur is thinking how good a cigarette would taste right about now. It's
been hours since he last had one, but how's he going to go about lighting
up when he's got this young, healthy lady lawyer over there on the passenger's side, her nose already turned up against the tobacco smell all around?

Jeremiah watches Sonya Nichols out of the corner of his eye, sees that
she is watching out the windshield as the countryside passes by. He tries to
make up his mind whether to ask permission to smoke a cigarette in his
own vehicle.

She says, "I suppose a good hard rain would come in handy at your ranch
right about now, wouldn't it?"

"I'd settle for a steady drizzle."

"I do not believe that I can recall ever before seeing the air this filthy."

Jeremiah had been just about to ask her would she object if he smoked.
He weighs how the question would sound, decides against it. "Beats all I
ever seen."

They drive on a ways in silence.

Then she says, "Captain Spur, I know that Elizabeth is terribly ill."

"Fact of the matter is, the cancer's gonna carry her off any day now."

"I know that. I don't want this to take any longer or be any harder on
her than absolutely necessary."

"I appreciate that. It ought not to be any other way, considerin'."

"Considering what?"

"Considerin' that I know for a fact you can eliminate her as a suspect."

"Nobody ever suggested she is a suspect."

"I reckon. Would it interest you to know why she ain't a suspect?"

"If you'd like to share it with me."

"In the first place she ain't the kind of person who would kill another.
But since I'm her father you'd expect me to say that."

"Well . . ."

"Of course, you would. But leaving that aside, the timeline don't work.
Lucy Brackett claims she seen Elizabeth with Sissy at a little past eleven
o'clock, in town. My wife is pretty sure Elizabeth got home before her

midnight curfew. That don't leave enough time for Elizabeth to have killed Sissy, buried the body, ditched the pickup, and got back home."

"Makes sense, I guess. Assuming, of course, your wife is right about when she got home. You know, assuming her memory hasn't failed her on that score."

Jeremiah thinks about how good Martha's memory might in fact be, since she had marinaded it in vodka every night for the last ten years. He starts to reach for his Camels, then stops himself. "Would it bother you if I smoked a cigarette?"

"I'd rather you didn't. Sorry."

After a while Jeremiah says, "Tell me about this case Clyde is workin'."

By the time Sonya has finished telling about it, they've reached the 610 Loop and are headed down the west side of town.

"So Clyde's gonna have the DPS check the prints from Uncle Freddie's against those in the Fletcher file?"

"Yes, sir. He ought to have the report tomorrow."

"Why's he got the print techs doin' it? Why don't he compare them hisself?"

"I don't know. Maybe he wanted to have an expert take a look."

"I could of done it if he wanted. Probably done that sort of thing a thousand times. What makes him think the two cases might be connected?"

"Nothing in particular. Just gut instinct, I guess."

"Well, it don't seem too likely to me."

They drive south on the West Loop in silence, a route Jeremiah has taken too many times, too many melancholy trips to the cancer ward. At least the other times he could have a smoke.

The traffic slows up south of the Highway 59 intersection, some kind of roadwork going on. Now they're creeping along bumper-to-bumper. Jeremiah's thinking maybe tomorrow he'll take 59 over to 288, spare himself all this tie-up.

He's wishing it were Martha with him today, instead of this young lawyer. God bless Jim Fletcher for opening his office up to them, opening Martha's heart up to the need for some kind of reconciliation with Elizabeth. Jeremiah hadn't known how it was going to turn out when they took their seats on that couch in Dr. Fletcher's . . .

Jeremiah is struck by a thought. "Sonya?"

"Yes, sir?"

"Do me a favor, would you? Go into that case file, fetch out the picture of that button what was found with the body."

"Okay." She rummages some, then says, "Got it."

"Have you studied that?"

"Not really."

"Take a good look at it. Tell me what you think it could have come off of."

They pull even with the construction, two lanes blocked off, guys operating heavy equipment, pushing hot asphalt around. Lots of black guys on this crew. Jeremiah checks his rearview mirror, sees Duke up, growling, being his usual intolerant self.

Jeremiah is thinking if Duke was a cop, he'd be in sensitivity training full-time.

By the time Sonya speaks again they've cleared the construction, Jeremiah's pickup taking the curve around to the South Loop at the speed limit, carrying him closer to the parking garage where he aims to light up a cigarette even if it harelips everybody in Harris County, including this health-nut lawyer.

"Well, this button, it's big and blue. It didn't come off any of the victim's clothes. It's not off a dress shirt. Could it be off a suit, or an overcoat of some kind maybe? I'm just kind of guessing here."

"What kind of overcoat?"

"You know, a big heavy wool one."

"Do you think it could of come off one of them trench coat–type deals?"

"Could be, I suppose. Most of them are more light-colored though. They tend to be olive, beige, you know."

"So you'd lean more toward a wool overcoat, like somebody would wear over a suit or a dress in real cold weather?"

"Yes, sir, I'd say, based on the size and color of it, that'd be a good guess. It would probably be impossible to trace to a particular garment."

"I ain't so sure about that. Brenham ain't much of a business-suit town, and given the climate it ain't an overcoat town at all. In fact, I do believe I've only seen one blue wool overcoat in Brenham in the last ten years. And I saw it yesterday morning."

"Where?"

"In Jim Fletcher's office. In a pile of stuff he was givin' away to charity."

"Now that's damned interesting. Maybe it's just a coincidence."

"I don't believe in coincidences."

"But still . . . He's pretty well alibi'd."

"By his own son."

"Yeah, but, look, if he were somehow connected with Sissy's death, he wouldn't have left something like that, something that might tie him to the case, out in plain view."

"He might of since he didn't know I was gonna get involved. He thought I had retired, didn't know I was gonna have anything to do with this investigation until I told him the sheriff asked me to pitch in."

"How'd he react?"

"He counseled me against it."

They are silent until Jeremiah parks the truck in the hospital garage, kills the engine. He turns to Sonya and says, "Tomorrow I think I need to go by and see Jim about the night of the dance, get his statement direct from him."

"But it's Sunday."

"I'll catch him after church. And I'm going to need to track that coat down."

He has a cigarette between his lips and lit before he closes the door to the pickup.

They make their way past the nurses' station, Jeremiah nodding to the ladies there. Directly they're among the patients' rooms, an area impoverished of color and laughter and pretty much everything else that makes life worth living, a place where souls slip away into the night, souls that go riding on the midnight express to the big Adios.

When they get to the door to Elizabeth's room, Jeremiah turns to Sonya and says, "Why don't you wait here a minute, give me a chance to see if she's awake and whatnot. Tell her about you and why you're here."

Jeremiah can see the lawyer hesitate, knows she'd a lot rather do the interview cold. That way she could spring her questions on the witness, not let her have even five seconds to get her story straight in her head.

But this is different, Jeremiah giving her a look back that he knows will remind her how different it is.

She says, "Okay."

He pushes through the door.

Elizabeth's awake, talking to Amanda and a third woman sitting between them across the room. They look up when he comes in.

"Hi, Papa," Elizabeth says. She makes it sound like she's glad to see him, but her voice is weak, her skin is gray, her eyes sunk back inside her head, the flesh hanging off her bones. Jeremiah thinks she's just about wasted away.

He crosses the room, gives her a peck on the forehead, moves around behind the bed, hugs Amanda, extends a hand to the third woman. "I'm Jeremiah Spur."

"Alice Redden," she says, taking his hand. "I'm a volunteer from the Houston Hospice Society."

Elizabeth says, "Alice helps people through the final stages of life, Papa. You know, gives them a hand, provides compassion to the loved ones."

Jeremiah looks around for a place to set his Stetson, finally parks it on top of a chest of drawers. "Is that a fact?"

"Yes, sir," says Alice. "Our group specializes in cancer victims, with emphasis on pain management. Once someone's had cancer, we are available to that person and her family, even if she's sick with something else. We were just finishing up for the day, but I'd be glad to stay a little longer if you'd like. If you think it would be helpful."

"What would be more helpful," says Jeremiah, "is if you was to come back tomorrow, say 'bout three o'clock, when Elizabeth's mother and I both will be here."

Jeremiah looks at Elizabeth, sees her smile, her eyes widen. "Papa," she whispers.

"That would be just fine," says the hospice lady. "We'll see you then."

She leans down, pats Elizabeth on the arm, turns to Amanda. "If you need me before then, just call. You have my numbers." Then she heads on out.

Jeremiah grabs a chair, pulls it up close to the bed. "How you doin', sweetheart?"

" 'Bout the same. They gave me a shot of morphine an hour or so ago, so I feel okay for now. Papa?"

"What is it, honey?"

"Is Mama really coming to see me?"

"She sure 'nough is. She wanted to come today."

"Why didn't she?"

"Well, now, that's where it gets a little complicated." He pauses, looks back at Amanda.

"I'm listening," Elizabeth says.

"You remember me tellin' you the sheriff's boys had dug up Sissy Fletcher's body out near Gay Hill?"

"Yes, sir. Papa, have you gone and gotten yourself involved in that?"

"Not on purpose."

"What are you saying, it was an accident? Papa, come on. I seem to remember that we talked about how you already had more than enough to say grace over, that you ought not to have anything to do with it."

"Which is exactly right. The only thing is . . . the sheriff told me yesterday they got an eyewitness says she seen you ridin' around with Sissy the night she disappeared."

Elizabeth closes her eyes, lets her head sink back into her pillow. After a spell she says, "So what if I was with her?"

"They want to take your statement, hon. They need all the help they can get on account of it's a ten-year-old case and they ain't got that much to go on concerning Sissy's KAs and so forth."

Elizabeth's eyes open. "KAs?"

"Known associates."

"I was seen with her, so I'm a 'known associate.'"

"Somethin' like that."

"So now I have to talk about this. About her. About that night."

Jeremiah shrugs, says, "Well, no, you don't really have to, not if you don't want to. You could refuse to cooperate, retain counsel, plead the Fifth Amendment if you want, I mean if you need to, force 'em to get a court order. It's up to you."

"Who's supposed to interview me? Is it you, Papa?"

"No, hon. It's an assistant DA, name of Sonya Nichols. She's just outside the door right now, waitin' to come in."

Elizabeth looks at Jeremiah, then over his shoulder at Amanda. "Amanda, honey. You know the story. What do *you* think I should do?"

Amanda hesitates, then leans in, one hand on Jeremiah's shoulder, the other taking Elizabeth's hand from the bedsheet. She says, "I think you ought to talk to her. Think of it this way. Alice says one way to take charge of your transition is to do all you can to minimize the number of loose ends you leave behind for others to deal with. That way you give yourself, and them, some peace. What harm can it do you now?"

Elizabeth is silent for a few moments.

Then she nods her head, looks at Jeremiah, says, "Okay, I guess. You can bring her in."

22

THERE IS NO GOD BUT THE LORD GOD JEHOVAH, AND MARTIN IS HIS MESSENGER.
Every morning that thought wakes him up, gets him out of bed, has his
heart started better than a pot of black coffee could.

It had him up before dawn on the morning of his sister's memorial service. It had banged around inside his head like the refrain to some song you
can't stop singing to yourself, except this was a song with only a refrain and
no other verses, nor music.

Martin is His Messenger. *I am His Messenger.*

Martin feels those words *ought* to be set to music, like the Hallelujah
Chorus from "The Messiah," which the choir performs at Christmas and
Easter in his daddy's church, music where they repeat the same phrase
again and again, like the point is to emphasize its meaning. Some com-
poser should set those words to grand, soaring music to be played on a big
organ somewhere, maybe in a Gothic cathedral in Europe, someplace like
that.

The Martin Chorus.

The Martin Chorus drummed away in his brain while he went out to
the garage, got his .357 Magnum out of the gun safe, sat there in the
dawn's early light and cleaned it of the cordite and residue left from the
other night. He shook the shells out, took the drum off, wiped it spotless,
dripped gun oil down the barrel, ran the brush after it, then the rag,
wiped down the outside until it gleamed in the light from the bare bulb
overhead.

Such that it was like new.

Such that it shone like the day he bought it out of the case at the gun
shop, a thing he had always wanted to own.

I am His Messenger.

King of Kings. Lord of Lords. And He shall reign forever and ever.

He took the empties and pocketed them, then reloaded and sat and
held the gun in his hand and admired it for a while, the weight and shine
of it, this little metallic deliverer, this punctuation sign for somebody's
entire life.

Directly Martin locked the gun back up in the safe, got in his pickup, drove around to the back tank, the one on his property that's farthest from the house. Parked the truck, got out, chucked the brass as far as he could into the water. Watched the ripples they made on the tank's surface, the water level so low now on account of the drought. The concentric rings of water were like the concentric rings of one of the targets over at the Gun Club shooting range, a target that with his mind's eye he could see stretching and growing until it was as big as a building, then lifting up, up in the air, and flying like a magic carpet across the county and dropping down on the courthouse.

When all the ripples were gone, he went back in his truck and drove to the house to get ready to go to church.

Later that morning Martin carried Linda and the kids down to the service, sat in the front row only half-listening, knowing where his daddy was going with it when he looked at the bulletin, saw that the Scripture reading was Matthew 7:1. He didn't want to sit there for an entire hour and be forced to think about his sister.

A week ago he wouldn't have thought of her for a hundred dollars. Now here she pops up after all these years, an integral part of a plan known in its entirety only to God, a plan that must have been set in motion somehow over ten years ago.

Martin sat there in that front pew wishing God could have come up with some other way to get His point across, even though he knew it was an impertinent thought.

He watched the tears roll down his daddy's cheeks, his daddy looking over his head, not down at him, looking out across the sanctuary at the congregation.

He thought to himself, *I am His Messenger.*

After the service was over they went to the parsonage, to the house that Martin had grown up in, a place that now felt strange to him, like the house of some other Martin unknown to him. He watched all those people trooping around, eating food the neighbors and folks from church had brought, and he did not think about what it had been like to grow up in that house because it was like the house of some other person.

Then he had that visit with the sheriff and Dr. Flatley, talked to Dud, made his decision inspired by God to change gears on his plans.

Any fingerprints on that duct tape could be traced back to him on account of it had come off his workbench. Before long the cops would be out here asking questions.

He left the parsonage as soon as it seemed proper, swearing to God Almighty he wasn't going to waste any more time. The Lord's Messenger would move with dispatch.

He got the family back home, helped them organize and pack, saw them off to spend a week at Linda's folks' over in Giddings, like they did every year when school let out. Martin never went. He and his father-in-law don't get along, what with Linda's old man being a drinker and prone to swear over much.

Martin didn't let on to his wife what he was up to since he felt like the Almighty would want all this to be on a "need-to-know" basis, and besides he wasn't entirely sure he could trust her with the knowledge. Linda had let the modern world get to her some, had become enamored of it, had become in recent years a wearer of makeup, a person who polished her nails.

He once came home, found her watching Oprah Winfrey on the sly.

It was a cause for concern.

So Martin is busy packing a bag of his own, throwing in camouflage and whatnot, a few boxes of shells for his wheel gun, his thirty-aught-six rifle, when Dud walks through the front door, hollering, "Anybody home? Hey, Martin. Where you at?"

"Upstairs," Martin hollers back.

Dud appears at the bedroom door, wearing jeans and boots, a T-shirt and a John Deere baseball cap, chewing a wad of gum. He leans against the doorjamb. "Where did Linda and the kids go?"

"They went to her daddy's for a week."

"What you doin' with them bags? You goin' someplace too?"

"Yep. So are you. The Republic of Texas. You ever been to Alpine, Dud?"

"Naw. I ain't been west of Austin."

"You're gonna love it. Lots of open country for a man to roam in, get lost in, good huntin', clean air. None of this filth and humidity in the air like we got around here. No cable TV to sit in front of, rot your mind."

"I got cable. I watch the WWF ever chance I get."

"That's what I'm sayin'."

"When you figger us to leave?"

"Monday."

"That quick?"

"Yep. I want to blow the courthouse Monday evenin', then get a good head start Monday night, before folks can figger out what hit 'em."

Corpses like refuse in the streets.

"Reckon I better pack my own self then," says Dud. "What do you suppose I ought to tell my mama if she was to ask?"

"Tell her you're leavin' town for a while with me."

"What about the cops? Ain't they gonna check up on her, see if I make contact?"

Martin closes the bag, chucks it on the floor, turns around, looks at Dud. "Partner, you and me are fixin' to light a fuse that is gonna set this entire country ablaze. Inside of a month, the cops, even the army, they'll have their hands so full fryin' such bigger fish, they will have all but forgot about the likes of us."

Martin and Dud walk into Wilson Feed and Supply an hour or so before closing time. The place is empty except for one old rancher in the back looking at some fencing.

Bobby Crowner is behind the counter wearing his official blue and yellow Wilson Feed and Supply apron, got a pencil stuck behind his ear.

"Howdy, fellers," he says. "What can I do you for?"

Dud steps up. "Hey there, Bobby. I'm lookin' to buy me about forty bags of ammonium nitrate. Y'all got that much in stock?"

Just like they'd rehearsed it.

"Let's just have us a look-see." Bobby punches some computer keys, peers at the screen. He looks up for a second. "Oh, by the way, Martin, I'm sorry about your sister."

"Thanks."

"Here we go. Yep. I can take care of you, Dud. We got that and a bit more in the back. You want us to deliver it?"

"No, thanks. I got my pickup here. Me and Martin, we'll carry it out. What do I owe you?"

Bobby totes up the bill, hands it over to Dud for inspection. Dud glances at it, reaches in his pocket, comes up with $650 cash money.

Bobby takes the money, starts counting it. Martin's thinking two days ago those bills lay in the cash drawer at Uncle Freddie's. Now a deputy sheriff is holding them, payment for bomb parts.

Bobby says, "Can't imagine what you need all this fertilizer for, what with the drought."

"Ain't you heard, Bobby?" Martin says.

"Heard what?"

"Weatherman's callin' for rain before next week's out."

"I sure hope you're right. This drought has durn near been the ruination of the feed and supply business. Mr. Wilson is sure gettin' tired of carryin' all this inventory, not to mention how his bankers feel about it. They'll be tickled pink for you to own all this AN come what may, but particularly if the weatherman is wrong as per usual."

Bobby rings up the purchase, closes the cash drawer. "Anything else I can do for you fellers? How 'bout you, Martin? You need anything today?"

"Nope. Just here to give Dud a hand."

"Okay then, we all set. Pull around back and we'll get them bags loaded for you."

An hour later they've unloaded the fertilizer into Martin's pole barn, breathing hard from the effort, dripping sweat in the hundred-degree heat. They walk back to Martin's house, help themselves to some iced tea from the refrigerator, try to cool down by sitting at the kitchen table directly in the path of the cold air blowing out of the window unit.

"You think a ton'll do it?" says Dud.

"It oughta. McVeigh used three and a half tons on the Murrah building but it was like twelve stories or something. The one in town only has two floors."

"Where we gonna get the diesel?"

"I got enough in my tanks to take care of it."

"What next then?"

Martin scratches at his beard. "We need a detonator."

"A what?"

"You know, somethin' to set it off with. A stick of dynamite or somethin'. You got anything like that?"

"Heck no, Martin, I ain't never had no need to blow nothin' up before. Where you reckon we could find such a thing?"

"I ain't exactly sure. I heard tell they use explosives for roadwork and such. If we could find a construction site we might be able to boost some kind of explosive."

"What about that overpass they're buildin' on 290, down near Hempstead?"

"It's worth a look, I reckon."

"Let's go then."

As they head south toward Hempstead, Martin says, "You know that nigger what works for the sheriff? Guy's name is Clyde Thomas or somethin' like that."

"Weren't he that big buck that walked out of Uncle Freddie's when we was over there casin' the place?"

"That'd be the one."

"I can't say I really know him, we ain't howdied or nothin' like that."

"You know anything about him?"

"Only what I heard 'bout him shackin' up with that young assistant district attorney, what's her name?"

"I don't know who you're talkin' about."

"I bet you seen her around. Tall, good-lookin' woman. Dark hair she wears long. It's a crime she would let that nigger so much as touch her."

"Wait a minute. You sayin' she ain't colored?"

"Nuh-uh. She's as white as you or me."

"Is that a fact? I think we ought to pop that spade."

"For livin' with a white woman?"

"Well, that would be one reason, I reckon. But the main reason would be I hear tell he's a pretty good cop, maybe the best they got down yonder. That's what Dr. Flatley done said to me at the reception. And the sheriff said he's the one workin' the Uncle Freddie's case. Plus they give him stuff to do on my sister's case when he's got the time. Dr. Flatley says he's got the brains to solve the both of 'em if he gets a chance. Hard for me to imagine, but that's what he says."

"Dr. Flatley's just partial to him on account of he's a blue gum."

"Yeah, I'll grant you that. But Dr. Flatley's a smart man. He ain't ignorant like the most of 'em."

"So you're thinkin' that if we can knock him off . . ."

"We can slow down the cops. Give us more breathin' room. Plus I don't want that shine diggin' around in my sister's past. I'd rest better if he was out of the picture."

"You know what? It might be kind of fun at that. How would we go about it?"

"I don't know. I ain't got it figgered out yet."

"Well, if we gonna blow the courthouse on Monday we ain't got a lot of time for much of anything else. When you thinkin' about tryin' to pull this off?"

"I don't know. The idea just come to me. Maybe tomorrow. We need to go down to Houston in the mornin', rent a panel truck, and pick up some fifty-five-gallon drums. Maybe we could try to pull somethin' together for tomorrow afternoon."

They are approaching the roadwork at Hempstead.

"Look," Dud says. "There's a trailer over yonder inside a chain-link fence."

"I bet that's where they work the construction from. Let's cruise by it real slow."

They pass it once, then turn around and drive by again.

"There's a padlock on the gate," Dud says. "But I don't see nothin' else to stop us. I don't see no dogs or security guards or nothin'."

"Tell you what," Martin says. "Let's go into Hempstead and get us a hamburger. Then we can come back out here after dark, see if we can bust into the place."

"You the boss."

Dud hits the accelerator and they head for the first Dairy Queen they can find.

23

JEREMIAH WALKS TO THE DOOR, LETS SONYA IN, TAKES HER OVER TO AMANDA who's standing by the bedside, watching the lawyer, the dread of the upcoming conversation about Elizabeth's past on her face even though she had counseled in favor of it. Seeing her like that, Jeremiah senses for the first time that her pain at the thought of losing Elizabeth might be in the same league with his.

"Sonya Nichols, this is Amanda Porter, Elizabeth's friend."

"How are you?" Sonya says.

"Fine, thanks."

"And this here," Jeremiah says as he steers Sonya to the side of the bed, "is my daughter, Elizabeth."

Sonya leans down, smiles. "Hey, Elizabeth. Nice to meet you."

Elizabeth's return smile comes across as nervous. "Visitors are always welcome in Room 1208B. Although I hear maybe you have more on your mind than just a mercy visit to a dying woman."

"I just need to talk to you a few minutes about . . ." Sonya glances at Jeremiah. "I guess you know what about."

"Yes. Your partner over there told me."

Elizabeth's trying to make a little joke here, Jeremiah is thinking. That's good.

Elizabeth says, "Why don't you have a seat?"

"I'll make this as quick as I can, so you can get back to resting up."

Jeremiah brings a chair over so Sonya can set up shop right next to the bed. She nods her thanks, takes her seat, sets down her briefcase. Pulls out the case file, a yellow legal pad, a miniature cassette recorder, holding it up where Elizabeth can see it.

"Do you mind?" she says.

"No. That's alright."

Sonya clicks a button on the recorder, sets it on the bedside table.

Amanda pulls a chair up to the other side of the bed. Jeremiah hooks his thumbs over his belt, leans against the wall near the foot of the bed so he can see the whole room, watch everybody's body language, facial expressions.

He can't help but notice the contrast of these two women of just about the same age. This lady lawyer who looks like she hasn't been sick a day in her life, probably works out at the gym all the time doing those dancing exercises women like, next to his daughter, her life vanishing while they watch, like the dawn mist that rises from Jeremiah's tanks during winter, spreading itself across the water for a little while and then burning off when the sun hits it square.

Sonya says, "Let me just get a few facts out of the way, for the record."

"Okay."

"What's your full name?"

"Elizabeth Barrett Spur."

"Date of birth?"

"October 10, 1970."

"Sonya?" Jeremiah says.

"Yes?"

"I can give you them kinds of facts, and I know from experience, Elizabeth ain't gonna have much stamina. So if you want to get this done, you best get to the point."

"Okay. Elizabeth, how well did you know Alicia Fletcher?"

Elizabeth's eyes move away from Sonya's face, focus on something in the middle distance, like folks do when they're working up a recollection.

"We knew each other but we were not what you would call close. I mean, she was, what, six, seven years older than me? I saw her around church growing up, then lost track of her for a while. She moved away, went off to college for a couple years. She came back to town just before I started high school and I would see her around now and then, at a high school football game or a rodeo. I wanted to get to know her some, but . . ."

"But what?"

Elizabeth looks over at Sonya. "But Mama . . . Mama discouraged it."

"Why?"

"She said Sissy was . . . I forget exactly how she put it. Not a high-quality person. Bad company. Something like that."

"Why did you want to get to know her better?"

"Well, she was different than most Brenham people."

"How so?"

"Do you live in Brenham, Sonya?"

"Yes."

"Then you know it's a country town, with country people living there. They live by a set of rules that they pretty much stick to, at least in public, a reality I appreciate more now that I've lived away, in a big city, for the last ten years. Country people are . . . How should I say it? Careful about how much of their real selves they let you see. That wasn't Sissy's way, though. She was an open book on every topic, how she felt, what she thought. At least she was once she came back from college. And a lot of the time she seemed to go out of her way not to abide by the rules."

"There's long been a 'preacher's daughter' stereotype. Was that it?"

"Maybe. But she was also real, real smart, not just looking to have a good time, and not afraid to show how smart she was, even around the gentlemen, if I can use that word, of Brenham, Texas. That made her unusual in a town where the men ran the show. They weren't used to a female making trouble for the social structure, such as it was. All of that made her more . . . interesting. It was that, that and the fact that, well . . . ."

"Go on."

"Do you have a picture of her? In your file there?"

Sonya opens the case file, flips back to a photograph, holds it up for Elizabeth.

"No, that's okay, you can put it away. That really doesn't do her justice. Because she was gorgeous. In the girl-next-door, Playmate-of-the-month sense. She had beautiful blond hair that she wore back in a ponytail most of the time, and blue, blue eyes. She had a great body too, athletic-looking legs. I don't know what she did to stay in shape, but wow. I used to see her driving around town in her pickup, blond hair pulled back, baseball cap, sunglasses on, and think what it would be like . . . I guess I had a crush on her would be one way to put it."

"Did you ever . . . Did anything ever happen between you?"

"Not before that night."

"Which night?"

"The night she disappeared."

"Why don't you tell me about that night then."

"What do you want to know?"

"Anything you can remember. Start anywhere. Start with the weather."

"Okay." Elizabeth shifts her gaze. "Amanda, honey?"

"Yes?"

"Would you get me some ice chips, please? All this talk is making me thirsty."

"Sure."

While Amanda fetches the ice, Elizabeth lies back, closes her eyes, rests. Directly Amanda returns with a paper cup and a spoon. "You want to sit up a little, let me give you some?"

Elizabeth's eyes open. "Great. Thanks."

She takes some ice chips, settles back down, swallows, does it a couple more times, then shakes her head no when Amanda offers more.

Jeremiah is surprised Elizabeth has gone on even this long. Talking about this seems to be tapping some source of strength in her somewhere, almost like it was putting her in touch with her past self, back when she had her health.

"'Start with the weather,'" she says. "Okay. I remember it was pretty darn cold. Cold enough for a hard freeze that night. Seems like we'd had a norther blow through a day or so before with a lot of wind and rain. Could use a blue norther right about now, couldn't you, Papa, and the rain it would bring?"

Jeremiah starts to say they're going have to wait 'til October for one of them, but catches himself in time. Instead he says, "I got a feeling it's gonna rain next week."

"Listen to that, Amanda," says Elizabeth. "Papa's turning into an optimist. Anyway, the front had cleared out by Saturday night and the wind was out of the north and it felt really good. Guess I'll never know that feeling again."

Amanda reaches out, pats her hand. Sonya stops taking notes for a moment, rests her pen on the legal pad in her lap.

"Anyway," Elizabeth says, "I went to the dance that night with a group of friends from school. Tommy Bledsoe picked me up at the house. Do you remember him, Papa?"

Jeremiah says, "Wasn't he one of them Bledsoes, worked land up near Burton?"

"Yes, sir. He was."

Sonya says, "Were you and he dating?"

Elizabeth smiles, reaches out, takes Amanda's hand. "Sonya, I'm gay."

"I guess I had sort of surmised that. But you knew, even back then . . ."

"Let's just say I wasn't attracted to any boys, including Tommy Bledsoe, who was sweet enough but dumb as a bucket of rocks and ugly as homemade sin. He and I were friends from school and from FFA . . ."

"FFA?"

"Future Farmers of America. We raised heifers together, to take down to Houston, to the fat stock show. It's funny, I guess. It turns out I wasn't one."

"Wasn't one what?"

"A future farmer."

Sonya smiles. "So you went to the dance with Tommy Bledsoe."

"And some other kids from school. We had agreed to meet, sit at a table together. Somebody was going to smuggle in some booze, vodka or rum or something. The plan was to do some underage drinking and dancing. Typical country Saturday night stuff. Except I didn't drink and nobody really wanted to dance with me."

"You mean Tommy and the other boys . . ."

"They had a pretty good idea about me. About what I was."

"So what happened at the dance?"

"Not much for a while. The band, I think it was Sandy and the Six-Pack, got started about seven-thirty. The lights went down, music started, people started dancing, people in my group danced and drank. You've been to one of those things, haven't you?"

"A time or two."

"Then you know what they're like. And they're all alike."

"I guess so. Even the same band was playing when I went."

"Well, there you go. See? I sat in a dark corner in the back drinking a Dr Pepper and feeling about as alone as a person can feel, wondering why I had bothered to come in the first place."

"Was Sissy there?"

"Yes."

"Was she there with someone?"

"I don't think so. I didn't see her come in so I didn't see if she came with anybody. If she did, she didn't leave with them."

"How do you know?"

Elizabeth takes some more ice, chews it, swallows. "Because she left with me."

"How did you all connect up?"

"I was sitting in my dark little corner and she came over and asked me to dance."

"Did you?"

"Of course. I was thrilled. I remember they were playing that old Judy Collins song, 'Someday Soon,' something like that, I forget its exact name. I loved that song."

"So you and she, you went out on the dance floor together?"

"Yes. That's where you dance at the American Legion Hall. On the dance floor."

Sonya grins, says, "I'll make a note of that. Did that attract any, uh, attention? I mean, two women dancing together would seem a little . . ."

"Yeah, out of place for Brenham. You bet it did. I felt like every eye in the place was on us. We did the two-step. She let me lead."

"Did you and Sissy dance a lot?"

"Just the one dance."

"Then what happened?"

"She said she needed some fresh air, wanted to get out of the cigarette smoke. She asked me if I wanted to go for a ride."

"So you left together."

"Uh-huh." More ice chips. "We got in her pickup and headed into town."

"Did you talk much?"

"She was in a mood to talk. She said she knew my mama didn't approve of her, hated her in fact. Said they'd had a run-in or two along the way, and Mama had turned against her, which was too bad, because she would have liked to have gotten to know me better, but now there wasn't going to be a chance for that."

"Did she say why?"

"She said she was planning to leave town soon. She told me I ought to, too. She said I was as much a misfit there in Brenham as she was and the best thing for me to do was to get out of there, go find people of my own kind. Go to San Francisco, she said."

"What did you say?"

Elizabeth glances at Jeremiah, then focuses back on Sonya. "I told her I hoped she might be a person of my own kind. I told her . . ." She pauses, takes some more ice chips, and then takes Amanda's hand in hers. "I asked her if she had any interest in . . . Basically, I made a sexual advance." She glances again at Jeremiah.

"How did she respond?"

"Laughter."

"That must have been pretty hard on you."

"It was very hurtful, although I don't think she meant it to be. I started to cry. I just felt so . . . I don't know. Alone. Rejected. Unloved. Right away she apologized, said she was sorry she hadn't been more sensitive."

"So she said she was leaving town because she didn't belong in Brenham."

"Yes. Plus she had some issues with her father, would be the way to put it, I guess."

"Did she say where she was going?"

"Some big city. She said she hadn't made her mind up yet."

"Someplace like Houston? Dallas?"

"Oh, no. Those places were 'too Texas,' she said. It was either going to be New York or L.A. She said it would be expensive, but she just about had that taken care of."

"How's that?"

"She said she and a partner had been working a business, been making good money, just about had enough stashed away to make a run for it."

"Did she say what kind of business?"

"Not in so many words. She called it 'Room Fifteen Enterprises' or something like that, then laughed about it, like it was some kind of joke. She mentioned something about somebody in town being a 'loss leader' or something."

"Do you remember if she said who her partner was?"

The strain of this much effort is beginning to show now in the lines in

Elizabeth's face, a face gone much older than her twenty-eight years. She pauses a long time, then she says, "It was a man, and she said his name. But no, I don't remember it."

"Anything more specific than that?"

"No. Not that I recall."

"Did she say when she was planning to leave town?"

"Not specifically. Just 'soon.' "

"This conversation you and she had. Where were you?"

"Just cruising around town. In her pickup."

"Did you go back to the dance together?"

"No. It was nearly midnight and I had a curfew, so I asked her to take me home."

"Did she say where she was going after she dropped you off?"

"No. She said she had a few loose ends to tie up before she left town, and she might try to see to some of them that night."

"Is there anything else you can remember from your conversation with her?"

"No. That's about the size of it."

Sonya checks her notes. "You said she had some kind of issues with her father. Can you be more specific?"

"My impression was that she hated him."

"Any idea why?"

"Not specifically. She just seemed not to care for the kind of person he was."

"What kind of person was he? Or maybe the better question is, what kind of person did she say he was?"

Elizabeth is fading pretty fast now. She sinks back into her pillow, eyes closed. She breathes awhile, almost appears to be asleep. Then her eyes open partially, and she speaks, but the energy is gone from her voice. "I'm sorry. This is beginning to wear me out."

Sonya says, "We should leave and let you rest."

"First, let me ask you a question."

"Okay."

"How well do you know my papa?"

"Excuse me?"

Elizabeth's eyes flick to Jeremiah, leaning against the wall behind Sonya. "How well do you know him? My papa?"

"Mostly by reputation. He's a legend in law enforcement. You probably knew that though. We only just met properly this morning."

"Well, let me tell you about my papa, so you'll know something about the man you've partnered up with here. He is a man of principle. He is completely devoted to doing what he sees as his duty. He is the most unselfish, least self-absorbed person I have ever known in my life. He is strong and brave and if he'd only quit smoking he would have no vices whatsoever. And, Sonya?"

"Yes?"

"Jim Fletcher may be a great preacher. But Sissy Fletcher would not have said any of those things about her daddy."

Elizabeth lies back, closes her eyes, and is asleep almost instantly.

Sonya fetches her tape recorder off the bedside table, places it and her legal pad back in her briefcase, rises from her chair, reaches across the bed to shake Amanda's hand, whispers, "Tell her when she wakes back up I said thanks. We'll try not to bother her anymore, but if she remembers anything else that might be helpful I would be grateful if you would give me a call."

"Okay."

Then Sonya walks out of the room.

Jeremiah Spur straightens himself up off the wall.

He walks across the room, stands by the bed, looking down at the sleeping figure of the only daughter, the only child, he's ever going to have. He bends down, kisses her forehead. Straightens up, looks at her for a moment longer. Then he walks around the bed to give Amanda a hug good-bye.

"We'll see you tomorrow," he whispers to her, then leaves the room.

Sonya is waiting for him in the hall. They walk toward the elevators together.

Sonya says, "She's a remarkable young woman."

Jeremiah makes no reply. He gets to the elevator, punches the button, looks up at the numerical display that tells him the elevator is on five, on its way up to fetch them. Once it arrives they get on, head down. It stops at near about every floor, Saturday afternoon visitors getting on to leave the hospital, go out into the heat and smoke.

When they reach the ground floor, Jeremiah says, "I have a hunch."

"What about?"

"About who the man is."

"Sissy's partner?"

"No. The other one. The one that Elizabeth said Sissy called a 'loss leader.'"

"Who do you think it is?"

"My wife said something about Joe Bob Cole, about how he knew a thing or two about Sissy and what Martha referred to as her dislike of men."

"Joe Bob Cole?"

"You know him?"

"Sure. Wasn't he the investigating officer when she disappeared?"

"I do believe he was. I think we ought to pay a call on him. Where do you reckon we could find him, of a Saturday afternoon?"

"Where you find all the middle-aged rednecks on Saturday afternoon. At the Brenham Country Club."

"Let's git on out there then."

24

CROSSING BACK OVER INTO WASHINGTON COUNTY NOW AT THE WHEEL OF HIS pickup, Jeremiah is thinking even with just the little bit they've been able to piece together so far this case is beginning to pick up some momentum.

Suddenly he's feeling half-glad he'd had to step into it after all, feeling right at home, doing what he does as well as anybody in the world, rooting out the bad guys.

"So what do we know about Joe Bob Cole?" he asks Sonya.

"Well, there's nothing in the case file, of course."

"Of course. He was the investigating officer. And he did a sorry job of it to my way of thinkin'."

"So what we know, or at least what I know, is generalized knowledge from around town. He was a sheriff's deputy from some time in the mid-1980s until Pat Patterson resigned under pressure, which would have been about 1994."

"When that prisoner died in custody."

"Right. The poor guy had been beaten to an absolute pulp. Joe Bob was implicated in it so they ran both him and the sheriff off. Joe Bob would have landed in Huntsville, too, if the other boys in the department could have been persuaded to testify. But they dummied up."

"What's he doin' nowadays?"

"He works at the Bluebonnet Ice Cream Company. Word around town is that he's gearing up for a run at the sheriff's job next year. And he seems to have attracted a meaningful amount of backing, mostly because of the widely held view that Dewey Sharpe is so ridiculous."

"I'm not sure I ever met this Cole feller, or if I did, I forgot what he looks like."

"He's a big guy, has to be at least six-five. Must weigh three hundred pounds."

"So he's a big ol' boy then. Big enough and strong enough, say, to cave somebody's skull in."

"Oh, yes. Absolutely."

Force equals mass times acceleration.

Sonya continues. "As for the rest of his appearance, he wears his hair long, got longish sideburns. Got kind of a late Elvis thing going. He's also spectacularly ugly."

They're closing in on the country club now, driving down a back road that runs alongside the golf course where they can see people out there, whacking golf balls, cluttering up the landscape in their peculiar golf duds. The road goes around a curve and Jeremiah sees the entrance. He pulls into the parking lot, slides into a space.

A few guys are loading golf bags off little carts into their vehicles, another day of golfing under their belts, another Saturday sacrificed on the altar of this curious god.

As they walk toward the clubhouse, Sonya says, "Are you a golfer?"

Jeremiah pauses to light a cigarette, take a draw. "I tried it a time or two when I was younger, then I give up on it."

"How come?"

He shrugs. "A thing can only be what it is. I couldn't see the point of spending five hours in the pursuit of something that made me look and feel stupid."

"It seems to be a popular game for retirees."

Jeremiah eyes Sonya, but decides she's just making small talk, not trying to get his goat.

Inside the pro shop, Jeremiah looks around at the stuff for sale, bags, clubs, what have you. Not to mention the clothes. Jeremiah is at a loss to explain your basic golfer's attire, which furnishes him yet another reason not to have his life beset with the affliction of this game. He can't imagine these getups appealing to anybody who has more clothes sense than a color-blind African pygmy.

There's one guy in the shop here, standing behind a waist-high glass counter, inside of which rows and rows of golf balls and other accessories are on display.

Jeremiah approaches him. "Excuse me. You the proprietor?"

The guy looks at Jeremiah over a large nose that has the look and coloration of a bunch of grapes that had been inverted. Jeremiah can smell the alcohol on his breath. "I'm the pro here." He jerks a thumb over his shoulder at a sign on the wall that says, "Brenham Country Club, Glenn Campbell, Golf Professional."

"You a singer too?"

"Very funny," says the Golf Professional. "It may come as a surprise to you, but you ain't the first person to say that to me. Now if you two is lookin' for a round of golf, I can't help you there. This here's a private club."

"Is that a fact?" says Jeremiah.

"Yep. There's a muni up in Bryan if you want to try up yonder."

"Well, as you can see, we're dressed like civilians, so we ain't lookin' to golf," says Jeremiah. "We're here to speak to a man. Name of Joe Bob Cole. He around?"

"You'll find him back yonder, in the locker room," says Glenn Campbell, Golf Professional, nodding in the direction of a brown door.

"Much obliged," says Jeremiah. He says to Sonya, "Let's go."

As they turn to go, the Golf Professional says, "Excuse me, ma'am, but you can't go in there."

"Why can't she?" says Jeremiah.

"Because it's a locker room. Guys walkin' around in there with no clothes on."

Jeremiah looks at Sonya, shrugs, says, "Okay. I'll bring him out here."

Jeremiah pushes through the door into the locker room, looks around at the crowd of guys talking, laughing, sitting in towels or getting dressed, a few guys in the back at a card table playing cards, a bar with a bartender at it, television going above his head, some kind of a golf game on. There's a couple guys sitting at the bar. One of them is big and fat, got long sideburns and more chins than the Hong Kong phone book, sitting there on a barstool, hunched over a cocktail.

Jeremiah walks up to him, says, "Pardon me. You Joe Bob Cole?"

Joe Bob shoots him a look. "What do you want, grandpa?"

Jeremiah's eyes narrow some. "My name's Jeremiah Spur. I'm helpin' out the Sheriff's Department with the Sissy Fletcher case, and I was wonderin' if you'd mind steppin' outside so my partner and me can ask you a few questions pertainin' to it."

Enough folks hear him say it to cause a noticeable reduction in the room noise in the vicinity of the bar, though in the back there's still plenty of racket. Jeremiah can feel this part of the locker room watching him.

Joe Bob looks back down at his drink. "Maybe you ain't noticed, but I'm kind of busy right now." He drains the glass, holds it up to the bartender so the man can see it's empty. "Why don't you call my office, make yourself an appointment, along about three, four years from now, when my schedule has done cleared up."

The bartender sets another drink down in front of Joe Bob.

Jeremiah says, "It won't take long. We'd appreciate the cooperation. You can even bring your other meetin' with you," he says, nodding in the cocktail's direction.

"Like I said. I'm busy."

"You don't look all that busy to me."

Joe Bob takes a swallow, looks sideways at Jeremiah, then back straight ahead. "You know what, old man? I don't even know you. I don't even know what authority you think you got. So why don't you go fuck yourself."

Jeremiah takes a last drag on his cigarette, thinks that what we got here is a serious case of truculent white trash.

A man can't escape his antecedents.

He looks around for an ashtray. " 'Scuse me," he says to the bartender.

"Yes, sir?"

"You got an ashtray?"

The bartender fetches one out from under the counter. "Here you go."

"Thanks." Jeremiah stubs out his cigarette. He looks at Joe Bob, who's studying his cocktail.

Jeremiah thinks to himself, force equals mass times acceleration.

He grabs Joe Bob Cole by the back of his shirt collar with both hands, hikes a boot up on the bar front, and jerks Joe Bob straight backward.

Joe Bob sails off the barstool onto the floor, cocktail following him backward in a wet arc, his fat ass crashing onto the floor where he lies, eyes bugged out, sucking air like a beached whale, his drink soaking the front of his black and yellow golf shirt.

Everybody in the locker room is watching now as Jeremiah leans over Joe Bob, says, "Rudeness is mighty unbecomin' in a fat man like you."

Jeremiah plants a boot on top of Joe Bob's right hand, applies some pressure. Joe Bob starts to thrash around, howl, "Hey, goddamnit, that hurts."

Jeremiah presses down a little harder. "You want to go outside and visit with my partner and me now, or you want me to keep this up until I hear bones breakin'?"

Guys start stirring around the room, like maybe they ought to step in, give Joe Bob a hand. Jeremiah looks around at them, letting them know without having to say it that that would be a poor way to top off their Saturday afternoon of golfing fun.

"Come on, man. Ow, fuck that hurts, goddamnit. Okay, okay, let's go outside."

Jeremiah eases off. "Get your ass up and out the door. You got so much ass that to haul it all might take multiple trips."

They leave the locker room to the sounds of some laughter, back through the door Jeremiah came in, Joe Bob walking kinked up from being smacked down on the floor with a thud worthy of a television wrestler, rubbing his hurt hand with the good one.

"You hurt my back," Joe Bob says.

"Bullshit," Jeremiah says. "All that fat give you plenty of cushion."

They meet up with Sonya in the pro shop. She sees Joe Bob all twisted up, dripping his favorite beverage, favoring his bad hand. She holds out her right hand to shake, says, "I'm Sonya Nichols. I'm an assistant district attorney."

Joe Bob grimaces, takes her right hand in his left, still got his right paw clutched at his side. "Joe Bob Cole. You work for George Barnett?"

"That's right."

"That's what I thought. He's probably the one what told you all about me and Sissy then. You know what?"

"What?"

"I think you ought to speak to your partner here about how folks got constitutional rights. He done violated a bunch of mine just now back yonder in the locker room, and in front of a busload of witnesses by the way."

"Well, I declare," Jeremiah says to Sonya. "Look what's happened now that the police brutality shoe has up and switched feet. This peckerwood's run off and joined the other side. Last time anybody checked he'd expressed himself on the subject of constitutional rights by helpin' to beat a prisoner to death. But now that I jerked his sorry ass off a barstool, he sounds like a card-carryin' member of the ACLU."

Sonya looks at Joe Bob, limping along, nursing his hurt hand. She takes Jeremiah to one side, says to him, "You know, Captain Spur, he's not wrong about . . ."

"Yeah, he is," says Jeremiah, making sure he says it loud enough for Job Bob to hear. "I'm a private citizen. I rough him up, he ain't got a constitutional claim. All he's got is an assault case, but my guess is he ain't about to go to the trouble of gettin' all lawyered up and bringin' it."

Jeremiah turns and looks at Joe Bob. "Are you?"

Joe Bob works his hand, has a sulk going, doesn't respond.

"That's what I thought. Well, let's get on with it then. Where around this private club do you reckon we can sit ourselves down and talk for a spell?"

"They's some lawn chairs out yonder by the practice green," says Joe Bob.

"Alright then."

They head out back, settle into the lawn chairs, by themselves except for some old codger in Bermuda shorts, dark socks pulled up to his knees, knocking golf balls around near the practice holes.

Sonya gets out her legal pad and her tape recorder. Joe Bob sits with his right hand cupped in his left. She walks him through the preliminaries, establishing name, address, occupation, what have you.

Then Jeremiah steps in. "How well did you know Sissy Fletcher?"

"I didn't kill her if that's what you're askin'."

"We'll get to that directly. My question was how well did you know her."

Joe Bob sneers. "You know how well I knew her if you've been talkin' to George Barnett. I knew her in the biblical sense."

"You care to elaborate on that?"

"Come on. Didn't George tell you already?"

"We'd like to hear your version of it."

Joe Bob rubs his hand. "I think you done broke some bones in my hand."

"You can git to a doctor when we're done here."

"This ain't gonna help my golf swing."

"Who gives a shit? You want to get on with it?"

"Okay. She and I had us what you might call an affair."

"When would this of been?"

Joe Bob knits his brow, says, "Sometime in 1987, I think, in the springtime."

"So tell us about it, why don't you?"

"It weren't long after I joined the Sheriff's Department. The other boys and me used to go over to the Farm-to-Market Café, across from the courthouse, for lunch. She waited tables there. We would come in every day about noon, grab a booth in the back, same booth every time."

"How come that particular booth?"

"On account of she worked it. She was the best-lookin' thing ever lived in this town." Joe Bob looks at Sonya. "No offense."

Sonya shrugs, makes a face that tells him "save your breath."

"Keep goin'," says Jeremiah.

"Well, right from the get go she was mighty flirtatious, 'specially with me."

"Had you known her at all before you started patronizin' her table at the Café?"

"Not really, just seen her around town some. She didn't pay me much attention."

"How come her to suddenly get interested in you then?"

"I honest-to-God don't know, unless it was the uniform, the position, bein' in the Sheriff's Department and all. That does it for some chicks."

Jeremiah is thinking he wore a uniform for a lot of years and it never caused him to violate his marriage vows.

He looks over at the old man with the dark socks pulled up, hitting the balls one by one at the hole, then going and fetching them back and doing it again and again. Jeremiah doesn't see the point. He's wondering how the guy knows when to stop, thinking maybe he does it until it gets dark and he has to quit or go blind, one.

Jeremiah tells his mind to stop wandering, get back to business.

"So," he says, "she starts gettin' friendly while she's waitin' your table."

"Yeah. Then one day I come in by myself, instead of with one or two of the boys as per usual. I'm sittin' there and she comes up to pour me a cup of coffee, says she would be interested in my opinion of an issue. I said 'what issue.' She said she would like to know where I stood on the issue of thong underwear."

"Imagine that," Sonya says. "A woman before her time."

Jeremiah turns and says, "What?"

Sonya says, "Never mind. Just something I read recently."

Jeremiah turns back to Joe Bob. "So what'd you say?"

Joe Bob is smirking again. "I told her deep down inside, I'm a serious student of such things. I don't like to hip shoot 'bout questions of such fundamental importance. I'd need me some more facts before I could venture any kind of an informed opinion. And she said if I'd care to meet her at the Adobe Inn later that afternoon, after she got off work, I could do some research. And that's how it got started."

"You and her over at the Adobe Inn."

"Yep."

"Where did y'all meet? In the lobby, at the registration desk?"

"No. In the actual room itself. She had done checked in. She give me the room number at lunch."

"What was it?"

"What was what?"

"The room number."

"Room fifteen."

Jeremiah glances at Sonya, then looks back at Joe Bob. "She ever say how come her to pick the Adobe?"

"Not right then. But she once tol' me she had a friend in management."

"How long did it last?"

"I don't know. Maybe fifteen minutes."

"Not that. The ever-what you call it. The relationship. This here affair of yours."

"Oh. I reckon about a year and a half, until a few months before she disappeared. We'd meet a time or two a month. Then she broke it off. She broke it off in me."

"What's that supposed to mean?"

"One day I come home and my wife had cleared out on me."

"She had caught wind that you'd been playin' around on her?"

"You could say that. She got an anonymous delivery, a bunch of photographs of the two of us, Sissy and me, doin' our thing down at the Adobe."

"Where'd they come from?"

Joe Bob shrugs, rubs his hand some. "Beats the everlivin' shit out of me. They just showed up, in a manila envelope, on our front doorstep. Next thing I know, my wife's as gone as this mornin's dew fall, movin' van shows up for the furniture, I'm bein' served with divorce papers, and ever-body in town is talkin' about it."

"You didn't ask Sissy where them pictures came from?"

"I tried to. I looked for her at the Café, at the Adobe, ever-where. She dropped out of sight for about a week, and then all of a sudden she showed up at the sheriff's office one morning while I was on duty."

"What happened then?"

"When I seen her come in, I started to get up, take her out for a cup of coffee, have a nice private visit somewheres where we wouldn't be seen, find out how come her to go out of her way to fuck up my life. She said right out loud, right where the whole squad room could hear, in front of God and ever-body, for me not to get up, for me to keep my seat. She'd just come by to say adios, we wasn't goin' to be seein' one another no more. Right there. In front of God and ever-body."

"You said that already."

"Well, it was."

"Was there a lot of people around?"

"Probably a half dozen. The sheriff, three or four deputies, couple of other people. It was like she timed it to get the maximum audience. She said her piece and started to leave."

"What'd you do?"

"I tried to stop her. I went runnin' after her, grabbed her arm, asked her what she knew about them pictures that had turned up at my place. She just laughed and kept on a-goin'. 'See you around, Joe Bob,' she said."

"Then what?"

"Then nothin'. She quit her job at the Café and I hardly ever saw her anymore."

"That was it? No further contact?"

"Believe me, I tried. But she didn't have no more use for me, I reckon."

Jeremiah pauses, lights a cigarette, watches the old golfer playing around with his golf club and balls. Part of Jeremiah's mind is working on what that golf club is called. They call it by a special name but he can't for the life of him remember what it is.

"Let's talk about the night she disappeared," Jeremiah says. "Where was you that night?"

"I don't remember."

"You don't remember."

"No. It was over ten years ago."

"Could you of been on duty?"

"I don't recollect."

"How about the rodeo dance? Could you of gone to that?"

"Maybe. I ain't much of a dancer. I just don't know."

"Did you see Sissy Fletcher that night?"

"I don't recall."

"Did you kill Sissy Fletcher, Joe Bob?"

"I already tol' you I didn't."

"But you had a motive, didn't you? She broke up your marriage, then dropped you like you had some kind of communicable disease."

"Doesn't mean I killed her."

"But you wasn't no big fan of hers."

"That don't make me the Lone Ranger."

Jeremiah takes a couple drags on his cigarette, looks off in the distance. He leans over, spits on the ground, looks back at Joe Bob. "You know what I don't get?"

"What don't you get?"

"I don't get why Pat Patterson picked you to run the investigation into her disappearance. You got an explanation for that?"

Joe Bob hesitates, says, "I'm a sumbitch if I know. You'd have to ask him."

"Be kind of hard to do, him bein' dead and all."

"That ain't my problem now, is it?"

"I looked at the case file."

"Yeah? So what?"

"It looked to me like you was just goin' through the motions."

Joe Bob shrugs, looks off into the distance now himself, rubs his thumb over the back of his hand. "I dug around, found out what I could, but it wasn't like anybody thought a crime had been committed. Ever-body figgered she'd skipped town with some rodeo type. We figgered she'd show back up someday lookin' like she'd been rode hard and put up wet."

Jeremiah stubs out his cigarette. He shakes another one out, lights it up, draws on it, looks at Joe Bob. "You ever owned a dark blue overcoat by any chance?"

"What would I need an overcoat for?"

Jeremiah taps the ash off on the sole of his boot, looks over where the old golfer is still at it. They call it a putter, Jeremiah thinks. He's over there putting around with his putter. Makes him look like a dimwit.

That thought triggers another thought. He says. "Did you ever see Sissy and Charlie Baker together?"

"Who?"

"Charlie Baker. The son of that lady runs the ice cream shop over at the bypass."

"You mean the re-tard?"

"From what I hear he ain't out-and-out retarded. Just kind of slow."

Joe Bob grins. "Hell, they was asshole buddies. I'd see him in the Farm-to-Market all the time, readin' comic books, her bringin' him soft drinks. We even picked him up a time or two, after we'd been, you know, together, and carried him out to get a hamburger. She had some kind of special thing goin' with that kid."

"How do you account for it?"

"I don't rightly know. She had some kind of soft spot in her heart for dumb asses, I reckon. That was Sissy, goin' out of her way to do kindnesses for re-tards, stray animals . . ."

"Obese deputy sheriffs?"

Joe Bob scowls. "I got me a glandular problem is all."

Jeremiah looks over at Sonya. "You got any questions?"

"Just a couple. Joe Bob?"

"Yeah."

"Did you all ever meet anywhere other than the Adobe?"

"No. Same place every time."

"Same time?"

"Generally. Mostly in the afternoons."

"Same room?"

"Oh, yeah. Always the same. It was like she had a long-term lease."

"Anything strike you as special about that particular room?"

Joe Bob knits his brow. "I don't know. It was a long time ago. Seems like the lighting was unusual, for a motel room."

"What do you mean?"

"Most motel rooms I been in, they tend to be kind of dark. This one here, it was lit up big time. And she liked to do it, you know, with the lights on. All of 'em."

Sonya looks over at Jeremiah. "That's all I have."

Jeremiah looks at Joe Bob. "'Preciate your time. Do me a favor, would you?"

Joe Bob goes to rubbing his hurt hand, gives Jeremiah a look like, Why would I be doing you any favors?

Jeremiah says, "Try to recollect where you was the night Sissy Fletcher disappeared, then give us a call. At Sonya's office."

Sonya hands him a business card. He tucks it in his golf pants, gets up, slinks away, leaves them sitting there, watching the old golfer putting his balls around.

Jeremiah says, "I don't get it."

"What's that?"

He motions toward the old golfer with his cigarette hand. "I don't get why a man would stand out there and do that for hours at a time."

Sonya looks over at the golfer. "I'm not sure there's a logical explanation for it."

Jeremiah jerks a thumb back in Joe Bob's direction. "You reckon he's lyin'?"

"About what?"

"About not bein' able to remember where he was the night of the dance."

"Maybe."

"Tell you what. Why don't you have your boyfriend—what's his name again?"

"Clyde Thomas."

"Right. Have Clyde check back through the work sheets in the Sheriff's Department, see if ol' lard ass was on duty the night of February 11, 1989."

"Good idea. What do you make of that business with Charlie Baker?"

"Don't know. Maybe nothin'. I think you ought to go check out the Adobe Inn tomorrow, see what you can learn over yonder. Then maybe go around, see Mrs. Baker."

"What are you going to do?"

"Like I said before. Go to church. Pay a call on Jim Fletcher. Then carry my wife down to the hospital to see Elizabeth. Come on. I'll give you a ride home."

They get up from the lawn chairs, start ankling to the parking lot.

Sonya says, "How long have you been married, Captain Spur?"

" 'Bout thirty-three years."

"Wow. How do you get a relationship to last that long?"

"What you really want to know is whether I ever let some woman tempt me the way Joe Bob let Sissy tempt him."

Sonya blushes. "Captain Spur, I didn't mean—"

"Am I right?"

"Sir, I—"

"Sonya, am I right?"

"Yes, sir."

"That's okay. The answer is no. I had a few chances to."

"A good-looking man like you, I'm not surprised."

"But I always passed 'em up."

"Not many men would."

They get to the pickup. Jeremiah unlocks the cab, opens Sonya's door for her, looks at her before she gets in.

"I look at it this way. There's a handful of things separate man from the rest of the animals. Without 'em, what we'd be is not much more than dangerous livestock that walk upright and can talk. One of them things is the ability to feel guilt. No animal ever felt guilty about doin' anything. Now people on the other hand, at least most folks, we feel it if we do some-thin' wrong, and it's a painful feelin'. We recognize it is a thing to be avoided, then we let the desire to avoid guilt guide our actions, keep us out of trouble."

Sonya's brow furrows. "What's a nice way to say this? Captain Spur, I guess I never would have figured you for someone who spent time thinking about such things."

Jeremiah shrugs. "You spend as much time as I have on stakeouts, you end up thinkin' about pretty near everything there is at least once. So how I see it is, it's a powerful emotion, guilt. And as applied to foolin' around with other women, I never thought it made any sense to spend an hour of my time doin' somethin' that was gonna make me feel guilty for the rest of my life."

"A lot of guys do it and don't feel guilty about it."

Jeremiah shrugs again.

"So that was it? That's how you were able to stay faithful all those years?"

"That. And one other thing."

"What was that?"

Jeremiah looks off into the distance, then back at Sonya. He smiles some, says, "You know, Sonya, I don't know you too well, seein' as how we just met today. But what I seen of you so far I like. You're a pro, and I respect professionalism in folks."

"Thank you, sir."

"So professional to professional, I'm gonna pay you the compliment of bein' blunt. Here's the deal."

"Yes, sir?"

"Even after thirty plus years, I still love my wife. I want to be a part of her future, and have her as a part of mine, always have had, ever since I done met her. I long ago figgered out that in order to make that come about, I was gonna have to make sure she was a part of my present, even when she wasn't anywheres nearby. And we been away from one another a lot during our marriage. Does that make any sense?"

Sonya smiles, says, "That's quite a romantic little speech coming from the legendarily tough Texas Ranger Jeremiah Spur."

Jeremiah shrugs one more time.

Sonya gets in the pickup. Jeremiah closes the door, walks around to the other side, gets behind the wheel.

Joe Bob Cole stands in the pro shop, watching Jeremiah Spur's pickup pull out of the parking lot. He says to himself, "It's true what they've always said about that son of a bitch George Barnett. The truth just ain't in the man."

Behind him the golf professional says, "Say what, Joe Bob?"

Joe Bob glances at the man, says, "Nothin'. I was just talkin' to myself."

He walks out of the pro shop, gets in his car. He figures he'll go home to do his drinking there rather than go back in the locker room and put up with whatever ridicule his rough treatment at the hands of a man twenty years his senior might have stirred up.

What he can't figure out is what to do about George Barnett. The man had assured him that Jeremiah Spur would keep his distance from the Fletcher case. Instead, not only is he giving Dewey's people a hand, he's coming around asking Joe Bob questions about things Joe Bob would just as lief not be questioned about.

It seems to him that George must have put ideas about him in the old Ranger's head. Why else would he be coming around here, ruining Joe Bob's entire day?

As he gets into his vehicle, Joe Bob is wondering whether maybe the DA had decided he didn't believe him after all when he denied that he killed Sissy, and that was why he had sicced Jeremiah Spur and that other one, that lawyer bitch who worked in George's own office, on him.

And now, with Spur on the case, Dewey's chances of finding the killer were looking up, which means Joe Bob won't necessarily be able to trounce Dewey in the primary next year like he had been planning on.

As he leaves the parking lot behind, Joe Bob is puzzling over how unfair life is, how fast a man's fortunes can go downhill on him through no fault of his own.

2 5

MARTIN CAN TELL THE SUN MUST HAVE JUST ABOUT SET BECAUSE IT'S TOO DARK to see more than a hundred yards or so. He punches the little button that lights up the dial on his Timex. Soon it'll be dark enough to go check out that construction shack, see if the good Lord has provided His Messenger with a detonation device.

Martin's feeling good about their prospects, the power of the Lord surging through him, through his body and out into his limbs, making him feel like some kind of a superhero, like David fixing to square off against Goliath and the entire Philistine army.

The power of the Lord is a profound thing.

He turns to Dud. "Let's give it another fifteen minutes or so. By then it ought to be good and dark."

"Fair enough."

"Did I ever tell you 'bout the time I went elk huntin' in Colorado?"

"Seems like you tol' me about it once. I don't mind hearin' about it again though since we just sittin' out here on the side of the road with our teeth in our mouth."

"Buddy of mine from the army and me went, in a national forest down in the southern part of the state. We found us a place to camp halfway up a mountainside. We'd go to sleep every night in our sleepin' bags laid out under the stars, next to a campfire dyin' off, listenin' to the coyotes howlin' way off in the distance. That's how we was meant to sleep, Dud, not in no bed with a air conditioner makin' a fuss in the wall."

"I reckon."

"Then every mornin' we'd get up before dawn, get the fire goin', eat some breakfast, get our gear together. We'd climb up on top of that mountain where there was a ridge that looked across a valley, over to another ridge. I'm gonna say it was maybe five hunnerd yards from ridge top to ridge top. There was pretty good cover down in the valley runnin' up the other side, but the far ridge top was mostly clear.

"We'd lay there, facin' west, sun comin' up over our left shoulders. It would light the far ridgeline first, turn it all goldenlike, then work its way down the side of the mountain until the valley floor was bright with it. We seen bobcats and coyotes and mule deer, but we wasn't huntin' them. We was there to bag ourselves a elk.

"We like to got skunked too, was out there our last mornin' until almost ten o'clock, actually talkin' about packin' it in when I seen him movin' real slow and careful just below the top of that western ridge. He was so far off I couldn't tell for sure it was a elk until I put the binocs on him. I got my rifle up on my shoulder, had the barrel resting on a log . . ."

"What was you shootin'?"

"My old thirty-aught-six. I put the crosshairs about six inches above and to the left of his front shoulders, tryin' to lead him just a tad, figgerin' the slug wouldn't fall much on account of the air is so much thinner up yonder. I slowed my breathin', tried to slow my heartbeat. I'm here to tell you, partner, I was havin' to concentrate hard not to let that old buck fever get me, my heart was goin' ninety to nothin'. I squeezed the trigger real careful-like. The next thing I knew he had dropped out of sight, disappeared from my scope. My buddy and me, we hightailed it down the mountain, up the other side, took us maybe twenty minutes to get over to where he was at, and sure enough, there he was. Just as dead as dead can be. Got him right through the heart."

Dud whistles. "One shot at five hunnerd yards. That's some fine shootin'."

Martin is thinking there's no God but the Lord God Jehovah, and His Messenger is a crack shot. "I believe I could do that again."

"Do what?"

"Hit a target from five hunnerd yards with my ol' thirty-aught-six."

"You back to that nigger deputy problem again, ain't you?"

Martin turns toward Dud. "I helped Earl Guidry fix a deer blind on his place about three years ago, and he let me hunt out of it last winter. I noticed while I was up there, a man has hisself a clear view of the parkin' lot over at the Rose Emporium, and it's about five hunnerd, maybe five hunnerd and fifty yards off."

"So you thinkin' . . ."

"Yeah. And I'm thinkin' there ain't no time like the present. I say we give that burrhead a call tomorrow, see if we can't arrange to put him out of his misery."

Once it's dark they get out of the pickup, make their way to the gate in the fence that surrounds the construction yard, both of them with flashlights, Dud carrying a bolt cutter. The fence is secured with a padlock, length of chain.

Martin looks at it, says, "Ain't no step for a stepper. I'll hold the flashlight while you do the cuttin'."

"Roger dodger," says Dud.

It takes about ninety seconds' work with the bolt cutter and then they're through the gate. They cross over to the front door of the construction shack. The door's held fast with a deadbolt. Martin tries it a couple times, then they walk around, looking for an easier way in. Over on the side is a window set up high in the wall.

Martin says, "You think you can fit through that window?"

Dud looks up at it. "I believe so."

"Let's give it a shot. Hand me that bolt cutter."

Martin takes the tool from Dud, swings the business end of it hard into the windowpane, ducks down to get out of the way of the glass that goes flying.

Then he sets his flashlight down, bends over, holds his hands out, makes a cradle for Dud, says, "Here you go, partner."

Dud takes off his boots, sticks a foot with a white sock on it in the cradle Martin has made, hikes up the wall. Standing up there, Dud uses the bolt cutter to clear the glass shards from around the inside of the frame. Then he reaches inside the window, unlocks it, swings the frame up. He looks down at Martin.

"How you doin' down there?"

"Just get on with it."

Dud works his shoulders through the window, then his trunk, gets stuck for a bit on his belt buckle, then he's over and in, sliding to the floor on the other side. He picks himself up, leans back out, looks down at Martin.

"I'm in. Hand me my boots."

Martin gives Dud's boots to him, walks around to the front of the shack. Directly the door opens and there stands Dud. They go inside, shutting the door behind them.

They click on their flashlights, scan around the little hut, see a couple tables with plans and maps on them, calendars decorated with naked girls hanging on the walls. A small refrigerator sits in one corner, and on the wall behind the door there's a desk with a telephone and some manuals on it. Back along the far wall is a set of cabinets.

Martin says, "Check the desk while I go look in them cabinets back yonder."

Dud carries his flashlight over to the desk, starts pulling drawers out, rummaging around in them.

All the cabinets are unlocked save one. Martin tries the unlocked ones first. He finds hard hats, safety vests, hand tools. He thinks about helping himself to a couple of Porter Cable drills, but decides the Messenger of the Lord had better be mindful of the Ten Commandments, steer wide of petty larceny outside the scope of his mission.

"You find anything?" he says to Dud.

"Nope. How 'bout you?"

"I ain't got nothin' so far. Down to one locked cabinet. You got a crowbar?"

"You bet, pardner."

"Go get it. I think I can bust into this sucker if I can get a purchase on it."

Dud is back in less than a minute, hands Martin the crowbar. He takes it to the cabinet, leans into it, busts the lock off its screws, shines his light in.

"I got me a box of somethin' here."

He leans down, opens the lid up, plays his light over it.

"Bingo," he says.

26

HE STIRS BEFORE DAWN, HIS DREAMS STILL LACING HIS BRAIN. HE'S STILL NOT
awake yet when a strong anxious feeling jumps sleep's claim to his mind,
and as he wakes up he searches for its source, tries to tell himself to stop
being so weak-minded.

He turns over, looks at the clock. Four forty-five in the morning. He listens to Martha's deep breathing, thinking about carrying her up to the hospital this afternoon, wondering if that's what has him on edge, has his heart
pounding in his chest.

That doesn't seem like it somehow.

Maybe it's the payment coming due on his note next month, and him
not having enough in checking to cover it, not even when you add in
whatever he could get from selling the fall-borne steers. It's an uncomfortable feeling all right, owing money you can't pay, but that isn't the sort of
thing that ordinarily sends his pulse rate up.

It isn't the smoke he can smell, drifting into the room from outside the
house where it hovers thick in the air.

His gut is signaling something to him though.

He gets up, feels his way to the closet, pulls out his clothes and boots,
eases out of the room and into the kitchen to dress, pour himself a cup of
black.

He's headed outside to smoke a cigarette, sit with his dog, watch the rest
of the night slip away, when that feeling in his gut turns him in a different
direction, draws him to the family room, past the bookshelves stuffed full of
books, from the bottom where the Encyclopedia Brittanica is, the set Elizabeth used when she was growing up, to the top, where Jeremiah can see
Martha's mama's old family Bible crammed in next to a set of the complete
works of Shakespeare, books nobody had taken down in years. Jeremiah
had never been able to sit still long enough to read much beyond the morning newpaper, hadn't picked up any kind of book to read, not even the
Bible, for as long as he could remember. But Martha had been some kind of
a reader back before the drink had locked up her mind, would sometimes
read a book a week.

There are pictures on the bookshelves too, of Elizabeth as a little girl and when she was older, sitting astride her horse Polly, in her graduation gown, pictures of Martha, from their wedding and later in life, still the natural beauty he married, even into her forties. A picture or two of him.

Jeremiah's gun cabinet sits next to the bookshelves. He stops in front of it, sets his coffee cup down, reaches up on top of the cabinet, pulls down his key from where he hides it, bends over, unlocks the bottom drawer.

There lie the two things he had kept when he left the Rangers.

One is his badge, a five-pointed silver "Lone Star" set inside a silver ring with the words "Captain" and "Texas Rangers," and scrollwork engraved there on it.

He picks it up between his thumb and forefinger, recollecting the day the governor had pinned it on his white shirt, at that ceremony up in Austin. That was the most proud he had ever been, in that moment when his boyhood dream came true for him. How many men have experienced a moment like that one?

Shaking the governor's hand. Looking down from the auditorium stage at his wife and his little daughter, standing out there in the audience applauding him for his accomplishment, along with all the other folks who had come out for the occasion.

He sets the badge down, picks up the other thing he'd left the Rangers with.

It's his Colt Commander .45, still in the shoulder rig, the gun belt next to it, lying just where he had laid it the day he came home, retired from the Rangers, out of law enforcement for the first time in more than thirty years.

He pulls out the gun and holster, pushes the drawer closed, grabs his coffee, goes out on the porch, gets situated in his cane-bottomed rocker. Lays his pistol on his lap.

Duke gets up off the floor, comes over walking slow, ready to keep him company.

Jeremiah is thinking a man who's got a dog can't be lonely. He's got immunity from it. He reaches inside his shirt pocket for his cigarettes, shakes one out, lights it, commences to smoke, scratch Duke behind the ears.

They sit there in the dark, a few patches of light bleeding out onto the porch from the family room. Jeremiah smokes, watches the sky lighten up to its cinder-block gray.

It's beginning to make some sense to him now, that feeling in his gut.

There's a killer loose in Brenham. Jeremiah's gut is telling him that he knows this, that somebody is out there. Somebody who thought they had gotten away with it, now for the first time in years worrying that maybe it's going to catch up with them.

Worrying that their luck is fixing to run out.

Jeremiah's seen others who found themselves in such a spot, seen how they had reacted, seen what they had done.

Jeremiah knows that queasiness is now.

That's his gut telling him there's a good chance folks are about to start dying around here.

Dr. James Fletcher walks into his office, beaming his big smile even before he sees Jeremiah. The preacher crosses the room, extends a hand.

"Jeremiah," he says as they shake, still smiling to beat the band. "Good to see you again. Please have a seat."

Jeremiah takes a chair facing the desk. He can't help but think back to twenty-four hours ago when the preacher had stood in the pulpit, displayed his grief in front of the entire town. How unusual that had been since the natural way of preachers is they are quick and persistent smilers even when the circumstances don't seem to warrant it.

Jeremiah shifts some, tries to get comfortable with the gun hanging beneath his sports jacket. It's the first time in a long time he's come to church with a firearm on his person. He reckons he could have left it in the pickup, but he felt the need to start getting used to having it strapped on again.

Jeremiah says, "I hope you don't mind me barging in here with no appointment."

"No, no, not at all," says the preacher as he shucks out of his robe, hangs it up on a coat rack that is set into the wall.

"That was a mighty fine sermon you preached this mornin'."

Dr. Fletcher sits down in his desk chair, smile growing even more. "The parable of the Good Samaritan. The ultimate expression of the Christian ideal. Love thy neighbor as thyself, as embodied, at the risk of being overly alliterative, in the suffering, selfless servant. Christ on the cross. St. Paul in prison. Christianity's greatest contribution to the Western belief system. Christians seek to gain enlightenment through their sacrificial service to others, a doctrinal distinction that elevates the faith above the Eastern religions, even above Judaism."

"The world sure would be a better place if more folks was to be that way."

"So, Jeremiah, what brings you in here, for the second time in three days? Would you like to revisit something about our Friday morning session?"

"No, sir, I got somethin' else on my mind this mornin'. Although I need to tell you, you were a big help to us on Friday. Martha's asked me to carry her down to Houston to visit with Elizabeth this afternoon, and we got you to thank for that."

"Well that's just splendid, just splendid indeed."

"Yes, sir. That's what it is, all right."

"So what else can I do for you?"

"We need you to answer a few questions about the night Sissy disappeared."

Some of the wattage flows out of the preacher's smile. " 'We,' Jeremiah?"

"I agreed to give 'em a hand. The Sheriff's Department, that is."

"I thought you had concluded that was a poor use of your time. I thought we had concluded that together."

"Somethin' come up that caused me to change my mind."

"Your parents named you well, Jeremiah."

"How's that?"

" 'I will discipline you with justice; I will not let you go entirely unpunished.' Words from your namesake. The words of God, spoken through the Prophet Jeremiah."

"You'd know more about that than I would. You mind if we visit some about Sissy's disappearance?"

The preacher sits forward, puts his elbows on his desk, straightens some papers, still smiling but not about to bust with it anymore, the corners of his mouth a lot tighter now. "No, no, not at all. I'm not sure how much help I can be, but let's by all means see what questions you have."

"How would you describe your relationship with Sissy? Were y'all close?"

"We were very close when she was a little girl."

"How about when she disappeared. When she was murdered."

Jim Fletcher cocks his head, looks up at the ceiling, breathes out a little sigh, looks back down at his desktop. "That's not a particularly apt description of our relationship at that time, no. Beginning with her teenage years, we had our share of differences we were always working on, trying to sort through. You have a daughter. You know what it's like. You love each other but there's often a clash of wills that . . ."

"What kind of differences?"

Dr. Fletcher tilts back in his chair. "Differences about religion, for one particularly stark example. Sissy was bright, Jeremiah, uncommonly bright. She had an unerring instinct for some of the more difficult issues posed by Christianity. The Christian doctrine of salvation, for example, bothered her to no end. She failed to see the logic in a system that denied salvation to good people who had not professed their faith in Jesus Christ. Good people of other traditions, other cultures, other parts of the world, people who may never have even heard of Christ, through no fault of their own. She saw that as a fatal flaw in Christian dogma and on that basis, among others, essentially renounced the church. As you can imagine, that was extremely difficult for me."

"Was there anything else that had come between you?"

The preacher's smile is beginning to look forced, even painful. He leans forward again, sets his arms on his desk, glances at Jeremiah, then goes back to studying his desktop.

"It should be easier to talk about this, especially with you. There are certain, ah, parallels between us as fathers, where our daughters are concerned. But that doesn't seem to make it easy, really."

"I'm not sure I understand what you're gettin' at."

"Your daughter, being gay, must have caused you some . . . I don't know, discomfort."

"A thing can only be what it is."

"I guess you're right. Sissy could only be what she was. And she was . . . promiscuous. Sexually speaking. At least, if the reports that made their way back to me were to be believed. I confronted her about it, and she didn't deny it. I tried to make her see how that made me look, but that didn't seem to be of much concern to her. There were times when, frankly . . ."

"What?"

"Well, it seemed like she did what she did specifically to *make* me look bad."

"Why would she of done that?"

Dr. Fletcher looks up and shrugs. "I don't know. I raised her the best way I knew how, after her mother passed away. I have tormented myself a lot of years about where I went wrong with her. I guess it doesn't matter anymore. For whatever reason, she was a bit out of control. And there wasn't very much I could do about it, except hope and pray it was a phase she would outgrow in due course."

"I heard she had some kind of bee in her bonnet where men was concerned. You got any idea about that?"

"I guess you might put it that way. It wasn't like she was a feminist, really. She was resentful of the powers that be here in town. She fundamentally disliked Brenham, and how the male-dominated power structure tended to be indifferent to the plight of little people. For reasons that are obscure to me, she saw herself as the guardian angel of the misbegotten. And believe me, it was a role she took seriously. She knew she really couldn't shift the balance of power in any meaningful way. But short of that, she had some kind of felt need to take the self-important types around town down a peg or two."

"I'll have to say, I don't completely follow you."

"And I'll have to say if I told you I understood it completely myself, I wouldn't be telling you the truth."

"We hear she was good buddies with Charlie Baker. What's the story there?"

Jeremiah sees something pass behind the preacher's eyes, his smile all but gone now. "That's a good example of what I'm talking about. Charlie is not too bright, and he sometimes has a bit of trouble relating to the real world. Sissy took an interest in him from early on, played big sister to him, looked after him around the church. It was her nature to take pity on the pitiful."

"That's all there was to it?"

Jim Fletcher shrugs again. "Pretty much."

"Where was you the night she disappeared?"

"Sitting right here, writing my sermon for Sunday morning, just like I have done every Saturday night for the last thirty years."

"Did you see her that night?"

"No."

"What about your son, Martin?"

"What about him?"

"Where was he?"

"He was next door, at the parsonage."

"How do you know?"

"Because he came in here while I was working to tell me good night. When I left here and went home, I checked on him in his room. He was in there asleep."

"What time would all of this have been happening?"

"He came in here about ten o'clock, and I worked until about midnight."

"Then you went home."

"That's right."

"The other day, when Martha and I were here, you sent out a stack of clothes with your secretary. What become of them?"

"She gave them away to charity."

"Which one?"

"She gave them all away."

"No, I mean to which charity?"

"I don't know. You'd have to ask her. Why do you ask?"

"I thought I saw a dark blue overcoat in the stack."

"You did."

"Was that your coat?"

The preacher shakes his head. "No, it wasn't mine."

"Whose was it then?"

"I don't know. Someone left it in the cloakroom a few years back and we kept it in lost and found all this time, but no one claimed it."

"So you give it away."

"That's right."

"Was it by chance missing a button?"

"I couldn't tell you. Why do you ask?"

Jeremiah considers what to say in response, then he decides he has rarely had occasion to regret something he didn't say. "No particular reason. Just curious. Your secretary around today?"

"No. She's up in Navasota visiting with her relatives."

"When is she gonna be back?"

"Tuesday, I think. Shall I have her call you?"

"That would be helpful. Thanks."

The preacher glances at his wristwatch. "Are we about done here? I mean, I need to start getting ready for the eleven o'clock service."

"Yep. I just got one more question."

"What's that?"

"When Sissy went missing, what did you think had happened to her?"

The preacher looks off into the distance. "I guess I assumed she had finally gotten fed up with life in this little town, and acted on her long-expressed desire to move away, find a life for herself on one of the coasts. She used to say, 'Brenham looks good in the rearview mirror.' But then, when I never heard from her again, I began to worry and wonder. Not that there was much I could do about it, except hope that someone would run across her someday, let me know she was okay."

"Did it ever occur to you she might of been a murder victim?"

"Not really."

"Do you know anybody who would have wanted to do her harm?"

The preacher looks at his watch again. "You know, Jeremiah, I really need to get ready for the next service. Why don't you let me think about that and get back to you?"

"Seems to me you would of already spent time thinking about that."

"Jeremiah, I—"

"Okay. Fair enough. You can get back to me." Jeremiah stands up to leave, and he and the preacher shake hands.

Jeremiah says, "Thanks again for your help with Martha."

The preacher says, "Let me know how it goes this afternoon."

"Be happy to. And have your secretary call me when she gets back in town."

As Jeremiah turns to leave the office, it occurs to him that the preacher isn't smiling anymore.

27

BY THE TIME HE FINALLY COLLAPSED INTO BED SATURDAY NIGHT, CLYDE Thomas had hardly slept for two nights running so it's already Sunday afternoon before he finally rolls over, prodded awake by a nasty dream of burned-up dead folks chasing him and his brother Leon down the street.

He shakes himself awake, thinking about Leon for the first time in a while.

Clyde had been twelve when Leon died. Leon was eighteen and Clyde's oldest brother. Clyde had thought Leon was the coolest thing God ever made. He had been an All-State wide receiver in high school, had four-four speed, hands like grocery baskets.

Clyde went to all the games Leon played in, watched his brother from the bleachers, was waiting for him when he came out of the locker room, hung around with him until his brother shooed him away so he could be with his own friends.

His senior year Leon broke four regional receiving records, was recruited by fifteen Division I schools, was headed to the University of Michigan on full scholarship.

One evening in late February, Clyde's mama had sent him to fetch Leon in for supper. Clyde knew just where to find him, too, hanging around with some other brothers on a street corner near a liquor store half a dozen blocks from the house.

Clyde had rounded the corner on his bicycle just in time to see the vehicle with the darkened windows drive by, the automatic gunfire belching from the passenger's side window, scattering the crowd on the corner by the liquor store.

Leon had bled to death in Clyde's arms, eyes fixed in a stare, mouth gaping.

Clyde turns his mind away from the memory, as he has learned over time to do.

He rolls over, looks at the radio clock on the bedside table.

"Oh, baby, that's what I'm talkin' about," he says out loud, even though there's no one else around.

He rolls back over, yawns, stretches, stares up at the ceiling, scratches himself. He swings his feet onto the floor, gets up to go to shower, then give Sonya a ring. See if she wants to get some lunch maybe.

When Jeremiah gets home from church, Martha's already waiting for him in the family room, sitting in an armchair, dressed and made up pretty, such that Jeremiah can see the beauty that she once was, the beauty that's still there in her. She's got a suitcase and a cosmetics case at her feet.

Jeremiah looks first at her, then at the luggage, then back at her again.

"I'm planning to stay down there with her," she says.

Jeremiah nods. "We'll find you a room in one of them hotels near the hospital."

"You could stay too if you wanted."

Jeremiah crosses the room, picks up the suitcase. "Maybe I'll come down later in the week," he says, and heads for the door. "There's some things I need to attend to, if I'm gonna work the fall-borne steers on schedule."

"It's not like you to stay for the fellowship hour."

"Beg your pardon?"

"I thought you'd be home a half hour ago."

"Sorry. I stopped in to see Jim for a bit."

"What about?"

"Just to go over a few points, 'bout the night Sissy died."

Martha's mouth thins out, eyebrows knit. "Work the fall-borne steers."

"Beg your pardon?" he says again.

"I don't think you're staying behind to work the fall-bornes."

Jeremiah shrugs, puts the cosmetic case under his arm, goes to open the door. Before he gets through it she says, "You're carrying your gun again."

"Only for a day or two."

Jeremiah walks out the screen door, catches it with his boot on its way back to closing so it won't bang, walks out to his pickup, puts the luggage in, waits while Duke mounts up, goes around to open the cab door for Martha, who has come out of the house behind him, locking the door as she goes.

The look she gives him when she gets in the truck tells him what she thinks about that shoulder rig he's toting around under his coat.

Sonya pulls into the parking lot at the Adobe Inn, shifts into PARK, says into her cell phone, "I'm really glad you got some sleep. You needed it. I could tell by looking at your face, you were pretty much out of gas."

Clyde says, "That's exactly right. Last night I felt like I'd been eat up by a wolf and shit over a cliff."

"Clyde, you can be so colorful sometimes."

"Now I got some sleep, got my deputy thing back, gonna crack this Uncle Freddie's case, pack some perp off for a dose of poison, lethal inject his murderin' ass up in the Walls Unit, everything gonna work out just fine, you know what I'm sayin'? So how's it goin' with you? How'd you and the Marlboro Man make out?"

"With him it's unfiltered Camels. The original coffin nail." Sonya fills him in on the interviews with Elizabeth and Joe Bob Cole, all the progress they had made.

"That sounds good, real good," he says. "Too bad the man got himself a racist dog, I might have got to likin' him. Now listen here, how 'bout you and me gettin' together for a little late lunch down at the Farm-to-Market Café, maybe take a nap after?"

"I'd love to, Clyde, I really would. But I've got some things I need to do on the Fletcher case. In fact, I'm just about to go into a witness interview. Tell you what. Let's meet at my place this evening, grill some steaks instead, have a nice bottle of cab."

"Now that there is a idea and a half. That'll give me a chance to put a little time of my own in, down to the office, see if the fingerprint techs done their thing yet."

"Great. Why don't you come around, say, about six o'clock."

"You on. I be bringin' the steaks."

"Since you're going to the office anyhow, would you do something for me?"

"All you gots to do is ask."

"Okay, here's the deal. Joe Bob claimed he couldn't remember where he was on the night Sissy disappeared. He didn't even know if he might have been pulling a shift for the Sheriff's Department."

"Hell, I can find that out. Just got to check the worksheets we got filed away."

"That's just what we wanted you to do."

"No problem, darlin'. I be seein' yo' sweet behind at six o'clock."

"See you then."

Sonya shuts off her phone, clips it onto her belt, allows herself a little smile. She kills the engine of her vehicle, grabs her briefcase, gets out, shuts the car door, walks through the front door into the reception area of the Adobe Inn.

She's wearing her usual summer weekend outfit that keeps her reasonably cool even if the temperature climbs way up—jeans, sleeveless blouse, fits nice, shows off her figure, comfortable pair of shoes. Hair pulled back in a ponytail.

The motel is a couple of two-story wings set perpendicular to the bypass on either side of a parking lot, with the office out front, big neon sign on top lit to say VACANCY. Sonya figures the market for this forlorn little monument to American mobility must be folks that get too tired to make it to a real city, like Houston or Austin.

The reception area is outfitted with green AstroTurf surrounded by cheap paneling and somewhere a window unit rumbles away.

An Asian guy sits behind the reception desk, reading the *Houston Chronicle*. He gets off his stool to greet Sonya. He can't be taller than five feet four.

"Would you like room?" he says.

Sonya reaches in her purse, pulls out her identification. "No," she says. "I'm Washington County Assistant District Attorney Sonya Nichols, and I just want to ask you a few questions concerning a criminal case I'm working on."

The Asian guy starts bouncing around behind the reception desk, going this way and that like he's got a snake in his drawers. "I no do something! I no do something!"

"Excuse me?"

"I no do something! I totally clean! I no do something!"

"No one said you did, Mr. . . . Excuse me, but what is your name?"

"I no do something! I pay all taxes I owe! Federal! State! I pay all taxes! Income! Sales! I no do something!"

"Sir, if you would just calm down a minute . . ."

"I no do something!" He reaches behind him, pulls a photograph of a young Asian man in a cap and gown off a shelf, shoves it at her. "This my son Nguyen! He a sophomore at Texas A&M University! He studying to be mechanical engineer! He straight-A student! I work hard, pay tuition, pay for books, pay for his room in big dormitory! I no do something! I pay all my taxes! I can show you receipts!"

He puts the picture back and runs around a wall into a little office. Sonya can see him through a glass pane. He opens drawers in a desk, pulls files, stacks them on the desktop, still hollering, "I no do something! I no do something!" As though those words were an incantation, calling forth some supernatural power to exorcise his front office of this intruder with her briefcase and her identification card.

Sonya walks around behind the reception desk, sticks her head in the office.

"Excuse me, sir."

"I no do something!"

"EXCUSE ME, SIR," Sonya shouts.

He looks up, files in his hands. "I show you tax returns! All tax returns done by accountant! I no do something! Anything wrong, is accountant fault!"

"Sir, please listen. The case I'm working has nothing to do with you."

"Not to do with me?" He stands there, tax files in his hands, looking at her like maybe she's going out of her way to lie to him.

"No, sir. Nothing at all. Would you please tell me your name?"

"I am Tran Van Minh."

"Thank you. Now, Mr. Minh, do you own this motel?"

The motel guy sets the files down, sits in his desk chair. "Not to do with me."

"Yes, sir, that's right. Now, can you tell me, do you own this motel?"

"I sorry. I had Internal Revenue in here, since four months. They very mean. They say they take motel away, I don't pay all withholding. I show them, I pay all withholding. Every penny. They want to know about Mexican maids."

"I'm sure that must have been very traumatic. So, this is your motel then?"

"Yes. I own motel."

"When did you acquire it?"

"Since five years about. I come to America since twenty-fo' years, from Vietnam. I work in shrimp business on coast ten years, then move up here. Get job in ice cream factory. Save all my money. Buy this motel, five years ago."

"Who did you buy it from?"

"I buy it from First State Bank, in town. They own it, put it up for auction. I highest bidder. They finance seventy-five percent, charge me prime plus two percent. Balloon note due in three mo' years. They say they refinance then. I not sure."

"Do you know who owned it before the bank did?"

"No. I not know that."

"Do you have your closing file?"

"Say again please?"

"The documents they gave you when you bought the motel. Do you have them?"

"Oh, yes. Yes, ma'am. They right here."

"May I see them?"

He opens another desk drawer, plunges in, holds up a file, got a big grin working, hands it over.

"Thank you." Sonya flips through the file, finds the abstract of title. "It says here that the bank acquired the subject property through foreclosure on March 16, 1993. The previous owner was . . ." She flips a page. "Here we go. The previous owner was Clay Johnson of Brenham, Texas. No other address."

She opens her briefcase, pulls out a legal pad, makes some notes, flips through the file some more, then hands it back to Mr. Minh.

"Mr. Minh," she says, "the case I'm working on involves certain, uh, activities that took place in room fifteen here at the Adobe over ten years ago. Could you show me that room please, sir?"

"Room fifteen."

"Yes, sir."

"Excuse me," he says.

He gets up, walks past Sonya to the reception desk, looks at a guest register.

"I have guest in that room. Mr. John Smith. This very popular American name."

Sonya thinks, *John Smith, come on, give me a break.*

"Well, if you don't mind, why don't you and I just walk around there and knock on the door and see if Mr. Smith would let us just have a look around the room some."

"Okay. If it that important."

"Yes, sir. It is."

They leave the reception area, head out the door into the heat and haze of the afternoon, turn right twice, walk down a sidewalk that runs the length of the motel's units. About halfway down, Mr. Minh stops at a door with a big number "15" on it, Ford pickup truck parked out front, one of the few occupied parking spaces back here where the rooms are.

He knocks, calls out, "Mr. Smith."

No answer.

Sonya says, "Try again."

He knocks harder, hollers, "Mr. Smith. Can you open door please?"

They hear someone moving around inside, then someone says, "Who is it?"

"It hotel manager, from front desk. Can you open door please?"

They hear the chain being worked, the door opens, and from behind it someone is saying, "This ain't a great time for a visit, I was just . . ."

The door opens, and Sonya says, "Good God."

Sheriff Dewey Sharpe stands in the doorway, nothing on but a towel wrapped around his substantial waist.

"Son of a bitch," he says.

And then he shuts the door.

28

SONYA STEPS UP, COMMENCES TO BANG ON THE DOOR. "SHERIFF SHARPE! OPEN up!"

Mr. Minh looks at her. "Why you say 'Sheriff Sharpe'?"

Sonya bangs on the door again. "Because that's his name. Come on, Sheriff! Open up! Let us in!"

"He not John Smith?"

Sonya looks at the motel guy, wonders how in the world he can have a son who's making straight A's in engineering at A&M. Kid must take after his mother.

"No, Mr. Minh. He is not John Smith. Do you have another key to this room?"

"Yes. I got other key."

"Go get it, would you please? If he doesn't let us in, we'll let ourselves in."

"But he can connect chain."

"What?"

"You know." He mimes a motion, like he's locking a chain latch.

"Oh, that. Well, I can kick in the door."

"No, no, no! Don't kick door. That tear up room."

"Just go get the key, okay?"

"Okay."

Mr. Minh heads back to the front office.

Sonya can see he is perplexed by the peculiar behavior of this American woman, exerting herself so on a hot Sunday afternoon, threatening to kick doors in. She goes back to banging on the door, breaking a sweat now, her blouse sticking to her in spots. She's thinking how she hates that feeling, sweat running down her face, rearranging her makeup, making her look like Picasso had painted it on her while he was half in the bag.

She reaches in her briefcase, fetches out a tissue to wipe her face with, get the sweat out of her eyes, wipe some of the mascara off her cheeks.

She's got half a mind to bust the sheriff's chops but good once she does get in there, retribution for locking her out here, forcing her to whale away at this door, make a spectacle of herself. She stashes her tissue in her jeans pocket, goes back to pounding.

"Come on, Sheriff. Open up!"

Directly she hears him fumbling with the chain latch—he had locked it, the little shit—then he swings the door open and yonder he stands wearing jeans and a golf shirt. He had even swiped at his hair with a comb although the part looks like an aerial view of a mountain road. Sonya is thinking that while he's not quite ready for his own spread in *GQ*, still it's a major improvement over his first appearance at the door, that cheap motel towel not quite making its way completely around his ample circumference.

That's a mental picture she's afraid she's going to be stuck with for a while.

Sonya nods at the sheriff, says, "I like this look on you better."

He says, "Well, dang it, I had just gotten out of the shower, didn't have time to get my drawers on before answerin' the door."

"My advice to you is always to wear as much clothes as possible, so as not to show the world any of your body. If you were to start going around with nothing but a towel on it might cause all kinds of problems. Motorists jumping curbs, dogs fainting—"

"Very funny. Now just what in the heck do you think you're doin', comin' around here, bangin' on folks' doors, makin' such a fuss?"

"I'm working the Sissy Fletcher case. What are *you* doing here, Sheriff?"

"I ain't sure it's any of your business."

"Would you rather I just draw my own conclusions?"

The sheriff scowls. "My wife and me had us a fallin' out is all. She indicated she thought it might be a good idea if we was to try separatin' for a while."

"What do you mean she 'indicated' that?"

"She threw my clothes out in the yard and locked me out of the house. So I collected my stuff and moved over here. Yesterday evening."

"Okay, but if that's all there is to it, why did you register under an alias?"

"It's a motel. Nobody uses their real name at a motel."

"They do if they don't have something to hide. Do you have something to hide, Sheriff? Other than your physique, I mean."

"Well, I'd just as lief the entire world didn't know Claudia had decorated our azalea bushes with my boxer shorts. But other than that I ain't."

"Why did you pick 'John Smith' of all things?"

"It was the only name what come to mind."

Sonya is wondering how Clyde can stand to work for this once and future truck salesman with his beer belly hanging off the front of him, his double-digit IQ.

"Have you been a long-time customer here at the Adobe, Sheriff? Have you used this motel a lot over the years by any chance?"

"Hell, no," he says. "This is the first time I even set foot in one of these rooms."

"You didn't maybe used to meet someone special over here from time to time? Someone whom you'd meet in this very room?"

"I ain't got any idea what you're talkin' about. I done told you this here's the first time I ever been in the place, and I never would have yet if my own wife hadn't locked me out of my own danged house."

Sonya's thinking he may be fat and disgusting and he may have a baloney sandwich where most people have a brain, but he doesn't sound like he's lying.

The sheriff says, "Now let me ask you somethin'."

"What?"

"What's the Fletcher case got to do with this here motel?"

"Why don't you invite me into your bachelor pad so I can cool off some and I'll tell you? Unless, that is, you're hiding something in there, 'Mr. Smith.'"

Dewey swings the door wide to let her walk through.

Sonya steps in, looks around. The room smells of cheap aftershave and cigar smoke.

It's a standard-issue rural American motel room, must be three hundred thousand just like it all coveyed up around every interstate and bypass in the U.S.A. You got a cheap table and two chairs next to the window, a double bed—unmade, of course—that takes up most of the square footage and that has a crater in the middle of it, like it had not been up to the task of supporting a certain overweight sheriff and had simply surrendered. There's a chest of drawers against the far wall that appears to have been designed and assembled by a team of chimpanzees wearing blindfolds. The television set over in the corner has a golf match on.

Scattered around, unceremoniously dumped on top of furniture and stuffed into drawers, hanging in the closet and the like, appear to be the wardrobe and other personal effects of Dewey Sharpe, sheriff of Washington County.

"*Très* Martha Stewart. You've got quite a flair for interior design, Sheriff," Sonya says. "You'll have to share your secret with me sometime."

"Very funny. I ain't had much chance to put this stuff away. Besides, I ain't plannin' to be here that long."

Sonya shifts her attention to the area around the bed. Track lighting hangs from the ceiling and there's a big mirror on the wall above the bed.

Dewey says, "You still ain't tol' me why you're here, how this place is connected to the Fletcher murder."

"Where's the light switch?" she says.

"Over here by the door. You want me to flip it on?"

"Please."

Dewey hits the lights. The track lighting stays dark.

Sonya points at the ceiling. "Have you had these on since you've moved in?"

"Naw. I don't think they work."

"Interesting. They would light this place up like a movie set if they did." She cranes her neck. "Hmmm. Hundred-watt bulbs. What do you make of this mirror?"

"Seems to be pretty strategically positioned, don't it?"

"You could say that."

Sonya goes to check it out, notes that it's not hanging. Instead it has been set flush with the wall itself, inside a big frame.

"You ain't answered my question yet," says Dewey, who's sounding cranky.

Sonya glances over at him, goes back to checking out the mirror. "Jeremiah Spur and I had a little chat with your buddy Joe Bob Cole yesterday."

"He ain't no buddy of mine."

"Whatever. His name has come up a couple times in the Fletcher case, so we decided to get him on record about a few things. Turns out he and Sissy were an item once, back when he was a deputy sheriff, which, by the way, would have been a disqualifying condition, in most law enforcement agencies, where his investigating her disappearance is concerned. But not, of course, in the Washington County Sheriff's Department. Anyway, turns out they used this very room for their illicit assignation."

"Their what?"

Sonya points downward at the bed.

"Oh. I get it. That Joe Bob Cole. He's a white trash piece of shit, ain't he?"

"You might say that. Anyhow, it appears that someone took a few photographs of Deputy Joe Bob and Miss Sissy during one of their little trysts, then delivered them to Mrs. Joe Bob, which caused his marriage to take the pipe. I don't know whether Mrs. Joe Bob took the intermediate step of turning her husband's wardrobe into yard art, as apparently Mrs. Sharpe did with you, or whether she went straight to filing papers."

"Claudia and me ain't gonna divorce. We just got a trial separation goin'."

"Whatever. All I know is, I came over here to check out the premises where all these things were going on, and I find you in this room, with the big mirror positioned above the bed and the landing strip lights in the ceiling, although I'll grant you the latter do not appear to be functioning at this time. Seems like quite a coincidence, doesn't it?"

Sonya pulls away from the mirror, looks at Dewey. "So, Sheriff, what has happened to undermine the marital bliss at the Sharpe residence?"

"None of your damn business. And we're gonna get it all straightened out, by the way. Just a little bit of a hitch in our get-along. Nothin' to get in a swivet about."

Sonya grins at him. "Like I said, I can draw my own conclusions. But you should think about the fact that there is such a thing as protesting too much."

"What's that supposed to mean?"

"Nothing. Forget it. You notice anything interesting about this mirror?"

Dewey looks at it. "Looks like a plain ol' mirror to me. It's a big 'un though."

"It's mounted into the wall."

"So what?"

"So I'd like to have a look at what's on the other side of this wall. Like I said, somebody photographed Joe Bob and Sissy doing their thing, which takes a lot of lights—"

She points at the track lighting.

"—and a spot where the photographer can hide."

She points at the mirror.

"So the logical next step is to take a look at what's on the other side of this wall."

There's a knock at the door, and they hear Mr. Minh say, "Hello. Hello?"

Sonya says, "Right on cue." She walks to the door, lets Mr. Minh in.

"Mr. Minh, I'd like you to meet Dewey Sharpe, sheriff of Washington County."

"You say you John Smith. But you not John Smith."

"Well—"

"You sheriff instead. Sheriff is like—"

Sonya says, "A sheriff is a kind of policeman, Mr. Minh."

Mr. Minh gets his stricken, I-no-do-something look, gives the impression that he's about to start hopping around again, doing his I'm-innocent-of-everything dance.

Sonya says, "Take it easy, Mr. Minh. He's not here on a case, are you, Sheriff?"

"No I ain't. I just needed me a place to stay for a couple days."

"Now, Mr. Minh," Sonya says. "I have a couple of questions for you. Do you mind?"

"I not mind."

"Good. First, tell me about these lights." She points at the ceiling.

"What about?"

"Have they been here ever since you owned the place?"

"Yes."

"How come they don't work?"

"Bulbs no good. They out."

"They're burned out?"

He nods.

"When did they burn out?"

"Always since I own Adobe."

"And you didn't replace them?"

"Not good idea to replace. Too much light. Electricity bill too high."

"Okay. Here's my next question. What's on the other side of this wall?" Sonya points to the wall with the mirror on it.

"Another room."

"Is there a guest in that one too?"

"No. Not today. It empty."

"Can you let us in there, please?"

"First I have to go get key."

Sonya can tell from the look on his face he's not happy about having to march back across the parking lot to the front office.

"That's fine," she says. "We'll wait here. And maybe if you have a master key, it would be a good idea to bring it with you this time."

As Mr. Minh slinks back out into the heat, Sonya is thinking his son must definitely take after the mother.

Since all the other boys are out on patrol, Clyde's got the squad room to himself except for Darlene working the dispatch booth way in the back. Clyde walks in, gives her a wave, she waves to him in return.

He walks over to his desk, sets down his half-finished can of Coca-Cola, sees the voice mail light on his phone flashing. The first message is from the fingerprint tech down at the DPS crime lab in Houston. The guy called sometime late Saturday.

"Hey, Clyde, this here's Russell Franks down in fingerprint analysis. I done that comparison you wanted of the prints in the Fletcher file against what you lifted off that duct tape from the liquor store job. I think you're gonna be real interested in the results. Give me a call, would you?" The guy says his phone number and Clyde writes it down.

Clyde saves that message, then goes to the other two, both of them being hangups from this afternoon, no message left.

Clyde dials up Franks, gets his machine, leaves a message for him to call back.

Clyde is thinking that now would be a good time to ease on back yonder to the file room, pull the departmental records, have a look at this Joe Bob Cole situation.

He lets himself into the file room, finds the file cabinet with the duty sheets from back in the Patterson days, all in chronological order. He pulls the file that says "Feb '89" on the label, heads back to his desk where he can sit down, sort it through.

Back at his desk now, he leafs through the file, finds the duty sheet for the eleventh, looks it over. It says Joe Bob Cole was on duty that night, pulled the late shift. Patrolling out in the northwest part of the county.

Out near Gay Hill.

Out where Clyde had found Sissy Fletcher's remains.

Clyde says, "That's what I'm talkin' about."

He's getting up to go back to the file room, get Joe Bob's personnel file, see if it's got his fingerprints in there like it's supposed to have, when his phone rings. He sits back down, picks up the receiver, hoping it's the Franks dude from down in Houston.

"Sheriff's Department, Deputy Thomas speakin'," he says.

"You Clyde Thomas?" says a voice he doesn't recognize.

"That's right. Who's this?"

"I'm a concerned citizen what has me some information relative to a recent armed robbery in which a couple folks died. You know the one I mean?"

"Yeah. What's your name?"

"I'd rather be 'nonymous, if it's all the same to you."

"What kind of information you got?"

"I don't want to tell it over the phone."

"Then what'd you call down here for, if you ain't gonna give me yo' name, and you ain't gonna give me this information you claim is so useful?" Clyde is thinking, *When is this cheap-ass outfit going to spring for caller ID?*

"I'm gonna give it to you, just not over the phone. You know where the Rose Emporium is at?"

"Yeah, sure."

"There's a split rail fence what surrounds the parkin' lot. In twenty min-utes I'm gonna staple an envelope with the information in it on the back of the third fence post from the gate. Now you give me until three o'clock, then you go down yonder and fetch that envelope. Don't come no sooner, on account of if I see your vehicle before three o'clock, I ain't leavin' the information behind."

"Okay. I'll be there at three o'clock."

The phone clicks and the line goes dead.

Clyde hangs up the phone, says to himself, "Sounds like a bullshit crank call to me, but I guess it don't do no harm to go out yonder, check it out, just on the off chance somethin' might come of it."

He gets up, goes back to the file room to fetch Joe Bob Cole's file, pull the fingerprint sheets, see what's up with the man.

Martin Fletcher hangs up the phone, looks at Dud. "I think he bought it," he says. He sees Dud's expression, says, "Now what's the matter?"

Dud says, "I don't know, Martin. I been thinkin' some about this, and I just ain't sure I see the sense in it is all. If we gonna blow the courthouse tomorrow afternoon and then be gone from here for good, you really think you need to put a bullet in that nigger deputy? Not that he don't have it comin', but it seems kind of risky."

"Why shouldn't we? There ain't no downside to it. Besides, there's more sense in it than you know. You ain't necessarily got the whole picture."

"I don't follow what you're sayin'."

Martin looks away, then back at Dud. "There's things I know what I can't tell you. There's reasons I got for gettin' rid of that boy that maybe go beyond the Uncle Freddie's thing."

"Such as?"

"Such as what Dr. Flatley said, 'bout him diggin' around in my sister's past where he don't belong. There ain't nothin' about her that him or you or me or anybody else needs to know. Beyond that I ain't gonna get into it."

"Did God tell you to pop that coon?"

Martin just looks at Dud.

Dud says, "Well, sometimes He tells you to do things, don't He?"

"That's between me and Him. And whether He did or not, we're gonna do it."

"It just seems risky to me. What if we was to get caught?"

"We ain't gonna get caught. Now that you bring it up, God ain't gonna let us get caught, because He's got work for us."

"You're sure about this."

"Yeah. I'm sure. I'll tell you somethin' else. I don't think too many folks around here would be upset if we was to wax that black sumbitch. I even got me a for instance."

"Let's hear it, then."

"His own boss is my for instance, Dewey what's-his-name. When I run into him yesterday, he said that nigger up and quit on him last week, called him a bunch of names he found offensive. What with an attitude like that, him sleepin' with a white woman and all, I bet even the sheriff hates his guts."

"You think so?"

"Now that I think of it, yeah, I'm pretty darned sure. There's a good chance that if we pop that boy, it ain't gonna create that much of a fuss."

"Okay then. I guess what we got to do is get ourselves out there, get you up in that deer blind with your rifle."

"I know a back way onto Earl's place. He won't even know we been there."

"Your rifle sighted in, partner? It's been almost six months since huntin' season."

Martin looks at him and says, "What do *you* think? Let's go."

He reaches in the corner where he'd leaned the Remington up, careful not to bump the scope, grabs it, shoves a box of shells in the hip pocket of his jeans.

They walk out into the yard, get into Dud's pickup.

29

THEY OPEN THE DOOR TO ROOM THIRTEEN AND WALK IN ONE AT A TIME, MR. Minh leading the way, flipping the lights on, pulling the curtains back, turning on the AC.

This room smells to Sonya of mildew and disinfectant, and she thinks about all the people who have passed through here on their way from one place to another. She turns away from the thought before it can cost her her mood. She says, "Besides having an unlucky number, room thirteen doesn't come with all the options."

"They ain't got the overhead lights in here they got over yonder," Dewey says.

"Nor is there a mirror that takes up half the wall," says Sonya.

"Other than that though, my room and this 'un are just two peas in a pod."

"I'm not so sure about that," says Sonya. "This one seems smaller to me."

She walks over, stands with her back to the wall the bed is up against, paces off from there to the door, goes back to the wall, paces off to the opposite wall. Then she goes outside, does more pacing, goes in room fifteen, paces off inside there some.

She comes back to room thirteen, pulls a legal pad from her briefcase, sketches on it.

"Check this out," she says. "It's about twenty-two feet from this wall to the near wall of room fifteen, but this room is only about nineteen feet wide. So there's a three-foot gap between the far wall in this room and the near wall in room fifteen Mr. Minh?"

"Yes?"

"Do you know what's between this room and room fifteen?"

The look on his face tells her all she needs to know.

"Whatever it is, it's news to you, I gather. Sheriff, let's see if there's some kind of access through this wall to the space between the two rooms. Give me a hand with that chest of drawers."

They each grab an end of the bureau, lifting the cheap little thing with ease. They set it aside, start checking along the wall's surface, feeling along it, looking for some clue as to how a person would access the space between the walls.

Sonya says, "This is kind of fun. I feel a little like Nancy Drew, looking for a secret passage in an old mansion."

Dewey says, "I feel a little like Helen Keller, looking for the bathroom."

"You know, Dewey, you're pretty much the exact opposite of Helen Keller."

"How's that?"

"Well, she was a woman, and you're a man."

"I follow you so far."

"And she could neither see, nor hear."

"And I can do both them things."

"And she had enormous brains and courage."

Dewey looks at Sonya like she had suddenly started speaking to him in Swahili. He says, "I ain't sure I get the Helen Keller thing."

Sonya stops working the wall and looks at him with her hands on her hips. "It's like this, Dewey. While you are a man who has possession of all his senses, you are also a man of untremendous brains and courage. Now, just keep looking for the secret passageway. Pretend you're Nancy Drew's helper leading a meaningful life doing useful things instead of a dismissable peckerwood sheriff stuck in the middle of nowhere."

Dewey runs his hands along the lower half of the wall. "You shouldn't go around insulting folks like that. It ain't polite. Hey! I think I found me somethin' here."

Sonya moves over, runs her hands over the spot he points out, a long crease in the wall under the wallpaper running parallel to the ground, about three feet from the floor. She runs her thumbs along the crease in both directions until it turns downward.

"Very good, Sheriff. Nancy is pleased. She might keep you around after all. And now, for extra credit, do you by any chance have a pocketknife?"

Dewey reaches in his pocket.

"Great. Why don't you further demonstrate your manhood by taking that pocketknife and slicing this elegant wallpaper along this lovely little crease?"

Mr. Minh says, "You tearing up room!"

Sonya says, "Relax, Mr. Minh. The county will pay to have this room repapered for you. You may have to reconcile yourself to a change in the pattern though. I expect it will be difficult to find this particular look anywhere west of the Iron Curtain."

Dewey starts slicing the wallpaper along the seam line first horizontally, then vertically, defining a patch about three feet square.

"Talk not enough. I need writing. You write down."

"I'll fax you a letter tomorrow."

Dewey finishes cutting, starts pulling the paper free.

He stands back, says, "Looks like this part of the wall done been built with particleboard or somethin', instead of sheet rock. What do you make of it?"

Sonya leans down, studies it, says, "Here's our access point. It's nailed in place."

"No fax tomorrow. I need writing today."

"Tell you what, Mr. Minh, if you would please try to scare us up a claw hammer, in the meantime I'll write out a letter in longhand for you. Is that a deal?"

"You give letter today?"

"Yes. Now be a dear and go find us a hammer, would you please?"

Jeremiah pulls his pickup into the hospital garage, lands it, kills the engine.

Martha says, "Leave the gun here, please."

Jeremiah hesitates, then takes off his coat, shucks out of his shoulder holster, stores the Colt behind the driver's seat.

"Thank you," says Martha.

Jeremiah gets out, closes the door to the cab, glances back in the truck bed where Martha's bags sit next to Duke, who is looking up at him.

Jeremiah says to Duke, "You keep an eye on them bags, you hear?"

Duke wags his tail, puts his head down on his paws.

Jeremiah and Martha catch the garage elevators down to the crosswalk that leads to the big tower where the cancer patients are kept, not a word passing between them. Jeremiah is thinking he would like to come up with something to talk about that didn't sound like he had come up with it just for the sake of having something to talk about.

He doesn't know what to expect from this abrupt ending of the years of estrangement between his wife and daughter, a separation that had its roots way back in the same time when somebody had caved in Sissy Fletcher's skull, then planted her remains in a pasture.

As they wait for the elevator to take them upstairs to Elizabeth's floor, Jeremiah turning his Stetson around and around in his hands, he imagines how the scene might unfold. He says, "You best better be prepared for a couple things."

The elevator door opens and lets them in.

"Such as?"

"Well, Amanda's gonna be there, for one."

"I figured as much."

"And Elizabeth, well, she looks—"

"Like she's dying of cancer? I don't expect her to look like she did when she barrel-raced, Jeremiah. I can imagine she looks pretty awful."

The elevator deposits them on Elizabeth's floor.

Jeremiah looks at Martha, says, "Imaginin' is one thing, seein' is somethin' else."

As they reach Elizabeth's room, the door opens. A little Indian guy in a white lab coat walks out, followed close behind by Amanda. She pulls the door shut behind her.

Jeremiah goes to Amanda, gives her a hug, steps back, and says, "Amanda Porter, I'd like you to meet Elizabeth's mother, Martha Spur."

Amanda holds out a hand, says, "Pleased to meet you, Mrs. Spur."

Martha hesitates for a heartbeat, then takes Amanda's hand, reaches with her other hand around Amanda's back, gives her a little squeeze.

They let go of one another, and Amanda says, "This is Dr. Guru Sandararaman. We call him Dr. Guru, for reasons that are probably obvious. And this is Jeremiah and Martha Spur."

They shake hands.

"Are you her doctor?" Martha says.

"No, ma'am," Dr. Guru says back. "I am just on duty today. We have had kind of a rough morning. She's been in considerable pain. There's not a whole lot we can do for her at this point, I'm afraid. I'm very sorry."

Amanda's eyes well up. "They say we don't . . . ." She falters, starts to dab at her eyes with a tissue.

Martha hugs her again. She turns to Dr. Guru, says, "May we go in now?"

He hesitates, sees the look on Jeremiah's face, says, "I guess so. But she's on some pretty powerful painkillers, and is only lucid at intervals. She sleeps a lot, which, frankly, is a good thing. So, please, don't get your hopes too high."

Martha puts her arm around Amanda. Together they push through the door, Jeremiah following behind, turning his Stetson in his hands, feeling awkward, out of place. He tells himself to be tough-minded.

Dewey takes the hammer from Mr. Minh, goes to work on the particleboard, having to put some effort into it to back the nails out, effort that causes him to grunt, causes his pants to slide down, giving Sonya yet another regrettable image for storage in her memory banks.

Sonya tries to ignore the sheriff's assault on the wall and its collateral effects and concentrate on writing out the county's promise to repair anything she and the sheriff damage. She signs it, hands it over to Mr. Minh.

"Here you go," she says. "There's my phone number at the bottom. All you have to do is get three estimates and call my office for approval."

Mr. Minh takes the paper, squints at it, looks back at her. "You pay in advance?"

"Just submit the invoices to us, and we'll cut the check to the contractors."

It takes Dewey ten minutes to get four nails backed out, but for all his grunting and display of butt crack he can't seem to get the one down at the bottom right loose.

"Dang it," he says. "Nailhead's buried. I can't get a purchase on it."

"Let me take a look," says Sonya, happy to have him back off for a minute.

Dewey stands up and she kneels down, examines the situation.

"Let me have that hammer a second."

She takes the hammer, works the claw between the particleboard and the sheet rock, then leans into the wall at the stud. The board and the nail start to back out together. She taps on the board around the nail head, gets enough of it exposed to slip the claw under it, then pulls it loose.

The board falls against her knees. She picks it up, hands it to Dewey.

She bends down, cranes her neck inside the wall.

"There's a passageway here all right. And we got some light coming into it from somewhere. I think I can just wiggle through here. I'm gonna go have a look."

She starts crawling through the hole.

Dewey says, "I'd like to join you but I don't think my butt is gonna fit."

She says, "Not in a hundred years."

"What?"

"Never mind."

She finds enough space between the walls to crawl through, stand up in. She moves along the wall to the light source.

The mirror into room fifteen is a one-way. She can see everything in room fifteen just as plain as day. "Candid Camera comes to Brenham, Texas."

They stand next to the hospital bed, looking down at Elizabeth while she sleeps.

"Sweet Jesus," says Martha.

She turns to Jeremiah, slumping into him, gripping his arm hard. He puts his arm around her, gives her some support, pats her gently, waits for her to commence crying.

But Martha doesn't cry.

She whispers, "She looks so old, so gaunt. More like a ghost of a woman than a woman. The cancer has made her a ghost already, even while she's still alive."

He had tried to warn her. He had known it was going to be a shock, a sight completely at war with Martha's memories of Elizabeth. But Jeremiah has to admit, his daughter looks a lot worse than she did even yesterday.

Jeremiah asks himself whether the interview Sonya conducted was too hard on Elizabeth, how much energy it had cost her, whether it had contributed to the pain she had been fighting today, made it worse. He wonders whether he should have stepped in, told the sheriff they'd take Elizabeth's statement over his dead body, forced them to get a court order, fought even that in hopes that he could stall it past . . .

He wonders if that's what a father who wasn't a cop would have done.

Maybe there's such a thing as being too tough-minded.

Martha has been quiet a long time. He thinks maybe this is too much for everybody.

"Maybe we'd best better go back out into the hall," he whispers to Amanda.

"No, please, let's don't," says Martha, looking up at him. "We've spent too much time apart, and that is mostly my fault. I'll have to live with that for the rest of my life. But right now I want every minute with her I can get, even if it's just watching her sleep."

She stares at Elizabeth for a while, then says, "I wonder if God is looking down on this little room right now. I wonder if He can find anything in it to be proud of."

Amanda says, "He can be proud of you. Of your coming to see Elizabeth."

Martha looks at Amanda, smiles a sad smile. "Please, child. I think He knows me better than that. But maybe I'm asking the wrong question anyway."

"How's that?" says Amanda.

"Maybe God doesn't feel pride when He looks down at all He's done. Maybe He just watches to see what happens. Like the ant farm Elizabeth used to have when she was a little girl. We put it together, put the ants in it, then we set it on a shelf so we could watch what happened. Sometimes it was interesting, lots of times it was boring. But we never felt it was anything to be proud about."

They stand there in silence for a while, looking down at Elizabeth, Amanda off a little to one side, working a tissue around her eyes.

Elizabeth's eyes commence to flutter, then they open. She looks right at the two of them, her mother and father.

Then she smiles and says, "Hi, Mama."

30

MARTIN FLETCHER LOOKS THROUGH BINOCULARS OUT THE WINDOW THAT HAS been cut in the side of the deer stand. It's a window with no glass so that a man can stick his rifle barrel through it, shoot a deer if one chances across the *sendero* down below.

"I hadn't figgered on this danged hazy air makin' the visibility so poor," he says to Dud. "I can't hardly make out the parkin' lot through all this crud."

"Let me have a look."

Dud slides his stool over. Martin hands him the field glasses.

"You ain't kiddin'," Dud says. "You reckon you can see good enough to shoot?"

"I ain't entirely sure." Martin lifts the rifle, sticks the barrel out the window, sights through the scope, left eye closed, right eye squinting. Off in the distance he can just make out people moving around in the parking lot.

Martin says, "It's gonna be close. I'm gonna need to try to catch him over there by the fence, standing by hisself. I don't want to send a slug whistlin' into some old boy what just come out here to enjoy the rose-bushes on a Sunday afternoon."

He pulls the rifle back inside, settles back on his stool, scratches his beard while he looks at the brush-covered country all around, the mesquite, scrub oak, prickly pear that provide cover for the game that had made this such a productive stand for old Earl.

Two long twenty-yard-wide alleys, called *senderos,* have been cut through the brush at right angles to one another. This deer blind sits at their junction.

"We all set now, ain't we?" Dud says. "Now that we got the panel truck and the fifty-five-gallon drums, got the detonator and the ANFO."

"Yep. Now all we got to do is go do it."

"How you figger to go about it?"

Martin leans back in his stool, takes his hat off, wipes his brow with his shirtsleeve, scratches at his beard. "We'll leave the house around five o'clock, say, with me leadin' in the panel truck and you followin'. You'll park over in the bank parkin' lot. I'll jump the curb with the panel truck, get it as close as I can to the courthouse, get out and run like blue blazes back to where you're at. That's where I'll trigger the bomb from. Then we'll drive down thirty-six until we get to I-ten and head west. The important thing is to stay under the speed limit, so the cops don't have no probability cause to stop us."

"No what?"

"Probability cause. I read about it on one of the militia sites on the Internet. The cops got to have a reason to pull you over, search your vehicle without your consent. If you just drivin' along, obeyin' the traffic laws, they ain't got that."

Dud scratches under his John Deere cap for a while. Then he says, "Martin?"

"Yeah."

"I ain't sure it's such a good idea to head straight down to I-ten once we blow the courthouse. Shouldn't we maybe think about takin' the back roads for at least the first couple hours, 'til it gets dark?"

Martin studies on that suggestion for a spell. "That might not be a bad idea."

"How long you figger it'll take us to get to Alpine?"

"It's about six hundred miles I reckon. We oughta be there by Tuesday mornin'."

"You know anybody out there we can contact?"

"Naw. I figger to get out there, do a little askin' around. If we start askin' the right kind of questions, they're bound to find us, instead of the other way around."

Dud takes the binoculars, looks through the window again. "Hey, Martin! I think he just pulled in!"

Martin looks at his watch. "Man, this guy is some kind of punctual. You go on down the ladder, get the truck started, so we'll be ready to make a run for it once I done finished off this son of a buck."

"Okay, partner. Good luck."

As Martin lifts the rifle to his shoulder Dud backs out of the blind.

Clyde pulls the cruiser into the parking lot, starts trying to find a place to land it.

"Look at this shit," he says to himself. "This here lot be about full, man. Lots of flower-lovin' sons of bitches out and about today."

Beyond the parking lot are the flower beds and gardens and such that give the Rose Emporium its name, filled with folks wandering around, staring at the various plant species that grow and bloom in the place.

Clyde takes two turns around the lot, finds somebody loading kids into a minivan. He positions the cruiser so he can slide in their place once they leave.

While driving out here he'd about decided that this whole anonymous caller thing was a bullshit waste of time. He'd given serious thought to just blowing off this trip to the Rose What-ya-ma-call-it, thinking his time would be better spent going and printing up Joe Bob, since sure enough there wasn't a fingerprint record in the man's personnel file like there was supposed to be. He was beginning to have a hunch that that racist dude might have eighty-sixed the Fletcher girl.

That had set Clyde to daydreaming about what it would feel like to get that collar, bust that big honky's ass for murder one. It'd probably get him interviewed by TV stations from Houston to Austin, might even make the East Coast papers.

Former cop busted for ten-year-old murder by up-and-coming Sheriff's Deputy C. Livermore "Clyde" Thomas of Brenham, Texas.

That would make his mama proud, make him a star the next time he goes back to Oak Cliff for a visit in the old neighborhood.

But in the end he'd decided to ride on out here, check out this business of the tip even though he suspects it's bogus. He figures he can roust Joe Bob later on, still solve the Fletcher case, have time to make it over to Sonya's for dinner and maybe some fooling around.

Then do the TV interviews tomorrow.

Clyde parks the cruiser, gets out.

Martin watches the cruiser through the field glasses, following it as it circles the lot, then parks.

Even with the binoculars at high power, Martin can barely see the deputy's Stetson once he stands up out of the car, the big cop all but obscured by haze. Martin can just make out the upper part of him, the part that's taller than the parked cars, from about the middle of his chest up.

Martin feels a little strange watching that man over yonder, standing now between a line of parked cars, looking around. Watching the last seconds of the man's life tick away, Martin knowing he'll be dead on the ground in less than ten minutes.

His heart starts racing like it never has before, not even on his Colorado elk hunt. He tells himself, stay calm, breathe slow, don't get the nervous high strikes or else your aim will be poor for sure.

He tries to concentrate, tries to imagine how it's going to play out, figures that if the cop does what Martin told him to do, he'll make his way to the front part of the parking lot, look for the fence post, bend over, not find anything, then straighten back up.

That's when I'll have my best chance, he says to himself. *I'll have me a fairly clear shot with that cop standing off by himself trying to decide if he misunderstood what I told him over the phone.*

He puts down the binoculars, shoulders the rifle, rests it on the windowsill, finds the deputy in the scope, sets the crosshairs on the impressionistic blur that is the big black man.

It's too far for a head shot. Martin figures the bullet's going to drop about a foot down here at almost sea level, given this humidity and the smoke all around. If he aims right below the man's Stetson, the slug will fall just enough to hit him in the chest.

Martin knows that will get the job done. He has seen what a thirty-aught-six slug does to an animal.

His heart is pounding hard, and the sweat has begun to run down his face. He squints through the scope, clicks off the safety, slides his finger onto the trigger.

Clyde walks to the front of the parking lot, counts off fence posts, goes to the third one, bends over, looks at it.

There's nothing there.

"That about fuckin' figures," he says. He goes to straighten up, then stops, his attention drawn to some dust he's picked up on his trouser leg, probably off one of the cars he had walked past. He leans over to brush himself off, trying to maintain the respectability of his appearance. While he's still brushing he turns, starts back toward his cruiser, in a hurry now to get out of here, get back to the office, grab a fingerprint kit, go find this Joe Bob dude, solve the Fletcher case, make a name for himself.

Martin watches the deputy through the scope as he bends over, starts to straighten back up, Martin's finger adding some pressure to the trigger now.

Then the big cop bends back down again. Martin loses him out of the scope, relaxes his trigger finger, moves the scope around gently, finally finds his target again.

"Dang it," Martin says to himself. "He's movin' too fast."

Martin tracks the deputy in his scope, furiously figuring the right amount of lead and where to place the crosshairs. His heart is going *ba-BOOM, ba-BOOM* in his ears.

He gets it set where he thinks it's right and tells himself, *Now. Do it now!* He squeezes the trigger slowly.

The rifle fires and kicks, the report loud inside the deer blind, setting Martin's ears to ringing. He levels the weapon again, looks through the scope to see if the Messenger of the Lord got the lead and the drop right.

31

JEREMIAH LEANS AGAINST THE WALL OF HIS DYING DAUGHTER'S HOSPITAL room, turning his Stetson around in his hands, studying the floor some, every once in a while looking out the window at the smoke hanging thick over Rice University, its orange tile roofs just barely visible. And from time to time he looks across the hospital room itself, watching the three women talking among themselves, paying him no mind.

Elizabeth is carrying her share of the conversation and then some, talking up a storm until she gets too winded to go any further, only then leaving it for Amanda or Martha to pick it up.

The first few minutes had been slow, awkward, the overburden of the past acting as a drag on the present, tying their tongues up a bit, producing silences that had tension built into them, the tension of not knowing how they would end. If they would end.

But then Elizabeth had said something about how nice it was to have them all there, but if she'd of known she was going to be hosting a family reunion today she would have gotten somebody to wheel her over to the hairdresser. That little spot of humor, lost on Jeremiah though it was, is what broke the ice, got them talking, feeling so much more comfortable with one another that you could actually see it.

Now Martha sits and holds Elizabeth's one skeletal hand in her two older hands, hands made rough from years of ranch life. Martha tells her news about kinfolks and other folks who aren't kin, who Elizabeth knew from school or from around town.

Elizabeth tells about San Francisco, about how she had met Amanda working as a volunteer in an emergency call center after the 1989 earthquake. How they had rented an apartment in an old "painted lady" over near the Marina. How they would sit in the evenings, watch the fog roll in off the ocean, fog like you never see in Texas. How she could hear the foghorn at night such that it would work its way into her dreams and wake her up early and she would get up and go down before dawn to run along the Bay where she could see the beacon rotating on top of Alcatraz.

How it reminded her of her papa, that beacon, on account of it was a light off all by itself. She looks over at him as she says it, and it causes him to turn the Stetson in his hands and look out the window at the smoke that is so unlike the fog of San Francisco.

Elizabeth tells how she and Amanda had loved to cross the bridge over into Marin County, to go for walks up in the Muir Woods, with the great redwood trees like the columns of a Gothic cathedral, their limbs like great fan arches, placed there by God, she thought, so that He would have something beautiful and eternal to support the sky.

Amanda sits on the other side of the bed, spoons ice chips, smiles through the profusion of face jewelry that makes her look like a member of some strange tribe of white Africans.

Jeremiah wonders if Elizabeth's story about her ride in Sissy Fletcher's pickup was known to Martha, whether Elizabeth had ever told her mother about the night of the dance. Jeremiah speculates that might explain a lot if she did. It might explain how a distance had grown between them. The way Elizabeth left home and whatnot.

It might explain the way Martha bristled when the Sissy Fletcher thing came up, how she reacted to his getting involved. However much his wife had known, she had never let on about it to Jeremiah.

But if the events of the night of the dance had indeed ever come between them, those are ghosts that don't seem to be haunting them now as they visit together.

It's a sight Jeremiah had never thought he would live to see, and yet yonder it is. So he leans up against the wall and marvels at it, hat rotating slowly in his big hands, looking at the floor, out the window, at the womenfolk chattering away.

Making sure he's got this one picture in his head for all time. Making it a part of his inescapable antecedents.

Too soon Jeremiah can tell Elizabeth is wearing thin from the effort. Looking at her now, making himself look at her and see the condition she's in, Jeremiah has to acknowledge another miracle. He has to acknowledge that it's a miracle she hasn't passed away yet.

He figures he's the one to do it, so he straightens himself up off the wall, walks over, puts a hand on Martha's shoulder, says to her, "Maybe we ought to give her a chance to rest up a bit while I run you over to the hotel, get you checked in."

Martha looks up, nods okay, leans over to kiss Elizabeth on the cheek, pat Amanda on the hand. "We'll be back in a while," she says.

———

George Barnett sits alone in the darkness of his family room.

He's saying into the phone, "I don't have the foggiest fucking idea where they heard about you and Sissy Fletcher. They sure as shit didn't hear it from me."

"Well," Joe Bob Cole says from the other end of the line, "they heard it from somebody. And they're closin' in on some stuff what's been buried for a hell of a long time, is the sense I get of it."

George chews his cigar, spits some flecks of tobacco on the floor for the maid to get. "They've come a long ways in just a couple days."

"Thanks to Jeremiah Spur."

"You got that right, m'boy. I never would have believed he would have let himself get all tangled up in this. I wonder how come him to get involved."

"Beats me. But he's in it up to his eyeballs now."

"I figured we could stop worryin' about all this once that nigger quit. I figured Dewey would flounder around, not get much of anywhere, case would pretty much stay unsolved. But it doesn't look like it's going to turn out that way now, does it?"

"No, sir."

They're silent for a while, George preoccupied with thought, working his cigar back and forth in his mouth.

At length he says, "Thanks for the report, m'boy. Let me know if you hear anything else, okay?"

"Okay, George."

Leroy Jones walks through the front door of the Christian Service Community Center, looks around at the racks with clothes on them, tries to think where to start.

A middle-aged white lady comes up to him, wearing a nice outfit, a kind smile.

"May I help you, sir?" she says.

Leroy says, "Yes, ma'am. I'se just here to see about gettin' a new pair of pants I can mop flo's in. Just landed me a job on a janitorial crew over at A&M, gonna start work tomorrow. They says I needs to wear khakis."

"Good for you," the white lady says. "Do you know your size?"

"No, ma'am. Can't say as I do."

"Let's just measure you then."

She produces a tape measure, checks Leroy's waist and his inseam while he holds his arms up like he's fixing to start flapping them and take wing.

"You're a thirty-two waist, thirty-six length. Let's look over here."

She leads him to a rack of trousers, pushes a few around, reaches in, pulls out some khakis. "How about these?" she says.

Leroy holds them up to his legs. "They look like they'll do. What do they cost?"

"Oh," she says, "they're free. Folks donate us their secondhand clothes, and we give them away to people in need."

"That's mighty nice of y'all," says Leroy, looking around. "This a nice place you got here. Let me asks you somethin', I mean, since I'm already here and everything."

"What's that?"

"My mama, she live up in Chicago, and I go see her every Christmas. Now, I ain't got the clothes for a Chicago winter, you know? I don't suppose you got somethin' would keep me from freezin' half to death when I goes up yonder, do you?"

"As a matter of fact," the white lady says, "we got a coat in here just the other day that might do the trick."

She leads Leroy to the back of the shop.

"We got it in so recently," she says, "that we haven't even had a chance to set it out yet. Not that many folks are going to be looking for a coat like this here in Brenham, especially this time of year."

She goes behind the counter, disappears into a back room. Directly she reappears, holding a navy-blue overcoat, and hands it to Leroy.

"Would you like to try it on?"

"Yes, ma'am."

Leroy shrugs on the coat, says, "It fit pretty good."

The white lady says, "Why don't you just take it then? It'll keep that cold Lake Michigan wind off you."

Leroy smiles, says, "No, ma'am. Chicago be in Illinois."

"I know. But the lake it's on is called Lake Michigan. I have a nephew who goes to school up there."

"Is that a fact? Well, I guess it don't much matter what the lake's name is, long as I got somethin' like this here coat on, keep me warm from the wind. Ain't that right?"

"I suppose so."

"Okay, I'm all set then. I 'preciate it."

Leroy walks out of the shop, turns left, takes another left at the corner, starts the slow walk two blocks down to where the tall dude with the head of white hair and the big smile waits in his car with fifty bucks to buy this old coat from him.

A coat the white dude had put him up to going and asking for, even giving him that jive story to tell, about having a job over at A&M, about his mama being in Chicago.

Shit, Leroy thinks, *I do yards for a living and my mama, she lives down in Houston, shacked up in the Fifth Ward with some dude, works over at the Ship Channel.*

As if Leroy would ever need any such kind of a coat.

But Leroy knows he can use fifty dollars. There's a lot of ways he can use that.

Leroy is thinking, *That's what I call easy money.*

Jeremiah carries Martha's suitcase into the hotel room, sets it down on the floor.

"Where you want it?" he says.

"Just put it on the bed. I'm going to visit the ladies' room."

"Alright then."

Jeremiah heaves the suitcase on the bed and goes to the phone while he's got the chance. He dials Sonya's cell phone number.

On the other end, she answers it.

"Just checkin' in," says Jeremiah.

"The sheriff and I just finished talking to Mrs. Baker."

"You and Dewey?"

"Yeah. I ran into him over at the Adobe, so he tagged along."

"Mrs. Baker know anything about Sissy?"

"Nothing to speak of. Just said she'd always been real sweet, real nice to her Charlie. I don't think it amounts to anything. But we hit pay dirt over at the Adobe."

She tells him about room fifteen with the one-way mirror, track lighting, the little room next to it where someone could stand and watch what was going on without being seen themselves.

Jeremiah says, "What did the owner allow about all that?"

"I don't think he had any idea about any of it before we showed up. He's only owned the place four or five years. Bought it from the bank at a foreclosure auction."

"The bank had foreclosed it, huh?"

"That's right. Before that it belonged to a Clay Johnson."

"I know Clay Johnson. Or I used to. He's dead now."

"That's too bad."

"His son's alive though."

"What's his name?"

"Greg Johnson."

"The same Greg Johnson Sissy was living with when she disappeared?"

"That's the one."

"He's a veterinarian, right?"

"That. And something else."

"What's that?"

"A professional photographer."

"When do you want to go see him?"

"This afternoon. When I get back. Let's meet at the courthouse at around four o'clock. We can go on over from there."

As Jeremiah hangs up the phone, Martha is coming out of the bathroom. "You need any help unpackin'?" he says.

"No. I can get it. Let me get that out of the way, then after you carry me back over to the hospital you can go on home. I know you're itching to get back to that Sissy Fletcher mess, even though you ought to spend the evening here with us."

Jeremiah starts to say something, then thinks better of it.

3 2

CLYDE STOPS. HE WAS JUST ABOUT TO SQUEEZE BETWEEN TWO PARKED CARS SO as to get back to his cruiser over there in the second line of cars. But he thinks, that would be a mistake, now wouldn't it, trying to go between these two cars parked so close together here. If he does that he's going to get his pants filthy again for sure, seeing as how both cars are just covered in dust and there isn't room enough to walk between them without brushing up against them.

He decides to go around the outside of this line of cars, come up on the cruiser from behind, from the other direction.

He walks around behind the end car, then turns back to his left and just at that moment, up close, the air makes a noise that sounds like *whhhit!* Three cars to his left, a back window glass explodes.

The next instant, way over to the right somewhere, Clyde hears a loud *crack!*

Clyde crouches down fast, knees just above the ground, says, "The fuck?"

Martin Fletcher's heart is going *ba-BOOM, ba-BOOM* in his ears, like distant tom-toms. He's searching the parking lot through his scope, looking for a body twitching on the ground or better yet lying totally still.

He can't see anything.

Dud hollers up from down below, "Did ya git him?"

Martin hollers back, "I'm just now lookin' to see."

He works the scope slow, squinting into it, straining to see through the haze.

There! He finds the big black guy, crouched over next to a car, farther to his left than he'd expected to find him. Martin is thinking he must have missed him, winged him at best. He lays the crosshairs along the guy's shoulders, relaxes his grip on the rifle stock, steadies his breathing.

The guy is starting to move again, low along the ground, making it hard for Martin to track him with the scope.

Martin draws his bead and squeezes the trigger again.

Clyde is thinking that loud *crack!*—that was a gunshot, from back to the east, the bullet busting out a car window over to the left.

He thinks, *Some fool deer hunter done cut loose with a shot at Bambi, slug strayed over here to where the flowers are.* Then he says out loud, "Shit, huntin' season is in the wintertime. This be a setup, man. Some motherfucker is tryin' to shoot my ass."

He stands up a little bit, tries to see back in the direction the shot came from. Just some woods and shit. Maybe the shooter is out there, hiding behind a tree.

Then he thinks whoever fired that round might be getting ready to squeeze off another shot over this way and here he is, exposed out here in the open, on the outside of this line of parked cars, nothing between him and those woods except a split rail fence.

Staying low, he reverses direction, moving fast, trying to get around and behind the car next to him, wanting to get that car between him and the shooter. He takes a couple steps.

The air goes *whhhit!*, a slug slams into the car just behind him, the rifle goes *crack!* somewhere off in the distance.

Clyde hits the deck, rolls a couple times, not worrying about keeping his pants clean now, gravel from the parking lot biting into his knees and hands.

On his feet now, he grabs his Stetson from off the ground, starts moving fast, staying low. He scrambles to the other side of the end car in the line, then lunges between two cars, the same two he'd decided not to walk between fifteen seconds ago.

Now he's got cover. He's out of the line of fire. He pauses to get his breath, jam his hat back on his head, thinking he needs to get in his cruiser, get out of here before the shooter plugs him, or drops some flower-sniffing bystander by mistake.

Martin searches the parking lot through the rifle scope, studying it, looking for a body, a pool of blood, anything that would tell him the second shot had bull's-eyed. He sees nothing to indicate he hit the man.

He tells himself he must have missed both times.

Martin thinks, *If it hadn't of been for all this smoke, it would have been an easy shot, the guy would be on the ground right now, well into his death rattle, maybe dead already, the devil carting his soul off to hell, using it for kindling.* He's thinking this poor air quality just makes it too hard for a man to see his target good enough to bust it.

Figuring he's got one last chance, he finds the cruiser in the parking lot.

All he can see of it is the top, the emergency lights, a bit of the roof. He puts the crosshairs on that part of the roof just above the driver's side, slows his breathing. Waits.

Clyde crawls over to the cruiser, leans up against the door on the driver's side. Tells himself to focus, think hard, think it through.

The cruiser's pointed south toward the highway, away from the gardens. If he gets in the cruiser and backs out, he would be exposed to the shooter, who is somewhere back to the east, the direction Clyde's facing now. When he shifts from reverse to drive, the car would be stopped for just a second or two, with Clyde profiled in the driver's seat.

That's got to be what Mr. Rifleman, who's missed him twice now, is counting on.

But he can't just stay trapped here. A hundred yards away are the gardens, full of civilians. Some of them will be leaving soon. They are all in danger as long as Clyde is hiding like some kind of fugitive here between the cars. It's a miracle nobody's been shot yet. The whack job out there with the rifle, he might decide to start plugging lawn and garden fans out of frustration.

Besides, Clyde's starting to get pissed off now. A minute or two ago, he might have been a little excited, maybe even a bit scared. He hasn't ever been shot at before. It's a scary kind of thing.

But he isn't really scared now, more just irate, righteous irate.

He needs to seize the initiative somehow, mess with Mr. Rifleman's plans. And he needs to be quick about it.

Martin sees the cruiser's door open. He thinks, *Now all I got to do is wait until that spade backs it out. When he stops to shift gears, I'll plug him, then vamoose.*

He stills his breathing, rests his finger lightly on the trigger, waits.

His eyes are starting to get dry from staring through the scope. He blinks a couple times, trying to get the moisture back in them.

Five minutes go dragging by. Martin shifts on his stool, trying to keep himself comfortable, relaxed, ready, all at the same time. He thinks, *The guy's trying to get me to let my guard down, get my attention to wander. He's probably going to back out fast, not give me much chance to draw a bead.*

Five more minutes go by and Martin spends them staring and blinking, shifting around as little as possible, afraid to take his eyes off the roof of that cop car, worried that in the time it takes to get his target sighted back in, the guy will back out and leave, ruin his chances. He blinks hard against the dryness in his eyes.

Then he hears something, way off in the distance.

Sirens. Cop cars. They're getting closer fast.

He tears his eyes away from the parking lot to look out into the distance and now he can see them out yonder on the highway that fronts the Rose Emporium, going flat out, their lights flashing.

The guy had used his radio, called in backup.

Two, three, now four cruisers, county, highway patrol both, converging on the Rose Emporium, bombing down the highway.

Martin pulls in his rifle, puts the safety on, backs out of the deer stand, steps onto the ladder that leads down to the ground, starts climbing down. Dud's at the bottom of the ladder, waiting for him. He can hear the sirens too. He's looking mighty nervous.

Martin says, "Let's get out of here."

Clyde is hunkered down low, stretched across the driver's seat of his vehicle, sweating through his shirt, listening to the sirens getting louder, some of them sounding like they're close, maybe even in the parking lot with him.

He sneaks a look out his back glass, sees a cruiser pull up behind his, the driver getting out, walking around the back of his vehicle, now opening the passenger side door.

Bobby Crowner looks in, grins, says, "It's okay, Clyde. Y'all can come out now."

Clyde looks at him, says, "That's easy for you to say. You ain't the one that's been set up to be shot. Ain't no motherfuckin' sniper trying to 'ssassinate yo' ass."

"What do you mean you was set up to be shot?"

"Some dude called this afternoon, told me he had a tip on the Uncle Freddie's job, said he was gonna leave it in an envelope tacked to a fence post out here. I got here and didn't find no envelope. Next thing I knows, there's rifle bullets comin' at me from somewheres. So I ain't comin' out 'til I knows it's safe, you know what I'm sayin'?"

Bobby stands up out of the car, looks around, leans back in. "We got about six squad cars workin' the roads around here. Ain't no way in the world somebody wants to shoot you so bad they'd run the risk of tanglin' with all of us."

Clyde sits up, puts his Stetson on, gets out of the patrol car, half talking to himself. "They must a wanted to shoot me pretty bad is all I got to say. I can't believe this shit, man. I coulda been gunned down, man, be lyin' out here deader than a canned ham."

Bobby says, "How many shots you reckon was fired?"

"At least two. One busted out a window of a car down that way, another plugged a Trans Am over yonder, missed my head by a millionth of a inch. Let me tell you somethin', man, it was so close I could feel the heat from it."

A crowd is starting to build now, people coming down from the hillside gardens to gawk at the two cops and at the squad cars with their lights going on top.

Bobby says, "Which way was he firin' from?"

"Over yonder way. He must of had some kind of elevation, 'cause they ain't nothin' I can see over there but scrub oak and mesquite and cactus and shit."

Bobby stands up on the floorboard of Clyde's cruiser, looks off in the distance. "I think I can just make out a deer stand, way over yonder. This guy must be one hell of a shot to try somethin' from that range with all this smoke and what have you in the air."

He gets back down, says, "I'll send somebody out there, get it checked out while we process the scene here. Clyde, you want to 'tend to this crowd what's building?"

Bobby reaches in Clyde's car, grabs the mike, commences to radio the other cops.

Clyde goes out to the people that are milling around, says, "Yo! You flower lovers! Y'all move along, alright? Ain't nothin' to see here. Git on back to lookin' at yo' rosebushes. Move it along now, you know what I'm sayin'?"

They make their way through woods and cow pastures, down back roads they know of only because they've lived in these parts their entire lives, hunted its fields, driven around them night and day. They head up north away from the sirens and when they hit the highway to College Station they turn back to the east, then south on Highway 6 and finally around the bypass toward Martin's place.

They ride along mostly in silence, with Dud focused on his driving, Martin praying quietly over what just happened, the implications of it for him and Dud.

The implications of it for the Messenger.

Martin's occupied with the thought that the cops might somehow link this situation back to him. He's not exactly sure why this possibility hadn't bothered him before he took it upon himself to try to put a slug in that boy. Maybe he was just so intent on doing an ashes-to-ashes, dust-to-dust number on the deputy that he didn't think it all the way through.

But now he's got to face the fact the cops are going to start looking for the shooter, and they'll be looking pretty hard since it was a cop just about got himself shot.

Okay, he says to himself, *they gonna launch themselves an investigation. What do they have that could lead back to me?*

There was that conversation he had with the sheriff yesterday, the sheriff telling him about this Clyde Thomas working the Uncle Freddie's case. Set that next to what happened today and it might raise some suspicions. But there's no hard evidence to . . .

The shell casings.

Martin reaches forward, grabs the dashboard to steady himself.

"What's the matter?" Dud says.

"Shut up a second. I'm tryin' to think somethin' through."

Each time the rifle had fired, it had ejected a shell casing into the deer stand, and he'd left in such a rush, he'd forgotten to stop, pick them up. He had personally loaded those shells into the rifle's magazine, and they'd have his fingerprints on them.

Those fingerprints would tie him to both the Uncle Freddie's job and the incident over at the Rose Emporium.

So what happens now, he asks himself. All those cops they stirred up, they'll look for the source of the gunfire, come across Earl Guidry's deer stand, find the shell casings, talk to Earl, go back to the courthouse, covey up over yonder, work through the night, fire up the coffeepot, every cop in the county, the ones working the Uncle Freddie's case, his sister's case too, the whole bunch so exercised about a guy taking a couple of shots at one of their own they'll be burning the courthouse lights late . . .

That's it. That's the answer. "Of course," he says out loud.

"What?"

They pull off the highway, turn down the dirt road that goes through the little woods that shields Martin's place from the road traffic.

Martin's so happy he could just about cry. The Lord God Jehovah has come to his aid one more time. God has delivered Himself of another revelation, beamed straight down from heaven into the Messenger's brain.

He grins, turns to Dud, says, "We stirred 'em up pretty good, huh, partner?"

Dud's return grin has got some nervousness to it. "I was worried for a while we wasn't gonna be able to shake loose from there, there was so many cops buzzin' around."

"That's what I know. That's what God sent us out there to do. We was on a mission from God and didn't even know it. I guess maybe He did tell me to go try to clip that soul brother after all, and I just wasn't aware of it at the time."

"Do what now?"

"The Lord sent us out there to take a couple shots at that boy, knowin' even before we went I'd miss, knowin' Buckwheat would call for backup, get all the cops within fifty miles all exercised, out racin' around now, lookin' for ever-who would bust a cap at a cop, then workin' overtime to find him, lock him up in the jailhouse, they so mad 'cause he tried to do the thing they hate most in the world. Which is kill a cop, of course. So it was the will of the Lord, what we just done."

"I don't get it. Why would He want us to do that?"

"Basically, to set 'em up for us. Tonight the courthouse is gonna be lousy with 'em, like I done said, them all workin' overtime. And we respond by hittin' 'em then."

"Tonight?"

"That's right. We gonna start this very minute."

"But I thought we was gonna bomb the courthouse tomorrow."

"God is settin' this schedule, not you and me. We gonna build our bomb and deliver it while all the cops got their attention focused elsewheres, while they done set up shop in town. Workin' through us, the good Lord has created the conditions for us to succeed in doin' His will."

Corpses like refuse in the streets.

"You sure 'bout this? This ain't the plan we talked about less than a hour ago."

Martin just looks at Dud. Then he says, "God reveals His will little by little. You got to keep your antennas up, listenin' for it all the time, His still, small voice tryin' to get your attention. I am the Messenger of the Lord, Dud."

"I reckon."

"Drop me off here at the house. I need to git a couple things. You drive on around back to the barn, start loadin' them drums into the panel truck. I'll meet you back yonder directly."

33

IT'S SUCH TIMES AS THESE THAT MAKE DEWEY SHARPE WONDER WHY HE wanted to be a cop. He hadn't set out to be, hadn't wanted to be one when he was growing up on a dairy farm just outside Brenham, the oldest of three brothers.

What he had wanted to be was a professional golfer, but that takes a body capable of muscle memory and a mind capable of concentration, qualities the good Lord had left out of his DNA. That at least was the enduring lesson of three years on the bottom rung of the high school golf team ladder. Hell, he had barely lettered.

Then he'd gone off to A&M, gotten his accounting degree, thought about business school, decided to take a job at County Line Ford until he could make his mind up.

He was still there ten years later, hustling F-150s to hayseeds, and bored to death. Would be there still if Pat Patterson hadn't been dropped in the grease over his boys beating that black prisoner to death, opening up the slot in the sheriff's office. Dewey had gone to his uncle Wilbert, the county judge, had told him he wanted a shot at the job, and his uncle had gotten the governor to appoint him to Pat's remaining term, and then the one time he was up for reelection he hadn't drawn an opponent in the primary so he sailed clear through.

But on days like today, he wonders if he wouldn't have been better off to continue pursuing a career in the automotive industry. At least there you get Sundays off, can get in a round of golf without your afternoon being bollixed up by some cotton-picking murder investigation.

So after Sonya drops him off back at the Adobe, Dewey sets about doing what he had been planning to do that afternoon before that obnoxious bitch woman lawyer had come barging into his room, asking personal questions, ordering him around, telling him to do this, do that, do the other thing, like she was his wife or his boss or something.

He gets in the county pickup he'd been using as a loaner, heads to the garage to swap it for his cruiser. On the way over there, he works himself into a swivet about Miss Lawyer Bitch, her mistreatment of him.

"'Untremendous brains and courage,'" he says to himself. "What the heck is that supposed to mean? Hell, she don't even know me. And for that matter I don't think there is such a word as 'untremendous.'"

Now that he thinks back on it, he knows what he should have said. He should have said, "Hey, you know what? The other day, I stood up for black folks like your danged boyfriend in front of an entire locker room full of redneck blowhards over at the country club. That right there takes a measure of courage."

But it hadn't occurred to him to say any such thing, so he had just let her insult hang there in the air, a verbal cloud throwing a shadow over Dewey's character, still making his ears burn when he thinks back on it.

Seems like it's always that way somehow, Dewey thinking of just the right comeback about an hour and a half after he needs it.

He promises himself if he ever gets half a chance, he's going to prove to Miss Lawyer Bitch his brains and courage are not untremendous, that in fact they are all kinds of tremendous. It's her kind of talk that's ginned up a primary opponent for him in the person of that lard-ass sadist Joe Bob Cole.

He pulls into the lot at the maintenance facility, gets out of the loaner.

Charlie Baker walks out of the garage, wiping his hands with a rag. He carries himself with his chin tucked into his chest such that he's always looking at you from under his eyebrows.

"Howdy, Sheriff," he says. "She's all ready for you." He holds the keys out for Dewey to take.

"Thanks, Charlie." Dewey unlocks his cruiser, gets inside, cranks the engine, turns the air-conditioning on full blast.

He stands up out of the cruiser, says to Charlie, "You gettin' along all right?"

"Yeah. I reckon," he says from under his eyebrows.

He turns to go back inside the garage.

Dewey gets back in the cruiser, says to himself, "There's somethin' ain't right about that boy."

He pulls out onto the highway, points his vehicle back toward the Adobe, figuring to watch the last few holes of the golf tournament on television, then maybe go out to the course, hit some shag balls once the heat of the day has receded.

At some point this evening he knows he's going to have to puzzle out how to work himself back into Claudia's good graces, and he's just fixing to worry on that subject some when his radio bursts into life, Darlene's voice sounding mighty exercised.

"Attention all units! Deputy Thomas has requested backup! His twenty is the Rose Emporium parkin' lot. Says he's pinned down by sniper fire!"

Dewey grabs the mike, says, "This is Sheriff Sharpe! I'm just leavin' the county maintenance garage! I'm on my way! ETA would be about fifteen minutes!"

He hits the siren and the lights, pulls a U-turn, and sticks his foot on the carburetor.

He goes howling around the bypass, turns down the county road that leads to the Emporium and is within a couple miles of it when he hears dispatch saying, "Deputy Crowner reports the parking lot situation is secure. He requests a unit check a deer stand east of there. He thinks that could be where the shots were fired from."

Dewey himself is driving in from the east, and now he's saying to himself, "Who's got a deer stand with a view of the parkin' lot over at the Emporium?"

He decides it's either got to be Earl Guidry or Luther Schoppe.

He grabs the mike, thumbs it, says, "This is Sheriff Sharpe, Darlene. I'm on it."

He heads over to the Guidry spread, which is the closer of the two. It takes him fifteen minutes to get to Earl's place, then let himself through the gate to Earl's pasture, make his way to the back part of the property where the deer stand is.

Dewey tops a little rise and the pasture road ends at the edge of some woods. Up ahead, on another rise beyond where the land dips into a little valley, sits a deer stand.

Dewey stops, throws the cruiser in reverse, backs down the hill until just the windows of the deer stand are in view. He watches for any sign it's occupied, looking to make sure there aren't any rifle barrels sticking out of it, thinking to himself, a guy of untremendous courage wouldn't be out here, exposing himself to the possibility of getting his ass blown off in the line of duty by a cop-killing sniper, now, would he?

He makes a mental note to point that out to Miss Lawyer Bitch the next time they cross paths.

He steers the cruiser around, across the pasture, looking for a way through the brush, finds a *sendero* that cuts through the brush from the south. From this angle he can see more clearly, can see the door to the deer stand is open, that there are no vehicles around its base. The thing looks to be empty.

Just to be sure, he watches the stand awhile, not wanting to rush in there, catch himself a rifle slug for his pains. Finally satisfied there isn't anyone in it, he gets out of the cruiser, fetches the service revolver he's got locked in the trunk, straps it on. Gets back in the cruiser, drives down the *sendero,* stopping at the base of the deer stand. Gets out of the squad car, walks around at the bottom of the deer stand, looking for tire tracks or any other indication a vehicle had been parked here recently.

The ground's too dry for tires to make an impression, but it does look like something had flattened some weeds over by the ladder that leads up the side of the blind. He goes over to inspect the weeds closer, decides that a man might conclude they'd been driven on recently from the looks of them.

He goes to the ladder, climbs to the top where he can peek inside the deer stand.

"Looky yonder," he says out loud to himself.

There's a couple spent shell casings on the floor.

He hauls himself inside the deer stand. There are two stools in here and that's it. There are windows cut into the sides of the blind so a deer hunter can look down the *sendero,* get himself a good shot at his prey. He looks out the window that points back west and sure enough there's the Emporium parking lot, got a couple squad cars in it.

He climbs back down to fetch his evidence collection kit.

Martin Fletcher walks through the front door of his house, heads straight to the desk in the family room. He opens a desk drawer, pulls out his ANFO file, shuts the drawer, looks around, tries to think of what else he might need from in here.

He's feeling excited now, sure he's doing the right thing, the very thing the Lord wants him to do at the very time the Lord wants him to do it.

There is no God but the Lord God Jehovah, and Martin is His Messenger.

He looks over in the corner, sees the television set standing there. He paid over $250 for the durn thing and never once turned it on, sat down to watch it. On a whim he goes over, picks the clicker up, punches a couple buttons.

The screen lights up and on this channel there is some kind of movie going, which sets Martin to wondering who would be sitting around watching this junk in the middle of the afternoon. He punches a button on the clicker and the channels commence to roll by.

Nothing on but junk, stuff that rots folks' minds, sex, violence, golf, beer ads, political talk. He stops on some political pundit show, a panel discussion, looks to be a bunch of Eastern liberals and a congressman from California, the one that has the bald head and the hair growing out his ears and on top of that is an out-and-out Communist, flapping their gums about gun control, going on and on about it.

"Wait a minute," Martin says. "That reminds me of somethin'."

He tosses the clicker on the sofa, just leaves the TV running, heads to the hallway, pulls down the ladder leading up to the attic.

That's where he hid the AK-47 so neither Linda nor the kids could find it.

Dewey doesn't see any evidence to be had other than the shell casings. He figures he probably ought to get a man out here to dust the place for prints just the same.

He climbs down the ladder, gets in his cruiser, heads back out the way he came.

As he finishes letting himself through the pasture gate leading into Earl's yard, Earl Guidry himself comes out the back door of his house to meet him.

"Whatta you doin' on my place?" Earl says to him, got a scowl on his old face.

Dewey walks over, says, "Howdy, Earl. I'm Sheriff Sharpe."

"What?"

"I said, 'Howdy, Earl, I'm Sheriff . . .'"

"Speak up you danged fool. I can't hear you if you is gonna whisper."

Dewey shouts, "I SAID, 'HOWDY, EARL. I'M SHERIFF SHARPE."

"I know who you are, you danged fool. Whatta you doin' on my place? You ain't asked my permission for it. You ain't got no right to drive around out here without my say so. This ain't Communist China, dammit."

"Sorry, Earl, we had us . . ."

"Speak up, durn it."

"SORRY, EARL, WE HAD US KINDLY OF A EMERGENCY. WE GOT A REPORT SOMEBODY WAS FIRIN' A RIFLE INTO THE PARKIN' LOT OVER TO THE EMPORIUM, FROM SOMEWHERE OVER IN THIS DIRECTION, AND I WAS JUST CHECKIN' TO SEE IF MAYBE THE GUNFIRE MIGHT OF BEEN COMIN' FROM THAT DEER STAND YOU GOT BACK YONDER."

Dewey holds up a plastic bag containing the shell casings. "I FOUND THESE ON THE FLOOR OF YOUR DEER STAND."

"So what? They coulda been from last huntin' season."

"MAYBE. YOU KNOW IF ANYBODY'S BEEN BACK YONDER THIS AFTERNOON?"

"No, they ain't. Leastwise, not that I know anything about."

"AIN'T NOBODY COME THROUGH YOUR YARD, GONE THROUGH THIS GATE, TO YOUR KNOWLEDGE?"

"No, sir. There ain't been nobody. Not today."

"IS THERE ANY WAY TO GET TO THAT STAND OTHER THAN THROUGH THIS GATE RIGHT HERE?"

"There's a couple other ways, through gates that front on the private road up on the north end."

"DID YOU HEAR ANYTHING THIS AFTERNOON? ANY GUN-SHOTS OR ANYTHING?"

"No."

"I reckon that figgers."

"What? Speak up, durn it."

"NOTHING. NEVER MIND. WHO USES THAT DEER STAND, BESIDES YOURSELF?"

"I don't use it. Never have since I put it up. My eyesight's no good, can't see to shoot a deer, leastwise."

"WHO DOES USE IT THEN?"

"My sons. Some of their kids. A few folks from around here."

Dewey knows Earl's sons, twins by the names of Brian and Ben, each of them with two or three teenage boys of their own. The Guidry twins lived in Houston, ran a pest control business. Word around town was that they were coining it down there, working night and day, trying to keep the roach population down in the low hundreds of billions. They don't strike Dewey as the kind of people who would come up to Brenham on a Sunday afternoon, start popping caps at folks over in the parking lot of the Emporium.

"WHO 'ROUND HERE HAS USED IT, SAY IN THE LAST FEW YEARS?"

"Well, the stand ain't been up but for about three years. I put it up on account of I started noticin' lots of deer tracks, deer shit back yonder, 'bout four years ago. Wanted somethin' for the grandkids to do when they came to visit durin' the holidays. So I bought me that stand, got some boys from over at the Gun Club to help me put it up. You ever been around them boys, Sheriff?"

"CAN'T SAY AS I HAVE."

"Well, they good boys, mostly. They got themselves a few oddball ideas about the gummint and whatnot, walk around in camo some. But they good hands at puttin' up a deer stand and since they pitched in on it, I let them use it when they want, when my own family ain't usin' it."

"LIKE WHO?"

"Let me think a minute. Rick Jessup is one. Buster Weems. Bo Jernigan. And the preacher's kid, I forget his name."

"MARTIN FLETCHER?"

"Yeah. That's him."

"ANYBODY ELSE?"

"Not that I can think of offhand."

"IF YOU THINK OF ANYBODY ELSE, YOU GIVE ME A CALL, OKAY?"

"Sure. I reckon that'd be fine."

"THANK YOU, EARL."

Dewey turns to go back to his cruiser, thinking to himself, *Martin Fletcher.*

I just seen him yesterday at the reception, at his daddy's house.

Talked to him and Dr. Flatley.

Told them about the Uncle Freddie's case.

Told them about Clyde headin' it up, what a good job he was doin' and whatnot.

Dewey stops, thinks a minute.

He thinks, *He looked at me with them strange eyes of his.*

Then he says, "Oh, Lord."

He jogs back to his cruiser, throws the door open, jumps in, grabs the radio mike.

"This is Sheriff Sharpe. Come in, Darlene."

"Yes, sir, Sheriff."

"Darlene, would you please radio Bobby and Clyde, tell them to meet me back at the courthouse when they're done at the Rose Emporium? And tell them to step on it."

"That's a roger, Sheriff."

Dewey signs off, cranks the engine, throws the cruiser into gear.

As he heads into town, all he can think of is, *Oh, Lord. Oh, Lord. Oh, Lord.*

Martin Fletcher walks out the back door of his house, headed to the pole barn where Dud is loading fifty-five-gallon drums into the panel truck they had rented. When he gets there, Dud's just loading the last of the drums.

Martin says, "Good work, pardner. Now all we got to do is mix the ANFO. I got the instructions right here."

Dud looks up, says, "That ain't all you got, is it?"

Martin holds up the automatic weapon, grins.

Dud says, "Where'd you come by that?"

"You'd be surprised what a preacher's kid with a clean record can buy himself at a gun show."

"That thing loaded?"

Martin taps the banana clip. "You betchem, Red Rider."

He opens the door to the panel truck, sets the AK-47 on the driver's seat, turns around, and says, "Now let's make ourselves a bomb."

34

ON THEIR WAY OUT TO TALK TO GREG JOHNSON, JEREMIAH TELLS SONYA THE "I-saids" and the "he-saids" from his visit that morning with Dr. Fletcher.

When he's done, she says, "You know what I think?"

"What?"

"I think he sounds like a man with something to hide."

"I kindly agree."

"Take that business about the coat, for instance. He claims he doesn't know where it came from. I'm not sure I buy it. Almost nobody in this town has need for a coat like that, and if someone were to leave it behind at the church, what are the odds they wouldn't come back for it at some point?"

"That's what's been goin' through my head too."

"And what about the fact that he decided to give it to charity the very week his daughter's body turns up, even though it's supposed to have been sitting in lost and found all these years? That's a strange bit of timing, don't you think?"

"We'll know more soon enough. I'm plannin' to find out from his secretary on Tuesday what she's done with it, go try to collect it myself. See if it's a match for the button what was found at the scene."

Sonya falls silent and after a bit Jeremiah glances over at her, sees her looking his way, got a funny expression on her face.

"Something on your mind?" he says.

"Yes, as a matter of fact. Mind if I ask you a question?"

"Go ahead on."

"Why are you wearing a gun?"

Jeremiah shrugs. "Just bein' careful, I reckon."

"Just being careful. You reckon."

"Yep."

"I see."

They turn into the gravel road leading to Greg Johnson's place, a double-wide set on a few dusty acres off Highway 36. There's two vehicles parked in the yard, some chickens running around loose, three kids on their hands and knees shoving toys around in the dirt. None of them can be more than six years old.

Jeremiah parks his pickup off a ways from the house, looks around, says to Sonya, "You see any yard dogs?"

"No, sir."

"Good. Neither do I. Duke don't care for yard dogs. They get him stirred up."

"Yard dogs and black men, huh."

"A thing can only—"

"I know. Whatever."

They get out, Jeremiah going around to the back of the truck to tell Duke to mind his manners. Then they walk through the chickens and the kids over to the door. Jeremiah does the knocking.

He turns to Sonya. "I known this guy a long time so I'll get the ball rollin'."

She says, "Fine."

A young woman answers the door wearing an apron, wiping her hands with a dish towel, her weariness apparent from the lines carved in her face, her sagging shoulders. She's a bit heavyset, and even though she looks to be only about thirty, her hair's already going gray on her. They can hear a baby howling somewhere in the back.

"'Scuse me, ma'am," says Jeremiah, taking his Stetson off, showing his respect for the lady of the house. "I'm Jeremiah Spur, and this here is Sonya Nichols. We're lookin' for Greg. Could we come in and have a word with him please?"

She looks the two of them over, makes a gesture with the dish towel, says, "He's around back. In his shop. You want me to go fetch him?"

"No, ma'am. That's all right. We'll go back yonder."

Jeremiah puts his Stetson back on and they walk around the double-wide where they see what looks to be a workshop set a couple hundred yards back of the house.

When they get to it Jeremiah does the knocking again.

The veterinarian opens the door.

"Howdy, Greg," says Jeremiah.

Greg Johnson is tall and so skinny Jeremiah figures he has to jump around in the shower to get wet. The animal doctor peers down at them through a pair of horn-rimmed eyeglasses that have lenses in them so thick they look to be made from bulletproof glass.

"Howdy, Jeremiah. If you got some sick livestock, you could of called. No need for you to come all the way out here."

He looks over at Sonya, says, "I don't believe we've met. I'm Greg John-son." He sticks his hand out.

She takes it, says, "Sonya Nichols, assistant district attorney for Washington County."

While they shake, Jeremiah says, "My livestock is all fine thanks, except they're way too skinny. Kindly like you, I reckon. You the only thing in Washington County that's skinnier than my herd."

Sonya says, "Dr. Johnson, the reason we're here is to ask you a few questions about Sissy Fletcher. As you may know already, her body was found—"

Jeremiah looks at Sonya, wonders if maybe she hadn't heard him when he said he would get the conversation started, because here she's already jumped in and—

"Yeah. I know," says Greg. He looks over their shoulders, back toward the double-wide. "Why don't y'all come in?"

He shows them into a little office furnished with a couple chairs and a desk. Greg and Sonya each take a chair. Jeremiah sits on the edge of the desk, one black calfskin boot hanging, one planted on the floor.

Jeremiah says, "What kind of operation you got back here, Greg?"

The veterinarian jerks a thumb over his shoulder, says, "Back yonder's my dark room, where I develop my photographs."

"The picture-taking business been any good lately?" says Jeremiah.

"It's been tolerable. Late spring generally is. You got your weddings and your proms and your graduations and whatnot. It's a cyclical business. This time of year and the holidays are the two best."

Sonya reaches in her briefcase, pulls out a legal pad and a tape recorder.

Greg looks at her, then at Jeremiah. Then he says, "Before you start asking your questions, I'd like us to get a few ground rules agreed to up front."

"Such as?" says Jeremiah.

"Such as I don't want my wife to know anything about this. She's not from around here. She's from Beaumont. She's never heard of Sissy Fletcher, leastwise she's never heard of her from me, and she doesn't know we once lived together."

"I'm sorry, Dr. Johnson, but we can't promise you that," says Sonya. "This is a criminal case, a homicide investigation. It's bound to become public at some point. If you can provide us with useful evidence, we may have to call you as a witness at the trial, which will be conducted in public, of course. It'll probably be covered by the media."

Greg Johnson takes off his bulletproof glasses, commences to polish the lenses. He replaces them on his head, says, "I'd rather not talk to you all then."

"Look, Dr. Johnson. You can refuse to talk to us. But sooner or later, we'll get your testimony. If I have to, I can get a court to issue a subpoena, force you to testify."

"Nobody threatened me with any such thing when the cops came around the first time, right after she disappeared."

Sonya is tempted to say something about there being a new sheriff in town, but gets a mental image of Dewey's butt crack, decides against it. "Not to be trite, but that was then and this is now. Back then there was no corpse, and people were apparently content to assume Sissy Fletcher had skipped town. Now we have a body and a medical examiner's report that says she was bludgeoned to death, and as a consequence we have a full-blown investigation in furtherance of which we need any evidence you can provide.

"Now, if a subpoena is what it takes to get your testimony, then all I need to do is get a judge on the phone and we'll have one before you can develop a roll of film."

She reaches in her briefcase, pulls out her cell phone. "In fact," she says, "thanks to the wonders of wireless technology, I can do it right from this chair. If you don't believe me you can hide and watch. So it would be a better idea if you tell us what you can today, and then you can find a good time to talk to your wife about your past, before the case goes public."

The veterinarian takes his glasses off again, commences to swipe at them.

Sonya says, "Maybe you would prefer that I dial up Judge Roberts after all. He's not going to like me interrupting his Sunday afternoon, and I'll have to explain what's precipitated it of course. Judge Roberts wouldn't by any chance use you to look after his herd, would he?"

She turns the phone on and it beeps a couple times, its little circuits coming audibly to life, helping her make her point.

The guy puts his eyeglasses back on, looks at Jeremiah and then at Sonya and then back at Jeremiah again, chewing away at his bottom lip. Then he gives a little shoulder shrug, switches to looking down at the floor.

"Alright," he says.

Sonya turns her phone off, puts it back in her briefcase.

Jeremiah says, "Anything else?"

"Yeah. I want . . . I can't remember the name for it. It's that thing the special prosecutor gave that woman, you know, the one that gave Clinton all the blow jobs."

He looks at Sonya, says, "Excuse my French."

Sonya says, "Do you mean you want us to give you immunity from prosecution?"

"Yeah. That's it."

Sonya hesitates, taps her ballpoint pen on her legal pad, says, "Well, obviously I can't offer that if you're the one that killed her."

"I'm not. And I don't know who did. And if that's all y'all want to know then you can get on out of here."

"We've got a few more questions than that," Sonya says.

"Well, then, there's some other stuff that, if it were to come out . . ."

Sonya thinks a bit more, doodles some on her legal pad. She says, "Captain Spur, could we step outside a minute?"

He nods, looks at Greg Johnson, says, "We'll be right back."

They get up and let themselves out the door.

Out in the yard, she says, "What do you think we should do?"

Jeremiah reaches up, scratches his gray stubble, says, "You're the lawyer, not me. But if there's anything collateral to the killing, the statute of limitations probably already run on it. So I reckon if it was me, I'd offer him use immunity, get ever-what we can from him would help us on the murder case."

She nods, says, "I think I agree with you."

They go back inside, take their same places back.

Sonya says, "Here's what we can do. I can offer you what we call 'use immunity' so that you'll not be prosecuted for any crime based upon anything you say with two exceptions. You don't get immunity on the Fletcher murder, and you don't get it for your own perjury. Do you understand what I'm saying to you?"

The vet nods. "I think so. Can I get it in writing?"

"I can write it up and send it to you first thing in the morning."

Greg looks at Jeremiah.

Jeremiah says, "If she says she'll do it, then she'll do it."

Greg nods, looks at Sonya, says, "Okay. Let's get on with it then."

She clicks on the tape recorder, sets it on the desk, says, "This is the statement of Dr. Greg Johnson, taken on Sunday, May 16, 1999, on the understanding that he will be granted use immunity. State your name, occupation, and address please."

"My name is Dr. Gregory Johnson, and I'm a veterinarian, a taxidermist, and a photographer. I live at 3177 Bellville Highway, Brenham, Texas."

"How long have you lived in Washington County, Dr. Johnson?"

"All my life."

"And how old are you?"

"I'm thirty-nine."

"Where were you living in February of 1989?"

"Right here. This same address."

"And were you living alone?"

"No, ma'am. I was living with Sissy Fletcher."

"How long had you known her before you started living together?"

"Since we were kids. We went to the same schools, and my folks went to her daddy's church."

"How long had you all been living together?"

"A couple years."

"Were you lovers, Dr. Johnson?"

"We weren't in love with one another, if that's what you mean."

"I mean that in part. I'm also asking if you were physically intimate."

"Yeah. On occasion."

"But you weren't in love, you said."

"No, ma'am. We was only intimate, to use your word, for recreation."

"If you weren't in love, why did you live together?"

"Well, there were a couple of reasons. I already had this place. I bought it when I got out of vet school over at A&M. She didn't have anyplace else to live, other than with her daddy, and she hated his guts. So I invited her to move in here, help share the expenses. But by the time I offered that up, of course . . ."

He licks his lips, his eyes shift behind his spectacles, dart around the room. Then he says, "Now we're getting into the part that I don't want y'all using against me. You see, we had us sort of a business partnership."

"You want to elaborate on that for me, please, sir?"

Greg reaches over onto his desk, picks up a hard rubber ball, squeezes it. "She came to me with this idea, you see. She was the one that thought it up."

"Excuse me. When was this?"

"Oh, probably late 1986, early 1987."

"Okay, please keep going."

"She said she'd been thinking about leaving Brenham for a while on account of she hated it so much here, and she was trying to come up with a way to get enough walking around money to make it to some big city, set herself up with a new life."

"Did she say how much she thought she needed?"

"At least a hundred thousand dollars as I recollect."

"That's some serious money for a single woman. Did she ever say why she thought she needed so much? Did she have a drug habit or something?"

"Sissy? No, she was clean as a hound's tooth. Drank some beer now and then, that was about it."

"Then what did she need so much money for?"

"She said once she left she wanted to stay gone. She used to talk about how she'd made a break for it once, got all the way to Austin to go to school, but then screwed up, got tangled up with the wrong crowd, had flunked out, had to come back here with her tail tucked between her legs for lack of the resources to do otherwise. She said she hated having to crawl back to this shithole—excuse my French—move back into the parsonage. That was embarrassing to her. I don't know that anybody actually ever carried her high about it, but she felt like, you know, folks talked about it, laughed behind her back about how she couldn't make a go of it out in the world. So she wanted to make sure she had a margin for error for the next time by staking herself to a big enough chunk to have something to fall back on if it took her a while to get established in some strange new place. Plus, I think . . ."

He stops, works that rubber ball hard, eyes like a rabbit's, blinking fast behind all that glass.

"Yes? Come on, you think what?"

"Plus I think there was more to it than just the money. She, well, she had a few old scores she wanted to settle along the way. Some kind of point she wanted to make on her way out the door. Kind of her last word for the folks of Brenham. She always liked having the last word."

"Okay. So she approached you and—"

"And she said we'd been friends a long time, and she'd hit on an idea, but she needed a partner for it."

He looks down at the rubber ball, passes it back and forth from one hand to the other, squeezes it until his knuckles turn white.

"She told me I was the perfect partner on account of I was a photographer and my daddy owned the Adobe Inn. She said her plan was to approach a few of the prominent men around town, prominent to their own way of thinking anyhow, and, you know . . ."

"No, we don't know. Spell it out for us."

"Well, seduce them, I reckon is the way to put it, get them in the sack with her over at the Adobe, which I happened to be managing for my old man at the time. She said we needed to arrange it such that while she was at it with them I would be positioned where I could take a few photographs, and then she would offer to sell the photos to her boyfriends, threaten them with disclosure if they didn't buy them back from her. She said she figgered they'd be more than happy to pay up, especially when they got an idea of what would happen to them if they didn't. She said it was a license to print money."

"How could she be so sure she'd be a success as a, uh, as a—I guess the word I'm looking for is seductress."

The guy squints at Sonya through his glasses. "You never saw her, I guess."

"I moved here after she disappeared."

"Well, the answer is, she was so good-looking it would have been hard for any man anywhere—here, in Houston, anywhere—to have resisted her. She once said the problem with having good looks is that after a while you actually get tired of being stared at by men, because you could always tell what they were thinking. And they were basically all thinking the same thing. And on top of that—"

"Yes?"

"She said that every guy God ever made just naturally thinks he's something on a stick when it comes to sex."

"Okay, so you bought into her idea."

"Sure did."

"What was in it for you?"

"Twenty-five percent."

Jeremiah's watching the look on the veterinarian's face, watching him give that rubber ball a workout. Jeremiah's thinking, yeah, that and the best entertainment you can get in Washington County, even if you got cable, plus the occasional freebie for the photography corps.

"So," Sonya says, "you all made a business deal."

"Yep. I fixed up a room at the Adobe with a one-way mirror and track lighting—"

"Room fifteen."

The veterinarian looks a little surprised, then says, "Yeah. Room fifteen. I built a wall in the room next door, which I made sure never got rented out. That wall created a space for me to hide in with my camera equipment. Then I'd go there every other day at about three o'clock in the afternoon, sit and wait for her to show up with the chump *du jour*."

"This time I *will* excuse your French. How long did this go on?"

"I don't know. Year and a half, two years maybe."

"How many, uh, 'customers' do you figure she had?"

"I don't think I recollect. But it was more than a few. As I recall, she focused on your more promising, more up-and-coming types, as well as some of the more established guys around town. You know, politicians, judges, cops, that sort of thing."

"Care to share their names?"

"No."

"Why not?"

He hesitates. "Well, for one thing, they paid good money for me not to. And for another thing, I can't remember who all they were."

"Whoa. Wait a minute. You can't *remember*?"

"That's right. It's been a long durned time. How am I supposed to remember the particulars of something that happened all that long ago?"

"I would have thought it would be pretty hard to forget, frankly."

"Well, I'm sorry, I don't recollect who they were. Besides—"

"Besides what?"

"Besides, even if I did, I figure it was one of them probably killed Sissy. If it's all the same to you, I'd prefer not to end up buried in a pasture."

"If one of them wanted you dead, don't you think he would have seen to it already?"

"Not necessarily. No one knew for sure I was working with her. She handled that entire end, made the demands, collected the money, delivered the photographs."

"But they could have put two and two together. It wouldn't have been that hard. People knew you were living together, knew you were a photographer, knew your father owned the Adobe Inn. Look, it took Jeremiah and me about five minutes to figure out you all were up to something together."

"Maybe. And maybe they figured after she disappeared, *I'd* put two and two together and keep my mouth shut."

"I'll get that subpoena if I have to."

"Get it then. I'll just say I don't remember, which is the truth. I don't."

They stare at one another for a few moments. Then Sonya goes back to her legal pad, looks at her notes. "How much money did your little shakedown operation make?"

"Each one of them was good for five to ten thousand bucks."

"Seems like a lot of money."

"They were all more than happy to settle their bill. Especially once they got wind of the fact that a guy had been thrown out by his wife on account of she got some of my work product hand delivered to her house."

"Joe Bob Cole."

"Maybe."

"Now that's the part I don't understand. Why would any guy trust her if word was around that she had set up Joe Bob?"

The guy shrugs. "They wouldn't have, and she knew it. That's why she waited until she had made the rounds, hit the sack with everybody she thought would make a good mark, before she lowered the boom on Joe Bob. When the rest of the mullets seen what had happened to him, it made it easy to collect from them."

"I get it. What did Sissy do with her share of the money?"

"She put it in the bank, I think."

"Which bank?"

"The First State Bank of Brenham."

"Where's that money now?"

"Still in the bank, I guess. I don't think she withdrew it before she disappeared."

"You're sure she didn't by chance withdraw it just before she died? Maybe give somebody who knew about all that money lying around a reason to disappear her?"

"Look. I've already told you. I didn't kill her. You think I'm lying about her not having withdrawn the money, then why don't you go down to the bank, check it out?"

"Oh, believe me, that is exactly what we're going to do." Sonya looks at her notes. "You said that Sissy hated her father. Do you have any idea why?"

"All I know is she said he was a hypocrite and a fraud and that one of these days the world would find out what kind of man he really was. She said she might even see to that herself when the time was right."

"Do you have any idea what she specifically might have meant by that?"

"No. I don't. But she had her stinger out for him, that's for danged sure."

"Okay. Let's talk about your whereabouts on the night she disappeared."

"Like I told the cops the first time, I went to the rodeo dance by myself. While I was there I ran into Sam Carter and we decided to vamoose. We went over to the Golden Cue, shot pool until about midnight, then left to go over to his place and drank whiskey 'til damned near sunup."

"And Sam Carter is—"

"Friend of mine from college—"

Jeremiah says, "He's a dentist. Here in town."

"That's right," Sonya says. "I've met him. So then on that Sunday—"

"I got up, sometime around noon I reckon, came home, but Sissy wasn't around. And her pickup was gone too."

"But you didn't call in a missing person's report."

"Not until the next day, when I began to wonder where the heck she was."

"So then you called the cops and they came out here, asked you a few questions, searched the place. You didn't tell them any of this good stuff about your arrangements over at the Adobe, I take it."

"Hell, no."

"Why not?"

"You think Joe Bob Cole would have given me immunity from an ass-whippin', much less prosecution?"

"I see your point. So they took your statement at face value, and that was it, so far as you were concerned."

The veterinarian puts down the rubber ball he's been working, says, "Yeah, that was it. Leastwise it was until that nigger cop—"

The look on Sonya's face stops him cold.

"What'd I say?" he says.

Sonya starts slowly tapping her legal pad with her ballpoint pen.

"So," she says, "let me see if I have this straight. You were an accomplice in an extortion conspiracy involving the daughter of Brenham's most prominent minister. You secretly photographed your friends and neighbors, some of them pretty powerful people from the sound of it, while they were engaged in sex with her and then stood by while she used those photographs to shake them down for money, twenty-five percent of which ended up in your Wranglers. You have hidden all this for more than ten years both from your wife and from the authorities. And last but not least you're an unreconstructed racist. Have I got it about right so far?"

The vet swallows, looks at the floor through his Coke-bottle-bottom glasses.

"Well, Dr. Johnson," she says as she clicks off the tape recorder and starts to pack her stuff away. "I made a deal to give you use immunity, and I'll live up to it. But I didn't say anything about keeping all this under wraps. Away from your wife. From your friends and neighbors. Some of whom are also your clients, no doubt."

She stands up, looks at the vet. "Or from my gentleman friend, Clyde Thomas."

She turns on her heel, walks out the door, slamming it hard behind her.

Greg Johnson looks up at Jeremiah. "Clyde Thomas? That's not the—"

Jeremiah heaves himself up off the desk. " 'Fraid so."

"Oh, shit."

"I ain't completely sure but I think you might of pissed her off."

"Oh, shit."

"If I was you," Jeremiah says as he heads out the door, "I believe I'd give her a call and try to apologize for your poor choice of words."

Jeremiah hesitates a second, then comes back in the office, letting the door close behind him. "I got one more question I'd like to ask if you don't mind."

"Go ahead."

"Was there anything special goin' on between Sissy and that Charlie Baker kid?"

"Who?"

"Charlie Baker. You know, the ice cream lady's kid."

"The re-tard?"

"I don't think he's actually retarded. Just kind of slow."

"You know what? I'd almost forgotten about that." The memory of it causes the veterinarian to tap the arm of his chair with his forefinger. "She was real partial to that kid. Treated him more special than anybody."

"She ever say why?"

"She said it was up to her to try to make amends for how he'd been mistreated."

"Mistreated? She say how?"

"No. Just that he'd been mistreated. By one of her kinfolks."

"But I take it she didn't name no names."

"No, sir. She didn't."

"Alright then. We'll let you know if we have any more questions. In the meantime, do yourself a favor. Call Sonya, tell her you're sorry you're such a dumb ass."

Jeremiah lets himself out into the yard, stops to light a cigarette, check his watch. Damn near five o'clock and it's still so hot the grackles are panting.

He walks around the front of the double-wide, sees Sonya over by the pickup, arms reaching over into the bed of the truck, scratching Duke behind the ears with both hands.

Sonya doesn't look his way when he gets there, just keeps scratching Duke, Duke's tail a-going with happiness from it.

Jeremiah thinks, Duke's done found himself a new friend.

She says, "I screwed up."

Jeremiah leans with his back up against the truck, puffs on his cigarette, since it seems like they're going to be visiting for a spell before they mount up. "How's that?"

"I shouldn't have given that miserable bastard use immunity. I should have subpoenaed his bigoted ass, drug him in front of a grand jury, and sweated him big time. Now he's going to skate on the shakedown, and what with the alibi he's got, he doesn't seem like somebody we can make for her murder."

"I agree. I don't think he done her in. But as to the extortion, I think I'm right on the statute of limitations anyhow. So it don't matter that you give him immunity."

"So he skates."

"Well—"

"Well, what?"

"There's skatin' and there's skatin'."

"Meaning what, exactly?"

"Meaning word'll get around. 'Bout what he done, that is. He ain't likely to have much of a future here in Brenham, as a vet or a taxidermist or nothin' else."

Sonya looks at him. "You really think so?"

Jeremiah takes a drag, squints at her. "One thing's for moral certain. I ain't usin' him no more. Not for my livestock, and not for my dog neither."

"How come?"

"I can't have a racist 'tendin' to my animals."

Sonya looks at Jeremiah, a grin beginning to break out on her face.

"Sometimes I'm not sure what to think about you, Captain Spur."

"I wouldn't spend too much time on it if I was you. I have a sayin', you know."

"I know," she says. " 'A thing can only be what it is.' "

Jeremiah grins, puts his cigarette out.

"Come on," she says, giving Duke a final pat on the head. "Run me back over to the courthouse so I can get my car."

Greg Johnson watches Jeremiah Spur's back disappear around the corner of his double-wide, then reaches over, picks up the phone, dials up George Barnett.

On the other end of the line, George says, "Yeah?"

"You were right. They were here, and they just now left."

"How'd it go?"

"The way I told you it would go. No names got named."

There's a pause on the other end of the line. Then George says, "They ask you if you know who killed Sissy, m'boy?"

"Yeah."

"What did you say?"

"I said that I don't know."

"And do you?"

"No, George, of course not."

"Okay. I've always wondered if you did."

"You know what, George?"

"What?"

"For over ten years now, I've wondered the same thing about you."

There's a pause at the other end of the line. Then George says, "See you around."

"Yeah. See you around."

The veterinarian hangs up the phone, goes back to worrying his rubber ball with his hands.

George Barnett hangs up, thinks about the file locked in his desk drawer down at the courthouse. He reaches in his pocket out of habit, touches the key to that drawer, assurance to himself that he's still got it.

It's a file that's served him well on many occasions over the years. Gotten a number of important folks, judges, county commissioners, a state legislator or two, even an otherwise incorruptible Texas Ranger by the name of Frank Cade, to see their way clear to doing the right thing which of course means the thing George had wanted them to do in any particular case, even if they were otherwise not inclined to be helpful.

He thinks that maybe a little later in the day he'll ease on down there, fetch it back to the house, lock it up in his safe here.

3 5

ON THEIR WAY BACK INTO TOWN JEREMIAH SAYS TO SONYA, "YOU KNOW Vaughn Ford over at the bank?"

"Yes, I do. I met him last year, on a DWI case involving one of his vice presidents."

"Why don't you give him a call this afternoon, see if he'd be willing to look for that account Sissy was supposed to have had when he gets to the office tomorrow?"

"I'll do it."

Sonya reaches down into the floorboard of the pickup to get her briefcase, answer the cell phone that's commenced to ring.

She fishes it out, glances at the screen, says, "This is probably Clyde calling. Hello? Hey, how—What? . . . Slow down, slow down. But you're okay, right? . . . Okay, okay . . . When was this? . . . Over at the Rose Emporium? . . . You got any idea who might have . . . Where are you now? . . . Who else is going to be there? . . . Okay, we're on our way in. See you in ten minutes."

She punches the OFF button, says, "There was some kind of an incident over at the Rose Emporium this afternoon. Clyde went out there to follow up on an anonymous tip on the Uncle Freddie's robbery and somebody opened up on him with a rifle."

"Is he all right?"

"Seems to be. He sounds pretty rattled."

"I'd say that would be enough to rattle a man. Where's he at now?"

"Over at the courthouse. He told me the sheriff wants to get together with him and Bobby Crowner. Apparently while Clyde and Bobby processed the scene in the parking lot, Dewey checked out a deer stand they think the shooter may have been firing from. He wants to talk to them about what he found."

"Why don't we go join 'em?"

"That's just what I was thinking."

At Sonya's suggestion they gather in a conference room in the district attorney's offices. The five of them take seats around the conference table. Sonya had brewed a pot of coffee and they take turns pouring themselves some.

Clyde takes a sip, makes a face, says, "Man! What's up with this coffee?"

Sonya says, "Hey!"

Bobby Crowner puts his cup down, says, "It tastes like it was brewed in a armadillo shell somebody got off a roadkill."

Sonya says, "Look, don't drink it if you don't like it."

Jeremiah takes a sip of his, says, "Y'all want to get down to business? Clyde, why don't you start off, take it from the top."

Clyde tells of the anonymous phone call, how he went out to check the Rose Emporium for the envelope that wasn't there. Next thing he knows he's being shot at.

"That's when I called for the backup, see? The way I seen it, if I'd uh tried to back my squad car out, they was a high potentiality of my ass gettin' shot the hell off."

Bobby says, "I picked up the call from Clyde and got there as fast as I could."

Jeremiah says, "And the shootin' stopped once you and the other boys arrived?"

"Yes, sir."

"And where do you think the shots was comin' from?"

Clyde says, "Back east of there somewheres."

He grabs a legal pad and pencil from the center of the table, sketches the scene. "Here's the parkin' lot, see, and here's where all the cars was lined up. I was standin' right next to this car here, when I heard the first shot, explodin' out the back glass of somebody's ride. Then the second shot just missed me, hit this car right here on the end. Now up that way is north, so over yonder would be the east."

Bobby says, "I eyeballed off that way when I got to the scene. At ground level I couldn't see nothin' but woods. But when I stood up in the car, I could see a deer stand way off in the distance and it had a view of the parkin' lot. The thing had to be a good five hundred yards away, and seein' as how there's so much danged smoke in the air, the guy must of been a heck of a shot even to get as close as he did. Anyway, I radioed for somebody to go check it out."

"Which is what I did," says Dewey. He places a plastic bag containing shell casings on the table. "I found these in that blind, which is over on Earl Guidry's place. We need to get 'em dusted for prints. But there's somethin' else."

Dewey is looking mighty uncomfortable all of a sudden, squirming around in his chair like his piles are working him over.

Jeremiah says, "You want to tell us what it is, or do you want us to try to guess?"

Dewey clears his throat, looks at the four pairs of eyes watching him while he twists and turns in his seat. "I spoke to old man Guidry about who's hunted out of that deer stand. He said his kids and his grandkids have, and some of the boys from over at the Gun Club. He lets 'em use it on account of it was them what helped him put it up."

Jeremiah says, "Did he say who in particular?"

"Martin Fletcher was one of 'em."

"Was he the only one?"

"Well, no, but . . ."

"But what?"

Dewey squirms some more, putting some real effort into looking miserable. "I run into Martin over at his daddy's yesterday, you know, at that reception after his sister's memorial service? And well, I sorta mentioned to him and Dr. Flatley from over at the black folks' church that Clyde was workin' the Uncle Freddie's case, you know, and doin' a good job, makin' real progress and whatnot."

The room is silent for a few moments.

Then Sonya says, "You are just unbelievable. Do you know that?"

"Hang on a second," says Jeremiah. "That doesn't necessarily mean he's the one that took the shots at Clyde, or that he knocked over the liquor store, killed the clerk and his mama. I don't know Fletcher myself, but based on what little I've ever heard tell of him, plus the fact that Jim Fletcher raised him, I have a hard time imaginin' him doin' any such a thing."

Sonya says, "Jim Fletcher also raised Sissy and given what we've found out about her I don't think he's a candidate for the Parent of the Year Award."

"That's a fair point," says Jeremiah.

"Check this out," Clyde says, leaning forward with his elbows on the conference table. "After I got back here, I had me a message to call a fingerprint tech down in Houston, been runnin' a comparison of the prints we done lifted off the roll of duct tape I found at Freddie's against the prints in the Sissy Fletcher file. Turns out there's a set that matches. Only thing is, the hands of the person was smaller back when they was printing up the Fletcher girl's pickup."

Dewey says, "What do you mean, smaller?"

"I mean smaller, man. I mean they was the same fingerprints, but off hands that was smaller. Like they belonged to a younger person, you know what I'm sayin'?"

Jeremiah says, "How much younger?"

Clyde says, "The dude say it was probably a teenager."

Jeremiah looks at Sonya, says, "And back when his sister disappeared Martin Fletcher was—"

"Sixteen years old," she says.

Clyde says, "And on top of that, the dude owns a white pickup truck."

Bobby says, "Who, the fingerprint tech?"

"No, man. Martin Fletcher."

Dewey says, "So what? That's mostly what the ranchers 'round here drive."

"I got me a eyewitness, says he seen a white pickup truck leavin' Uncle Freddie's around ten-thirty the night of the robbery."

Bobby Crowner says, "I seen Martin yesterday too."

Jeremiah says, "Where would that of been?"

"Him and his sidekick Dud Hughes come into the feed store, bought themselves a ton of ammonium nitrate."

"A ton? Right in the middle of the worst drought in fifty years?"

"They said they'd heard it's gonna rain this week."

"Plenty of time to buy fertilizer once it's commenced to rain," Jeremiah says. "Maybe they ain't plannin' to use it for crops."

"What else would they use it for?" says Clyde.

"To make ANFO with."

"What's that?" says Dewey.

Sonya says, "It's a bomb. It's what McVeigh used in Oklahoma City."

"You know somethin'?" says Dewey. "Old man Guidry did say somethin' about them boys down at the Gun Club havin' some of them militia-type tendencies."

The room gets quiet again, everybody thinking about all that's been said.

Sonya says, "What do you make of it, Captain Spur?"

Jeremiah reaches into his shirt pocket for his Camels, shakes one out, lights it, takes a drag, taps the ash off in his coffee cup. Then he says, "First, the print match on the duct tape means we got to bring Fletcher in for questionin' on the Uncle Freddie's case, and have him fingerprinted. Maybe he wasn't the only teenager that had access to Sissy Fletcher's vehicle when she disappeared, but he's sure one of 'em that did."

Clyde says, "You mean go out yonder and arrest his ass?"

"If he won't come voluntarily. What do you think, Counselor? We got PC?"

Sonya says, "Based upon what we know now, yeah, I'd say so. Plus, given that we have a reasonable suspicion that he and his buddy—what's his name?"

Bobby says, "Dud Hughes."

"Dud. What kind of a name is that I'd like to know? Anyway, since he and Dud might be up to some serious mischief involving ANFO, I think we can even proceed without a warrant."

"Good," Jeremiah says, "which gets me to my second point. If they're usin' ammonium nitrate to make ANFO, we best better get high and behind it.

"Third, this business over at the Emporium means we got to be careful, send three or four guys out there at least."

Clyde says, "Let's do it, man. We got four guys sittin' right here. Let's do it right now, before this crazy motherfucker kills any mo' black folks."

Jeremiah nods. "I think we should. But you need to dance down a little."

"What the fuck is that supposed to mean?"

Sonya says, "It means you need to chill."

"Alright, alright, I'm chillin'."

Jeremiah says, "Tell you what, I'll ride with you. Dewey, why don't you and Deputy Crowner come in a second car. Anybody know where Fletcher lives?"

Bobby Crowner says, "I do. I'll lead you all over there."

Sonya says, "What about me?"

Jeremiah takes a drag, squints at her, says, "You stay here. Try to get Vaughn Ford on the phone, see if he can help us with that bank account."

Clyde says, "What bank account?"

Jeremiah pushes back from the table, says, "Let's get goin'. I'll tell you about it on the way over."

3 6

IT'S DUSK BY THE TIME THEY FINISH LOADING THE PLASTIC DRUMS WITH THE ANFO. Dud watches while Martin rigs the dynamite with a radio-activated detonator they had boosted along with it. The detonator links back to a switch Martin carries in his pocket.

Dud says, "Where'd you learn how to do that?"

"Buddy of mine from the army showed me one time. It's real simple once you get the hang of it."

They close the back doors of the rented van, get in their vehicles, pull around to the front of Martin's place, park there.

Martin gets out, goes over to the driver's side of Dud's truck. "I'm goin' in the house, get my bag. Did you pack gear like I tol' you to?"

"Yeah," Dud says. "I got it at my house."

"Why don't you head on over there then? I'll get my stuff and meet you there. Then we can drive on into town, do this thing that needs doin'."

"Okay, partner." Dud pulls out, headed for his place.

Martin walks up the porch steps, through the front door, up the stairs to his bedroom, past the family room where the television is still running, playing for no one.

Two minutes later he's back in his front yard, his bag in his hand.

He takes one last look around his ranch. In the distance he can hear his neighbor's dog barking at something. He can hear cattle lowing. Cicadas saw away in the trees.

He had loved the country life and there had been some good years out here, before the drought set in, before the cattle market collapsed. But recent times had been hard, and a dime looks like a manhole cover to Martin now. If God hadn't reached down, chosen him as His Messenger, Martin knows he would have been bankrupt by Christmas. They were going under fast, even with his wife Linda working two jobs, one at the dry cleaners, the other waiting tables at the truck stop out on the bypass, where truckers used foul language in front of her, made passes at her, pinched her on the behind. His daddy would have helped if he could, but he was rich in spirit, not in legal tender. Linda's daddy was a worthless drunk. Martin wouldn't have asked him for a single thing.

Martin is thinking, *None of that matters one bit no more, now that I been anointed by the Lord to do His will.*

He's going to be a long time gone, a soldier in the coming struggle to reclaim the country for those who own it by right. He has faith God will provide for him and his family, of that he is sure. He only needs to do this thing God has set out for him to earn his place in history.

To earn his place in heaven.

He opens the door to the rented truck, chucks his bag on the passenger's seat next to his automatic weapon, gets in, cranks the engine. He reaches in his pocket, pulls out his bag of Red Man, gets himself a wad, stuffs it in his cheek.

As he pulls onto the highway headed west toward Dud's place, two Sheriff's Department cruisers are five miles away, driving toward his ranch from the east.

Sonya says into the phone, "Good evening, Mr. Ford. This is Sonya Nichols calling, from down at George Barnett's office?"

"Hi, Sonya, how are you?"

"Fine, sir. Listen, I'm sorry to bother you at home, but we need your help in an investigation we are conducting."

"How can I help you?"

She describes for him what she wants him to do the following morning.

When she's done, he hesitates for a minute, then says, "Look, I'd like to oblige you all if I can. But I'd kind of like to talk to my lawyer first. Would that be okay?"

"Sure."

"Where can I reach you?"

"I'm in my office at the courthouse."

She gives him the number and he says he'll call her back.

Outside she can hear somebody coming through the front door of the office.

She checks her watch, says out loud, "They can't be back already, can they?"

She gets up from her desk, goes to the door, just in time to see George Barnett's back disappearing into his office. She's wondering what in the world he could be doing up here late on a Sunday afternoon.

Five minutes later, she hears him leaving.

They follow Bobby Crowner's cruiser as it pulls off the highway onto the dirt lane leading through the thick stand of woods and brush that screens

Martin Fletcher's two-story house from the highway. As they roll up in the yard Jeremiah says to Clyde, "Pull over there next to Bobby's car."

Clyde slides his cruiser up next to Bobby's, slips the transmission into PARK.

Jeremiah gets out of the car. He can see some lights burning inside the house. It looks like maybe a television is on in a front room. It's nighttime now, pitch-black out here with no moon, hard to see well, but back behind the house, he thinks he can just make out a barn with a light on in it. There's a white pickup parked next to the house.

No sign of people though.

He goes over to Bobby's car, Dewey sitting on the passenger's side, the side nearest to Jeremiah. Dewey slides the window down so they can talk.

Behind Jeremiah, Clyde has switched off the vehicle, gotten out of the squad car, is checking his Glock.

Jeremiah leans over, looks in at the two cops sitting there.

"Ain't no way to know for sure," he says, "but my guess is he's inside watchin' TV. So Clyde and me are gonna go knock on his front door, try to get him out here."

Dewey says, "You want us to just wait here?"

"No, sir," says Jeremiah. "It's also a possibility he's in the back yonder, where that barn is. I think I can see some lights back that way. Why don't y'all walk on back there and check it out? But be careful, okay? Watch yourselves."

Bobby kills the engine. He and Dewey get out, walk back toward the barn.

Jeremiah looks over at Clyde, says, "Let's go."

They walk up the porch steps to the front door. Clyde takes a position to the right of the door and turned partways toward it, got his gun out, both hands on it, barrel pointed up at a forty-five-degree angle.

Jeremiah knocks on the door. "Martin? Martin Fletcher? Washington County Sheriff's Department. Open up. We need to have a word with you."

Jeremiah stops to listen, looks at Clyde, says, "You hear anything?"

Clyde shakes his head. "I think I can hear the television goin'. That be it."

Jeremiah knocks again. "Martin! Open up."

He waits five seconds, then reaches inside his coat, takes out his Colt with his right hand, tries the front door with his left.

It's unlocked.

He looks at Clyde, gives a little jerk of his head that says, let's go in. He pushes the door open, goes in fast and low, gun out, got the entry hall covered.

There's no one there.

There are rooms off to the left and the right and a staircase straight ahead. He motions to Clyde, telling him with hand signals to check the room with the television going in it, the one on the left.

Clyde moves through the door, over to the room on the left, whips around the corner, gun out.

He looks back at Jeremiah, shakes his head.

Jeremiah moves over and checks the room on the right. No one there either.

He gestures to Clyde to check the rooms in the back of the house. He points to himself, then to the staircase, then upstairs, telling Clyde what he's going to be doing.

Slowly Jeremiah starts moving up the stairs. He makes it to the top, moves from room to room. In what looks like the biggest of the bedrooms, probably the master, someone has left the lights on.

The bed is unmade. Drawers are pulled out of a bureau. The closet door is open.

Inside the closet now, Jeremiah is looking at the clothes hanging there. Women's things on one side, men's on the other. Overalls, khakis, jeans, work shirts. Looks like the inside of Jeremiah's own closet, only bigger.

Footwear on the floor. Work boots, cowboy boots, a couple pairs of dress shoes.

The shelves above are stuffed with hats, sweaters, some boxes of ammunition. Jeremiah reaches up, pulls down a green and yellow box. The lettering on the outside says it holds thirty-aught-six cartridges.

Jeremiah holsters his Colt, opens the box. It's empty.

Jeremiah heads back downstairs.

When Dud comes out of his place with his gear, Martin is already there, sitting in the driveway in the yellow rental truck with the engine idling, chewing on his tobacco wad. Dud walks up to the driver's side window, holds up a duffel bag for Martin to see. "I'm all set, partner."

"What'd you tell your mama?"

"I told her we was goin' out of town on militia bidness, be back in a couple days."

"What'd she say?"

"She said, who's goin' with you? I told her you was. She said that's good, with you along, she knows I'll stay out of trouble. Ain't that a stitch?"

Martin grins a Red Man grin, his teeth all brown and speckled. "Yeah. Okay, you know what to do?"

"Come on, Martin. I ain't ignorant."

"Tell it to me anyhow."

Dud telegraphs his exasperation with a sigh. "I'm to follow you into town, wait for you in the bank parkin' lot. Ain't a damn thing to it."

Martin nods, shoots a brown stream of tobacco juice onto Dud's St. Augustine. He says, "I figger to get this rig as close to the front door as I can, then run over to where you're at to trigger the detonator. Grab my bag and take it with you to your truck, would you? I don't want to be hauling that around with me."

Dud walks around to the other side of the truck, opens the door, grabs Martin's bag, says, "See you there, partner."

Martin slips the truck into gear, starts backing down the driveway.

Clyde is waiting in the entry hall for Jeremiah. "Ain't nobody here, man," he says.

"Nobody upstairs either."

"Found the dude's collection of firearms, though, in a gun cabinet in back. Couple shotguns. No deer rifle that I could see. No handgun neither."

"He's got to own him a deer rifle, though." Jeremiah reaches for his cigarettes.

"How come you to say that, outside of the fact that every redneck from here to Abilene probably has themselves one?"

Jeremiah shakes a cigarette out, taps it on his thumbnail, lights it, takes a drag. "I found an empty box of Remington cartridges up in his closet," he says, cigarette smoke streaming out his nostrils.

Clyde waves a big hand in the air. "Yo, man. Watch it with the smoke. Find anything else up yonder?"

"Drawers pulled out, looked like some men's clothes might be missing."

"Whatta you mean?"

Jeremiah takes another puff. "There wasn't no camouflage clothing in his closet. These militia types, they tend to be all about the gear. Walkin' around in camo is part of the attraction. Makes 'em feel like soldiers."

"So you're thinkin' . . ."

"I'm thinkin' our man has hightailed it with his rifle and his militia apparel."

"But the man's truck still be in the yard."

"Must be with that other one he runs around with. The one calls himself Dud."

"You think maybe we ought to go check his place?"

"Seems like a good idea, don't it?"

They walk out the front door just as Dewey and Bobby are coming around the house from in back.

"What did y'all find?" Jeremiah says.

"Bunch of empty AN sacks, that's about it," says Dewey.

"It's that load I sold 'em yesterday, all right," says Bobby. "Dud tol' me it was for him, though."

"Empty sacks, huh," says Jeremiah. He takes a drag on his smoke, says, "Sounds like they might of done made themselves a bomb."

"Wasn't there nobody home?" says Dewey, pointing at the ranch house.

"No, man," says Clyde. "Me and the cap'n here, we was just sayin', maybe we ought to go check out where this Dud dude lives. Huh. 'Dud dude.' That's kind of funny, ain't it?"

"I know where he lives," says Bobby. "It's over west of here. I've delivered feed to his place before."

"Whatta you think, Cap'n?" says Clyde.

Jeremiah Spur takes a last drag on his cigarette, flicks the butt out in the yard. He pushes the brim of his Stetson up with a weathered hand so he can scratch a spot at the top of his forehead. "Where would them peckerwoods be goin' with a bomb?"

Dewey says, "Probably a federal building, down in Houston, or up in Austin maybe. You know how them militia types are when it comes to the feds. They all think Janet Reno is a dyke communist who's personally gonna come to their houses with a team of Uzi-totin' ATF agents, confiscate all their weaponry."

"Maybe," Jeremiah says. He looks at Bobby. "It was just yesterday they bought the fertilizer?"

"Yes, sir. After the reception over at Martin's daddy's place."

Clyde says, "What do you make of it, Cap'n?"

Jeremiah tugs his Stetson back down, reaches for his cigarettes, shakes one out, lights it, says, "I ain't completely for sure. But I think we ought to split up. Sheriff, why don't you and Deputy Crowner go on out to Dud Hughes's place and see if them boys is there. But be careful. You see 'em, you call for backup."

Dewey says, "Where you all goin'?"

Jeremiah glances at Clyde, says, "I was just thinkin', maybe we ought to go back into town. I got me a hunch them crazy sons of bitches might be headed to our own danged courthouse."

Clyde says, "Shit. I ain't thought of that."

"I'm thinkin', if Fletcher was the one that knocked over the liquor store, then took a shot at you, at the same time he was settin' out to make himself a bomb, he's got some kind of agenda he's hard at work on. Could be it has somethin' to do with his sister's body turnin' up in that pasture. Maybe that was what stirred him up, and I reckon it's possible he could have got it in his head that . . ."

"That what, man?"

Jeremiah shakes his head. "I don't know what he could of got in his head. I just think we better play it safe, is all."

As he finishes speaking, they can hear the sound of passing traffic out on the highway a couple hundred yards away.

Two vehicles. A yellow panel truck, followed by a white pickup, headed east, toward town, going just over the speed limit.

37

CLYDE THOMAS SAYS, "YOU KNOW WHAT, MAN? I THINK I AGREES WITH YOU. We better bounce on out of here, get down yonder, you know what I'm sayin'?"

As they jog over to the cruiser, Clyde says, "You mind drivin'?"

Jeremiah says, "Makes me no never mind. How come?"

"I wants to call Sonya, tell her to get the hell out of there, her and everybody else, 'til we can track these crazy-ass motherfuckers down."

As they get in the cruiser, Jeremiah says, "Good idea." Clyde hands him the keys and he cranks the engine.

Directly Jeremiah is pulling the cruiser out onto the highway, hitting the siren and the lights once he gains the pavement, heading east into town, followed by Bobby Crowner driving the other cruiser, who turns in the opposite direction.

Clyde unclips his cell phone from his belt, finds where he's saved Sonya's office number for one-touch dialing, punches the SEND button.

"Come on, baby," he says. "Answer the phone."

Sonya had forgotten that the bank's counsel was Walt Turner, the nerdiest, most anal-retentive lender's lawyer in the history of nerdy, anal-retentive lender's lawyers, until her phone rang and she heard his nasal whine at the other end, launching without preamble or even a "howdy" into a recitation of various common and statutory law principles, principles designed to protect the customer's right to privacy and that could be invoked in a lawsuit by a contingency fee lawyer representing a depositor against the bank were it to be so imprudent as to comply with her request of Vaughn Ford.

After she had sat through ten minutes of his diatribe she finally got a chance to say something herself. "Walt," she is saying, "I'll grant you, you're very learned and I've always wanted to hear an extemporaneous lecture from you on this very subject, but maybe you haven't heard. The depositor is, or was, Sissy Fletcher, and absent the first resurrection of the dead in two thousand years, she is not going to be suing your client."

Halfway through her comments she notices her second line has lit up, somebody trying to get through to her while she's busy explaining to Mr. Two Hundred Dollars An Hour that dead folks have a long tradition of not filing lawsuits.

"But what about her next of kin, huh?"

"What about them?"

"They might have a claim, some kind of derivative cause of action. What about that? Is the county ready to indemnify my client if her relations sue?"

Half her brain is listening to this nitwit ask for indemnification and the other half is thinking that whoever is trying to reach her on her other line is mighty persistent.

She says, "Walt, can I put you on hold a second?"

He says, "Sure."

She punches HOLD, then the button for her second line. All she gets is dial tone.

Martin slows the truck down as he enters the city limits, not wanting to risk being pulled over for speeding, not with a truckload of ANFO that God Almighty Himself is relying on him to deliver. In his rearview mirror he can see Dud following behind him in the pickup.

Martin is rehearsing what he'll do in his mind one more time.

Taking a left onto Main Street, he knows he's less than two miles from the courthouse. He'll come down the street, reach the courthouse at its southeast corner, turn onto the property halfway down the block, drive up the sidewalk, park his truck right by the front door.

Then he'll grab the AK-47, jump out of the truck, run west, toward the bank parking lot where Dud will be waiting. When he gets there he'll trigger the detonator. Then they'll make for the Big Bend country, lose themselves out yonder for a while, at least until the uprising gets some wind in its sails.

In the distance he can see the town square, with the courthouse sitting in the middle, visible in the light of the streetlamps all around.

There is no God but the Lord God Jehovah and I am His Messenger.

He rolls down his window, spits out his chaw of tobacco. The action is fixing to commence and the Lord's Messenger doesn't want to run the risk that he might swallow his chaw if things start getting lively.

Clyde hangs up the phone, says, "Goddamnit, she ain't pickin' up the phone. Won't this fuckin' ride go no faster, man?"

Jeremiah is staring out the windshield at the road. He says, "I'm doin' a hunnerd now. We'll be there in less than ten minutes."

"Okay. I'll try her again."

He hits the REDIAL button.

"Sorry about that, Walt," Sonya says, back on line one now. "Are you telling me you all want some kind of indemnification from us?"

"Yes."

"For what?"

"Anything and everything. Costs, fees, expenses, liabilities, incurred by the—"

Sonya notices her second line lighting up again. She waits for a break in Walt's speech to ask for permission to put him on hold again.

"—bank, it's officers, directors, agents, counsel—"

"Counsel?"

"Yes. Especially its counsel."

"Walt, can I put you on hold again?"

"Sonya, I've got dinner company—"

"It'll only take a second. Thanks."

She punches two buttons, says, "Sonya Nichols."

"Sonya! Get the fuck out of there! Get out of there, right fuckin' now!"

"Clyde? What's going on?"

"We ain't sure but we think maybe Fletcher and Hughes might be headed up yonder with their truck bomb! Now go!"

"Oh, my God."

She drops the receiver, jumps up, grabs her purse, runs out the door of her office.

Out in the hall now, she hits the fire alarm.

All over the courthouse, sirens begin to sound.

The panel truck roars into the courthouse square past a pickup that's parked at the southeast corner. Martin has to swing around it.

In front of the pickup now, he jerks the steering wheel hard to the left, stomps on the accelerator, jumps the curb, drives up the front sidewalk.

Duke is sleeping on his side in the bed of Jeremiah's pickup when the sound of an engine racing wakes him up.

He stands up, shakes himself, watches the panel truck roar past him.

As the panel truck jumps the curb and heads toward the front door of the courthouse, he growls.

Sonya figures the quickest way out is the front door.

As she runs down the hall toward the staircase leading to the ground floor she hears the sound of an engine roaring, getting louder, coming her direction from down the street, somewhere off to the right.

Running down the stairs now, she looks out the front windows of the courthouse. She watches the headlights of a panel truck as it jumps the curb, then drives down the sidewalk toward the front door, where it slides to a stop and the driver's side door opens.

She gets to the bottom of the stairs, jerks the front door open, starts to run past the panel truck, wanting to get away as fast as she can, across the lawn to safety, when a powerful hand reaches out, grabs her arm, turns her around.

She looks up into the wild, grinning face of Martin Fletcher, his eyes above his beard wide, staring, such that she can all but see the madness behind them. His fingers dig into her arm.

"I am the Messenger of the Lord," he says. "And you are my prisoner."

"NO!" she screams. "TAKE YOUR HANDS OFF ME!"

She starts hitting him with her purse on his arms, his chest, his shoulders, scared now, wishing she had some kind of a weapon, something more effective than a Gucci handbag. She is screaming, "LET ME GO! LET ME GO, GODDAMNIT!"

With his free hand he slaps her across the face, stunning her. Her free hand goes to her cheek, her mouth drops open in surprise.

He holds her arm with one powerful hand while he reaches inside the panel truck with the other, lifts an automatic rifle off the seat, and says, "You're coming with me. So stop making trouble."

He turns her toward the street, just in time for both of them to see a big black Labrador retriever, ninety pounds plus of teeth and muscle and heart, running flat out across the lawn toward them.

Duke leaves his feet, takes to the air like a hurdler, hits Martin Fletcher in the chest with his front paws.

The force delivered by almost a hundred pounds of flying dog causes Martin to lose his grip on Sonya at the same time it knocks him to the ground. Duke stays on top of him, growling, going for his throat. The automatic weapon skids under the panel truck.

Martin hollers, "GET HIM OFF ME! GET HIM OFF ME!"

Sonya turns away from them, runs across the lawn as hard as she can.

Behind her she can still hear the preacher's son screaming for help, can hear Duke growling, right up to the point when the world explodes.

The heat and the light from the bomb going off turn the night into noontime in hell.

The sound of it is ungodly loud, a tremendous, eardrum-shattering blast. Even though Sonya is more than a block away by the time the bomb explodes, the shock wave knocks her to the ground.

As the force of the blast slams her into the pavement, her mind goes black.

38

JEREMIAH AND CLYDE ARE CROSSING THE TOWN LIMITS WHEN UP AHEAD THEY see a bright flash, followed a few seconds later by a dull boom.

"Motherfucker!" Clyde says.

"Yeah."

They race through the darkened town streets, getting to the courthouse in a few minutes. Jeremiah pulls up to the curb a couple blocks away. In the distance they can hear sirens, the local volunteer fire department scrambling its three-truck fleet.

Ahead of them, the front wall of the courthouse is completely blown away. The rest of the structure is on fire, the collapsed wall, whole sections of the roof, the inside of the building, everything burning, the flames stretching high into the night sky. When they get out of the cruiser they can feel the heat on their skins, the smoke burning their nostrils. The fire generates so much light you could read a newspaper.

"God Almighty damn. Look at that shit, man."

"Yeah. Them boys must of built themselves one hell of a bomb. Sure hope ever-body got out in time."

"I'm gonna see if I can reach Sonya on her cell phone." Clyde unclips his cell phone, punches in the number of Sonya's cell phone, hollers, "Shit! Fuckin' voice mail." He hits the END button, returns the phone to his belt.

"My truck is over on its side," says Jeremiah. "I wonder where my dog is at."

A crowd has started to gather, local people, folks that live nearby, coming out to gawk at the burning courthouse, forming a ring around it, kept back by the heat.

"Maybe Sonya is in the crowd somewhere," Clyde says. "I'se gonna go see if I can find her."

"I'll look too. You go round yonder way, and I'll go the other direction. Keep an eye out for my dog, would you?"

"Yeah, man."

Clyde starts working his way through the crowd, looking for Sonya. A couple minutes later three firetrucks come screaming up, horns blaring, sirens howling, lights flashing. The firefighters pull up as close to the court-house as the heat will let them, get out, run around their engines, hook up their hoses. They start pumping water on the fire, generating great clouds of steam that rise hissing into the air.

All the townspeople stand, watch, talk among themselves. Clyde can see their looks of shock at what had become of the Art Deco style seat of county government. Off toward the First Church of the Lamb he sees Jim Fletcher standing on a corner.

Clyde goes over to him, says, "You seen yo' son Martin lately?"

The preacher turns his eyes toward Clyde. Clyde can see the worry in them.

Then the preacher turns away, walks back in the direction of the church.

Clyde hollers after him, "We was just out at his place, found a bunch of empty fertilizer bags. We inclined to think this might of been his doin'. Y'all let us know if you hear from him, you know what I'm sayin'?"

The preacher keeps going. He does not respond. He does not look back. He walks slowly toward the church, his head crowned with white hair, hanging down.

Clyde keeps moving around the square, looking in all directions, stop-ping people every few feet, asking if they had seen Sonya Nichols, seen a big black dog. They all say they just got here, and they haven't seen either one.

He runs into Darlene, the dispatcher, looking like she's about half in shock. "Glad to see you made it out," he says.

"Somebody pulled the fire alarm. I heard people hollerin' and runnin'. I got out down the back stairs just in time."

Clyde looks at the burning courthouse. "Man, that's some shit, ain't it? Was there anybody else in there?"

"Not in the Sheriff's Department. The squad room was empty."

"You seen Sonya?"

She shakes her head no.

"She was in there. I called her, tol' her to get her ass out. I don't know if she made it or not. I can't find her."

"I'll keep an eye peeled."

"Thanks, man."

Directly his cell phone rings. He jerks it off his belt, hoping it's her on the other line. Caller ID says "D Sharpe."

Clyde says, "Fuck."

He answers the phone. "Yo, Sheriff, what's up, man?"

"What's happenin' down there, Clyde?"

"The courthouse done been blowed up, man. Fuckin' thing is a bonfire. The homes from volunteer fire is tryin' to put it out, got three trucks sprayin' it. I can't find Sonya. Cap'n Spur's dog is missin'. Bunch of folks is standin' around watchin'. It's totally fucked up, is what's happenin'. Where y'all at?"

"We're headed back into town."

"I don't s'pose y'all found Fletcher or the other dude."

"No. We spoke to Dud's mother, though."

"Yeah? What she say?"

"She said Dud left a while ago with Fletcher. Said they had some militia business out of town."

"Yeah, well, their militia business was in town, man, you know what I'm sayin'? I'se fuckin' lookin' at it."

"We'll get there as quick as we can."

Clyde hangs up, sees Jeremiah coming his way through the crowd. "You have any luck?"

Jeremiah shakes his head.

"Me neither. I ain't found shit."

"Let's try down these streets that shoot off the square. I'll take these two and you take them two over yonder. Meet you back at the cruiser when we're done."

As he heads down a side street Clyde is starting to have a real bad feeling about all this.

Forty minutes later the fire department is making progress getting the fire under control, and Clyde has walked half a mile down each street. No sign anywhere of Sonya or the old Ranger's dog.

When he gets back to the cruiser Captain Spur is already there, smoking a cigarette. Dewey and Bobby have arrived, parked their cruiser behind his. A couple of Department of Public Safety types had pulled up in their highway patrol cruisers, gotten out to talk to the Washington County boys.

The look on Jeremiah's face tells Clyde all he needs to know about whether he had come across Sonya.

The state troopers nod at Clyde when he walks up, then move on off to their own vehicles. Clyde takes his Stetson off, wipes his brow with a handkerchief, says, "I been up and down them fuckin' streets. I ain't found shit. Goddamnit, where the fuck—"

He's interrupted by the chirping of his cell phone. He takes it off his belt, looks at the display, answers it. "Sonya! Where—"

But it's a man on the other end of the line. He says, "Guess again, watermelon."

3 9

THERE ARE A COUPLE OF THINGS ABOUT WHAT HAD HAPPENED DOWN AT THE courthouse Dud can't get out of his head as he sits over at the Washington County Gun Club, nursing a beer he had fetched from the refrigerator, trying to decide what to do next.

One is how unreal it had all seemed, how it had been as though he had driven his pickup onto the back lot of some movie studio where they were filming a movie picture, some kind of action-type deal with Tom Cruise or Arnold Schwarzenegger.

He watched it all happen from his pickup. He saw Martin jump the curb with the panel truck, saw the courthouse door open, saw that woman, the one that lets that nigger deputy fuck her, run out, saw Martin grab her by the arm, go back into the panel truck for the AK-47, saw that big black dog leap out the back of a pickup, go hauling ass across the lawn, knock Martin down, pin him there.

Then that woman ran away from the courthouse, ran in his direction, while Martin fought with the dog. He watched it right up to the moment when they disappeared, they and everything around them, in an enormous burst of light and sound.

Just like in the movies.

Taking his best friend since forever to his reward in heaven.

Dud had been surprised at how big a blast it was. It rattled the windows in Dud's own pickup even though he was three blocks away, caused his ears to ring. He saw parts of the panel truck go flying off every which way.

Damn, it was loud.

It even knocked that lawyer down in the street.

Dud himself moved as if in a dream, slipping his pickup into gear, driving to where the woman lay unconscious on the pavement.

He got out of his truck, picked her up, surprised at how little she seemed to weigh, wondering absently if the excitement and danger of the moment was giving him superhuman strength like he read about, the kind that lets a man lift an entire automobile off somebody so as to save them.

He set her in the bed of his pickup along with her purse, then took off, headed away from the sirens he could hear howling his way off to the west, headed east, in the direction of the Gun Club, a double-wide trailer house set back in the woods a good ways from town.

The lawyer was still unconscious when he got her over here. He carried her over his shoulder like a sack of potatoes, laid her on a couch inside the Gun Club, bound her hands, found a length of rope in a cabinet, fashioned a hobble out of it so she could shuffle along if he needed her to. No way she could run.

He went back outside, got her purse, went through it, found her cell phone.

That's when he had his idea about what to do next.

He got himself a beer, sat down, thought about the other thing that he couldn't get out of his head. How unfair it was.

Martin Fletcher, the bravest, most God-fearing man Dud had ever known, tackled by a damned dog, then blown to bits by his own bomb.

It doesn't square with what Dud had been raised to believe about the world, that good things happen to those that do good, and bad things happen to bad folks.

Martin had been the finest man Dud had ever known. Sure, he had had his eccentricities, tended to hear God speaking to him from time to time, but who among us is without an oddity or two?

The fact remained Martin had led the best Christian life of anybody in these parts. The man was practically a saint, didn't drink, gamble, mess around with women, beat his kids. He was constantly in search of God's will for his life, spent more time in prayer and Bible reading than most guys do watching sports on TV. He went to church every Sunday, talked with his kids at the dinner table about the Bible, wouldn't have allowed them to have a television set if his wife Linda hadn't nagged him half to death to get one. Martin had thought television was an instrument of the devil, generally speaking.

Now that good, decent man is dead.

"It ain't right," Dud says to the unconscious woman on the couch. "It's all that damned nigger's fault, too. None of this would of happened if that nigger had left poor Martin's sister be, left her where she was out in that pasture. When he done dug her up, that's when all the trouble started."

On top of that, one of the last things his friend Martin tried to do on this earth was wax that jungle bunny. Dud is feeling like he ought to finish the job, as a memorial to his friend, to correct the injustice of it, Martin being dead and that deputy still walking the earth.

Dud takes a long swallow of beer, working himself into a swivet over the whole affair. The more Dud thinks about it, the madder he gets.

"Martin needs to be averaged," he says, although the word he is actually looking for is "avenged."

When he had hung around with Martin, Dud had always let Martin take the lead, had never asserted himself, had even gone so far as to alter his behavior to be more like Martin, more Christian-like. Martin never cared for that part of Dud that could be badass.

And Dud could be plenty badass.

When Martin was away in the service and not around to act as a governor on Dud's wilder side, Dud had gotten himself arrested twice for DWI and once for knifing a peckerwood in a barroom fight, some guy who had made a pass at Dud's girl right in front of him. Dud had fixed his little red wagon, just about chopped that man's ear off.

Since it was his first offense they let him out after six months in county.

Dud looks up at heaven, where he knows Martin is at this very minute, looking down on him. Dud says, "I'm gonna square it for you, partner. I sure as hell am."

Dud figures it's not safe to spend the night here at the Gun Club, figures they'll eventually come looking for him, once they get the situation under control in town.

He had only come over here to give himself a chance to figure out what to do.

Besides, the Gun Club is just about Dud's favorite place in Washington County.

There's an extra large Confederate flag that takes up most of one wall, some broken-down furniture, a coffee table and a countertop with gun and hunting magazines scattered around, an old refrigerator and a stove that hardly ever gets used. A bulletin board has been hung up on one wall, it's got a few gun show fliers and Texas Parks and Wildlife notices on it, plus a picture of the first lady, target superimposed over her face, bull's-eye right above that smile of hers, that smile that lets the world know how superior she thinks she is.

The firing range is out behind the trailer house, long rows of double-level benches with sandbags where guys sit, rest their weapons, fire at targets set at various distances in front of a little rise that's just high enough to stop a wayward round from flying off, dropping some heifer in its tracks somewhere.

If he had more light to work by and wasn't at the moment a fugitive from the law, Dud would get Martin's thirty-aught-six out of his pickup, go back yonder and sight it in, since he's got use for it in the morning.

Dud thinks, *It'll be a danged good thing to use Martin's own firearm to eighty-six that coon.*

He finishes his beer, reaches into his shirt pocket, pulls out the lawyer's cell phone. It's just like the one his cousin Arlene has. Arlene had even showed him how to use hers, how to find the last bunch of numbers that a person had called.

He turns the phone on, hits the SEND button, scrolls down the list of numbers until he gets to one that says "Clyde-Cell."

Dud punches the SEND key.

The deputy answers on the first ring. He says, "Sonya, where—"

Dud cuts him off. "Guess again, watermelon."

"Is that you, Fletcher?"

"No it ain't. Martin is dead. This here is his partner, Dud Hughes."

"Where'd you get that cell phone then?"

"I got it out of your girlfriend's purse is where."

"Where's she at? She be all right?"

Dud smiles. "I got her, watermelon. She was running away from the courthouse when the bomb went off, knocked her out. I scooped her up off the pavement and now she's my hostage. But if you a good boy, I might give her back to you tomorrow."

"Yo, man. You best listen up. If you hurt her—"

"Yeah? What you gonna do, huh?"

"I'm gonna tear your head off, motherfucker, you know what I'm sayin'?"

"Yeah, well, fuck you, man. Tell you what. If you want to see this bitch again, be by your cell phone tomorrow morning around six o'clock. We'll talk again then. Sweet dreams, watermelon."

"Wait, man. Hang on a second. Jeremiah Spur wants to talk to you."

Another voice comes on the line. "Dud Hughes? This is Jeremiah Spur."

"Howdy."

"Was you here when the courthouse got blown up?"

"Yes, sir."

"Did you see what happened to my dog?"

"Was it a big black one?"

"Yep."

"It tackled Martin while he was trying to get away, knocked poor Martin flat on his ass, rolled around on the ground with him. Somehow that triggered the bomb switch what was in Martin's pocket. Caused Martin to get blowed up his own self. I think your dog got blowed up too."

"Shit. That was the best dog I ever had."

"Well, he should of left Martin alone."

"I'd wager Martin did somethin' to provoke him, or else they'd both be alive."

"I reckon. Look, are we about done here? I need to shake a leg."

"No, we ain't. I ain't got to the main point, which is you need to turn yourself in. You need to bring Sonya Nichols with you. We can work somethin' out."

"Bullshit."

"It ain't bullshit. We're going to find you sooner or later. You turn your-self in now, we might could make some kind of deal."

"I ain't comin' in. I owe it to Martin, try to square accounts some."

"Martin's dead now and you're in enough trouble already. In addition to the courthouse, we make you and him for the Uncle Freddie's robbery, murder of them two folks. That's a capital crime, lethal injection is what you get for that. You better come on in and try to plead somethin' out."

"I didn't touch them niggers. Was Martin that put the pistol to 'em."

"The law don't give the remotest shit, son. But it might make some amends if you come on in, turn in your hostage unhurt, take the opportu-nity to 'splain yourself. Might be some mitigation in it. Wasn't your idea to blow up the courthouse, either, now was it? It was Martin's, I'd be willin' to bet. That means we might could make some kind of deal, based on the fact, Martin was just taking advantage of your gullibility, see."

"It wasn't Martin's idea."

"Was it yours?"

"No."

"Whose was it then?"

"Martin said it was God's. God told him to do it."

"Do what?"

"He said he was on a mission from God."

"What made Martin think God wanted him to blow up the courthouse?"

Dud shrugs, says, "He was the one what did the talkin' to God, not me, so I ain't completely for sure."

"You didn't go to the trouble to quiz him, satisfy yourself 'bout all this before you jumped in the middle of it?"

"Look, the way I figger it, when your best friend tells you he's gettin' messages from God, you either believe him or you get yourself a new best friend. Anyway, it seemed like he had some kind of notion that God was actin' through him to mobilize the people against the gummint."

"What people?"

"You know, The People. Your regular folks, your hardworkin', God-fearin' types who feel most of the effects of they own gummint workin' against 'em. Martin hated the gummint, all forms of it, thought it was athe-istic and evil. He thought God wanted him to start a rebellion, somethin' like that."

"And this rebellion of his was gonna get kicked off by him blowin' up the Washington County courthouse?"

"Yeah. That was the gist of it. Kindly like the Boston Tea Party."

"The Boston Tea Party?"

"Yeah."

"What about his sister? Did this have anything to do with her?"

"I don't rightly know, although it did seem like she was all tangled up in it somehow. It was almost like he thought that nigger findin' his sister's body was God's way of focusin' him on the courthouse, gettin' him pointed in the right direction. He once said he wished his sister would of stayed buried but God let you all find her as a signal to him about what God wanted done. I got to say I agree with him about one thing."

"What would that be?"

"I wish that blue-gum had left his sister alone."

"Do you think Martin killed his sister?"

Dud shrugs. "I ain't sure, but I kindly doubt it. It's fair to say he acted funny where she was concerned but I knowed him pretty well, and killin' his own sister don't seem like somethin' he would do."

"What if God told him to do it?"

"Why would God tell him to do such a thing? It'd be against the Ten Commandments."

"Well, it sounds to me like the God Martin listened to wasn't all that hung up on adherence to the Ten Commandments."

"I ain't sure I'm followin' you."

"Never mind. How long did you and Martin know one another?"

"Since we was itty-bitty. We growed up together."

"How tall would you say he was when his sister disappeared?"

"Do what now?"

"I'm askin' you how tall he was. 'Bout the time his sister went missin'."

"Let's see. He would of been about sixteen years old. I'd say five-five, five-six."

"But he grew to be about six-three or so, right?"

"Yeah. But he didn't start growin' good 'til his senior year in high school. Grew about six inches that one year. Look, I got to go. You tell that nigger to be by his cell phone tomorrow morning like I told him to."

As he cuts the connection he can see the woman on the couch is coming around, starting to stir some. He tucks her phone in his shirt pocket, crosses the room to where she is, starts shaking her shoulder. "Hey, lady," he says. "Wake up."

Her eyes open. She blinks a few times, looks up at Dud, then down at her hands. She swings her legs around so she can sit up. She shakes her head a time or two, looks around the room.

"Where am I?" she says.

"The Washington County Gun Club. You my hostage."

"Who are you?"

"My name's Dud Hughes."

She looks at him, then down at her hands, at the hobble around her ankles, then back up at Dud. "Man, do I have a headache."

"I could try to find you some aspirin."

She looks at him, says, "I don't want anything from you."

He shrugs, says, "Suit yourself."

"Tell me something," she says, "what the hell kind of name is 'Dud'?"

40

JEREMIAH CUTS OFF THE CELL PHONE, HANDS IT BACK TO CLYDE. "HE SAYS HE needs you to be by your cell phone in the morning."

"What you think the dude's got workin', man?"

Jeremiah fires up a cigarette. "Beats me. We'll just have to wait and find out."

Clyde shakes his head. "Fuck that. I ain't waitin'. I'm gonna go find the racist motherfucker, pop a cap in his ass."

"Clyde, he could be 'most anywhere," says Dewey. "He may not even be in the county anymore. It ain't smart to spend all night runnin' around all over the place."

"Yeah, well, it ain't yo' girlfriend he's got his hands on, neither. What if the dude was to bitch out, try to make it to Mexico or somethin', carry Sonya down yonder with him? You think uh that?"

"I'm just sayin' you're way better off tryin' to get some rest tonight, see what kind of a play he makes in the mornin'. Ain't that right, Captain Spur?"

Jeremiah takes a drag on his cigarette, then says, "I suppose so. I think he's probably gone to ground somewhere. I didn't hear no road noise over the phone so I don't believe he's out there drivin' around. It'd be my guess he's probably hidin' out. I got to say, the odds don't favor you findin' him by mornin', Clyde."

"I just hates sittin' 'round, waitin'. It's jive bullshit, is what it is."

Jeremiah says, "I understand, but I can't see a better option. Dewey?"

"Yes, sir?"

"I don't see why we got to do all the work. Why don't you go over there to one of them DPS boys, tell him we need 'em to put an APB out on Dud Hughes, that he's got hisself a hostage, is armed, dangerous. Tell 'em we also need 'em to get a man to watch his house. I doubt he'd go back there tonight, but it's worth doin' anyway."

"That's a roger." Dewey starts over toward the highway patrol.

"Hold it a second," Jeremiah says. "Was all your department's gear, your Kevlar and whatnot, in the courthouse?"

Dewey stops, says, "Yes, sir. It was all in storage up in the office. It's about turned to shit now, I reckon."

"Alright, then. While you're at it, why don't you ask the DPS if they can get someone down here tonight with four or five sets of SWAT gear, you know, helmets, vests, sniper rifles, just in case we need it tomorrow."

"Okay, Captain."

Dewey is gone for five minutes, then comes back. "The highway patrol says they're more than happy to oblige us, ought to have the SWAT gear here by midnight."

From over by the courthouse, they see Bobby walking their direction. "Hey, fellers," he hollers.

"Yo," Clyde hollers back. "What's up?"

"Rose has opened the Farm-to-Market, so she can feed the folks what are gatherin' 'round. Y'all want to get somethin' to eat?"

Dewey says, "That there's a pregnant idea."

The Farm-to-Market Café sits directly across the street from the court-house. When the four of them round the corner they can see that the Café's plate-glass windows, the ones facing the street, had been shattered by the blast. Just inside the door, sweeping up rubble, is the proprietress, Rose Emory.

Jeremiah is partial to Rose. Just about everybody in Brenham is. If they gave a trophy every year for the best liked, happiest person in Brenham based on a vote of the folks in town, Rose Emory would have retired it long ago. She's a big-boned woman in her mid-forties, grew up with a dozen brothers and sisters in an Irish Catholic family up in St. Louis, moved down here twenty years ago, got in the restaurant business.

Folks drive from four counties over just for a bowl of her chili.

She looks up from her broom work as they come trooping through the door. She's wearing the first frown Jeremiah has ever seen on her face, an expression that's as out of place there as a mute is at a sing-a-long.

"Howdy, boys," she says, the Midwest accent still in her voice.

"Hey, Rose," they all say.

"You all come on in, take any seat you like. I'll be with you in a minute. Help yourselves to some iced tea or coffee. We got fresh pots sitting in the back."

They thank her kindly.

She shakes her head, says, "I can't believe something like this would hap-pen here. Beats anything I've ever seen. Word is that Martin Fletcher might have been the one that did all this damage."

"He is," says Dewey.

"Was," says Clyde. "Dude blew hisself up along with the courthouse."

There are a few customers sitting at tables in the middle of the room. After they fetch their drinks, Dewey leads the four of them to a booth in the back where they can talk without being overheard too much.

They park their Stetsons on an empty table, take their seats, Clyde on the same side with Jeremiah, sitting across from Bobby and Dewey. They scan the menu, order bowls of chili and corn bread from Rose when she appears with her pad and pencil.

After she's taken their orders, Dewey says, "Rose, I got an uncle in the glass business down in Houston. Why don't you give him a call, ask him to send a truck up here, replace them windows. Tell him you're a friend of mine and he'll do it at cost."

Rose smiles her big smile for the first time that evening. "Thanks, Dewey, that's awfully nice of you." She writes down the name and phone number Dewey gives her, then moves off to tend to her other customers.

Dewey looks at Jeremiah, says, "So, what did Dud allow?"

Jeremiah summarizes his conversation with Dud Hughes, and while they're studying on that, he reaches over, grabs an ashtray, lights up a cigarette.

Clyde looks sideways at Jeremiah, says, "So what are you thinkin', man? You thinkin' maybe ol' Martin offed his sister, then pulled all this other shit, like blowin' the courthouse all to hell, so's we wouldn't trace it back to him?"

Jeremiah takes a drag on his cigarette, says, "I don't think so." He holds up a big hand, starts ticking points off on his fingers. "First, while I guess it's possible Martin might of been the one that killed his sister, it don't seem too likely. The coroner's report said the killer was taller than her, that the blow came from above her somewhat."

Clyde says, "You know what? I been thinkin' 'bout that. That conclusion assumes she was standin' at the time she got it. But we ain't got no evidence to say whether she was or she wasn't. She could of been sittin' or kneelin', either one. Then the killer wouldn't need no height advantage."

"Good point. That part of the ME's report has been botherin' me too. But that ain't the only thing. Martin would have had to have been mighty strong to cave her head in, stronger than most five-foot-five-inch sixteen-year-olds.

"However, and this is point number two, you could make a case based on how he's been acting that he was tryin' to protect the identity of the real killer. That might explain this crackpot notion of his, to blow up the courthouse, since he could of figgered out the investigation would be run out of there, and that if he was able to pull it off, it would destroy a lot of evidence and maybe even kill some of the folks workin' the case. If that is what he was up to, who do you reckon he would most want to protect?"

Dewey says, "The only person I can think of would be his father."

Jeremiah nods, says, "Yep. Point number three. Jim Fletcher tried real hard to talk me out of gettin' involved in this case. Plus I was over yonder the other day and I seen an overcoat in his office that might match the button y'all found at the scene. He said it wasn't his, said it had been left behind by someone. I think he was lying about that. I think it was his coat, it figgered into the murder somehow and he had forgot about hangin' on to it until Clyde found Sissy's body. That's when he decided to get rid of it.

"Finally, there's the stuff with the Baker kid. There was more goin' on there between Sissy and him than we know. Greg Johnson told me today Sissy felt it was incumbent on her to try to make up for how the kid had been mistreated by one of her kinfolks. My gut is telling me that mistreatment is tied in here somehow. And I think Jim Fletcher knows how it ties in."

Clyde says, "So you think maybe the dude offed his own daughter?"

Jeremiah shrugs, stubs out his cigarette. "Maybe. I ain't sayin' I'm sure. I think it's a possibility though. It's about the only thing I can think of, would explain the way Martin twisted off like he did."

Dewey says, "But what reason would Jim have to kill his daughter?"

Jeremiah shrugs again. "I'm a sumbitch if I know."

Dewey shakes his head. "I ain't sure I buy it. I'll grant you, there's a lot to what you say, and it sure don't sound like Jim has shot straight with us. But that whole shakedown Johnson and Sissy were running—don't it seem more likely that one of their marks would have been the logical one to pull her plug?"

Jeremiah says, "I've been thinkin' about that. But I really don't buy the notion that a guy would murder Sissy and let Greg Johnson walk away untouched, since without the vet there wouldn't have been no shakedown."

"Okay. I see your point there."

Jeremiah says, "Martin had to have been trying to cover up for Jim. Why else would the guy conjure up orders from God to bomb the durn courthouse?"

They sit quiet, cogitating on this, while Rose brings them their bowls of chili, corn bread, hot sauce.

Clyde takes a bite of chili, looks at the other three, says, "Seems like we might ought to go see the preacher man this evenin', check the dude out."

Jeremiah nods. "Let's you and me go over yonder right after we're done eatin'."

41

BY THE TIME CLYDE AND JEREMIAH GET TO THE CHURCH, IT'S A LITTLE AFTER nine o'clock. They can see some lights on in the back of the church.

Jim Fletcher meets them at the door, reading glasses on his nose, a Bible in his hand, wearing a force-of-habit preacher's smile that disappears when he sees them like a raindrop disappears when it hits a puddle. He has everyday clothes on, slacks and an oxford cloth shirt, makes Jeremiah wonder if this is the first time he's ever seen the preacher dressed in something other than a business suit or a clerical rig.

"Evening, Jeremiah," the man says, looking at Jeremiah over his glasses.

"Jim. Have you met Clyde Thomas?"

The preacher looks at Clyde. "Not formally, no. We spoke out on the street earlier this evening. How are you, Deputy Thomas?"

He sticks out his hand and they shake.

"I'm fine, Dr. Fletcher. How you doin'?"

Jim Fletcher smiles a sad smile. "As well as can be expected on this tragic night, especially if what you said to me when we saw one another is true. Do you all really think Martin had something to do with that awful business down at the courthouse?"

Jeremiah says, "Fact is, Jim, that's why we're here. Mind if we come in?"

"No, not at all."

The preacher swings the door wide and they step through. Dr. Fletcher leads them into his study, over to the little group of chairs where Jeremiah and Martha and Jim had sat together just last Friday morning. Jeremiah and the preacher sit down across from one another. Clyde sits off to one side where he can see them both.

Jeremiah reaches for his shirt pocket, says, "It bother you if I smoke?"

"No." Jim pushes an ashtray over toward Jeremiah.

Jeremiah lights his cigarette, exhales a cloud of smoke, says, "I hate to be the one what has to bring you bad news, Jim. Your son, Martin? He's dead."

The preacher visibly starts. "What?"

"I'm sorry."

"How?"

"Near as we can figger, he made the bomb that blew up the courthouse.

We think he drove the truck it was in up to the front door, parked it there, was on his way to someplace safe where he could detonate his bomb, when a dog, my dog as it turns out, jumped on him, knocked him down, triggered the switch that set the whole thing off. Leastwise, that's what his partner, Dud Hughes, tol' me on the phone this evenin'."

The preacher's face has gone white. "Are you sure about this?"

"Not completely, since all we got is Hughes's version of it, but we ain't got any reason to doubt it. I reckon we'll find out more once we take Hughes into custody. He's runnin' from us at the moment, has himself a hostage, a local assistant DA by the name of Sonya Nichols, a good friend of Clyde's here."

"Oh, my God."

Jeremiah takes a drag, tips his ash. "Bad as it is, that ain't all. I had gone with Clyde out to Martin's ranch this evenin', to bring him in, talk to him about the Uncle Freddie's liquor store job you may have heard tell of. We think Martin and Dud might of been behind that, and behind an incident at the Rose Emporium this afternoon, where somebody tried to clip Clyde with a deer rifle. It was while we was out at his place lookin' for him that he come down here with his truck bomb. If there's any good news it's that at the moment we think everyone got out of the courthouse alive. We got an APB out on the Hughes boy. You know him, by the way?"

The preacher's face is in his hands. He sobs softly. He nods his head.

Jeremiah says, "I don't know about you, but I don't think he knows c'mere from sic 'em. He seemed right confused about what was behind this plan of Martin's. He allowed as how Martin said he had orders from God to do it, and it seemed to have somethin' to do with Sissy."

Dr. Fletcher lifts his head, sits back, tears running down his cheeks.

Jeremiah leans over, taps the ash off his cigarette, pushes the tissue box in the preacher's direction, the same tissue box Martha had been dipping into Friday morning.

Jeremiah says, "You and I go way back. And I've always made you for a real smart man. The way I figger it, you must have some idea what it was in your son's antecedents that would cause him to hear God tellin' him to blow up the Washington County courthouse, and how Sissy would have figgered into it. Am I right about that?"

Dr. Fletcher reaches for a tissue, wipes at his eyes. "I can't believe he's dead."

"I'm sorry, Jim."

"I can't believe he's dead," he says again. "It's all my fault, too. I should have recognized his problems for what they were years ago, gotten him treatment. It's . . ."

"It's what, Jim?"

"It's . . . it's tragic, it's sad, and now he's gone and I'll never, ever forgive myself. I guess I just didn't want to face the fact that he was a really sick young man. Someone who is given to hearing voices, having paranoid fantasies about the government, like he did, had to have been. Did you know that his mother was schizophrenic?"

"No, sir."

He nods, wipes his eyes. "She was in and out of state institutions when the kids were little. She killed herself, slit her wrists while she was in the bathtub. Martin found her, the first great trauma of his life, but not the last, not by any means. I should have done something, long ago, when I started to see the same symptoms in him."

"But that ain't the whole story, is it, that he was mentally ill?"

The preacher shakes his head. "No."

"Now would be a good time to get it off your chest, ever-what it is."

He sobs quietly some more, his head bent over, his shoulders shaking. Then he sits back, wipes his eyes, nods. "There is wisdom in that. I tell people who are dealing with times like these to get it all out on the table. Then they'd understand why the most optimistic words in the Bible are 'it came to pass.' Implying that whatever their problem of the moment is, it didn't come to stay."

"I ain't sure I follow you there."

Jim looks up at Jeremiah, tries a weak smile. "Sorry. That's what passes for preacher humor. Tell me, Jeremiah, have you had any practice at taking confession?"

"Some."

"Where would you prefer that I begin? The night of the dance?"

"Tell you what," Jeremiah says. "Why don't you begin with Charlie Baker?"

Dr. Fletcher brings his hands up to his face, rubs his eyes hard, clears his throat. "You asked the other day about my relationship with Sissy. The truth is, she hated me, and over time I grew less and less fond of her. Martin got caught in our crossfire, was forced to choose sides, ultimately took my part in it, and . . . I think it must have done something to his mind, along with the genetic deck being stacked against him. And yes, it all goes back, in a way, to poor Charlie Baker. You see, to my everlasting shame, I once had an . . . unnatural affinity for young men. Boys, even."

He looks Jeremiah in the eye. "I want you to know, I did overcome it after ten years of therapy, working very hard with an extraordinarily talented psychiatrist in Houston. I am over it now and I have been for years. While I was still in thrall to it, I uh . . . sometimes I . . . There is no easy way to say this . . . I sometimes violated the faith and trust placed in me by the parents in my congregation."

Jeremiah works his jaw. "Seems to me like a pretty easy way to say it."

The preacher closes his eyes. "Charlie's mother so wanted him to go through confirmation, despite his being somewhat dull, intellectually speaking. I told her I doubted he could keep up with the other children, that he needed special attention.

"One afternoon I let the staff go home early. He and I were together here in the office. Sissy must have been about sixteen years old. I had thought she was at school, at cheerleader practice, but she came home early, feeling ill, and walked in here and . . ."

He looks up at the ceiling. "I guess I had forgotten to lock the door."

"After that," Dr. Fletcher says, "well, Sissy changed, as did our relationship. I tried reasoning with her, tried explaining that I was the victim of a disease over which I was powerless. I begged her for forgiveness. I promised to seek treatment. But she shut me out, and before long we stopped speaking altogether. As time went on, she became increasingly rebellious and . . . Ultimately she just spun wildly out of control.

"After she went away to school, I tried to keep her apprised of my progress in therapy, hoping it would lead to a foundation for a better relationship. But college was a disaster for her and when she returned home she was even more bitter and full of hate than when she left, all but destroying my hope for a return to a more normal relationship. Indeed, she appeared to enjoy embarrassing me publicly. She only called me to taunt me, to remind me she held my reputation in her hands, to report her many affairs with married men here in town. The only time she actually came around here was to get Martin, who was just learning how to drive. She let him practice driving her pickup, probably as a way of maintaining some kind of relationship with him."

Jeremiah lights up another cigarette, takes a drag, says, "What happened the night of the dance, Jim?"

"It was late—around midnight—when she came here. I was working here in my office, on the next day's sermon, as is my custom. It was very cold that night, and as we were having some budget problems, rather than heat the whole church so I could work here, I kept the heat off, and worked in my overcoat."

"The one I seen on the couch the other day?"

He nods, says, "Yes. I lied about it not being mine, and I apologize for that. Of course it's my coat. I have always loved that coat, you see. I bought it years ago, on a trip back east. I don't usually place great store in material possessions, but that coat, well, it is a very fine article of clothing, of which I was perhaps unduly proud. Even the children knew it, knew that when I was wearing it, they were to keep their distance, lest they soil it. I was afraid to tell you it was mine when you asked, afraid you would conclude I had killed my own daughter, since I assumed you had found the button that was missing from it."

"Let's come back to the coat later. Tell me what happened the night of the dance."

The preacher nods. "Okay. Like I said, while I was working in here, I heard someone pounding on the door that you all came in through tonight. I went down the hall to see what was going on, and I saw her standing outside, banging and shouting to be let in. So I opened the door.

"She had been drinking, but I don't think she was drunk. She pushed past me into the sanctuary, down the main aisle, all the way to the altar. I followed her. I could smell the stale beer on her. The cheap perfume. I can still remember every detail, every word of what we said to one another.

" 'So here we are in the house of God, the God of the great Reverend Dr. James R. Fletcher, the child molester,' she said. She was talking very loudly, almost shouting.

"I tried to shush her. I told her to get out, go home, sleep it off.

"She said she wouldn't leave until she had said good-bye one last and final time to her father, the hypocrite and fraud, and to get from me what she was owed. She said she was getting out of Brenham and not coming back this time.

"I asked her where she was going. She said as far away from here as possible.

"She said that every day she had to spend in this pissant town, she was reminded of how I'd fooled these sorry country fucks, as she put it, and it reminded her how much she hated my guts. She said if she had to stay here another day, she'd go completely mad.

"I asked her what she was planning to live on, and that's when she told me she had been blackmailing people for months, had put away almost sixty thousand dollars.

"But she said she wasn't sure that would be enough, and so, she said, I had to kick in some too. She wanted me to make it a good round number, a hundred thousand dollars. She said if I didn't, then she'd just write a letter to the local paper, tell about my, my failing, so why didn't I just make it easier for both of us by cutting her a check?

"I told her I didn't have that kind of money and she knew it. She said, well, the church does. 'Write me a check out of that account,' she said. 'You've got the authority. It's the least you can do after all the years of shit you've put me through.'

"I told her I couldn't possibly do that either, and wouldn't do it, even if the church weren't having trouble paying its own bills.

"She said, 'Why not? You're smart enough to cover your tracks.'

"'That's not it,' I said. 'God would never forgive me for stealing from Him.'

"She laughed at that. She said, 'Oh, please! Don't tell me you're afraid of Him! C'mon, Father, He's not going to lay a finger on you! If He were, He'd of done it already. Compared to child molestation, a little embezzlement doesn't amount to a hill of beans.' She said that of all the things that bothered her, maybe what bothered her most was that God had never troubled Himself to punish me for what I had done.

"I said God had punished me with the loss of the love of my daughter, and there could hardly be a worse punishment than that."

"She said that was twentieth-century talk-show bullshit, that real punishment involves pain or death and sometimes both. She said that sometimes it made her wonder, whatever happened to the Old Testament God? The God of wrath and vengeance, the God who got things done? The God that sent the angel of death to kill the firstborn of the Egyptians, that smashed the Egyptian army, that caught David screwing Bathsheba, and then killed David's baby, to teach him a lesson?

"She said, 'If He's still around He's asleep at the wheel. Or maybe He's just sort of given up, you know, after all these centuries, gotten tired of keeping track of these miserable, good-for-precious-little souls scrambling around on this planet, with their petty lusts and five-and-dime agendas, gotten to where not that much pisses Him off anymore. What do you think it takes to get His attention these days, huh?'

"She said, 'What if you and I did it, Father?'

"She unzipped her jacket and took her blouse in both hands and ripped it open. She held her breasts up in front of my face.

"'Would that do it?' She was shouting by now. 'What if you raped me *and* poor Charlie right here on the altar, would that be enough to get a rise out of the God of vengeance?'

"I had had enough. I told her to get out. Leave the church, leave Brenham. I told her I never, ever wanted to see her again.

"She looked at me, and I could see in her eyes how deep her hatred ran. Then all of a sudden she smiled, zipped her jacket up, reached into her pocket, produced a pocketknife, opened it, started walking toward me. Jeremiah, for a moment I thought she was going to kill me."

"Is that why you caved her head in?"

Jim Fletcher looks at Jeremiah. "Jeremiah, you have to believe me. I did not kill Sissy. At that moment, I would not have been sorry had she died, but I didn't kill her. She walked toward me with the knife, placed it right under my chin, like this"—he holds his index finger upright, the tip touching the bottom of his chin—"and she said, 'Are you sure you can't make some modest contribution to the Sissy Fletcher Liberation Fund?' I said I couldn't. Then she did a very strange thing. She smiled, looked down at my coat that I loved, moved the knife slowly down the front of it, like this."

His hand moves down the front of his shirt.

"She said, 'You've always loved this coat, haven't you, Father? Loved it for the same reason that I have hated it.'

"'What reason is that?' I said.

"'Because it makes you look so distinguished, like the man you want the world to think you are, the great, high-minded intellectual saint among us, instead of the poor white trash country preacher you are, with your dark little secrets and obsessions, just another miserable lost soul God has given up on.'

"Then she cut off a button and pocketed it. 'Something to remember you by,' she said. And then she said, 'Now, my little business here in town had a silent partner who's got plenty of ready cash. I believe I'll stop by and see him, get what's owed me, then I'll be history. In the meantime, be sure to pick up a copy of the next issue of the *Brenham Gazette*. You'll find a story in there that will interest you. And your congregation.'

"Then she left."

Jeremiah says, "So that was it?"

The preacher sighs, says, "Would that it were so. Our encounter had drained me, so I sat in one of the pews to rest and pray. I had my head down, my eyes closed. Then I sensed someone was there with me, and I looked up, and I saw Martin. He must have come over from the parsonage at some point, come in and hidden in the narthex, listened to us quarreling. You could tell from the look on his face that he had heard what she said, or enough of it at least. I will never forget how he looked at me.

"I sat him down in the pew next to me, and told him as gently as I could about Charlie Baker, which was very, very hard to do. But I also told him about the efforts I had made to overcome my affliction. I told him I thought my past was about to come to light, that Sissy was going to go to the press with the story, that he should be prepared for that. That since he was my son I owed it to him to make sure he heard the truth from me before he read about it in a newspaper. That I was sure to be exposed to considerable ridicule, perhaps even criminal prosecution, and that at a minimum we should prepare ourselves for the possibility that we would be forced to leave Brenham in disgrace.

"We sat and cried together, and he told me he loved me no matter what.

"We spent the next few weeks basically holding our breath."

Jeremiah says, "But instead she disappeared and there was no newspaper story."

"That's right. Time went by and nothing happened. It seemed like a miracle. I made no effort to find her. I had ceased to care what had become of her. I prayed to God that she would never return."

Jeremiah lights a cigarette, takes a drag, looks at the preacher, says, "Sorry, Jim."

"What? You don't believe me?"

"Seems mighty thin to me."

"I can't help it if you think it's thin. It's what happened."

"Then how do you explain Martin's wanting to blow up the court-house?"

The preacher examines his hands for a while. "I'm not sure I can, other than to say this. After Sissy had been gone six months or so, he came in to see me one day, here in my study. He said, 'Father, remember the last night we saw Sissy? Remember what we talked about in the pew?' I said I did. He said, 'I think God made Sissy disappear so your secret will always stay a secret.' Then he hugged me and he left the room.

"Then, the other night, when the sheriff came by and told me they had found Sissy's body I called Martin to tell him. I told him that this would undoubtedly lead to a murder investigation, and that the old things, the bad things, things he and I had thought were behind us might come to light. I told him he needed to think about what he would say to his own wife, maybe even to his kids if . . . if my secrets came out.

"He listened and for a while he didn't say anything.

"When he spoke, his voice sounded very funny, very tense, and what he said was something like, 'Father, I don't care who killed Sissy. But God will not allow the past to be revealed. He will not allow it. He will not allow it.' He said it over and over again.

"I think he was mortally afraid I was right, that your investigation would lead you just where it has, to my revelations tonight. I think that fear, com-bined with his mental imbalance, caused him to do what he did, gave him whatever mad justification he thought he needed. In the end, I think he destroyed himself, out of a desire to protect me."

Jeremiah Spur crushes his cigarette out in the ashtray, stands up, looks down at Jim Fletcher. "I only got one problem with what you're tellin' me."

Fletcher looks up at him. "What's that?"

"I think you killed her."

"I didn't, Jeremiah. Honest to God, I didn't."

"I think you did. And if I can figure out a way to prove it, I will. Now I want to know where I can find that overcoat."

"Why?"

"I want to have it run through forensics, checked for bloodstains and whatnot. You want to tell me what you did with it? Because if you're inno-cent like you claim, you won't mind us takin' a look at it."

Jim Fletcher stands up, looks Jeremiah in the eye.

"Wait here," he says. Then he leaves the room.

Jeremiah looks at Clyde. "What's your gut tell you?" he says.

"I think the dude is dirty, man. I think he's the one that done it."

The preacher returns directly, the overcoat draped over his arm. "I managed to retrieve it this afternoon, after our little chat this morning. Since you said you were going to look for it, I thought I had better get my hands back on it first."

"You got to admit, Jim, that don't sound like the behavior of an innocent man."

"I suppose not. At the time I guess I thought I might hide it, until it was safe to try to get rid of it again. You must understand, I wanted my past to stay secret, as much as Martin apparently did, and this coat seemed like it could lead to problems where that was concerned. But if you want to test it, well, then, please, be my guest. The results won't do anything but substantiate what I have told you already. Not that in the end it will matter much anyhow."

"What's that supposed to mean?"

"Just take the coat, Jeremiah." He hands the coat over to Jeremiah.

"Now, if you gentlemen will excuse me, I've lost my only son today, and I believe I would rather be left alone."

They walk back toward the town square together, the big black deputy and the old Texas Ranger, Jeremiah carrying the preacher's coat.

Clyde says, "I'm tellin' you, man, sounded like jive to me, what the dude said. Sounds to me like what was distressin' ol' Martin was, his daddy crushed his sister's skull, then buried her ass. I bet the kid even seen it and that's what caused the dude's soundness of mind to bounce up and hitchhike to Kansas or where the fuck ever."

"Could be, I reckon. Seems more likely than that story Jim was peddlin' just now."

"Yeah. That's what I'm talkin' about. Maybe we ought to haul the man in, print him up."

"Let me study on that some. Somethin's botherin' me about the way that conversation ended."

They stop to look at the wreckage of what once was the Washington County courthouse. The air is thick with the smell of smoke, charred wood, the whole town square smelling like the inside of a chimney that needs cleaning out. Firemen still hosing down the rubble, rescue workers searching the steaming pile of junk for bodies. Guys from over in Waller and Burleson Counties have arrived to give the local boys a hand.

Somehow somebody had gotten Jeremiah's truck turned right side up. The window glass had been blown out and the windshield is spiderwebbed.

Other than some damage to the body, it looks okay, looks like it might be driveable.

Jeremiah says, "Why don't you go on back to the Café? I want to see if my truck can get me home."

"Okay, man. But if it can't, I can."

"Thanks. I'll join y'all in a minute. Go ahead and tell the others what Jim told us if you want. And here, give this coat to Dewey if you don't mind, see if he can get the DPS to check it out for us."

As Clyde walks off with the overcoat, Jeremiah opens the door to his pickup, sweeps glass off the seat with his hand, gets in behind the wheel, broken pieces of glass crunching under his boots. He slips his key into the ignition, cranks the engine. It turns over right away. He shifts into drive, pulls forward a little ways, listens for anything scraping.

Satisfied it will at least get him home, he kills the engine, gets out, closes the door behind him. He sees four firefighters in black and yellow raincoats standing off on one corner of the courthouse lawn. At their feet are a couple of body bags.

He walks up to them, says, "How many victims y'all got?"

One of the firefighters, a guy in his twenties, looks at him, says, "You're Jeremiah Spur, ain't that right?"

"Yes, sir."

The fireman sticks out a hand. "Kurt Schoppe. I went to school with Elizabeth. How's she doin'? I heard she has the cancer."

"Yep. She's in the hospital, down in Houston. Don't know how much longer she's got."

"Bless her heart. I'm real sorry to hear that, sir. You were askin' about victims?"

"That's right."

"We only got them two so far, a man and what looks like an animal, probably a dog. Both of 'em was pretty near burned up."

Jeremiah looks down at the body bags. "Which one is the dog?"

"Let's see. That would be the one on the left."

Jeremiah goes over to the body bag, leans down, grabs it by its corners, starts to lift it.

The fireman says, "Captain Spur? You mind if I ask you what you're doin'?"

Jeremiah straightens up, says, "This here was my dog. His name was Duke, and he was a good 'un. We got an eyewitness, says he got hisself blown up tryin' to stop one of the bombers. I 'spect what's left of that bomber is the one who's in your other body bag yonder. Anyhow, I aim to take him home, give him a burial."

"Let me give you a hand then."

The fireman walks over, grabs a corner of the bag.

" 'Preciate it. That's my truck over yonder."

"Looks like you're gonna have a bone to pick with your insurance company."

"Yeah. But it's driveable and that's all I need tonight. I'll worry about 'pretty' tomorrow."

They carry Duke to the curb, set him inside the truck.

Jeremiah closes the tailgate, looks down at the body bag for a long time.

Then he says, "This here dog used to park hisself at my feet when I was sittin' in my rockin' chair on the back porch. Ever-when I'd stand up, he'd hop to, sure as a dog can be that if my butt wasn't in that chair it was fixin' to be behind the wheel of my pickup, and he wasn't about to miss none of it. I never seen a dog that loved ridin' so much. Now that I know my truck is workin', I might ride him around some tonight, one last time, before I head home. I reckon he would of liked that."

The firefighter says, "I heard someone say one time all dogs go to heaven."

Jeremiah says, "I don't hold with the notion. Never have."

"That dogs go to heaven?"

"That there even is a heaven."

"Might be easier if you did, what with your daughter and all."

"Yeah. I know. 'Preciate the help. And thanks for askin' after Elizabeth."

"Yes, sir."

Jeremiah walks away from the truck, headed for the Café.

Twenty minutes later Clyde and Jeremiah have finished telling Bobby and Dewey about their interview with Jim Fletcher.

Dewey says, "What do you make of her sayin' she had a silent partner?"

Jeremiah says, "I ain't sure. I ain't completely convinced she said it to begin with. But even if she did, I got to say, it don't seem to me it matters much."

"How come?"

" 'Cause I think Jim Fletcher's the one that done it. She sure give him plenty of motive, and if she went by there that night, he had all the opportunity he would of needed. But I'm damned if I know how to go about provin' it was him."

"What do you think we ought to do now?"

Jeremiah looks at his watch. "Well, it's gettin' kinda late. I think we ought to all go home, get some sleep, meet somewhere tomorrow mornin' before dawn so we're all together in one place when the call comes in from the Hughes boy."

Dewey says, "I been on the phone with the county judge. There's a vacant floor over at the First State Bank building they're willing to let us use for a while, until we can figger out what to do long-term. I'm goin' by Vaughn Ford's house when we're done, pick up a key, then come back over here, wait for the DPS to show up with the hardware we asked for. Y'all want to meet over yonder, say around five-thirty in the morning?"

"Yeah, let's do that." Jeremiah looks at Deputy Crowner. "Bobby?"

"Yes, sir?"

"Tomorrow morning, why don't you get Judge Roberts to issue warrants to search the Fletcher and Hughes places, see what we turn up."

Clyde says, "What about the parsonage?"

Jeremiah hesitates, then shrugs, says, "Yeah. Search that too. And get that coat down to the DPS."

"Okay."

"Now," Jeremiah says, "let's think about what we might need for tomorrow morning."

After another fifteen minutes, they get up and leave together except for Bobby, who had promised Rose he would stay behind, help her lock up, as much as you can lock a place up when the windows have been blown out of it.

42

THE PICKUP BOUNCES DOWN THE *SENDERO* IN THE PREDAWN, ITS HEADLIGHTS picking up jackrabbits scurrying for cover, their tawny backs and cartoonish ears hopping away from the engine noise and high beams, a few hops taking them back into the nothingness outside the reach of the headlights, lensed and diffused by the smoke and haze. But the armadillo's paleolithic design precludes speed, and from time to time Sonya sees one for a split second just before she can hear its shell crunching under the wheels of the pickup.

She knows she's somewhere out in the country and that's all she knows. Nothing is visible outside the wash of the headlights, the darkness of a moonless night made complete by the incessant smoke, such that the world could have been enfolded within a black leather glove. In the headlight beams the smoke is layered. It moves and shifts like a veil, like a thing alive and menacing.

Ever since they had left the double-wide with its big rebel flag, broken-down furniture, smell of gun oil everywhere, Dud Hughes had kept to roads so far back in the country Sonya can't imagine why they were ever built in the first place. He has driven in complete silence, directing neither glance nor word at her, his jaw set, his eyes fixed on the blacktop ahead, the dashboard lights giving his skin a greenish cast under his John Deere baseball cap.

Fifteen minutes ago he had left the pavement, pulled up to a gate set a ways back off the road, gone through the awkward process of getting out, letting himself through it, closing it behind him.

She thought about trying to make a run for it then, when he was out of the truck tending to the gate, but what with her hands and feet trussed up, she didn't figure she would make it very far, aside from the fact that it's so black out here she wouldn't be able to see where she was going anyway. She is conscious of the pistol Dud has jammed in the waistband of his jeans, a wordless argument for biding her time.

Now they are lurching down the *sendero*, the mesquite and cactus that line it on both sides occasionally visible in the headlight beams.

She looks at the dashboard, says, "Is that right?"

"Is what right?"

"Your clock there. Is it four o'clock in the morning?"

"No. I ain't reset it for daylight savings time. It's a hour later."

"Why don't you reset it? Don't you know how?"

"It ain't worth the trouble. In five more months it'll give the right time again anyway, and in the meantime I just add an hour to the time in my own head."

"Yeah, right. I bet you don't know how to reset it."

"I do too."

Sonya snorts. "I doubt that anybody who would get himself mixed up in that courthouse business has the basic smarts to reset a dashboard clock. That's like a baseline intelligence test in America. If you can reset your dashboard clock, you're smart enough to stay away from imbecile bomb plots. If not, well, then you're Dud Hughes."

"I can reset the clock."

"Let's see you then."

He ignores her, keeps his eyes focused out the windshield.

"That's what I thought," she says. "Stumped by the baseline intelligence test. Stuck choosing between Door Number Two, life in prison, or Door Number Three, lethal injection."

"Shut up."

"Don't forget to add kidnapping to an act of terrorism, plus more than likely murder. They give you a gurney ride for some or all of that."

"Shut up."

"And I still would like to know what the hell kind of name 'Dud' is."

"I said shut up."

Directly he stops the truck, backs it up a bit, turns it to the right so that the headlight beams shine on the brush line running along the edge of the *sendero*. He shifts into park, gets out, goes to the back of the pickup. Sonya can hear him rummaging around in a toolbox back there.

Then he appears at the passenger's side of the vehicle, opens her door, grabs her arm with one hand, jerks her out of the pickup. In his other hand he has a length of rope.

He starts walking her across the *sendero*. With her feet hobbled and the ground uneven, her pace is slow and she stumbles every few yards. Dud jerks her back to her feet each time. They're headed in the direction of a tree, a big oak. She has a moment of panic, suddenly fearful that this jerkwater goat roper has gotten it into his head that he ought to lynch her. She's wondering if it was prudent to lip off about his being too dumb to operate his dashboard clock.

But it turns out lynching is not what he has in mind. He positions her against the big oak with her back to the trunk, and starts tying her to it with the length of rope.

"What's up with this?" she says.

He makes no reply. She can hear him straining to get the rope tight, fix the knots. The rope cuts into her skin across her legs, torso, upper arms.

Then she realizes what he's doing. "Oh, I get it," she says. "You know, this is not particularly good thinking on your part. You should be using what's left of the night to put some distance between you and local law enforcement, because if they find you in the neighborhood when the sun comes up they are going to put you under the jail. Dud."

She can hear him laboring on the other side of the tree, the effort to secure her combining with the bad air, causing him to wheeze some. She thinks, *Maybe I'll get lucky and he'll stroke out.*

She says, "You're dumber than I thought, wasting your big chance to escape like this, playing these dumb revenge games out here in the sticks in the middle of the night. No wonder you couldn't pass the dashboard clock test."

Then she hears him close to her ear, breathing hard. He says, "Listen. The way I got it figured is this. I'm the most wanted man in the state of Texas right now, so it don't do all that much good to run. They gonna have cops at every intersection in the state, so even if I did try to make it out to the Republic of Texas, odds are they'll find me and I'm probably gonna end up in the jailhouse before too long."

As he is talking they can hear sirens way off in the distance.

"See what I mean?" he says. "So either Martin was right, and we got the revolution kick-started last night, which means it won't be long before the white hats come and spring me from the clink. Or Martin had it all wrong, and you're right, and I'm lookin' at life in prison or maybe worse. So it don't much matter what I do this mornin' other than see if I can't square accounts while I'm still out here with no bars between me and what needs doin'. The one thing I don't need on my conscience when the sun goes down this evenin', ever-where I may be, is the notion that that boyfriend of yours is still walkin' around loose and I could of done somethin' to prevent it."

"Your issue with Clyde is what, again?"

"He could of prevented all this from happenin' in the beginnin' if he had just minded his own damn bidness, left Martin's sister in the ground where she was."

"Funny. Some people would say it was his business that he was minding, responding to a call for assistance from a citizen. Since he is a cop, after all."

"Don't change the fact that Martin is dead, and it all goes back to that burrhead."

"You know what? I really think you need to lose the racial insensitivity before they park you in Huntsville. They have a Welcome Wagon up there that might make it kind of rough on you if you don't."

He makes no reply.

She listens as he returns to his pickup, closes the lid on the toolbox, gets inside, closes the door behind him.

He drives the pickup a hundred yards down the *sendero*, parks, kills the engine.

With the lights off, she can't tell for sure what he's doing. But it sounds like he is climbing a ladder. She hears a door open, the sounds of something scraping around.

Then it becomes quiet. The only sounds are sirens and coyotes howling in the distance, and armadillos snuffling in the grass closer at hand.

43

THEY COLLECT IN A CONFERENCE ROOM ON THE THIRD FLOOR OF THE FIRST
State Bank of Brenham, sunrise, such as it is, still a half hour away.

Dewey arrived first, at five-fifteen, opened up the building, set out
doughnuts and coffee he had picked up at a place over on the bypass.

Then, at five-thirty sharp, Clyde and Jeremiah pulled into the parking lot
at the same time, Clyde driving his cruiser, Jeremiah at the wheel of
Martha's white Buick. He left his pickup at the ranch, Duke's body still in
the truck bed, it having been too late when he got home last night to bury
his dog.

They sit around a conference-room table, not talking much, chowing
down on the doughnuts, dusting the powdered sugar off their shirtfronts,
glancing from their wristwatches to Clyde's cell phone which he has set on
the conference-room table, the mouthpiece flipped closed, a little green
light flashing on it. They finish eating and sip their coffee. Jeremiah smokes
one cigarette after another, Dewey doodles on a legal pad, Clyde paces the
room, looking at his wristwatch every other minute. Through the windows
they watch the day brighten to what hunters call shooting light.

While he smokes, Jeremiah is thinking about what he'll do with the rest
of the day once this episode is over. Thinks he'll probably go home, dig a
grave for his dog, then get cleaned up, drive down to the hospital, look in
on Elizabeth and Martha.

He called Martha at her hotel when he got home last night, aiming to
get a report on Elizabeth. He awakened her but she said she didn't mind.
She said Elizabeth seemed to be holding her own, which was the best anyone could hope for.

Then she asked him how the Sissy Fletcher thing was going.

He told her about all that had happened, about the courthouse and
Duke, about his suspicions where Jim Fletcher was concerned, about Dud
taking Sonya hostage, about what he expected might happen this morning.

She was quiet for a while after he finished talking. Then she said, "I'm
sorry about Duke, Jeremiah. I know how much you loved him."

He said, "I'm sure 'nough gonna miss him."

"Maybe you ought to get yourself another dog."

"I don't know. I'll think about it. Ain't likely I'll ever find me one like Duke."

"You never know."

"Can I ask you somethin'?"

"Sure."

"Would you mind if I buried him just to one side of the pumphouse? I'd like to be able to look at his grave while I'm sittin' on the porch."

For a second or two, he thought he heard her crying. Then she said, "Yes. Of course," the words sounding like they scratched her throat on their way out.

Now Jeremiah is thinking that the other thing that needs doing is some of that Bible reading Dr. Fletcher assigned Martha and him the other morning. The fact that the man probably killed his own daughter doesn't mean Jeremiah's got license to ignore his pastoral counsel, and he's already three days behind on account of all the time and energy he has devoted to this Sissy Fletcher operation.

He knows he's fooled around with this sorry mess way too long already. He needs to get back to the business of tending to his own family, get back to his own life.

"Boys," he says, "after sleepin' on it, I'm more inclined than ever to think Jim Fletcher killed Sissy. I think he done it when she called on him the night of the dance, that Martin knew about it somehow, and that's what sent him around the bend. I think that button y'all found just about proves it, but it probably ain't quite enough just by itself. If y'all gonna make the case, it's gonna be on ever-what other evidence you can get from runnin' forensics on his coat, searchin' his house and the church and what-not."

Dewey says, "I expect you're right 'bout that, Jeremiah."

Clyde looks at his watch, sees it's six-oh-five. "Goddamnit," he says. "I hate it when motherfuckers is late."

Jeremiah says, "If it's all the same to y'all, once we get Sonya away from Dud Hughes, I'm gonna back out of this thing, leave y'all to your own devices. I got me a sick daughter and problems in my ranchin' business, and they both need attendin' to. That in keepin' with the deal we made the other day, Dewey?"

Dewey says, "Yes, sir. I believe it probably is. By the way, I never did tell you, I'm sorry 'bout your dog."

"Yeah, man. That's fucked up, what happened."

"Thanks."

On the conference-room table Clyde's cell phone commences to ring. He snatches it up, flips it open, says, "Yo. Deputy Thomas speakin'."

On the other end of the line a voice says, "Good mornin', watermelon.

I hope you slept good. Hope you ready to step and fetch for the white man bright and early today."

"Where's Sonya at, man? She okay?"

"I think so. No reason why she shouldn't be. Hang on, let me check."

There's a few moments of silence, then he comes back on the line. "Yeah. I think she might be asleep. She must be awful tired, to be sleepin' tied up to a tree. I'll tell you somethin' else, watermelon."

"Yeah. What?"

"I gotta hand it to her. I'd have a hard time takin' a nap if someone had me in the crosshairs of a thirty-aught-six."

"A thirty-aught-six, huh? Wait 'til I get my hands on you, mother—"

"Here's the deal, watermelon. I got your punch staked out 'bout a hunnerd yards up a *sendero* that runs south from a deer stand on Earl Guidry's place. That's the very same place Martin tried to nail you from yesterday. I'm sittin' in that deer stand, and from this distance it would be an easy shot, rifle slug would blow the back of her head plumb off, and the coyotes would get to what's left of her before you could."

"You lyin', man. You ain't gonna shoot nobody. How do I even know you still got her, ain't already dumped her somewheres?"

"The only way to know is to come look, ain't it? Now, it oughtn't take you more than an hour to figure out where I'm at, and to get your sorry watermelon ass out here. In one hour or less, I better see you walkin' over that little rise in the land what's south of here, the one that's between this here deer stand and the Guidry place. If I don't see that happen inside of an hour, I'm gonna shoot your girlfriend yonder. If you come over that rise in a vehicle, I'm gonna shoot your girlfriend. If anybody but you comes over that rise, I'm gonna shoot your girlfriend. If I hear helicopters flyin' anywheres near here, I'm gonna shoot your girlfriend. You got any questions, watermelon?"

"No, man."

"The clock is running, boy."

Clyde clicks off the cell phone, tells the others what Dud Hughes had said.

Jeremiah says, "The dumb ass has gone and trapped himself. He must want you pretty bad. Dewey, you were out there yesterday. Give us the lay of the land."

Dewey flips to a clean page in his legal pad, sketches a few quick lines, then turns it so the others can see. "Here's the deer stand, up on a little rise here, and here's the rise south of there he wants you to walk over."

Jeremiah says, "Can you see to the other side of the rise from the deer stand?"

Dewey scratches his head, says, "No, sir, I don't believe you can. The land slopes down from there, all the way to old Earl's place."

"How far you reckon it is from the top of that rise to the deer stand?"

"I'm guessing six hundred yards."

Jeremiah lights another cigarette, studies Dewey's hand-drawn map, then says, "We ain't got much choice but to play by his rules, long as he's got Sonya. Them DPS boys, did they deliver the SWAT gear like you asked?"

"Yes, sir. Kevlar, sniper's rifles, helmets, the works."

"Alright, then. Y'all grab three sets of that gear and meet me at Clyde's cruiser in ten minutes."

He gets up, starts to walk out the room.

"Yo, man," says Clyde. "Where you off to?"

"I'm gonna go see if the Farm-to-Market Café is open yet."

As Jeremiah leaves, Clyde says, "Didn't you get enough to eat already? Shit."

44

DEWEY PARKS JUST BELOW THE TOP OF THE RISE THAT'S SOUTH OF THE DEER stand and they all get out. Jeremiah and Dewey are wearing bulletproof vests under their shirts. Clyde wears Kevlar over his T-shirt, carries his uniform shirt in his hand.

While Dewey goes to the trunk to fetch a couple sniper rifles, Jeremiah says to Clyde, "Turn around here, let me get you rigged up."

Using duct tape, Jeremiah fixes two freeze-lock bags loaded with tomato sauce to the back of Clyde's Kevlar vest. Then Clyde pulls his uniform shirt on, buttons it up.

Dewey hands Jeremiah a rifle, and Jeremiah checks to see that it's loaded.

Clyde says, "Yo, man, you sure you know what you're doin' with that thing?"

"I won the Rangers' top marksmanship award five years runnin'. Let me get into position before you go out into the open, okay?"

Jeremiah starts walking toward the right side of the *sendero*.

Clyde says, "Was that with a pistol or a rifle, man?"

Jeremiah keeps walking.

"Yo, man. Was that with a handgun or a rifle, you know what I'm sayin'?"

Near the crown of the rise, Jeremiah gets down on his belly, starts crawling forward, pushing the rifle in front of him until he's at the top. He arranges himself in a shooter's prone position, rifle butt on his right shoulder, stock resting in his left hand.

He would prefer to be wearing camouflage for this affair but he figures that against the dead brown grass and dirt his khakis will be a challenge to spot from any distance.

He looks through the scope at the deer blind, barely visible through the smoke, almost a half mile away, the rectangular box made indistinct by the poor air quality, even with the help of magnification. Down to the right some, a little closer to his position, he can just make out what might be Sonya, slumped against a tree.

Shifting his focus again, he pans the little valley between him and the deer stand.

Jeremiah turns his head, gives Dewey and Clyde a leathery thumbs-up sign.

Dewey turns to Clyde, says, "Good luck."

"I ain't got such a good feelin' 'bout this." But he walks to the top of the rise.

The night his brother Leon died, the cops came to his house, took a statement from him. He remembered the two big white men in their blue uniforms, smelling like leather and sweat, their hair slicked down under their cops' hats, smacking their chewing gum. He remembered them checking out his crib, the contempt he could see in their eyes, even though his mama worked hard to keep their place clean, tidy, unlike most of the shotgun houses folks lived in around there.

Those cops had made him feel small, him in his secondhand jeans and sneakers, his old Dallas Cowboys sweatshirt that he had changed into when he got home, his skinny wrists sticking out of it, while he told them about seeing the vehicle rolling past the corner, seeing the gunfire, seeing the bodies hit the ground, sights that had branded his mind. No, he had told them, he couldn't remember what kind of vehicle it was, what numbers were on the license plate. It had just driven away like the folks in it had somewhere they needed to be, like they thought watching his big brother die on the pavement wasn't worth hanging around for.

He had studied them while they tried to talk to his mama, his poor wailing mama, her going on and on about how the devil had come and snatched her baby from this earth. He remembered studying the gunbelt one of them wore, studying it so as to have something to do other than bear witness to his mama's misery, staring at all the gear that was riding there, the black grip of the pistol that was strapped down in the holster, the can of Mace in its little holder, the walkie-talkie, the baton, the handcuffs.

That's the night he decided to become a cop someday.

He wanted to be the one wearing all that righteous gear, the one to collar those folks who rode around his town, fired bullets into other people's bodies. Folks like those that snuffed the brother he had adored. He fantasized about that for years, saw himself hunting them down, busting into their cribs with his gun on full cock, saying, "You under arrest, motherfucker, for the murder of Leon Thomas. Come on, get on the flo', all of you. Don't give me a reason to bust a cap in yo' ass."

He dreamed of watching as they finally got what was coming to them, after they had been marched through the criminal justice system, dreamed of being there when they were strapped down to a gurney in the Walls

Unit, the needle biting into their flesh, the fear of what waited for them on the other side like heat lamps in their eyes.

It was a dream that had gotten him through high school, through college, and through the endless miserable shit that went with being a black man on the DPD.

The cops never came around to his house again after that first night, never did any follow-up questioning, never called to say how the case was going. Now and then his mama would call down to the police station, ask where things stood. Every time they had the runaround waiting for her there such that she never got a satisfactory answer.

After he'd been on the force about five years, he decided to go downtown to homicide, check out the jacket on his brother's shooting, see for himself what had become of the case.

It took the file clerk a while to find it, since he hadn't known the case number. Finally she brought it over to him, to a desk he was sitting at, dropped it.

"This file's as skinny as a soda cracker," she said, and walked away.

He handed it back to her three minutes later.

The only witness statement in it had been his. There were some ballistics. Other than that, nothing.

He thought about how they gave his mama the runaround every time she called, told her there were no new leads, but they were working the case, hoping for a break.

A couple days later Clyde tracked down a friend of his, a Homicide detective, the dean of the black Dallas cops, T. J. Williams, a twenty-year man with gray in his goatee, lines on his face, eyes that drooped at the sides like a basset hound's. Clyde caught him at his desk in the squad room at the big police station downtown.

Clyde told him what he had found, that the DPD hadn't lifted a finger to catch whoever had killed Leon. Clyde asked him did he have an explanation for that.

T. J. looked at him a long time. Then he glanced around the squad room, at the other cops sitting there, all of them white, and said, "Take a walk with me, son."

They walked out the police station, down the sidewalk, toward the park downtown where they got statues, bronze cowboys driving a bronze herd of cattle, the trail drive frozen in position for so long as there's a Dallas.

It was a while before T. J. spoke. Then he said, "A lot of these drive-bys, like the one your brother got himself caught in, happened back when budgets was bein' cut and everything was bein' operated on a shoestring, you might say. The department was strained for resources, had to pick the cases they were going to work based on . . ." He paused, stopped by a bronze longhorn, leaned against it, gazed off toward the big skyscrapers downtown like something about those big buildings standing tall against the sky had just captured his attention.

Clyde said, "Yeah? Based on what?"

T. J. looked away from the skyscrapers, looked back at him. "Based on the likelihood of getting a collar, for one thing."

"But there was somethin' else, wasn't there? Somethin' you ain't sayin'. Come on, man, the dude was my brother."

T. J.'s face had a smile on it like the one a man might have if he had remembered something funny about a friend that had just passed away. He said, "Friend of mine, brother who retired a few years back, was assigned to IAD back at the time of all the drive-bys. Him and another cop was workin' a case involvin' a couple Homicide detectives they thought was dirty. They had wired these two dudes' ride, taped the conversations that passed between them. One day the subject of drive-by shootings come up. Set these two yardbirds to laughing, about how everybody went through the motions, nobody ever wanting to break a sweat. One of them allowed as to why that was."

"Yeah?"

"He said, 'Why should the DPD do anything to get in the way of the de-niggerization of Dallas?' "

They would say to her, No, Mrs. Thomas, we ain't got no progress to report yet. We're working on it though. Why don't you call us back in another month or so?

The next week, Clyde had put in for the Washington County job.

As he crosses over the rise this morning, barely able to see the deer stand in the distance up ahead what with the smoke all around, Clyde Thomas is thinking, once he gets Sonya back from this whack job Dud Hughes, he's going to tell the homes back there he's reached his quota, he's not available to be shot at with a rifle from a deer blind anymore, at least for the rest of the month.

And he's wondering if sometime in the next fifteen minutes the Washington County Sheriff's Department is fixing to be de-niggerized.

Sonya had fought it for as long as she could but at length her discomfort had yielded to her fatigue and she had dozed off in the darkness, tied there to an oak tree.

Daylight had already arrived when she comes to with a start, not knowing where she is at first, then remembering it all in a burst of recollection stapled to a headache, her head smarting from lack of sleep and dehydration, she guesses. Her lower arms have lost most of their feeling from being tied. Up ahead she can see Dud Hughes's pickup truck parked under a deer stand, but no sign of her tormentor himself.

She looks up at the deer stand, at the window cut in its side, sees a rifle barrel emerge from the darkness inside. She tugs at her ropes in panic, wondering why that crazy bastard would tie her to a tree and then shoot her from a hundred yards away when he could have simply put a bullet in her with that pistol he has tucked into his waistband.

She looks back at the deer stand again, sees that the rifle isn't pointed at her.

It's pointed off to the left and farther up the *sendero.*

She tries to turn her head around to see behind her, in the direction the gun is aimed, but the rope restricts her range of motion too much.

Watching through the rifle scope now, Dud Hughes can just see the outlines of a man emerging from the smoke, walking toward him down the *sendero,* a lone figure, the photographic negative of a man, a black man emerging from a white background.

Dud knows that as a marksman he can't hold a candle to Martin Fletcher. That's why he had hogtied the black man's chick to a tree within a hundred yards of the deer stand. To get to her, the deputy has to get that close to where Dud sits now, sighting down the rifle barrel.

At a hundred yards, that's an easy shot, even if the man is wearing Kevlar. A head shot at that distance would be duck soup.

Dud figures to waste the big uppity wise ass, then go down yonder, fetch his woman before any more cops can materialize, use her as a hostage, bargain his way to somewhere safe. Mexico maybe.

Watching the deputy through the scope, Dud can feel his excitement building. He clicks the safety off.

Lying facedown in the grass at the top of the ridge Jeremiah Spur has the crosshairs resting just at the top of Clyde Thomas's shoulders, mentally allowing for the drop the slug will make over the distance, some four hundred yards. If he gets that wrong, Clyde Thomas is at best crippled for life. At worst, he's dead.

He shifts some, tries to stay relaxed, tells himself to be tough-minded, be patient, wait until Clyde is within a couple hundred yards of the deer blind.

Dud Hughes watches the deputy in his brown uniform with the yellow trim growing larger in his scope, the crosshairs resting just on top of the man's head, on the crown of the Stetson he's wearing.

"Come on, watermelon. Just a little bit farther," he mumbles.

The sound of the rifle shot in the distance causes Dud Hughes to flinch, lose his view of the deputy in his scope. He swings the rifle around to check on his hostage. She's still there all right, twisting and turning in the rope he had cinched her up with.

He pivots the rifle barrel, searches for the black man through the scope, then finds him, lying motionless, facedown on the ground, a stain spreading on the back of his shirt.

"What th—"

The sound of the lawyer's cell phone ringing in his pocket cuts him off.

He pulls the cell phone out, looks at the display, the name "D. Sharpe" showing up on caller ID. He says into the phone, "Who the fuck is this?"

"Hey, Dud. It's Sheriff Sharpe. How'd you like that shot?"

"Do what?"

"I said, how'd you like that shot I just made from up here?"

"Where?"

"Look at the top of the rise, Dud, the one that spade just come over."

Dud checks the top of the rise through the scope. Way off yonder he can just make out through the haze the form of a fat man, waving a rifle at him.

Dud says into the phone, "What, are you tryin' to say you shot your deputy?"

"Fuckin' A, bubba."

"I don't believe you. I don't believe you would shoot your own man."

"Can't you see the blood on him, Dud?"

Dud looks back through the scope. It sure looks to him like the man is bleeding. He says into the phone, "He must of knowed what he was comin' out here for. How come him not to be wearin' a bulletproof vest?"

"All our gear was stored in the courthouse. Your boy Martin blew it all up, or did you forget already?"

"I reckon he did, didn't he? Well, I mean, sumbitch, what did you want to go and shoot your own man for?"

The sheriff says, "Hell, I been wantin' to shoot that goddam nigger ever since I first laid eyes on him. I was forced to hire that shine against my own durn will and I ain't had nothin' but trouble from him since. I was tellin' Martin 'bout it the other day, at his sister's reception. Didn't he tell you?"

Dud is thinking, Martin did say something like that, now didn't he? He says, "But I wanted to be the one to plug his sorry ass."

"Don't worry, Dud. I'm gonna be sure and tell ever-body it was you that done it. You know, I got to say, I 'preciate you settin' things up like you did.

It couldn't have worked out no better if I had planned it my own self. Now I'm shed of that buck nigger. He won't be hangin' around in this white folks' town, pissin' ever-body off all the time, costin' me my reelection, insultin' me for no particular reason. You should of heard the names that boy called me. On top of that, he was livin' in sin with a white woman. Our daddies never would of stood for that, Dud. Ain't that right?"

"But, goddamnit," Dud says. "I wanted to be the one to shoot him. I got about half a mind to shoot his girlfriend."

"Go ahead on."

"Do what?"

"I said, have at it. If you don't, I'm gonna have to myself on account of she's the only person in the world who can say you wasn't the one what did it."

That checks Dud up short. Now he has another reason to keep that lawyer alive. Not just as a hostage, but as a possible witness too.

"Dud! Hey, Dud!" The sheriff is shouting into the other end of the phone.

"What?" he says.

"I got a proposition for you."

"What would that be?"

"I need to be sure that nigger is all the way dead, and on top of that, if you ain't gonna do it, I need to put a round into his lady friend. So I need to come down yonder."

"I don't think I want you no closer, Sheriff."

"You ain't heard what's in it for you, yet."

"Okay. What's in it for me, then?"

"A fresh set of license plates, for one thing. You can swap 'em out for yours, make your vehicle harder to identify. I'll drop 'em by that shine's body and you can pick 'em up when I leave. Plus, I been listening to the police radio this mornin', done figgered out which roads you ought to take, give you the best shot at avoiding the patrols that is out. I got 'em written down on a piece of paper I'll leave with the tags. With any luck, you can make it across the border to Mexico by tonight."

"Why would you do that for me?"

"Like I said, I don't want no witnesses around that can say it wasn't you that shot that coon."

"Let me think on it a minute."

Dud doesn't entirely trust this situation, but he's not sure it isn't worth a try. He's thinking, if he makes the sheriff leave the rifle up yonder, such that he only has a sidearm on him, and the sheriff doesn't come any closer to the deer stand than where he has that lawyer positioned, Dud can take the man out before he can pull off any kind of trickery or deception that he might have in mind.

Then he thinks, *That's just what I ought to do anyhow.*

Shoot the sheriff, trickery or not.

That way he can take the license plates and the woman both, still have himself a hostage. A new set of license plates would come in mighty handy, not to mention a set of directions out of here. "I ain't such a dumb ass after all," he says to himself.

"Okay," he says into the phone. "But don't come no closer to me than where I got that lawyer tied up. And when you're done, you're to skedaddle."

"Fair enough. I'm headed down there then."

"First let's see how far in this direction you can chuck that rifle."

He watches while Dewey rears back, then swings his arm forward, sending the rifle spinning in a lazy arc down the slope toward the deer stand. Then the sheriff disappears from the top of the rise.

Directly a Sheriff's Department cruiser appears there, moving slowly, Dud following its progress through the rifle scope. Once it gets close to the deputy's body it parks, its nose pointed off to the left a bit. Dud looks it over through the scope. He doesn't see anybody in it other than that fat sheriff behind the wheel. He watches the sheriff get out of the vehicle, walk up to the deputy's body, position himself over it, pull his sidearm, fire one round down in the direction of the deputy's head.

Then the sheriff goes back to the cruiser, reaches inside the passenger's side window, rummages around, pulls out what looks like a set of license plates, holds them up for Dud to see, then drops them by the deputy's body.

The sheriff starts walking toward the lawyer.

Dud follows his progress through the rifle's scope as he moves down the *sendero.*

Jeremiah hides on the backseat of the cruiser, his knees folded up against his chest, holding himself as still as he can. He hears Dewey fire a round into the ground, then hears Dewey return to the cruiser to get the license plates.

Dewey leans in, whispers, "I see her. She's another hundred fifty yards farther down on the right. Give me sixty seconds after you hear them license plates hit the ground."

"Roger," Jeremiah says back to him.

Then Dewey backs out of the cruiser, holding the license plates high. They hit the ground with a metallic click, and Jeremiah starts counting under his breath. "One-Mississippi, two-Mississippi, three-Mississippi . . ."

When he gets to fifty-Mississippi, he eases the sniper rifle around such that he can get the barrel out the window and pointed toward the deer stand. Moving the rifle and his body with care, he positions the rifle butt against his shoulder, the very end of the barrel sticking out the window. He looks through the scope. He sets the crosshairs at the top of the deer stand window.

He can see Dud Hughes's rifle barrel sticking out the window, pointed at a forty-five-degree angle to his position.

He steadies his sight, takes a deep breath, exhales slowly, squeezes the trigger.

Through the rifle's scope Dud can see the fat sheriff waddling down the *sendero*. Dud follows him in the scope, can see the dark spots on the sheriff's shirt where he has sweated through it.

Dud clicks off the safety, slips his index finger inside the trigger guard.

The sheriff is about fifty feet from where the woman is tied up. He's reaching into his holster, taking out his pistol.

At that moment something slams into Dud's right shoulder, knocking him backward in the deer stand, sending Martin's thirty-aught-six clattering to the floor down beside him. He struggles to get up, pain screaming down his entire right side.

He feels the warmth of his own blood flowing down his arm.

His ears are ringing and the pain is so intense it makes him want to spit up. He pushes himself up with his left hand, fetches Martin's rifle off the floor, goes back to the window, determined to get a shot off, put a slug in that double-crossing sheriff.

As soon as he hears the report from Captain Spur's rifle, Dewey starts running. He runs wheezing until he has covered the rest of the distance to Sonya, planting himself between her and Dud Hughes, hoping the old Ranger's aim was good, hoping that if it wasn't he can trust the Kevlar on his back, Kevlar that feels like a ski parka out here in the heat.

Sonya's head is hanging on her chest when he gets there and for a moment he's afraid she's dead already.

Then she lifts her head, looks at him, says, "I suppose you're here to collect your apology for that brains and courage crack, huh?"

Clyde is on his feet, Glock in his right hand, running for the deer stand as hard as he can from the moment he hears Captain Spur fire. Any second he expects to see the man up yonder appear in that window again, deer rifle aimed at him, trying to put a round through Clyde's bald head.

In fifteen seconds he's close enough to hear Dud Hughes thrashing around in there.

No way to know if he's been hit, or how bad he might be hurt.

Clyde gets to the deer blind, thinks about running under it, filling it full of lead from the bottom, decides against it. He pulls up short, aims his Glock at the window, holds it in both hands, widens his stance.

With his left hand Dud Hughes manuevers the rifle out the window, points it off to the left, where he had tied up the lawyer, moves to put his shoulder against the butt.

That's when he first realizes his right shoulder is pretty much gone.

Down below he hears a voice say, "Freeze, motherfucker."

Dud looks down.

Clyde Thomas has a pistol pointed right at him.

Dud Hughes starts to pivot the rifle over and down.

As Jeremiah runs up to the deer stand he sees Clyde fire two rounds, sending Dud Hughes reeling back inside the deer stand. Then Clyde walks under the deer stand, aims his Glock upward at its plywood bottom, empties the rest of his magazine into it.

The deer stand vibrates with each round Clyde fires into Dud's body.

Jeremiah thinks, *Force equals mass times acceleration.*

Dud Hughes's blood drips through the punctures Clyde has made with his nine-millimeter in the bottom of the deer blind, thick drops of crimson rain in the gray morning light, like something out of a scene from some lost chapter of Exodus.

Clyde holsters his weapon, walks up to Jeremiah, says, "That oughta about do it."

Jeremiah looks at the blood dripping down, says, "I reckon."

"Yo, man," Clyde says, stripping out of his shirt. "You want to give me a hand with the sacks of Ragu back yonder? I don't want to be around Sonya smellin' like I spent the night sleepin' in a big ravioli or some shit."

45

WASHINGTON COUNTY'S TWO WORKING AMBULANCES RARELY SEE SIMULTANE-
ous action. Dewey had used his cell phone to request them both to come
out to Earl Guidry's place, one to carry Dud's body to the morgue, the
other for Sonya to ride in to the emergency room to get her checked out
after her rough night.

While they wait for the ambulances they collect the rifle from the top of
the ridge, search Dud's vehicle, listen to Sonya tell about her experience as
Dud's hostage.

After about a half hour the sheriff is fixing to call his request in again
when a lone ambulance tops the rise off to the south and rolls slowly their
way.

The ambulance parks and two EMTs get out, help Sonya get situated in the back. Clyde climbs in next to her, holding her hand, the
musculature of his black arms and shoulders highlighted against his
white T-shirt. One of the EMTs stays in the back with them to check
Sonya's vital signs and whatnot while the other walks with Jeremiah and
Dewey to the front of the vehicle, gets in behind the wheel, ready to
drive off.

"We gonna have to wait long for that other ambulance?" Dewey says.

"It's going to be a little while, I expect," the driver says. "We had another
call right before y'all's. That's what's holdin' up our other rig."

"Yeah? Where was that?"

"Over at Dr. Fletcher's house."

"Do what?" says Jeremiah.

The guy turns the key in the ignition. The engine fires up. He looks out
the window at them. "The preacher's maid called first thing this morning,
all hysterical. She went over yonder to get her workday started, found the
preacher's body. Looks like he shot himself in the head, sometime last night,
probably. Reckon he couldn't live no more with the fact his son was a nut-
case that had blowed up our courthouse."

The EMT slips the ambulance in gear, pulls away, goes bouncing up the
sendero until he disappears over the rise to the south.

"Son of a bitch," says Dewey. "I reckon that tells us what we needed to know."

"I reckon," says Jeremiah Spur.

Later, while Jeremiah is on his way home, he decides he'll brew himself some coffee once he gets there, read some of the Bible verses Dr. Fletcher had assigned, try to get some kind of spiritual state of mind working before he buries his dog.

He'd just as lief not think about the last twenty-four hours, the tragedy of it, but it's damned hard to get out of his mind.

He should have figured that if Jim Fletcher was getting shed of his secrets like he was, that he was planning to do his own self in. He should have tried to do something, maybe arrested the preacher, if for no reason other than protection from himself.

He had told the sheriff when they took their leave of one another a while ago that Dewey ought to do what he could to finish up the Fletcher case, do the searches they had discussed, run the forensics, talk to anybody else that might have evidence, even though it seemed pretty clear Jim Fletcher was the one that had caved in his daughter's skull.

The one thing Jeremiah can't quite understand is why the man didn't own up to it last night, when he was telling his story about the night of the dance, if he had been planning all along to swallow his own pistol. Jeremiah speculates that maybe he had been afraid Jeremiah would run him in, deprive him of the chance to end his own misery.

Bobby Crowner and Jake Goodman reported that they had been all through the preacher's house and his study over at the church but hadn't found a suicide note. Jeremiah figures one will turn up at some point, and maybe that's where Jim Fletcher's final confession will be found, his confession to having killed his own daughter.

After he gets home, gets his coffee started, Jeremiah sets about trying to find Martha's Bible, the one she carries with her to church, that she had fixed little tabs in to mark the beginnings of each of the various Books. After ten minutes of rummaging around, he decides she must of taken it to Houston with her, so she would have it handy while she was down yonder.

He's about to offload his Bible reading plans when he remembers Martha's mama's Bible, high up on the top shelf in the family room. That'll do just fine, he decides.

Even though he's well over six feet himself, he has to stand on tiptoe, stretch up high to get the Bible down.

He gets ahold of it with his right hand, pulls it down toward him, almost dropping it, grabbing the front cover and some of the text to keep from los-ing his grip on it altogether. Something falls out of the Bible, flutters to the floor, some kind of yellow envelope. He is bending over to pick it up when he sees the mailing label.

The sight of it freezes him in place.

4 6

CLYDE TELLS SONYA HIS STORY FROM THE NIGHT BEFORE WHILE THEY RIDE IN the back of the ambulance with the EMT hovering over her. Clyde tells her nobody but Jeremiah's dog and Martin Fletcher died in the bombing, thanks to her pulling the fire alarm, giving everybody time to get out. He's fixing to tell her about their interview with Jim Fletcher when the EMT looks up from what he's doing, says, "Jim Fletcher? The preacher?"

"Yeah, man. You know him?"

"Can't say as I do. But we got a call this mornin' to come fetch his body."

"Say what?"

"Yeah. The guy pulled his own plug last night."

Clyde and Sonya exchange looks. Clyde says, "He musta been the one then. Man must of waxed his own kid."

Clyde tells Sonya Jim Fletcher's story, about what had happened between him and the Baker kid, his version of the doings at the church on the night of the dance.

Sonya says, "But you all think he lied about killing Sissy."

"That's what the cap'n thinks alright."

Clyde then tells how they had set Dud up to be taken out by Jeremiah, hiding with a rifle in the backseat of the sheriff's patrol car.

Sonya says, "So it was Captain Spur's idea to fake Dewey's shooting of you, to get you all close enough to take out Hughes?"

"Yeah. Dewey done tol' us he had mentioned to Martin Fletcher and Dr. Flatley that me and him had had ourselves a fallin' out, exchanged words. The cap'n, see, he figgered Fletcher and Hughes was so tight, there was a good chance Fletcher would've passed it on to the man. So the cap'n said if we could make it look real enough, that dumb ass Dud might buy off on Dewey shootin' me his own self out of revenge or spite or on general racist principle, 'specially if we threw in some special effects like a gallon of tomato sauce, then mixed it with an offer to ol' Dud of a get out of jail free card."

"Seems mighty risky."

"No shit, it was risky. We was like all out of low-risk options, though.

The key to it was to think like the man thinks, try to imagine yo'self as a redneck with the IQ of a baked potato, see what a dude like that would make of the situation."

"Thank God Captain Spur has a good shooting eye."

"The man has himself a righteous shootin' eye. He tol' me he was the best marksman of all the Texas Rangers for like all kinds of years runnin'. I forget the number exactly."

"Too bad about his dog, though."

"Yeah. Even though it was a racist dog, it be like a real hero and shit."

Sonya spends about forty-five minutes with the emergency-room doctor, a good-looking kid with a thick mop of brown hair, a lopsided grin, and a shy way about him. When he's done he tells her everything is operating within what he calls "normal parameters."

She dresses in her smelly clothes from last night, walks out into the waiting area where Clyde is looking at a six-week-old news magazine, some early morning talk show blaring from a television set over in the corner.

She says, "Thanks for waiting."

He smiles, says, "Hey, man, no problem. You check out alright?"

"Fine as can be."

Clyde's eyes roam the room, then come back to her. "The uh—"

"What is it, Clyde?"

"The dude didn't, like, touch you or nothin', right?"

"Of course he touched me. How else could he get me in his truck to begin with?"

"I don't mean like that."

Sonya sighs. "You want to know if I was raped?"

"Well—"

"The answer is no, Clyde. He kept his johnson in his drawers."

Clyde's grin returns. He comes over, gives her a hug. "Seein' how much lead I put in the man, that's just where it's gonna stay too, you know what I'm sayin'?"

Sonya is wondering what he would have done, what he would have said, if the answer had been otherwise. She starts to ask, then thinks better of it, thinks she's way too tired for a Clyde Thomas psychoanalysis session here in the waiting room at the Washington County Hospital.

Clyde says, "Listen, I talked to the sheriff a little while ago. The man say if we can wait a few minutes, he'll be on over here, give us a lift back to the courthouse, you can pick up yo' ride, go home, get yo'self some rest."

"Okay," she says. "It would be nice to get cleaned up, get something to eat."

"Shit, I didn't think about that. You want to go find a cafeteria or somethin'?"

"No, thanks. I'll just wait until I get home."

They sit down facing one another. Sonya says, "Is my car okay?"

"Yeah, man, it's fine. Was on the other side of the courthouse, see."

"But I don't have my car keys. They were in my purse, and I have no idea where that is."

"Dewey found it in the bed of Dud Hughes's truck. He's bringin' it with him."

"That's great. I wonder what we're going to do for offices."

"They's some unused space, over at the bank. They gonna let us hang out there for a while, 'til we can sort through all this shit."

"It's going to take some time to get it sorted out, what with computers and case files and everything else blown to smithereens. I need to talk to George about . . ."

She stops, drops her head down, suddenly lost in thought.

" 'Bout what?"

She looks up, says, "I was going to say, I need to talk to him about getting continuances in all the cases we're working on. Then I remembered something. Last night, before you called me to warn me that Fletcher was headed my way, I saw George kind of sneaking around his office at the courthouse."

"So what? It be the man's office. He can sneak around it if he wants, I 'spect. You think it means somethin'?"

She shrugs. "I don't know. It may not mean a thing. It's just not like George to be lurking around there late on a Sunday afternoon."

"Maybe he was tryin' to get hisself a jump on the work week."

"Yeah. Maybe." They sit in silence awhile.

Then Clyde says, "You sure the man didn't—"

"Give it a rest, Clyde."

When the sheriff walks into the room, Sonya gets up to shake his hand.

Dewey says, "How you feelin'?"

She smiles, says, "Fine. Nothing wrong with me that a bath, some clean clothes, a bowl of tomato soup, and about twenty hours of sleep won't cure."

"Okay. Let's go." Dewey turns to leave.

Sonya says, "Sheriff?"

Dewey turns back. "Yeah?"

"I do want to say, in all sincerity, that it was wrong of me to question your courage. You showed plenty of that this morning. Thank you."

Clyde says, "Yeah, man. Thanks. I'se gonna make sure word gets around amongst the children, they all needs to turn out on election day, vote for you. They got theyselves a telephone tree, you know what I'm sayin'? We can turn all they asses out."

Dewey shrugs, smiles, says, "It wasn't nothin'."

As they walk to Dewey's cruiser, Dewey says to Sonya, "What about brains? You ain't said nothin' about that."

Sonya looks at the sheriff, thinking what to say. Then she says, "You know what they say in the oil business, Sheriff. 'When you hit oil, stop drilling.'"

She opens the door, starts to sit on the passenger's seat of the cruiser, sees her purse lying there, picks it up.

Dewey says, "Your cell phone is in there too. It was kindly covered in blood. We cleaned it as best we could. You might want to think about getting a new one, though."

She reaches in the purse, fetches out the cell phone, turns it on. The battery could stand a good recharging, but other than that it seems to be working.

They get out of the cruiser at the town square, stand for a while staring at the smoldering pile of ruins that once was the Washington County courthouse. The fire had caused all the walls to cave in and the grounds are littered with debris—papers, furniture, office equipment, parts of the building. Workers pick their way through the rubble, trying to see what they can salvage, guys in black windbreakers with "ATF" stenciled on the back working there with them.

Television uplink trucks from Houston, Austin, and Dallas are parked down the street, camera crews loitering around.

Dewey says, "I was watchin' CNN this mornin'. They had a report on us. Said right-wing militia blew up the courthouse. Said an investigation was underway."

Clyde says, "Ain't nothin' to investigate no more. Ever-body dead already."

Sonya says, "Seems that way. I guess we'll be needing a new courthouse."

"Yeah, man. This one here is for shit."

Inside her purse, Sonya's cell phone starts ringing. She reaches in, gets it, looks at the display. Caller ID says "Jeremiah and Martha Spur."

She says, "What in the world?"

47

DIGGING IN THIS HEAT IS WORK AND IT HAS HIM DRIPPING SWEAT RIGHT OFF. Fighting the hardpan puts him in mind of the other day, when he had had to replace that fence post, when Duke had just about tangled with that rattler.

Now Duke is dead, and he's got to bury him.

Gives him something to do while he's waiting for Sonya Nichols to call, tell him what she learned over at the bank. He had called her, asked would she mind checking the bank records of Sissy Fletcher and Greg Johnson before going home to get some rest. Told her there was just the one loose end the preacher had mentioned, the "silent partner" angle, that needed looking into. Told her he would like to know what she could figure out from those bank records before he heads into Houston to see his wife and daughter.

She said she'd be happy to check it out.

He thinks, there's been so much death. His dog. Dud Hughes. All the Fletchers, going way back to the mama. The thought of it makes him dig harder, and the sweat boils out of him and runs down his body. He strips out of his shirt, tosses it over on the ground, the skin of his torso white next to the nut brown of his arms, his face, his neck.

He had watched them load Dud Hughes into the body bag, his eyes wide in their death stare, his body a mass of wounds, the image captured now forever in his mind, there for so long as he walks the earth, enshrined in his memory as though it were something to be treasured when in fact it is anything but. His mind is like a camera for just such as that, he can call such images back from memory at any moment.

And then his mind sometimes brings them forward of its own accord, in his sleep, when he dreams his barbecue dreams.

He's never talked about them to others, but that's the name he gave them when it first happened, years ago, after he had had a big mixed plate of links and brisket down at Otto's in Houston one evening for dinner. It must have been something about that thick spicy sauce or the beans or the potato salad that didn't sit well with him.

That night he'd tossed and turned, at length fell asleep and dreamed his dreams.

And now it can happen to him without a meal to trigger it. Any night they might come to him, in his barbecue dreams. Images his mind has captured of victims from the cases he has worked over the years. They bust out of the place where his mind has them locked away, and they come calling on him in his sleep.

Corpses with heads blown off. Bodies that have been dismembered. Or stuffed in old refrigerators or the trunks of automobiles. Hanging from ropes. Floating, swollen and grotesque, on the banks of some bayou, some river, some mud lake. Patrolmen, young guys with families, dead on the ground with massive chest wounds, opened up on with shotguns at point-blank range by crazed boys, boys that had been stopped for speeding or making a turn without giving a signal.

Other images from long ago, some of the worst, from way back when he was in Vietnam, civilians dead of napalm or mortar shrapnel, GIs who had been cut down by automatic weapons fire or who had fallen into one of Charlie's booby traps.

In his barbecue dreams, they rise up, silently fling their challenge at him, dare him to put his questions to the Almighty on Judgment Day.

Jeremiah thinks, *Far be it from me to challenge the Almighty. Especially when I might have need of Him.*

When he has finished the hole, he tosses the shovel aside, backs up his truck to where the empty grave awaits the fulfillment of its purpose. He hauls the body bag containing Duke out of the back of the pickup, drags it into the hole, covers it with lime, commences to shovel dirt on his dog's remains.

Directly, when he's done, he stands, looks at the pile of rocks and turf and dirt, tries to think of what to say.

At length, he looks up, says only this:

"Lord, I always figgered you made me tough-minded enough to tend to myself, so you'd have more time to see after folks what need the help. So that's why I ain't spent a lot of time askin' you for this or that or the other thing. But I got this to ask of you this mornin'. I'd like to see my dog again someday. And my daughter, too, once you've taken her from me. I'd appreciate it if you could arrange it. I'll try to hold up my end of it down here."

He throws the shovel in his pickup, collects his shirt, turns toward the house.

Then he stops, looks up again, says, "Amen."

Inside the house he goes into the kitchen, pours himself a cup of black, sits at the kitchen table. He picks up the envelope that had fallen out of Martha's mama's Bible, turns it around in his hands.

The mailing label is the type businesses use, with the sender's name and address printed at the top, then a blank space below that's for the addressee's information. The printed part says "Johnson Veterinarian and Taxidermy Services: Either Way You Get Your Dog Back!"

Jeremiah used to find that kind of amusing. This morning he doesn't.

Under that someone had hand printed the address of Nadine Barnett.

Jeremiah thinks about the two items he found inside the envelope.

One is a newspaper clipping from an April 1987 issue of the *Brenham Gazette*, about a one-car accident in which the driver of a late-model Lincoln Continental had died, her car slamming into a concrete pillar out at the bypass, going at a very high rate of speed. The cops who were at the scene were quoted as saying she didn't appear to have been wearing her seat belt.

The driver had been George Barnett's wife, Nadine.

The other item is a photograph.

The telephone rings, and he gets up to answer it. "Jeremiah Spur," he says.

"Captain Spur, it's Sonya."

"Howdy."

"Listen, I just finished at the bank. There were large deposits, very large deposits, in Greg Johnson's accounts that were not matched by deposits in Sissy's. They can't be traced back to either of Johnson's businesses. In fact, so far as I can tell, they can't be traced anywhere at all."

"What happened to the money in Sissy's account?"

"She was declared legally dead after she had been missing five years. The money was released to her next of kin. Which would have been her father."

"Okay. Thanks. You don't by any chance know where I could find George this mornin', do you?"

"No, sir. I'm calling you from our temporary offices at the bank, and he's not here. My guess is that he's working out of his ranch house."

"Okay. Thanks again. Go get yourself some rest."

"Captain Spur?"

"Yes?"

"What do they mean?"

"Beg your pardon?"

"What do these deposits mean?"

"I ain't sure. Maybe nothin'."

"Let me mention one more thing to you, while I've got you."

He listens as she tells him about George Barnett's strange behavior at the office the night before.

"Can you make any sense of all this?" she says.

Jeremiah hesitates a minute. Then he says, "I don't rightly know."

He says good-bye, hangs up, heads into the bathroom to get showered and shaved.

4 8

JEREMIAH FINDS THE VETERINARIAN SITTING AT A PICNIC TABLE BACK BEHIND his place of business, unwrapping a tuna salad sandwich, fixing to have his lunch. Greg gets up to shake Jeremiah's hand, offers him a seat on the bench across the table from him.

"You hear about Jim Fletcher?" says the veterinarian, taking a bite, peering at Jeremiah through his spectacles, the lenses making his eyes appear to be larger than they are, less human, like the eyes of some kind of aquatic creature.

"Yep."

"The talk is that he killed Sissy. Hard to believe, but I suppose it could be."

"I reckon."

"Sorry to hear about Duke, by the way. That dog was a good 'un."

Jeremiah reaches in his shirt pocket for his Camels, fetches the pack out, pops it in his palm a couple times. "Best I ever had."

"You want me to see if I can preserve him for you?"

"No, sir. Body was too burned. I done buried him."

"Damn. That's a shame."

"I need to ask you somethin', Greg."

The veterinarian wipes his mouth with his napkin, sets his sandwich aside, takes a sip of a soft drink, folds his hands in front of him, watches Jeremiah with his fish eyes while Jeremiah lights himself a Camel.

"Go ahead on."

Jeremiah shakes the match until he kills the flame, then flicks it over against the back wall of the veterinarian's shop. He takes a drag, then he says, "Last night I went by to see Jim, before he killed himself."

"I heard as much."

"I accused him of killin' Sissy. He claimed it wasn't him that done it, even though she did go up yonder to see him the night of the dance. Accordin' to him, she left his place alive, headed off to see someone else."

"Did she say who?"

"She said to Jim you all had a 'silent partner' in your shakedown operation, and she was on her way to see him, collect off him what she could."

The veterinarian shifts his gaze off into the distance. "Can't imagine what she would of meant by that."

"That's too bad. I was kinda hopin' you could clear it up for me. There's somethin' else."

Greg looks back at Jeremiah, his marine eyes expectant.

"We checked your bank records this mornin', for the two-year period what commenced in March 1987, yours and the Fletcher girl's both. We seen a number of large deposits to your account during that time period that didn't match up to deposits in hers. I'd be willin' to bet that extra money of yours come from your 'silent partner.' "

"I ain't got nothin' to say 'bout that."

"What you got to say about this, then?"

Jeremiah reaches in his pocket, produces the photograph that had been in the envelope that had fallen out of Martha's mama's Bible, hands it across the picnic table.

The vet takes it. The color drains from the man's face. "Where'd you get this?"

Jeremiah ignores the question. He takes a drag on his cigarette, then holds it between the index and middle finger of his right hand, uses it to indicate the photo. "You can't tell who the woman is, but the man is plainly George Barnett, although the lighting ain't so good. I ain't person-ally been over there myself, but I'd be willin' to bet that shot was taken through a one-way mirror set in the wall of room fifteen over at the Adobe, and that you're the one what took it."

The veterinarian hands the photo back to Jeremiah, takes his glasses off, sets them on the picnic table, rubs his face with his hands.

Jeremiah slips the picture back into his shirt pocket, finishes his cigarette, crushes the butt on top of the picnic table, drops it to the ground.

"Was George Barnett your silent partner, Greg?"

The veterinarian quits playing with his face, puts his glasses back on his nose, looks off into the distance like he just heard his name being called from over there.

Then he says, "He called me sometime in early spring, 1987, said he needed a place where he could meet a certain lady in the afternoons, and since he knew I was managing the Adobe he wanted to know, could I help out. At the time I had just finished outfitting room fifteen, see. Quite a coincidence, huh?"

"I used not to believe in them things. Reckon I'm gonna have to rethink that."

The vet shrugs. "I reckon. Anyway, I was more than happy to oblige him, thought I could use his situation as a trial run for our little setup. I asked him when he needed it, then arranged for the room key to be delivered to him, and for myself to be situated behind the one-way mirror when he come over.

"Well him and his . . . lady came and did their thing and I took some photos, and they were all underexposed, pretty much like this one here was. You could recognize George alright, but not the woman. I showed 'em to Sissy, thought she'd be pleased that I had tested the arrangements, plus I needed to let her know we would be delayed until I had fixed the lighting. I should of guessed what she would do, but that possibility never crossed my mind until George come by the shop a few weeks later."

"After his wife had died."

"Yeah. After that. He told me Sissy had come to see him, told George about the pictures, threatened to show them to Nadine, if he didn't pay up. I guess she had decided to test her part of the operation too, even though it hadn't been her that was with George. He told me he threw her out of his office, told her to go to hell.

"Two weeks after Sissy called on George, Nadine Barnett crashed her car into a concrete pillar over on the bypass. He told me he found an envelope with the pictures in it when he was goin' through her effects after she died. Sissy must of gotten her hands on the photos somehow, sent them around to Nadine when George wouldn't play ball."

"What did he want when he came to see you?"

"He said he had figured out what we were up to, and he wanted in on it. He offered to pay me for a second set of prints, and he gave me a list of potential marks, offered to pay a bonus for each one we was able to land. We got almost all of 'em, too. You're one of the ones we missed."

"Is that a fact?"

"Yes, sir."

"I take it you decided not to cut Sissy in on this side deal of yours."

The veterinarian shakes his head. "Wasn't my decision. It was George's. He said it had to be that way. He said that bitch had killed his wife and he didn't want her to have nothing to do with his end of the deal. She found out about it though, toward the end there, right before she disappeared."

"How'd she figure it out?"

"Same way y'all did. I went hunting one weekend and she went rooting through my stuff, found my bank statements, made a study of 'em, compared 'em to hers. She was wicked smart. Didn't take her long to put it all together, I reckon. Then when I got home she confronted me, asked me if I had something working on the side with George. I asked her why she thought it might be George. She said he was the most logical choice, since he had some knowledge of what we were up to, was smart enough and ruthless enough to try to capitalize on it. I told her yeah, I had a side deal."

"Why did George Barnett want the photos, Greg?"

"You'd have to ask him that."

"Okay. Then let me ask you one more thing."

"No, Jeremiah."

"No, what?"

"No, I ain't gonna tell you who the woman in that picture is."

"That's fine," Jeremiah says as he stands to leave. "I'll go ask George."

As he turns to walk off, the veterinarian says, "I reckon all this probably ain't done much for your opinion of me, huh?"

Without looking back, Jeremiah says, "A thing can only be what it is."

4 9

GEORGE BARNETT'S RANCH HOUSE LOOKS LIKE HOLLYWOOD'S IDEA OF A RANCH house, a white, two-story job with dark trim, with dormers and gables, sprawled on top of a little hill, surrounded by porches with swings and rocking chairs on them, red barns and farm equipment sitting out back, white fencing all around.

Not at all like Jeremiah Spur's little cracker box of a house that always needs something done to it, with its nondescript sheds and barbed-wire fencing.

Jeremiah parks Martha's Buick in the front drive, starts walking up the steps.

The door opens before he can knock, George standing there, puffing on a cigar, wearing dungarees, blue oxford cloth shirt, loafers with no socks. He says, "Word around the campfire is you want to ask me a question or two, Jeremiah."

"I figgered Greg would call you."

"That he did." He opens the door so Jeremiah can come in.

The front door opens up directly into a family room, dark paneling all around, bookshelves crammed with books and pictures, mostly of George, trophy game mounted on the walls, stone fireplace directly across from the door, oriental rugs spread out on the dark hardwood flooring. At the back there's a staircase leading up to the second floor.

"Have a seat," George says.

"You disappoint me, George."

Jeremiah remains standing, just inside the door, looking at the DA.

"How's that, Jeremiah?"

"Mixing yourself up in that shakedown Greg Johnson and Sissy Fletcher had workin'. I figgered you for a better man than that."

"No man is so good that he's above his own self-preservation."

"I don't understand why you'd have a hand in it."

"Let me see if I can explain it to you, then." The DA crosses the room, settles into an armchair behind a glass-topped coffee table next to the fireplace, set of fireplace tools by his side. He leans forward, stubs his cigar out in an ashtray full of old cigar butts, ash. "Let's start with a question."

"I ain't got time for games. I'm overdue at the hospital down in Houston."

"What is it most folks in small-town Texas fear more than anything in the world?"

"I said, I ain't got time for games."

"Scandal is the answer you're looking for. After all, what's the point of living in some dog ass little town out in the middle of nowhere if you can't wallow in those good, wholesome, small-town values? If you can't look down your nose at the degeneration of the big city, feel morally superior, high and mighty compared to somebody like the president with all his highfalutin' education and whatnot?"

The DA pauses long enough to cut the end off a new cigar, light it, puff out a cloud of smoke, spit some tobacco flecks on the floor.

"It's all bullshit though. Weight for age there's as much sin and degeneration in a place like Brenham as there is in Houston, or New York City, or Paris, France. But that's not the way folks want to think of themselves, and that's sure not the way they want *other* folks to think about them, or about their loved ones."

He leans forward, taps his ash.

"I understood this, see. I understood that if a man was thinking about doing something I had a problem with, say, holding the wrong way in a case if he was a judge, or running against me in the primary if he was a lawyer, or getting too close to a situation I'd just as lief was let alone, if he was a lawman, then he probably could be dissuaded from his course of action by a conversation with someone who had documentary proof that he, or his brother, or his cousin, might not be able to maintain that most important fiction in small-town Texas life. Take Frank Cade, for example."

"What about him?"

"Frank's one of them that fell for Sissy's peculiar brand of charm. Greg Johnson's photographs turned Frank from a loose cannon into a man you can actually work with. I tried to get Dewey to see the sense of bringing old Frank in on this Sissy Fletcher business, but he wasn't having any of it. If Dewey had just listened to me, you and I wouldn't be having this conversation, and things would have stayed settled down around here. Now everything's in an uproar, Jim Fletcher's gone and killed himself, and you're still nosing around like there's somethin' to find."

"I think there is somethin' to find."

"But it's all turned to shit and gotten out of control, Jeremiah. Don't you see how much better it is when somebody like me, somebody who sees the entire chessboard, can use a little leverage on folks, keep them on the reservation? And all you need to get the right kind of responsiveness from folks around here is threaten them with the loss of that precious fiction of theirs."

"What is this fiction you keep talkin' about?"

"Why, the one I started talking about. The fiction that they are superior, morally speaking. That they have the right Christian pedigree, belong in the company of good folks, from small-town Texas."

He takes another puff, leans back in his chair, says, "Folks like Jeremiah Spur."

"A thing can only be what it is, George."

"Yes. I expect you're right about that. Anyway, all I did, once I figured out what Greg and his girlfriend were up to, was go around, see Greg, offer to make it worth his while if he could steer her in the right direction where her customer base was concerned, and furnish me with my own set of his work product."

"He says your list included me."

The DA shrugs. "Can't blame a fellow for tryin'. I didn't hold out much hope for it though."

Jeremiah works his jaw muscles. "Did you kill Sissy Fletcher?"

"Did I kill her? No, I did not."

"Did she come here the night she died?"

The DA nods, fishes with an index finger inside his lips for a piece of tobacco, pulls it out, inspects it, then flicks it on the floor.

"Yes. She did. She wanted what she called her part of what I had paid Greg Johnson. She said she wanted it that night, on account of she aimed to be gone from Brenham before the sun came up. She said if I didn't pay her, she'd let the world know what kind of man I really was, was the way she put it, I think. I told her to get lost."

"You sure? You sure you didn't kill her, then shallow bury her?"

The DA taps some more ash, then sits back in his chair, puffs his cigar. "Like most folks, Jeremiah, I am guilty of numerous sins. But murder ain't one of them. You're right about one thing, though."

"What would that be?"

"She didn't leave here alive that night."

"Who was it that was with you then?"

The DA leans forward again, taps his ash, looks up at Jeremiah. "Jeremiah, what do you want to go into all this for? What possible good can it do?"

And just like that, Jeremiah Spur knows who killed Sissy Fletcher.

Jeremiah says, "I'm overdue down in Houston, at the hospital. When I get back, I'm comin' to see you, and I'm gonna collect two things from you. One is your resignation as district attorney. Effective immediately. So you might want to start callin' folks you know, tellin' 'em you've decided to hang it up after all these years."

"I'd rather not."

"I don't give a shit what you would rather do. Have it ready."

The DA shrugs. "Okay. But you said there were two things you wanted."

"I want that file of photographs." He starts to walk out the door.

George calls after him, "I don't have the photographs."

Jeremiah turns around. "Do what?"

"I said I don't have those pictures. They were in the courthouse. They're gone."

"Don't bullshit me, George. Sonya saw you up yonder yesterday evenin', actin' funny. My guess is you went to fetch 'em after I braced Greg Johnson so you could make sure you had 'em tucked safely away somewheres. Have 'em ready for me when I get back. Along with your resignation."

Jeremiah walks out the front door.

5 0

AS HE WALKS DOWN THE STEPS IN FRONT OF GEORGE BARNETT'S HOUSE HEADED
for Martha's Buick, Jeremiah is all of a sudden feeling old, beat up, tired,
sleepy even, like he does at the end of a day spent working his herd, a
thought that reminds him, he still has the fall-borne steers to work sometime this week.

He decides he's too sleepy to go directly to Houston, decides instead to
swing by his place first, get some coffee in him.

Plus there's something there he needs to fetch, carry with him down to
Houston.

Halfway toward Martha's car he stops, gets the feel of the wind blowing
soft out of the northwest, takes the measure of it.

The weatherman is wrong again, by God.

Rain is coming.

The shift in the wind makes the afternoon air feel good.

Directly he's out on the highway, driving over to his place. Way off in
the distance, Jeremiah can see flashes of lightning in the clouds.

"Looky yonder," he says to himself. He pulls off the county road into
the drive leading up to his house, drives around back, parks.

Jeremiah can hear the thunder rumbling way out in the distance, out
toward Caldwell. He figures it's probably raining in Burleson County
already.

He walks in the house, starts the coffee, stops at the kitchen table where
the yellow envelope that had been hidden in the Bible still sits. He takes the
photograph out of his pocket, looks at it for a moment or two, then returns
it to the envelope, which he sets back down on the kitchen table.

Then he heads out to the back porch, figuring to have himself a cigarette, look at Duke's grave, wait for the coffee to brew.

He sits in his rocking chair and lights a Camel.

The storm is getting closer now, first the lightning followed maybe
twenty seconds later by the thunder, which would make the lightning a
couple miles off.

It doesn't seem real to him, sitting here, watching the rain clouds getting closer, the memory of the events of the last few days filling his brain, taking root in his mind.

He thinks about how strange folks are, how odd their behavior can be.

The wind freshens and he can hear it moving through the trees in the woods west of the house, the breeze telling him the rain is closing in.

He can hear the phone in the kitchen ring.

He catches it on the fourth ring. "Hello?"

Soft crying at the other end of the line.

"Hello? Martha?"

"She's gone, Jeremiah. Our baby's gone."

"When?"

Martha can barely speak through her sobs. "Just now. She started going downhill this morning. I've been trying to call you since late morning but there was no answer and . . . Oh, my God, oh my God."

Jeremiah holds the receiver to his ear and listens to his wife's crying.

He says, "I'm on my way."

He hears her hang up her end of the line.

He cuts off the coffeepot, starts to walk out of the house, then stops, goes back into the kitchen.

He opens a drawer, pulls out a dish towel, goes in the pantry, gets a paper sack.

Then he goes to the cabinet where Martha keeps her liquor. He opens the door, reaches up with the dish towel, grabs Martha's half-empty vodka bottle, careful not to touch it other than with the towel. He places it in the paper sack, closes it, then walks out of his house, through his backyard, to Martha's Buick. He opens the door, gets in, sets the paper sack next to him on the seat.

He puts the key in the ignition, starts to turn the thing.

The first raindrops hit the windshield and the hood together, big, fat drops that sound almost like hailstones.

He's thinking, *They make kindly a lot of noise for just being drops of water.*

There is lightning and thunder all around now for the first time in months, and the darkness brought on by the advancing clouds lights up every time there's a flash, and the thunder happens right after, and the lightning makes his place—his barn, his house, his fields—it makes them look like old photographs in a picture album.

As if he ought to be able to see his young wife in them, holding his little girl by the hand.

And he starts to look for them, then shakes his head at himself, knowing that it's all starting to get the better of him.

Inside of a minute, it's raining so hard he's straining to see anything that's more than a hundred yards off. He can see just well enough to watch little streams of rainwater already building out in his field to the east, starting to trickle down toward his tank, the one that had gotten so low.

He reaches in his shirt pocket for his cigarettes, starts to shake one out, then stops. He looks at the package resting there in his hand.

He stares out the windshield, watches the rain come streaming down, then looks back down at the cigarette package.

With his left hand he hits the button on the door that rolls the window down, the wind blowing the rain inside the car now, making dark brown spots on his khaki shirt.

With his right hand he pitches the cigarette package out of the window. He watches as it hits the ground and rolls into a puddle. He rolls the window back up.

Then he puts his head down on the steering wheel and tries not to cry.

51

THE CONTINUING HARD RAIN MADE THE TRIP HOME FROM HOUSTON SLOW such that it's after dark by the time they get back to the little ranch house in northwest Washington County. Jeremiah parks the Buick around back, pops the trunk, fetches Martha's suitcase from it while she walks ahead of him into the house, turning on lights.

When he gets to the kitchen he finds her looking down at the yellow envelope that he had left on the table. She has picked it up, and stands there now, holding it in her hands as though it were a telegram containing news from the end of time.

Jeremiah says, "I couldn't find your Bible to read the verses Jim had assigned, so I went to get your mama's down. That fell out of it."

She glances at him, sets the envelope back down on the kitchen table, walks in the direction of her liquor cabinet.

"Your vodka bottle ain't there," Jeremiah says.

She turns and looks at him. "Where is it?"

Jeremiah sits down in a chair at the kitchen table. "I took it. Before I came down to the hospital yesterday, I dropped it off with a fingerprint technician at the DPS. He checked it this mornin', found prints that matched those on the steerin' wheel, door, and tailgate of Sissy Fletcher's truck."

She's quiet for a bit. Then she says, "I liked you better before you quit smoking."

"Maybe you better come sit down, tell me about you and George Barnett and Sissy Fletcher."

She sighs, comes and sits at the kitchen table. She had made her face this morning, washed her hair, blown it dry, put on one of her nicest dresses, as if losing a child was like church, a cause for dressing up. The lines on her face are like markings left behind by a dying race of men.

She puts her hands on top of the table, studies them. They are the strong hands of a woman who has lived a hard life, a country life. There is no polish on her nails.

"I dated him some, you know, before we got married, while you were off in Vietnam, when I wasn't sure from day to day whether you would be back. He was in love with me, I suppose, but you had won me early on. When the army took you away, he was still available. Had a student deferment, as I recollect. So I went out with him some when he asked, rather than just sit around worrying.

"When you came home, you and I picked right back up where we left off. And for years there I rarely even saw George. I would bump into him in town now and then, and that was about it."

She looks up from her hands, into Jeremiah's eyes. "Then, after you became a Ranger, you were gone all the time and I got lonely, living out here on this farm, doing the hard work a farm requires, no one to share it with night in and night out. Do you realize two, sometimes three weeks would go by, and I wouldn't even hear from you, not a single phone call? It was as though you were back in Vietnam again."

Jeremiah knows two things right now. One is that she is right in what she says. The other is that it was terrible bad judgment to give up smoking yesterday.

She says, "I married you because I wanted a companion, someone to spend my life with. Instead I got a rebellious daughter and an empty bed."

She drops her eyes to her hands again. "George Barnett, with his unerring nose for human frailty, figured that out. And he took advantage of it."

Jeremiah can hear his pulse pounding in his temples, going *thump thump, thump thump*, like the rocker arm over at the Gibson place. He clears his throat of the obstruction that has lodged itself there, says, "Over at the Adobe."

She nods. "The particulars of how we ended up there don't matter, I suppose, just that we did, and that neither one of us knew we were being watched. Photographed.

"Two weeks later Nadine Barnett died in that car wreck. I put it all together pretty quickly prompted in part, I guess, by my own guilt about what we had done and by what I knew about Nadine, how dependent she was on George. Anyway, I confronted George about it. He owned up to her having found out that he had been unfaithful, told me about some pictures she had received."

She looks up at Jeremiah, the tears beginning to work their way down her cheeks, spoiling the makeup she had applied. "I was horrified about the whole thing, what I had done to Nadine, to myself, to us. I told George I never wanted to see him again. He begged me not to leave him alone, said he wanted to marry me. I know it's hard to imagine George Barnett pitiful, but that's what he was. I walked away from him and thought that was the end of it, that the only guilt I would have to live with was the guilt from what I had done up to that day.

"A few months went by and then I got a call from him one night, while you were away on a case. He sounded like he had been drinking. He brought up the pictures again, the ones he said someone had sent Nadine. Basically, he threatened to have them fixed so he couldn't be recognized, then send them to you, anonymously. Unless . . ."

"Unless what?"

"Unless I . . . spent a night with him. That is, one night for each picture."

Jeremiah's jaw is set. "How many were there?"

"Ten."

"So you started barterin' them back."

"Yes. I thought I was doing it to save us, Jeremiah, our family. And that brings me to the other problem I was struggling with then, which was Elizabeth. You see, I knew what she was, what she was becoming, even before she did."

"How?"

"A mother can just tell. There are little signs that you read." She smiles weakly. "Call it female intuition. I knew one thing for sure, though, and that was that Elizabeth was infatuated with Sissy Fletcher. Elizabeth would catch a glimpse of her at a football game or in town somewhere and she would come home and talk about her for days after. I told you that I told Elizabeth to stay away from Sissy."

"Yeah."

"I didn't tell you that I told Sissy to stay away from Elizabeth. A few months before Sissy . . . disappeared, I went to the Farm-to-Market Café, while she was still waiting tables there, sat at one of her tables in the back long enough for the lunch crowd to thin out. When there were just the two of us, I asked her to sit down, and I told her she was never to go near my daughter. She asked me why. I said that Elizabeth was at a stage in life that was very confusing for her, and that I was frankly concerned that Sissy, based upon what I had been hearing around town, was not the kind of company Elizabeth should be keeping. I think that made her mad. She said we both knew what Elizabeth was, that Sissy could tell it by the way Elizabeth looked at her body. I said she had better keep her body away from my daughter. She said what she did with her body was her own business. I got up to leave and she said, 'Be sure and tell George Barnett I said hi.'

"I had suspected, based on what I was hearing around town, that Sissy had something to do with the pictures George was using to manipulate me. That confirmed it, confirmed that Sissy was the reason Nadine Barnett was dead, the reason I was being so badly used by George."

"She had a hand in it, I reckon. But you was—"

"I know, I know. But my own part in it didn't stop me from working up a blind hatred of that bitch. The only thing I couldn't figure out was why you hadn't gotten a set of pictures like Nadine did. Anyway, the night of the dance George called, said he knew you were out of town, said he wanted me to come over. I told him I couldn't until Elizabeth got home. I was watching out the window for her when Sissy's pickup pulled into the yard. I could see Sissy at the wheel when Elizabeth got out because the dome light inside the cab went on. Elizaebeth came in crying and she went to her room and locked the door but soon it got quiet, she had gone to sleep. I went over to George's then.

"Anyway, George and I were upstairs when we heard someone downstairs pounding on his front door."

"Sissy."

She nods. "Yes. He went down to see what was going on. I got dressed and walked partway down the stairs. I could hear them fighting, her demanding money, him refusing to let her have it, telling her to leave before he called the police. She said, 'You're not about to call the police, George, because then they'd find out you're sleeping with Jeremiah Spur's wife. I recognized her car out front when I drove up. I saw it earlier tonight, when I was dropping her daughter off at their ranch.'

"I think that actually surprised him, that she had found us out.

"Then she said she had suspected all along it was me in those pictures that Greg Johnson had taken, but Greg had never been willing to say who it was and she couldn't be sure because the lighting was so poor, too poor for the pictures to turn out well. She said George had one more chance to pay her what he owed her and if he didn't she would leave town anyway and make sure once she was safely gone that the story about him and me got around to everybody. Especially you.

"He told her to go to hell.

"She said, 'Fine, we'll play it your way.'

"I stepped around the corner then. She saw me, said, 'Hello, Martha.'

"I said, 'I told you to stay away from my daughter.'

"She said, 'Your daughter is gay, Martha, alright? She needs someone she can trust to talk to. Can she trust you, Martha? Obviously your husband can't.'

"I asked her what she did to Elizabeth to make her cry.

"She said she had done two things. She said Elizabeth had made a pass at her and she had turned it down. That was one. She said, 'And I told her to face the facts about herself, go somewhere, start a new life, get out of this godforsaken shithole where she would be whispered about forever. I told her that was what I was going to do. I hope she'll take my advice. I plan to make it easier for her, by the way, by making sure word gets around, not only that you are fucking the DA, but that she's a dyke. You see, Martha, when I'm done, there won't be any secrets left in Brenham. Not a one. We'll see how much y'all like your small-town paradise when you know the truth about one another.'

"Then she walked out the front door."

"But she never made it to her pickup, right?"

Martha shakes her head. "I have never felt such hatred in my life. All my shame and humiliation and frustration about myself, about my daughter, about the mess our lives had become, found a focal point, and it was that blond-headed bitch who had just walked out the door. I grabbed a fireplace poker and caught up with her in the yard. She never heard me coming. I hit her once across the back. That knocked her to her knees. Then I swung it as hard as I could at her head."

Jeremiah lights a cigarette, takes a drag. "That explains it."

"Explains what?"

"How the medical examiner got the notion she was killed by someone taller than her. She wasn't standin' when you caved her head in."

"That's right."

Her eyes look into Jeremiah's. Hers are begging.

His are stone.

"I took no pleasure in it, Jeremiah. I did it because I had to, because I couldn't let her destroy my family."

"What do you call what you were doin' there with George?"

"I'm so sorry. You can't possibly imagine how sorry I am—"

"Finish it up. Did you bury her body?"

"Yes. George had seen it all from the front porch. He helped me load her into her pickup, gave me a shovel, told me where to go with the body, told me where to meet him when I was done. I took her out into that pasture and dug her a grave and pulled her into it. Then I drove back and met George on the north side of town. That's where we left her pickup. Then he took me back to his place so I could collect my car and get home. I got back here before dawn, before Elizabeth woke up. I started a fire in the burning barrel and burned all my clothes and all the pictures that George Barnett had of us."

"He gave them all to you?"

"They were in the front seat of the car when I got back to his place. I didn't know until I saw them that you really couldn't tell the woman in them was me. That's why you didn't get a set, and poor Nadine did."

Jeremiah picks the yellow envelope up. "But you didn't burn them all."

She sighs. "No. Even though George swore he would never tell anyone what had happened that night, I didn't think I could trust him. I kept this one as, I don't know, insurance maybe, something to give me some kind of leverage with him, use it to try to tie him to his wife's suicide somehow, should he change his mind later, decide to make trouble for me. I stuck it in Mama's Bible because I couldn't imagine you ever taking it down off that shelf. In more than thirty years of marriage, you haven't touched that Bible, not once. Anyway, I guess that's where I was wrong."

Jeremiah says, "You was wrong in more ways than I can count, Martha."

"And, to be completely honest with you, I stuck that envelope away so long ago, I had forgotten it was still there. I guess that's what drinking too much will do for you. I should have gotten rid of it long ago."

Jeremiah pushes his chair back, stands up, starts walking out of the house.

"Where are you going?" she says to his receding back.

"I got somethin' I need to do."

George Barnett is in his bathrobe, smoking a cigar, when he opens the door to let Jeremiah in his house.

Jeremiah says, "You got what I want?"

The DA points at a box sitting on a chair by the front door. "Yonder it is," he says. "Sorry to hear about Elizabeth."

Jeremiah walks over, opens it. Inside he can see a letter and a thick brown file folder with an elastic band stretched around it. He picks them up, looks them over, puts them back in, closes the box lid.

He looks at George. "You better not have made copies of any of them pictures."

"I haven't. Anything else you want before you get the fuck out of my house?"

"Yeah. I want to show you somethin', George."

"What would that be?"

Jeremiah's right fist slams into George Barnett's jaw, sending the DA sprawling backward, crashing through the top of his glass coffee table, landing hard in a tangle of busted glass and arms and legs and terry cloth, his cigar cartwheeling through the air, dropping into his armchair, commencing to leave a burn spot there.

Jeremiah Spur kicks his way through coffee-table debris, stands over George.

Then he says, "I just wanted to show you a small piece of what you can expect if you ever come near my wife again. And that ain't nothin' compared to what I'll do to you if you so much as breathe a word of what happened the night of the dance."

Then he turns, collects his box, leaves the house, walks out into the rain, leaving George Barnett on the floor, spitting teeth on his oriental rug.

That night, after he had torched George Barnett's file in the burning barrel, putting enough lighter fluid on it to make sure it burned down completely, leaving nothing but ashes despite the driving rain, he sits on his porch, watches the rain coming down lit by the yard light out back, the one mounted on the roof of the pumphouse.

Martha had gone to bed early, but before she did, Jeremiah had sat her down, told her how woefully disappointed he was in what she had done, told her he needed to sort out what he was going to do next.

Told her he still loved her.

He asked her what Elizabeth had known about this whole sorry mess.

She said, "Nothing."

He said, "You sure?"

"Yes. Very sure. She slept late the next morning, almost until noon. She came into the kitchen where I was fixing lunch, blurted out that she wanted to get out of Brenham right after graduation, move to the West Coast. Find herself, she said. I told her I had a pretty good idea where she got that notion and that I wouldn't stand for it. Our relationship had gotten pretty rocky already, and it went downhill fast from there."

That started her crying, and it took her a while to stop.

When she did, Jeremiah told her she knew him well enough to know he needed some time to sort through his duties, try to figure out how to reconcile them all.

She smiled at him through her tears. She said, "I'm so sorry, Jeremiah. I'm so sorry to have hurt you, and to have created all these problems for you. You deserve better than me. I'm just so sorry."

He said, "Show me."

"How?"

"Here's how. I done give up smokin', on account of our Elizabeth, God rest her. Now I want you to give up drinkin', and I want you to try harder to be happy. Even allowin' for the fact we both got some grievin' to do yet. I don't want you to be miserable for the rest of our lives. It's a waste, is what it is."

She started crying again, and told him she would try her level best.

He said, "That's all I ask. Now I need to go burn this file."

Now he sits alone, watches the rain falling hard on his dog's newly dug grave. He sits and wonders what the future will bring for his ranch, his wife.

He sits there a long time until finally he decides that if the world wants to think that Jim Fletcher killed his own daughter, that's going to be okay with him. He's not the kind of man who arrests his own wife, no matter what she may have done. His duty as a husband, his duty to protect his wife, trumps his duty as a lawman, pure and simple.

Martha tagged him pretty well the other night when she said turning away from one duty to respond to another is what makes him who he is.

Now that he's made up his mind, he's glad he had decided not to take Martha's vodka bottle in to be dusted for prints, decided instead to tell her that fable about her prints matching some found on Sissy Fletcher's pickup, to see if she'd call his bluff.

Instead, he pitched her bottle in a trash can down at the Medical Center.

So only he, and Martha, and George Barnett would ever know the truth.

His mind made up, he gets up to go inside to bed.

In their bedroom, he feels his way in the dark, shucks out of his clothes, tries to make as little noise as he can, tries not to disturb Martha, whose soft breathing he can hear coming from the other side of the darkened room.

He gets in bed, lies there, listening to the rain falling. Since the weather has turned cooler Martha has cut off the air conditioner, cracked a couple windows. The sound of the rain is like poetry to Jeremiah. The north wind causes the curtains to move and shift.

Maybe there's a way to save the ranch, he thinks. What with the rainfall they're getting, maybe the pastures will green out, the cattle will take on some body mass, such that he can sell them for enough to get his bait back, maybe even turn a profit.

Maybe this here change of luck where the weather is concerned will be enough to get the bankers to back off for a while.

As sleep begins to cover him like a benediction, he knows he's made the right choice about Martha, about leaving the past be.

Just one of life's mysteries, how he loves her. To him, life without Martha is beyond imagining.

A thing can only be what it is.

EPILOGUE

A WEEK TO THE DAY AFTER ELIZABETH SPUR DIED, JEREMIAH SPUR IS DRIVING A rental car across the Golden Gate Bridge, his wife Martha over on the passenger's side, Amanda in the back, cradling the little urn in her arms.

Over to Jeremiah's left, he can see the Pacific Ocean, the first time he's laid eyes on it since he shipped stateside from the 'Nam, the white breakers rolling up, waves endlessly churning, spending themselves on the rocks below, like wayward messages from a distant world.

To the right lies San Francisco Bay, the sailboats white against the blue water, the ferry carting tourists back and forth between Alcatraz or Marin and Fisherman's Wharf.

Jeremiah has to admit it's nice to see the sun again. It had rained every day for a solid week back home, now that that big high pressure system had moved off and the drought had broken.

All the pastures were already looking green again. His biggest tank is filling back up to where it needed to be.

The bank called on Wednesday, told him they needed to sit down together, talk about restructuring his loan or something like that. He told them he was going to be out of town a few days, would be back toward the end of this week, they could do it then if they wanted. He'd give them a call once he got back.

Martha recommended that he talk to her nephew, a young lawyer there in town, get some advice from him before going in to see the bankers.

Amanda leans forward, says, "Captain Spur—"

"Call me Jeremiah."

"Okay. You want to take the next exit."

They exit off Highway 101 and follow the signs to Muir Woods. The road takes them through a couple of little towns, then commences to climb up green hills, switching back and forth through hedgerows, high grass, eucalyptus trees.

Amanda says, "How's it going, Jeremiah? Giving up smoking, I mean."

He glances in the rearview, then looks back at the road, says, "The English language may have words that are adequate to describe how miserable it is, but I can't claim to have them words in my vocabulary."

Martha looks at him, says, "She would have been proud of you. Wouldn't she, Amanda?"

"All your girls are proud of you, Jeremiah."

He says, "I reckon."

Directly they get to the entrance of the park, Jeremiah nosing the rental car into a space, killing the engine. There are hardly any other cars around. It looks like they have the park pretty much to themselves.

The three of them get out, look up at the giant redwoods, make their way into the park, Amanda carrying the urn.

It had never occurred to Jeremiah that trees could get so big. They stretch up so high, he can't get his head back far enough to see their tops.

He says to the ladies, "Look at the trunks on these here trees. You want to walk all the way around one, you best better pack a lunch."

They stop on a bridge that crosses a little creek, water bubbling along, running over stones down the hillside.

From there they look all around, at the great old trees, at the wildflowers blooming in their shade. They listen to the wind moving in the treetops and the birds up there somewhere hidden from sight, singing their songs.

Jeremiah's thinking maybe he should have thrown in a sweater. He's also thinking that it'd be nice to be able to light up a cigarette just about now.

Martha looks at Amanda, says, "I can see why she loved it here."

Amanda says, "These woods were a cathedral to her. She said she found God every time she came here."

They stand in silence for a while, looking at the beauty of the place around them.

Then Martha says, "Do you know the spot she was talking about there towards the end?"

Amanda says, "It's just up that hill a ways."

The three of them set off walking in that direction, hand in hand.